SHADOW NOTES

A CLARA MONTAGUE MYSTERY

LAUREL S. PETERSON

woodhall press
Norwalk, Connecticut

This is a work of fiction. Names, characters, places, and events described herein are products of the author's imagination or are used fictitiously. Any resemblance to actual events, locations, organizations, or persons, living or dead, is entirely coincidental.

Shadow Notes: A Clara Montague Mystery
Clara Montague Mysteries, Book 1
Copyright © 2016 Laurel S. Peterson (www.laurelpeterson.com)

Edited by Ti Locke
Proofreader: Penny Farthing
Cover Artist: Jessica Dionne

ISBN Trade Paperback: 978-1-949116-36-6

Library of Congress Cataloging-in-Publication Data Available
Second Edition: June 2021
Printed in the United States of America

woodhall press
Norwalk, Connecticut

DEDICATION

For my father, who never said there was something a girl couldn't do, and for my mother, who showed me how to hang on even when things got rough.

Thank you.

CHAPTER 1

ll I wanted was to blow this little Spanish town and my soon-to-be ex-husband, head to Paris, and bathe my wounds in Chanel and walks along the Seine. But I'd had a terrifying dream. The last dream predicted my father's death. This one predicted my mother's:

> *I'm standing at the edge of a vast green field. The field slopes up and loses itself in the bluest of blue skies, pure like the polished cobalt that stretches out over the Sangre de Cristo Mountains outside Santa Fe, New Mexico. In front of me is a paddock with three lean and muscular horses, brown and sleek in the bright afternoon sunshine. The afternoon breeze fluffs their tails. I recognize this place as home, although I have never lived anywhere that looks anything like this.*
>
> *In the distance, I see my mother running down the hill. Her arms stretch out toward me, overbalancing her, and she stumbles, falling to her knees in the soft grass. I can't see what frightens her. The pasture is empty. She screams my name: "Clara! Look out!"*
>
> *I turn. Behind me hangs a dense cloud, green-black like the sky before a tornado. This cloud, though, is more like a mass, something palpable, living and dense and suffocating. It is almost upon me. I turn to run toward my mother, only to find a dark mass almost upon her as well. If they shroud us, I know we will never find our way out, we will never find our way to each other. Mother is weeping in the middle of the field. "Clara, please. Help me." When I finally reach her, she is laid out, as if for a grave, arms folded across her chest, her face as white as empty paper.*

I woke exhausted, shivering and cursing into my pillow. I couldn't fall back to sleep, no matter how I tried to calm myself with restful thoughts—salmon antique roses against a grey stone wall, the lull of rain pattering on stone courtyards. All the reasons I didn't want to go home kept intruding.

Going home meant returning to Mother; it meant dealing with my own guilt. I'd never told her my dream about father's death, how I'd seen the sleek black casket, the priest, my father's face made up all waxy or plastic, as if he belonged at Madame Tussaud's. I'd never told her he'd whispered from the casket, "Heart attacks happen, Clara." I knew when he'd said it that I could prevent it, but I hadn't. I blamed myself. I blamed her.

Mother lied. When I was little, before I knew better, I would tell her my dreams, and she would get this frightened look on her face. The look intensified whenever my dreams corresponded to real life. Like the time I dreamed that Timmy Lefkowitz would throw up blood, and then he did on the playground the next day. I shouted at her that if we'd told Timmy's mom or the teacher, they might have kept Sean Gallagher from beating Timmy half to death in the bathroom because Timmy said the Virgin Mary was just another girl, not a saint.

She said no one believed in dreams or intuitions until after something happened. She claimed nothing I could have said would have changed what happened, and telling people only made them frightened of me. I was going to have to get used to that, and if I didn't, people would call me crazy. In fact, until I gave up telling her much of anything, she would say, "It's just a dream, Clara, a coincidence. You mustn't tell anyone about your dreams." She'd make me repeat it, as if I were in detention, writing a hundred times "I will not tell lies."

Then I'd had the dream that predicted my father's death, more terrifying than any dream I'd ever had. Was it symbolic? Real? She would tell me to ignore it, as she had all the others. I didn't want to frighten my father, in case it wasn't true, and I didn't want to stay silent, in case it was. While I was paralyzed by indecision, he died. I hadn't forgiven myself for ignoring my intuition. That was fifteen years ago.

Now, here I was again and this dream felt the same: if I didn't act on it, Mother would die. She'd pushed me away, but she was my mother, and no matter how angry I was with her, I couldn't lose another parent. If I saved her, maybe then I would have done something right, and if I'd done something right, maybe she would be the mother I wanted.

I rolled over and looked at the clock: six a.m. Sliding out from the covers, I shivered for a moment. On the floor lay three open, packed suitcases.

I picked up the phone and dialed United's international desk. "I need to change a flight," I said.

CHAPTER 2

ugh Woodward was my date at Mother's annual Christmas Fête. Twenty-four hours later he was dead. I'd arrived home two days earlier from Girona, Spain, where my ex-stockbroker and soon-to-be ex-husband was in an early mid-life crisis. He was an annoyance of a man with rimless glasses and too much chest hair who, at forty, believed he still had a shot as a professional bike racer. Mother was startled to see me, and that was the only emotion she expressed—the only *thing* she expressed—in the entire two days. In fact, other than greeting me at breakfast and asking after my day when she arrived home around ten p.m. after some function, she said little to me. She absolutely refused to be available for the conversation I needed to have with her.

On the day of the Fête, Mother ended up with an odd number for dinner because Mary Ellen Winters canceled at the last minute with some excuse about a crisis in her brother's special election campaign. The incumbent had dropped dead of a heart attack on the Senate floor a week after Labor Day, providing Andrew Winters with an early opportunity to declare his bid for the seat. The special election would be held in early February, so none of the Winters made it that evening.

That left Hugh Woodward, an old family friend, without a dinner partner. Mother always invited the whole town to the party, friends and foes alike, and insisted on having an even number of guests at the table: an etiquette rule she refused to break. I was conveniently available. "Clara, darling, you will help me out, won't you?" Just a touch of guilt, just a touch of intimacy—my mother's trademark.

I hated these parties. Most of the people were perfectly nice, but the ones who weren't—the ones who played political games, did frenetic charity work, pretended to like people because they had more social status or money, or used Botox while making sly little digs at someone else's skirt size or cellulite—those were the ones I couldn't wait to ditch when I left town, even though they existed everywhere, even inside me.

"Of course, Mother."

She lifted her cheek toward me, and I kissed her. That's what one did.

Mother held her fête in early December, after the first snow had fallen, but before the roads had clogged with angry shoppers. Connecticut was particularly beautiful, her green hills and pearl lakes just crisp, not frozen, the dust of winter newly laid, glittering with red decorations of holly berry and window poinsettias.

Mother's house—she'd inherited it along with a pile of money from her family—was a long, low Frank Lloyd Wright-ish affair crowded round by woods and overhung with pines. Father had landscaped thirty years ago with privet and holly, rhododendrons and grass; only the holly and privet were left, the rhododendrons and grass having given up the ghost when the sun disappeared into the clouds of green leaves, and my mother's disapproval became so strong it floated from the house like the scent of burnt toast.

All that green stood out spectacularly against the weathered grey stone of the house. One summer, *Better Homes and Gardens* had even done a spread. They'd planted flowers in father's garden; he'd had them dug up again at the end of the day.

Promptly at 7 o'clock on the evening of the fête, I presented myself in a short red cocktail dress and silver sandals. One didn't show up late to Mother's parties expecting a flexible cocktail hour. Show up at 7:45 and one had only fifteen minutes to gulp down the first martini before being called to dinner. Besides, being on time let me scope out the room for candidates likely to give up Mother's secrets. My dreams of a civil conversation with her hadn't lessened any, now that I was home, but her reticence required new tactics.

The downstairs rooms twinkled with gold, red and green trim, and tiny white lights. The window drapes and throw pillows had been changed to red, green and gold velvet, two large coffee tables held elaborate crèches, and a pine bough garland festooned with crimson bows and real-looking fake cranberries draped the fireplaces.

Mother's Christmas fête was strictly black tie. Women in body-draping dresses, thinner than they were at seventeen, their skin professionally smoothed, decorated men distinguished with early grey hair and tuxedos, whose eyes roamed the room for women more good-looking than their wives and men richer than they were. Their superficially delighted expressions registered underlying anxiety, perhaps at their own sense that they weren't having as much fun as they should be. Perhaps because that anxiety was roughly akin to the seventh grade schoolyard, they wielded an exacting social power, determining in a glance wielded like a Michelin four-star chef's paring knife whether or not a newcomer was worthy. It was exhausting to be part of their world and devastating to be rejected.

Martini in hand, I'd gotten trapped by Hetty Gardner, stepdaughter to my father's business partner, Ernie Brown. She was an organic lamb farmer and claimed she was selling to the biggest chefs in New York—which meant her business had a slightly better than fifty percent chance of survival. She'd cornered me by my mother's stadium-sized Christmas tree and was holding forth on the merits of homeopathic remedies for sheep diseases, while shooting glances at Hugh. Unable to pry myself loose from her without a small shower of ornaments traveling with me, I suffered through her litany until Mother rang the cowbell for dinner.

So much for checking out the crowd.

Of course, Mother created seating charts. She alternated men and women, broke up couples, and put rivals (usually) at opposite ends of the table. I was seated next to Hugh, a not unsurprising choice, given that I'd replaced Mary Ellen Winters, my mother's oldest enemy. Their enmity began long before I was born, and Mother had never deigned to tell me its source. What amused me was the subtext: Mary Ellen would see being seated next to Hugh Woodward as a message from my mother: "Get some help."

Hetty sat across from us, watchful, her bare, buff arms shining in the candlelight. Mother sat at the far end of the table, with a polished-looking man, silver-haired and square-jawed, to her right. Hugh Woodward was also handsome, but the softness in his cheeks and gut would soon shape him like a whiskey bottle. He had been my mother's therapist for twenty years. I'd overheard gossip in town that an affair between them broke my father's heart. Whether it was true or not, Mother's independent self couldn't be touched by either my father or me.

The line between therapist and friend was blurred early on. Hugh frequented our family dinners and often spent holidays with us. After my father died, Mother always mentioned Hugh in the Christmas and birthday cards that never failed to find me, no matter where in the world I was hiding. He was the perfect person to answer my questions.

I looked down the table at Mother, this woman whom I mirrored in so many respects. Both petite and lithe, we shared the same blonde hair, the same green eyes with the littlest uptick at the corners, and the same long, thin toes that made finding sandals difficult. We both laughed with a gurgle. We liked Mendelssohn and take-out Chinese. Not that she told me these things: I knew from watching her, seeing the take-out cartons in the refrigerator, and eavesdropping on her conversations. I knew she kept a stash of detective novels by her bed; at nine or ten years old, I'd snuck into her bedroom when she was out for a forbidden read. Curling into the pillows on her bed, I smelled her perfume, lay where she lay, tried to become her for those few precious hours.

Unfortunately, rumors like the one about Hugh Woodward and my mother linger in the community brain, making inroads like worms in dirt. I know part of the motivation for what I did was that rumor, a pure, driving need to know my mother. But finally, we are all unknowable, the psyche impossible to collapse into a package that can be dissected and neatly labeled. It didn't stop me from trying, from trampling into the spaces others wished to keep private.

"So, Clara. Constance tells me you might be job-hunting in the new year." Hugh spooned up some of the delicate scallop soup that comprised my mother's first course.

Leave it to Mother to share my life along with her own. "Yes. Maybe." *If I hadn't returned to Paris.*

"Something using your degree in landscape architecture?" It sounded patronizing, but it was hard to tell since his mouth was full of roll.

"Mm. My Ph.D. From Harvard." I couldn't resist.

"Yes, I remember. What have you been doing with all that education?" he asked.

"A little of this, a little of that."

As Hugh knew, I didn't have to work. I'd inherited my father's money, half his landscape architecture business, and his passion for the land. While that passion had propelled me through graduate school, I had never taken on my half of the business, and had instead let father's partner handle it for the last fifteen years. Any work I'd done had been short-term because I needed to explore the world.

Hugh said, "You don't sound thrilled."

I laughed and drank a little more wine. I had to finish this glass. A different wine would be served with the next course. "It's kept me busy enough I suppose."

At the laugh, he'd turned and looked at me, assessing. He seemed to notice everything—the blonde hair, the green eyes, the pointy chin and freckles, the skinny, pale mouth. Some men found the combination appealing, but Hugh's thoughts weren't clear. I suppose psychologists have long practice in bland, neutral faces. "We haven't seen you in a long time, Clara."

Mother's servers came by right about then and unloaded another half bottle of wine—a new one—into my Baccarat and Hugh's. Cleared the soup. Brought the first course, a pasta tossed with golden caviar on a gold-rimmed plate. I dizzily twirled some around my fork, noticed Hetty staring at Hugh again.

"I've been avoiding the place." I laughed once more, taking in the voluptuous flower arrangements, the crystal chandeliers, the excess of small, white, glittering candles, Hetty's intense and inquiring face across the table.

"What a lovely laugh you have," he said. "So different from your mother's."

After that, it was easy. Hugh and I slipped out separately, after the dessert course, upstairs to my childhood bedroom, redecorated to Mother's taste in black, white and gold silk. No one would interrupt us here.

We returned in time for after-dinner brandy. Mother always brought in the Methodist church choir to sing carols (strange, as we were Episcopalian, but our choir never was worth much, except in their stock portfolios). They'd reached "Joy to the World." Mother, still seated next to that handsome man: silver-haired, distinguished, knowing—someone I'd never seen before—slid Hugh a cool look. Me she ignored. Nothing new about that. She didn't say anything later either.

And then, Hugh was dead, and I figured we didn't have to talk about it at all.

CHAPTER 3

fficers Joe Munson and Pete Samuels showed up the next day at noon to inform us that Hugh had been beaten to death with a fireplace poker and to question Mother about the murder. My third feeling, after the shock of realizing Mother was considered a suspect and sadness at losing Hugh, was uncharitable frustration that my prime source of information had dried up. Never mind that, when I'd lured him upstairs the night before to ask if he knew about Mother's trouble, he'd told me to ask her myself. And of course, Mother wouldn't kill Hugh. They were friends. Why would Mother kill Hugh?

Mother wouldn't kill Hugh, would she? No. Too messy. Too uncontrolled. Not possible.

The interview began cordially enough. Mother seated the officers in the living room and asked if they wanted tea. They did. She left me to entertain. The room smelled of cinnamon with an overlying hint of old champagne. Someone must have spilled on the carpet.

"You live here with your mother?" Samuels asked.

"Temporarily."

He looked like he thought I was a bit old for that. His mistake was thinking I cared what he thought. He leaned back on the couch, shoved a throw pillow to the side.

Mother arrived with the tea tray. She'd used the silver, complete with pot, sugar, creamer, and four of her daintiest china cups. Super-thin sugar cookies left over from the fête formed a flower shape on a delicate porcelain plate. Intimidation via Bernardaud. Even so, the tray must have been heavy, as it shook a little when she set it down. She poured; they set their cups on the coffee table on top of the linen napkins she passed them. They didn't drink.

Munson began. "Since Dr. Woodward spent most of his evening here, you might have seen or heard something that would be useful."

Mother's eyes flicked at me, but she nodded.

"Did Dr. Woodward have any enemies?"

"Everyone has enemies."

"Is that a yes?" This from Samuels. If he hadn't been a cop, he would actually be kind of hot. Yet another reason why I shouldn't be allowed out of the house on my own.

She shrugged. "I guess so. I don't know."

"How about someone who might hold a grudge against him?"

"No."

"Was he involved romantically with anyone?" Munson again.

Samuels sipped at his tea cup. He looked remarkably comfortable with it given that his body looked useful for bulldozing through doors.

"Me, I suppose." Mother leaned back and tapped her index finger on the armrest.

All the rumors were true, then? I liked Hugh, but wasn't it déclassé to date one's therapist? Mother must have been really lonely. How surprising.

How sad.

"Involved how, ma'am?" Samuels set his tea cup down and leaned forward, flexing his fingers, as if he wanted to wrap them around Mother's throat.

Munson leaned back. His gesture seemed to calm Samuels, who let his hands go slack.

"He was my analyst, and, well, there were all those rumors. Rumors tend to create a relationship of a kind."

They nodded again, a pair of those bobble-head dolls that used to appear in everyone's rear car windows. "Yes, ma'am. We need to know if the rumors are true."

My mother glanced in my direction. "Where there's smoke, officer..." Her voice drifted off while her fingers traced the paisley pattern in the chair's fabric.

"Is that a yes, ma'am?" Munson waited, pencil poised over his notebook.

She inclined her head, but barely, like Princess Diana.

"Were you intimate with Dr. Woodward last night?" Samuels seemed to prefer the salacious questions.

"Why would you think that?" Again, that little glance slid my way. For a woman of iron control, it was a remarkably uncontrolled gesture. Surely, Munson and Samuels could see her doing it. What did she think we'd done upstairs anyway? *Oh my god.*

"You've just confirmed the rumors."

"Yes, officer, but that has nothing to do with last night."

She couldn't have been with Hugh. I'd watched his car leave, and Mother hadn't gone out, had she?

"We have a witness who claims you entered Hugh's house around the time of the murder." Samuels dug a bit of dirt out from under his fingernail and flicked it onto the carpet.

"And who would this be?"

"We will need a DNA sample, ma'am."

My stomach dropped. Shouldn't she have a lawyer?

Samuels asked, "Did you kill him, ma'am?"

"Don't be ridiculous."

"Is that a 'no,' Mrs. Montague?"

She sent him a withering look. Samuels, maybe the first human ever, seemed impervious. "You need to come down to the station, ma'am."

"Are you arresting me?"

"We'd like to ask you a few more questions." Munson threw me a look.

"Clara, call Bailey." She stood.

Had something happened between her and Hugh? If I'd been home earlier, could I have prevented it? I pulled out my cell phone and started toward the coat closet.

"I don't need you, Clara. Just *stay here.*"

She collected her coat and handbag, then walked out without a word, Munson and Samuels behind her. The front door snapped closed.

I dialed Bailey, who assured me she would meet Mother at the station. "You won't be able to see her. Seriously, Clara, let me assess the situation first, okay?"

I disconnected and slid the phone into my pocket.

Mother was now definitely in trouble and completely out of reach. With nothing for me to do, the house felt claustrophobic. I left the dirty tea service for the maid, pulled on a pair of wooly boots and a sheepskin coat, and grabbed the keys to the Land Rover. I needed advice, and Richard and Paul were just the ones to give it to me. At this point, they were my only friends, unless you counted the barista at Starbucks, and I didn't feel like hanging out alone with a latte and the inevitable idiot at the next table speaking importantly into his cell phone about butter futures or his prostate exam.

They knew I was home, but I didn't know how they would take my just showing up on their doorstep. Faithful Paul had always sent regular missives by email or text, whether I replied or not, and I'd seen them over the years, but my communication was erratic, and that was a kind word for it.

I shut and locked the front door. It had started to snow and for a moment, I sat in the Land Rover and watched the flakes collect on the drive. Had the dreams been warning of Mother's arrest? Why would someone kill Hugh? At least I knew now why I'd come home. I shoved the car in gear.

Ten minutes later, I pulled up in front of a sweet little house by the water. In the summer, the herb garden puffed over the walk and made the air smell like a perfumed bath. Today, the snow-dusted path led to the porch with its purple front door, around which the house gleamed pale yellow like some grandmother's fairytale home. They'd spent a lot of time fixing it up before Richard was diagnosed with HIV two years ago, finding pleasure in working on it together.

Now, Paul's recent messages communicated an ongoing tension, a waiting for bad news that ate up any excess energy.

Paul opened the door. He looked tired, his hair ruffled upright and his shoulders stiff, but his eyes brightened when he saw me. "Oh good! Just what we need to cheer us up." He pulled me into the house, calling to Richard, who loped through the kitchen door into the living room that stretched across the front of the cottage.

"Hey lady!" He engulfed me in a bear hug, and I relaxed. Richard was six-foot-three and about two-hundred and fifty pounds. He reminded me of a cat who was all muscle and swagger until he got into your lap, and then he was nothing but purr. Paul, in contrast, was lithe and slender and topped with brush-cut dark hair.

"You sure this is a good time? You guys look like you just got in from a night of partying."

Richard was still in his robe and Paul's eyes were bloodshot; Paul clutched a mug of coffee.

Paul shook his head. "We were hashing over the week." He gestured toward the kitchen. Grateful, I draped my coat over a maroon leather recliner, Paul's one concession to Richard's tastes in the room. The rest was decorated with heavy brocades in dark green and navy and lightened with photographs of the sea Paul had taken on their annual trip to Bermuda.

In the kitchen, a cheery haven of yellow, green, and ruffled plaid seat cushions, a plate of bagels with cream cheese and lox sat in the middle of the table. Richard grabbed another plate from the cupboard and shoved cream and sugar in my direction, while Paul poured coffee.

"What's up?" I asked.

They looked at each other. Paul said, "Richard's HIV has been outed at work, and everyone freaked."

"I thought that stupid behavior left with the eighties."

Richard tipped his head in defeat. "Seems not."

I reached for his hand. "What are you going to do?"

"Nothing. They can't fire me, and no one is overtly rude, just nervous. They don't want to talk to me; they don't want to work with me. They even want to meet in the conference room instead of in my office, like I've contaminated the space I work in. I now know why shunning was so effective."

"Oh, Richard..."

"They're scared and ignorant." He shrugged.

"Time to find another job?"

"I like the one I've got. Anyway, we can't do without my income."

Richard was the VP of a small technology firm in New York City. Paul owned his own herbal shop and was a healer and therapist. Briefly, I wondered what Hugh had thought of Paul's kind of therapy.

Paul must have seen the shadow cross my face. "What's the matter, Clara? You didn't come to hear our problems."

"You make it seem like I don't care."

"That's not what I meant, and you know it."

He stood to fetch the coffee pot. I ran my finger around the lip of the mug.

"Hugh Woodward was murdered last night, and Mother has been arrested for the murder. On top of that, she's acting weird."

Richard said, "Murdered? How?"

Paul said, "Honey, your mother's never *not* been weird."

"Someone beat him to death with a poker—and she's weirder than normal."

"How is that possible?" asked Richard.

"Stop," said Paul.

Richard shrugged, grinning.

"True confessions first: last night I dragged Hugh up to my bedroom between the dessert and the after-dinner drinks."

Richard leaned back and guffawed. "Home for less than a week, and she's already seduced Mama's therapist. Was this for fun or profit?"

"Oh god. That's what Mother thinks too. But I didn't. It was the only place I could think of that was truly private. You know what those parties are like. I'd been trapped by the Christmas tree with Hetty Gardner for a half hour before dinner. Not even a second martini could help me through that tedium."

"So what did you do if you didn't, you know....?" Paul put the coffee pot back and sat down again. I rolled my eyes at him.

"I asked if he knew anything about Mother's troubles. He waxed rhapsodic about his professional ethics and how much he loved Mother and would never, ever hurt her."

"Never ever?" This from Richard.

"You're not helping," said Paul.

"When the police came today, Mother told them she was with Hugh last night. But unless she slipped out after I went to sleep, she's lying."

"How do you know?" Paul asked. "You haven't talked to her for fifteen years. They could have been involved."

"I—" He was right. I knew hardly anything about Mother's life and understood even less. "My god. Do you think she did it?"

Richard laughed drily. "You mean, did she assume that her daughter had slept with her lover and killed him in a jealous rage?"

I blew out a breath. "You're right. My mother doesn't have jealous rages."

"Betcha didn't think she had lovers, either." Paul draped some lox over half of his bagel and took a bite. "Why would you think something was wrong with your mother?

I pinched a corner off a bagel and rubbed it into crumbs on my plate. "My dreams."

"You're having dreams again?" Paul put down his bagel, alarmed.

I explained about the dreams of blood and the appeals for help. "Maybe her being wrongly accused is what the dream meant. Or maybe she committed this crime to prevent a greater one? I don't know. Asking Hugh was my best idea."

"Why don't you ask her?"

"I can't. She won't tell me."

Paul looked at me speculatively. "That's two different answers."

Richard threw in his two cents. "Talk to her friends. She had a houseful of them last night."

"Right. Then the most private woman in the world finds out her daughter is asking questions of everyone in town, and that's the end of that."

"The end of what?"

"Good point. There is no *there* there, is there?"

Richard shook his head. "Lord save me."

"Fine. Me. It's the end of me. If I ever want any relationship with my mother, my prying will kill it. Anyway, isn't that the police's job?"

Paul said, "Do you want a relationship with your mother? I would have a hard time telling if you did. C'mon, Clara. You show up after fifteen years with some wild story about your mother being in danger, corner her therapist in the bedroom and demand private information. How do you think she'll feel if she finds out?"

"I've tried to ask her directly." That wasn't exactly true. "I might be able to draw out some gossip, but Hugh was my best shot—discreet and knowledgeable. I needed him. My dreams are getting worse, and you know what happened last time."

Paul teetered between irritation and worry. "I remember flying to Switzerland to check out that Zurich clinic for you. I remember you curled up in hotel bed, where you'd been for a week without eating." He paused, shook his head. "The dreams will tell you, but you have to give them time. You know that."

"I don't want to lose her." To my horror, I felt myself tear up.

"Oh, honey, of course not." Richard handed me a paper napkin for my nose.

"At the reading of father's will, she told me she'd be here when I was ready to come home, only she's exactly the same woman I left fifteen years ago. It's still impossible to connect with her!"

I blew my nose. "Sorry," I said. "I'll get hold of myself, I promise."

"You know," Paul speculated, "Maria Leiber might talk to you confidentially."

"Who's that?"

"Hugh's wife."

"Hugh was married?"

"Sure," Paul said. "Forever." He noted my shocked expression. "Forever is about fifteen years, give or take—after you left at least."

"I never heard about a wife."

"You haven't been around to hear about much of anything, have you?" He raised his eyebrows at me. "Hugh and his wife have—had—an open marriage. They used their money and social connections to help each other, but didn't want to be tied down. They both had open affairs for years, but from everything I saw when she visited, they adored each other fiercely. All very pragmatic. Anyway, she spends most of her time at that monstrosity of a house they own in Helena."

I said, "You've been to her house in Helena?"

"No, hon, she showed me pictures. Wanted to outfit a room for massage and aromatherapy, and paid me to consult."

Richard said, "I imagine the police called her. When she arrives, I'm sure she'd talk to you."

"How would she know anything about Mother?"

Paul said, "Maria and Hugh talked all the time. If something was going on that Hugh could talk about, Maria would know."

I thought about my dreams: the blood on Mother's hands, her pleas for my help, her locked up in jail, someone seeing her going into Hugh's house last night. I'd long wondered if she had the same gift I did, and if she did, could she be sending me the dreams—or was that wishful thinking? At least it would be some kind of communication. "Even Maria, it'll get back to Mother, and she'll be furious with me," I repeated.

"She doesn't have magical powers," Paul said, eyeing me.

Richard said, "If she's going to know anyway, you should start with the person who can give you the most information."

I sighed, resigned. "Fine. Let me know when she arrives and I'll call her."

"Maria isn't who I mean."

I looked at him, puzzled.

"Think. Who else has the goods and wouldn't care who she dished to?"

It took me a minute. Then, suddenly, light. "Mary Ellen Winters."

"She'd be the one."

"She'll tear me to bits."

"We'll patch you up." Richard shrugged. "Anyway, you have nothing better to do."

CHAPTER 4

other was detained by the police overnight, so the next morning I met Bailey at the police station. There had been an eyewitness, a police officer, which gave them more of a case than I'd anticipated. Bailey had taken her retainer from my hot little hand, saying, "You can't be a party to my conversation with her, and I can't allow you to see her before they talk to her again this morning. They might want to speak to you, and you need to keep your stories separate."

"But—"

"You can see her when we're done."

Bailey and I had been friends once, but competition interfered. We couldn't both have the prizes we'd wanted: highest SAT score, lead in the school play, soccer team captain. Sometimes I really missed her; I missed having women friends. It seemed like a long time since I'd had any.

Bailey left me cooling my heels in the lobby, while she and her tight, grey, pinstriped self clicked down the hall on spike heels. Every cop in the place peered after her. I settled myself as comfortably as I could into one of the orange molded plastic chairs that lined the vestibule, and tried not to picture Mother locked in a concrete room with no windows.

At ten o'clock in the morning, station activity amounted to a series of people crisscrossing the lobby, some in uniform, some not. I let their monotonous circling and patter and the sleepy heat put me into a half-dream about Mother and me running in circles with buckets of water trying to extinguish a fire.

I was startled awake by a deep voice.

"Miz Montague."

I nearly slid from the chair as I looked up into a pair of topaz eyes, which didn't help my state of mind any.

"Your mother is ready to go. May I show you the way?"

I shook my head a little to clear out the dream. "What happened to Bailey?"

"Your lawyer's gone."

And left me snoozing in the lobby of the police station. *Nice.* We could talk about that when her bill arrived.

He led the way, allowing me to be diverted by his incredible, uh, shoulders. They filled out a taupe wool suit that looked custom made. No wedding ring on his left hand. His black hair curled tightly around a dark skull and a thin rim of bright white shirt gleamed between the dark skin of his neck and the collar of the suit. I imagined he was a detective, since he wasn't wearing a uniform—and what a nice detective package it was. Then I chided myself. Checking out the guy who jailed my mother wasn't cool. I distracted myself by wondering if it was a challenge to be a black police detective in this oh-so-white town.

Mother sat at a table in a grey box of a room. The one door contained a small window threaded with wire through which I could see the guard. I sat down opposite her. Even after a night of questioning, she remained regal. The only sign that all was not well were her eyes, which seemed pinched, as if she'd rubbed them after cutting up jalapenos.

"Clara."

"Mother."

"Thank you for calling Bailey." The thaw was akin to flake ice. Not solid, yet still ice.

"Of course. What evidence do they have?"

"None." Her right shoulder moved up a quarter of an inch and then down again, her version of a shrug. "Some meaningless fingerprints. I handled the fireplace poker the last time I visited Hugh; I'm better at keeping fires going than he is."

"And the witness?"

We stared at each other. I didn't know what she was thinking. I had never known what she was thinking.

Then I remembered Paul's suggestion that I ask her. What I really wanted to know was whether or not she had had an affair with Hugh, but I didn't ask that. "What's going on, Mother?"

Finally, she said, "You must be *very* careful, Clara."

I spread my hands out in front of me to make the universal gesture of what-the-hell-are-you-talking-about.

She looked away. "Fire."

"Fire? Are you kidding? Because of some poker—"

"Talk to Paul." She wouldn't meet my eyes.

I remembered my dream in the lobby and got one of those weird little shivers. I wondered if I should tell her about it, but I didn't feel like listening to her dismiss me yet again. I had accepted that she would never acknowledge my intuition. But now I had to try to reach her across the divide my dreams had created.

"Mother, I—"

"Thanks for coming," she said.

"Have they arrested you?"

"No, but I assume they will shortly. The witness took a photograph, Clara."

"What? Did you go to Hugh's last night?"

"No." Her shoulders sagged a little, then straightened, as if the ice in her spine had melted and refrozen. "But someone wants it to look that way."

"You think you're being set up? Who would do that?"

But she refused to say anything more.

I couldn't do anything else, at least not here. The guard asked if I needed help finding my way out and I told him no. Big mistake. It took me ten minutes to find my way back to the lobby, but that could have been more about my confused state of mind than the layout of the police station.

Blood coated Mother's hands, clothes and face. Blood-glazed bone poked through the skin of her knees. She tried to crawl, using her elbows to pull herself toward me. Red varnished her face. As I watched, it grew and spread, as if it were alive. It flowed from her eyes like tears, down her body, reaching across the dead space between us...

I'd woken myself from this dream four times tonight, pain like electric shocks radiating across my chest. Even when I forced myself awake, it took several minutes before the pain eased, and, if I fell back to sleep, the dream picked up where it left off. At three a.m., exhausted and panicky, I turned on the light and sat with my arms wrapped around my knees until the sun eased over the horizon.

I slumped down to the kitchen in my white flannel PJs and made coffee, doctored it with sugar and real cream, and took it into the solarium, where I curled into a settee and stared out through the floor-to-ceiling windows to wake up. The dreams often left me feeling both drugged and anxious, as if I'd taken a sleeping pill and couldn't quite shake the effects. The dreams before my father died had caused insomnia, anxiety, and finally panic attacks. It wasn't a state I wanted to return to.

Outside, a gentle hill sloped to a pond just skimming with ice. Once, when I was ten, my mother had held a skating party for me and four of my friends. Mother rented skates for the girls who didn't have any, and when we had had enough of giggling and falling on our butts and tramping through the snow in our skates, she set us up in the solarium with a hot chocolate party, complete with new stuffed animals, gingerbread cookies, tea sandwiches, perfect little cakes with icing strawberries and flowers, and a new fairytale book for each of us. I still had the book. Come to think of it, she'd even gotten the editor to sign them for us. It was the only memory I had of her doing something for me that wasn't coldly practical.

I wondered what had happened to those girls. They could still be living around here, married to stockbrokers or IT specialists or hedge fund traders or wannabe politicians. After all, that's the kind of girls we were, after we went to graduate or law school. Had to have the education, even if we never did a thing with it. Like me. All my education and I'd never put it to use. And if I stayed? If I somehow persuaded Mother to let me help her and our relationship became more of what I wanted and less of what I remembered, what then? Would Ernie want me as a working partner in my father's business or did he prefer me as a silent one? Would I even want to commit myself to a "real" job? Would Mother even want me to stay?

Then what drifted through my befogged mind was that, no matter what I did, Mother wouldn't like it. Even that idyllic afternoon was colored with the faint stain of disapproval—for what I couldn't remember. If I stayed to help, she would be angry. If I left, she would be angry. If I talked to her friends, she would be angry. If I didn't do anything, she would condemn me for my laziness. And that gave me a lot of latitude.

I had always wanted her to accept my gift. She never had, so I'd gone through life defensive. Now, I felt a bit of that defensiveness fall away. I would use my gift, because it was the right thing to do, and maybe because it would help me know her. Knowing her mattered to me. Father was gone. We only had each other.

Most of all, I needed to know if she had the intuition, too. I'd long suspected she did, but if so, she'd kept it a state secret. Things she'd said in passing about "that kind" of experience led me to believe she knew exactly what kind it was. Knowing who we were, how those genetic connections played out in me, would make me feel less alone in the world—and maybe her, too. My talking to Mary Ellen Winters would jeopardize my finding out, but I couldn't see any other way forward.

Mary Ellen was Mother's age, which made her about fifty. The last time I'd seen her, seven or eight years ago on a surreptitious visit to Richard and Paul's, she'd looked good—buff from lots of time at the gym and on the masseuse's table. She liked designer clothes, Thierry Mugler and Prada, things that only looked good on women who seemingly hadn't eaten for the last three months. Her hair was streaky blonde, her hands free of rings. Hadn't she been married? I wondered what had happened to him. Wasn't he a doctor of some kind? No, that wasn't quite right. I'd met him at one of my mother's parties, maybe one of the summer ones. I seemed to remember sails and blue water. Had she rented a boat and sailed us all around for twilight cocktails or something? Why would we have been invited? Maybe it was a party like the fête, where everyone got invited whether you liked them or not.

Hugh told me Mary Ellen was working on her brother's campaign, and, in the murky back of my brain, something buzzed about her and the local Women's League. Mary Ellen would have the inside scoop on my mother and Hugh's relationship and would gloat over any misery in Mother's life. The tricky part would be convincing her I wasn't on some conniving mission from my mother—if I could get her to talk to me at all.

Thirty minutes later, I was dressed in Mother's pink Chanel suit with a pair of patent leather boots. If you were going to meet the enemy, it was best to wear camouflage. Not that I didn't love Chanel suits. I tossed a cashmere pashmina over my shoulders, grabbed the Land Rover keys and hoped I was doing the right thing.

Paul said Mary Ellen manned the phones at the Women's League headquarters on Mondays, the perfect place to beard the bear in her den, or something like that. I pulled into the League parking lot at noon, in time to see Mary Ellen tripping out in her Uggs and miniskirt. Not very appropriate wear for a fifty-year-old fashionista. She must be having a bad day.

I called to her. She turned slowly, red-rimmed eyes focusing with trouble. She looked like she'd stayed up all night partying. "Clara." Her voice was flat. "I heard you were back in town. How nice for you. What do you want?"

"I was hoping you could help me. I'm looking for a cause." I smiled my most winning smile. Years of practice learning those social skills Mother demanded.

Her shoulders slumped. "I don't have time for your mother's games today. Go home."

"I'm sorry?"

Her head, which had swiveled toward her car, swiveled back toward me. "What?"

I felt as if we were playing "who's on first."

"I understand you had a crisis the night of Mother's fête. I'm good at putting out fires, thought I could help with Andrew's campaign." I smiled. "Lots of time as an administrator." Exaggeration for a good cause.

She looked briefly disconcerted, then recovered. "You're a Republican?"

I shrugged and felt four generations of liberal Democrats fly over me with their wings of death.

"Constance would never approve."

"Exactly," I said.

Her eyes narrowed. "I need lunch. Come." She gestured toward her alarmingly clean BMW. I wondered if she kept the chauffeur in the trunk to polish it between drives. She beeped, the car unlocked. Stepping carefully around the ice patches, I opened the passenger door and slipped into the smell of new leather and systematic betrayal.

She drove with assurance. It was a standard transmission, and she moved from gear to gear without hesitation, sensing what the car needed and when to give it. Within a matter of minutes, we pulled up at an elite restaurant down by the water where, it was rumored, local businessmen and lawyers met their mistresses for lunch. Mary Ellen, it seemed, had a standing reservation. The maître d', a slender, olive-toned man—the color of all the service personnel in this town—took us immediately to a window table.

Without asking, she ordered us two Bombay Sapphire martinis, straight up with olives, and the maître d' left us to look at the menus and the view. I didn't usually drink at lunch; staying awake for the rest of the day was a problem, and it was a worse problem when one hadn't slept much the night before, still felt slightly out of it, and needed all one's wits to pull off a con. When the waiter returned with the drinks, I asked for a large glass of water and prayed for the best. Mary Ellen lifted her gin in a silent toast and drank half of it down.

She said, "I recommend the duck, the Caesar salad with chicken and any of the fish dishes, especially the scampi." By the time the waiter returned to take our order, she'd finished her drink. She ordered the scampi and another martini. I ordered the Caesar salad.

"So," she said. "You're still rebelling, is that it? And you've come to me because I'm the sure-fire way to get back at your mother. Never mind that she's locked up for murder, being gone for fifteen years isn't enough rebellion for you?"

Her sharpness stung. Had I been merely rebelling all this time? I considered it self-protection, not some extended adolescent tantrum. I put part of the truth on the table. "I want to know about my mother and Hugh. She won't tell me.

I also need employment, and if it's something my mother doesn't approve of, maybe it will annoy her enough to get her to open her mouth." Which appeared to be sewn shut with braided titanium fishing line.

"The girl has guts." She laughed again, with a little meanness. "But really, Clara, why would I help you? Having her locked up in jail is amusing. And what's in it for me, aside from pissing off Constance? I haven't had any trouble doing that for the last thirty years."

The waiter brought her second martini. She took a long sip, but not as big as the first one.

I looked out at the water. The clouds had lowered again, and whitecaps skipped across the tops of the slate waves. I felt more than saw Mary Ellen swing her UGG-fitted foot rhythmically, in sync with the muted music issuing from speakers above our heads. I thought of the blood on Mother's hands in my dream. I couldn't be fainthearted.

I smiled that good society girl smile again. "But what a betrayal to have her own daughter working for the woman she hates the most. Can you really top that, Mary Ellen?"

Her lips pinched together, probably to keep her from shrieking yes. She leaned across the table, her eyes feverish and bright. "I'll tell you about your mother on one condition. You give as good as you get."

I hedged because she would expect it and to recover my breath at her malice. "I've been gone for fifteen years."

Her eyes glittered. "You know enough. I promise you."

"Fine. But the deal comes with sponsorship into the Women's League and invitations to your parties, as well as that job with your politician brother and his campaign."

"Want a plaid headband, too?" she mocked.

"Of course." Two could play that game.

She tapped one long nail on the table. "You don't know what you're asking, Clara. Some secrets should stay buried, and there are people in this town who will do whatever it takes to make sure they do."

My heart flip-flopped in a moment of self-doubt. What if I didn't really want to know what Mother had hidden all these years?

The waiter arrived with our meals, setting them carefully in front of us, and wiping the edges of the plates of imagined bits of stray food or dust that had accumulated in transit. He bowed slightly and left, but not before Mary Ellen ordered her third martini. I asked for more water. I hadn't even lowered my drink to the level of the olives, and already I felt woozy. Mary Ellen enjoyed her food and ate all of it—unusual for a woman of her skeletal shape—sopping up the extra sauce, or perhaps the gin, with bread. She seemed to have forgotten what I'd asked and chatted casually about a garden club open house planned for Christmas and her family's upcoming post-holiday trip to Vail. Only when we'd made it to double espressos and chocolate mousse (for Mary Ellen—I couldn't eat that much, and certainly not at lunch, or I'd be the size of Grand Central Terminal) did she finally say, "Agreed."

Our conversation had gone so far afield since my initial demands that it took me a minute to figure out what she was referring to, which might also have been influenced by my finishing the martini and her droning voice. She must have seen my confusion, because she said, "Friday at noon, my house. Women's League planning meeting for the Christmas Bazaar. We need lots of slave labor, since the event is less than two weeks away. You can interview Saturday evening at my brother's campaign fundraiser. I'll put in a good word for you—you do have some skills, don't you?"

I described my employment history.

"Good. The money's a pittance, but it's not like you need it." She sniffed and waved at the waiter for the check. I started for my wallet, but she said, "Oh please."

I tried one last time through the fog in my head to get information. "Were my mother and Hugh having an affair?"

She looked at me with what seemed like pity, if it were possible for her to feel such a thing. "Of course. They had been for years." She leaned across the table and tapped that one long, red nail on the table again. "Broke it off not long ago, though. I don't think Hugh was happy about that. I heard he kept coming around. Somebody told me Constance was thinking about getting an order of protection."

"You 'heard'? 'Somebody told you'?"

She stared at me. "You really don't understand how much your mother hates me, do you?" The waiter set the bill on the table, and Mary Ellen, without glancing at it, dropped a stack of twenties and handed it back. She threw her wallet into her purse. "We *are* enemies, after all. I don't know *everything* firsthand." She gave me that malicious smile again. "But you do."

Her driving on the way back to the Women's League headquarters was no less assured than it had been on the way out. I wondered what neuroscience would have to say about a specimen like her. She parked in the same space she'd vacated and popped open the BMW's locks. "Now, git." She twizzled her perfectly manicured nails in my direction—so I got.

On the way home, a slightly sickened feeling settled in my stomach, as if I'd sprayed a perfectly healthy plant with Round Up. I decided to believe it was the effect of a martini without enough protein, even though I knew I had done something unforgiveable in approaching Mary Ellen. Mother spoke of her rarely and always with contempt.

What had I gotten for my troubles? If I believed Mary Ellen, I had confirmation of Mother's affair and a motive for her to commit murder—nothing I really wanted.

CHAPTER 5

riday's Women's League meeting about the Christmas Bazaar consisted of women in plaid headbands, sitting in an eight-thousand-square-foot over-decorated mansion, talking about how they could save the low-income locals by selling expensive jewelry and crafts to each other. Maybe I was missing the big picture, but it seemed more self-serving than serving. But then I was hardly an innocent, having learned with the best of them how to polish off a bottle of wine, get rid of a husband, avoid my issues, and check out which of my neighbors might be useful to me. Anyway, Mother had pleaded not guilty at her hearing, and I was a little distracted.

Saturday night was the political fundraiser for Mary Ellen's brother, Andrew, where I hoped not only to lock up a job in his campaign, but also to talk to some of Mother's friends, cry a little on their shoulders, and see what kind of information I could elicit. The Winters hosted the event at their mansion. It started at seven p.m., so the attendees could get home in time to sleep off their excesses before the limo picked them up for church the following morning. The mansion itself was a huge error on the part of the Winters, a purchase, it was rumored, meant to give the family historic credibility. Apparently, their first choice had been a home in which President George Washington had slept, but they'd settled for one where John Adams had stopped on his way to the First Continental Congress in 1774. Since then, the walls had been sheet-rocked, floors evened out, and an industrial-quality kitchen, a second story, and "architecturally-appropriate" additions had been fitted on. The result was a cross between the bridge of the *Enterprise* and a badger sett. Apparently, *Architectural Digest* didn't agree with me, as they'd done three spreads on the house so far.

Andrew Winters was running for a U.S. Senate seat against Sherilyn Ambroise, an African-American Democrat. He looked like a sure win, given all the money behind him: Mary Ellen's contacts from her volunteer work and their husbands, and his friends from Yale Law and Harvard Business. His corporate law clients, General Electric, Pitney Bowes and World Wrestling Entertainment, would contribute. Andrew played the humble card, emphasizing that he'd started his career as a public servant on the school board, before an appointment to city council. He volunteered on nonprofit boards and was seen at the right political fundraisers. He might have run for governor if this seat hadn't opened up.

What was apparent about five seconds into meeting him was that he craved power and attention, but the evening was so populated with power-hungry, attention-seeking guys I almost forgot there were other kinds of men. At least half of them, the married half it seemed, came on to me. Some forgot they'd already come on to me and tried again after they'd had their third or fourth martini. This got in the way of my making friends with their wives.

At some point, it occurred to me to wonder how I had grown up among these people but not become one of them. Well, a little. Definitely in my closet. I loved Chanel and Calvin Klein and Roberto Cavalli shoes with the best of them.

Maybe what kept me separate were all the secrets I had to keep, like maybe my mother had an affair with her therapist; or that only fifteen years in age separated us; or that sometimes from her room, I heard strange noises, like someone keening.

"It was nothing," she would say if I mentioned the noises. "Really, Clara. You must stop making things up."

Sometimes I wondered what it would have been like to grow up in a home where I didn't feel split in half.

And now, what was I getting myself into by volunteering for the most high-profile activity in town, one that would certainly get my activities scrutinized like no other? Was it a short-cut to the information I needed or a path back to crazy?

A drunk, fat guy wobbled in my direction. I turned away fast and collided with someone tall and substantial in a lovely charcoal wool suit. I wanted to rest my cheek against that comforting fabric, but managed to drag myself off. I looked up into topaz eyes.

"If it isn't Miz Montague," the voice attached to the eyes said.

"I'm so sorry." I felt myself blush. "It appears I'm incapable of being graceful *and* conscious around you."

He laughed. A nice laugh, like melted chocolate. "I'm Kyle DuPont."

I shook his hand. It was warm, like the laugh, and it sucked me in, even though he was police, and they were not on my side at the moment.

"It's Clara, please."

Before I could get any further, Mary Ellen had her claw around my upper arm. "C'mon," she said. "Time for your interview."

I shrugged at Officer DuPont as she dragged me through the crowd, whispering under her breath about how *tragic* it was that my mother was in jail, especially with that new African-American cop. You just never knew with *those* people...

I yanked my arm away and thought if I could find Hugh's murderer, I'd pay him to do one extra job before they locked him up.

Andrew stood in front of a large stone fireplace in a bouquet of matching honey-wheat-blonde women. Not hard to do, mind you, in my town. The hairdresser I'd seen before Mother's party was already after me to add a little color to my hair, and I didn't even have any grey yet.

They all wore the same suit but in different colors and fabrics, and their eyes lingered on each other's jewelry, as if figuring out how to steal it. The shortest clung to Andrew's arm, as if he were a tree trunk and she a lizard. I had to admire the way he slid from her grasp to take me aside.

Andrew was a little older than Mary Ellen, but equally well-preserved. Gold and platinum hair, thick and solid, but not yet fat, an oval face, clean shaven, as all politicians were, so the voters could convince themselves he was telling the truth. He had discarded his suit jacket in favor of the rolled-up-shirtsleeves look, and fine hairs glimmered on his pale arm. "Clara. How lovely to see you. Your mother and I were so... close."

That was news. I watched him assess my hair, my chin, my breasts, waiting for a reaction, and stilled my revulsion.

"My sister has told me what an asset you would be to my campaign." One of his arms slithered across my shoulders like a boa constrictor. "When can you start?"

Pretty short interview. "Whenever you want."

"How about Monday? It's only part-time for now, but as the campaign heats up, there will be room for promotion." He dragged the word out. I wondered what he thought I would be willing to do for eight-fifty an hour.

"Sounds good," I said. Mary Ellen gave me a sharp look, but didn't say anything. The boa constrictor slid to the middle of my back.

"Tell me about your skills." The gin on his breath should have killed the boa dead of alcohol poisoning.

"I have solid research skills from my Ph.D. at Harvard. I worked in France for—oh," I waved my hand languidly through the air as if the companies were of no consequence and my tenure at each far longer than the few months it had actually been, "Moët, Chanel, Versailles—doing event and PR work." I moved slightly away from him, but that turned out to be a mistake, as the boa constrictor slid still further south, almost below the equator.

"Perfect. Just what we need. I think I'd like you to start by reviewing our donor files. Mary Ellen, don't you think she'd be great at planning fundraisers?"

Mary Ellen nodded, her right eyebrow slightly quirked.

Just as the boa started to head south of the border, two things happened simultaneously: I turned to face him, pulling myself free, and someone grabbed my shoulders and tugged me backwards, almost making me lose my balance.

"Miz Montague. I've been looking for you."

Kyle DuPont inserted his bulk between me and Andrew, slapping the maybe-senator's shoulder. Andrew winced. "Mr. Winters. How are you?"

Andrew said to me, "I see you've met our new chief of police."

"*Chief* of police?" My surprise showed like red underwear under white pants. This town *had* changed if they'd hired a black man to lead their police force.

Andrew cocked his head and Kyle DuPont rescued me. "I gave Miz Montague directions the other day. I think she thought I was a detective."

I nodded, grateful. Everyone knew my mother was in jail, but who wanted it said aloud? "You were looking for me?"

"Only if you're done with Mr. Winters."

I looked a question at Andrew. He gave a hearty slap to DuPont's shoulder, a gesture that backfired, as DuPont didn't seem to feel it, but Andrew looked as if his arm was vibrating. "No, we're done. A pleasure to meet you, Clara, and I'll see you in the office on Monday at ten." Mary Ellen watched the interchange, a bemused look on her face.

Chief DuPont guided me to a secluded corner. French doors looked out over a stone patio lightly brushed with snow. The trees, wound with little white lights, glowed. "You okay?" he asked.

"Why wouldn't I be?" I'd gotten what I wanted, but it settled uneasily on me.

"Guy has a reputation. Moved in on you pretty fast."

"I'm not fifteen, for god's sake."

He nodded, his eyes focused on Winters across the room. "You should watch out for him anyway." The coterie of blondes had returned, goldfish around an outstretched hand. Before I could ask him what he meant, he said, "Isn't that Hetty Gardner?"

"Where?" I turned again to look.

"The one not dressed like anyone else."

Hetty stood just outside the circle, her long woolen skirt and heavy clogs a thick counterpoint to the other women's delicate couture. The silver-haired man from Mother's fête lounged casually on a hot pink loveseat behind her. His eyes were watchful.

"Yes, why?"

"It's rumored she holds some kind of weird pagan ritual out at that farm of hers. Fire and sheep guts under the dark of the new moon."

"Is the chief of police supposed to spread rumors about his residents? And to a virtual stranger?"

He focused on me. "You're not a stranger. I know everything there is to know about you."

"You've researched me?" I think I squeaked. The light through the windows played across the planes of his face, deepening the shadows around his nose and mouth. "You arrested my mother. Why would you research me?"

"I have files on a lot of people."

"I didn't do anything." From squeaking I moved on to sputtering.

"We'll see."

My laugh came out like a cough. The muscles in my torso had contracted to a pinpoint, making it difficult to breathe. "Just when I was warming up to you, you had to ruin it by adding me to your suspect list."

He shrugged. "It's my job."

"So you rescue me from Slimebag Winters there just so you can throw me in the lockup?"

"'In the lockup'?" he mimicked, grinning suddenly. "What is this, a bad episode of CSI?" He leaned in. "And I wouldn't use that pet name of yours for Mr. Winters too loudly." He flicked his finger in a half circle. "Lots of ears in this room."

"Speaking of, how did you get invited?"

"Campaign has to court the town officials."

"This is the town-est of the town officials, all right." Nat Mueller, the mayor, sidled up to us and shook DuPont's hand. Mueller was thirty pounds overweight in a square, bulldog sort of way, but he carried it like a boxer, light on his toes.

The chief nodded in my direction. "You've met Clara Montague?" He didn't realize that I knew everyone in town. It was he who was new.

"I believe we renewed our acquaintance," Mueller drawled, "one or two martinis ago."

At least the man had the grace to remember and I smiled at his sort-of apology. "In fact," Mueller continued, "I've known Clara and her mother all their lives, but I hadn't seen her in so long, I forgot what she looked like." He patted DuPont on the arm, still addressing me. "Your mother did us a great favor when she pushed us into a nationwide search for police chief. We got ourselves a good man."

"Mother was involved in finding a police chief?"

"Your Mama's pretty influential around here. Not everybody likes that."

Hetty Gardner chose that moment to interrupt. "Clara."

"Hi, Hetty."

"I'm sorry about your mother." She held her head to the side slightly, as if shielding her comment from the men.

"Thanks." I glanced at Nat, not sure what he knew.

"Yeah, terrible thing, Clara. You got a good lawyer?"

"Bailey Womack."

Hetty sucked in her breath sharply, then coughed.

"You okay?" I asked.

"I, uh..." She snuffled a bit and rooted around in her pocket. A large handkerchief emerged to cover almost her entire face. If she blew, it was silent, and a moment later, the handkerchief disappeared again. "She and I didn't really get along at school."

"Hetty, you were, what, three grades behind us?"

"One," she snapped.

"Sorry," I said. "I don't remember it all that well. Actually, I've tried to forget most of it." I gave a cocktail-party laugh.

Chief DuPont leaned against the doorframe and scanned the room.

"You were pretty oblivious." Her sharp tone surprised me.

I hardly remembered interacting with her at all other than on the bus. We hadn't lived far from each other then, but later—if my fuzzy brain recalled accurately—I thought her parents moved to another part of town. After that, I hardly saw her, even though her mother's second husband, Ernie Brown, had been my father's business partner.

"I imagine forgetting wouldn't be that hard."

"What are you talking about?"

She just shook her head. "If you don't remember...."

I made the mistake of looking at the chief and he raised an eyebrow at me. "I knew you'd been misbehaving, Miz Montague."

It was all I could do not to burst out laughing. Hetty harrumphed.

Mueller changed the subject, rescuing us all. "So Hetty, how are those sheep doing? We've still gotta contract for the town picnic this summer, right?"

Hetty nodded. "Five lambs and tomatoes, lettuce, radishes—all the vegetables you ordered. I've got it all worked out. I'll butcher the lambs a week or so before, so the meat will be really fresh. I even have a couple of the high school kids lined up to help me with packing and transport." She ducked her head, presumably in deference to the mayor and his kindness in ordering from her farm.

"Sounds great," he said, a bit too heartily.

I was thinking about the lambs—little, fluffy, playful lambs. "I need another drink," I said. "Can I get anything for anyone else?"

"What's the matter, Clara? Can't you take the blood and guts?" Hetty stared at me, her eyes dark and triumphant. I could see why people thought she was dancing naked while praying to the moon goddess.

"Frankly, Ms. Gardner, I'm not sure I can either," muttered Mueller. He took my arm and guided me away from Chief DuPont and toward the bar, buried six-deep in bodies in a low-ceilinged dining room. Mueller's beefy hand stayed on my arm as we threaded our way through. It was good it was his left hand, because he needed his right hand to shake with almost every person we passed.

When we reached the relative sanctity of the bar itself, Mueller said, "I've known your mom a long time. You'll let me know if there's anything I can do, right?"

It was what people said when they didn't really want to do anything of the kind. I wanted to ask him if my mother and Hugh had had an affair. I wanted to know if they'd broken it off, if Hugh hadn't stopped coming around, as Mary Ellen said, but I didn't. "You went to school with her?"

He nodded.

I had the bartender pour me a glass of seltzer water. It was getting late and I was feeling the drinks I'd already had.

"What was she like?"

"She treated everybody the same, no matter what side of the tracks they grew up on, if you know what I mean. She was always telling stories and making plans. She wanted to be a dancer."

"A *dancer*?" I couldn't remember Mother on any dance floor.

He nodded. "She spent more time at that ballet studio than at school, but she always had time for the school newspaper—not that we had much to write about in seventh and eighth grade—and the drama teacher got her to help choreograph one of the school musicals. She was something, your mother."

"Why did she change?"

The question startled him. "I, uh... I'd have to think about that," he hedged, running his hand down his tie and patting it flat against his stomach's bulk. "The person who knew her best was Hugh. So tragic. You just say the word, and I'll do whatever I can to help." He picked up the fresh martini from the bar and then someone caught his attention, and he turned away, patting vaguely at my arm.

I looked around the room. It was as empty as any room I'd ever seen, even jammed with people. So much money and ambition couldn't fill this space with anything more than fizz. What would any of these people ever tell me that would give me the kind of insight into Mother I so desperately wanted? Mueller was right. Hugh had been my best bet, but Hugh was dead.

CHAPTER 6

 came home at two a.m. with a hangover in the making to a house too empty and quiet, and switched on some Miles Davis for company. I poured myself a huge glass of water, kicked off my shoes, and curled up on the couch. The music, or the lingering effects of the alcohol, or my exhaustion from the past couple of days, must have caught up with me because the next thing I knew, light was streaming through the windows, and I had a terrible cramp in my neck.

At least the gin had anesthetized the dreams, and although my head was fuzzy, I'd slept through the night for the first time in two weeks. I crawled into a sitting position and tried to remember what day it was. *Sunday.* Today was Hugh's memorial service. He was gone, but he was still my ticket into my mother's head. Chief DuPont had given me an idea with his reference to keeping files on people, but for it to succeed, I needed camouflage.

I called Paul, bought bagels, cream cheese, lox, red onions, and the papers; and loaded them into the car alongside a bottle of champagne from Mother's wine cellar. I needed the bubbles to cheer me up, make the hangover recede— and help persuade my audience.

Paul and Richard's walk had been shoveled but not salted. About halfway up, my heel slid into the snow and I ended up in a contorted pose worthy of a *Vogue* model. I yanked my heel out just as Richard opened the door in his bathrobe. "Hope you can take us *au naturel*. We'd barely gotten up when you called." It was almost noon.

"Another tough week?" I stepped inside and kicked off my shoes to avoid tracking in garden mud and snow. In the kitchen, Paul turned from making coffee to kiss my cheek.

Richard shook his head and opened one of the bags, inhaling the scent of the warm bread. "Ah... the greatest smell on earth."

Paul said, "People are still treating him like he's contagious. They'll get over it—"

"Maybe!" Richard interjected.

"They'll get over it," Paul repeated, "but it's going to take some time."

Richard rolled his eyes. "Pollyanna over there thinks in a few days everything will be back to normal, but we all know that isn't going to happen. I have to figure out how to handle things the way they are now, since that may be the rest of my career at this company."

I touched his shoulder. "I'm sorry." I knew what it was like to be ostracized.

"How about you? Have you learned anything?" Paul pulled mugs from the cupboard while Richard sliced bagels in half.

"Men are weird and stupid," I said.

Paul passed me a plate with his eyebrows raised.

"Present company excepted," I amended lamely.

"We're so grateful," said Richard.

"Where does this earth-shattering revelation come from?"

I slathered a bagel with cream cheese. "I went to a fundraiser for Andrew Winters last night."

"As I recall, you begged Mary Ellen for that privilege."

"That on top of the Women's League meeting I had to suffer through on Friday makes me very aware of why I've avoided them for so long."

Richard laughed. "Is your butt black and blue this morning?"

"Shut up." I wrinkled my nose at him and took a large bite.

Paul sat down opposite me. "How is your mother?"

"Also weird."

"Maybe she's secretly a man?" Richard suggested.

I almost snorted cream cheese out my nose. Paul handed me another napkin. When I could breathe again, I said, "Actually that's why I'm here."

"Because your mother's a man?" Richard pretended incredulity.

"Would you stop?" Paul tapped his hand playfully.

For I moment, I envied them so deeply it hurt.

I said, "I need to get into Hugh's therapy files."

Paul shook his head. "Oh, no, Clara. Absolutely not."

"Hugh is still the best source for information about my mother—"

"Except for your mother herself."

"Who won't talk to me, so—"

"Clara!" Paul's anger shook me, seemed to shake the whole room. The bright yellow curtains glared at me.

I stopped, felt my eyes tearing up. *Oh joy.*

"You are not above the law."

"I'll return her file after I find out why she might be in danger."

"Have you considered the consequences of reading it? Like that you might find out things you don't want to know? Maybe even about you?"

"I already know what she thinks of me."

"Do you?" he snapped. He got up and starting clearing the table, even though we had barely started eating, his movements agitated and quick. Plates crashed onto the counter, and the refrigerator door slammed shut. He turned around. "You're trying my patience. If you intend to find out who your mother is, you need to start taking responsibility for yourself."

"What does *that* mean?"

"It means that, for a long time, you've blamed your mother for all the negative things you feel and do. While she is responsible for initiating some of those patterns in you, you are now an adult and it's time you thought and behaved as a responsible grown-up."

I sat there with my mouth open even though, as a well-bred, upper-class girl, I would never do that.

Paul held my gaze as his words worked their way through my defenses, like a needle through the layers of a quilt. Mary Ellen said I'd been "just rebelling," as if I'd had an adolescent temper tantrum. I knew I'd been hiding for the last fifteen years, but I'd also been grieving—for my father, for a childhood, for the kind of family I would never have. And I'd been reconciling myself to a gift I never wanted and that my mother had tried to deny out of me.

I said, "Thank you for acknowledging that she was responsible for the beginning." I stopped. I had to say the rest of it, but the breath wouldn't move over my vocal chords and across my tongue. It was stuck in my chest. I had too much practice sticking things there.

Richard took my hand again, and that helped.

"You're right," I said. "I've gotten away for a long time with sidestepping the truth. You're right," I repeated, emphasizing it to myself. "But Paul, I'm trying to do the right thing, trying to help her and she won't listen. I need to know who I am, too. I do care about her, even if I'm not sure what that means, and I'll do what it takes to make sure she's safe, even if my actions aren't within the ethics of your profession or the law."

"So you can leave again?"

"Maybe." I thought of Paris.

Paul just shook his head, but when he looked away, Richard squeezed my 35 hand.

Hugh's house was in the woods. We arrived right at four, but had trouble parking. The road was narrow and only about a car-and-a-half wide. God forbid two cars going opposite directions should try to pass each other. Someone would have to back up a half mile.

My town ran the gamut from lavish waterfront estates to hip downtown condos to horse farms to luxurious and discreet hideaways. Hugh's house was nestled in among the rock slabs that had slid through here during the last ice age. In the summer, shade gardens and a slate patio surrounded a blue-green pool. Today, the pool was tarped and sifted over with snow.

The slate theme had been carried into the house in the floors of the vestibule and the kitchen, which was straight down and at the end of the center hall. Floor-to-ceiling windows looked out from the kitchen over the pool deck. To the right and down a step was the living room, carpeted in white. I wondered whether that had been Maria's decision or Hugh's. No woman in her right mind would install white carpet; it would be white with a beige path in about six weeks, no matter how good the maid was.

Rows of chairs faced the fireplace and an elaborate silver music stand. Next to the stand, a small table was set with a white cloth and a silver-framed picture of Hugh. The house was crowded with people, but each sat nearly silent holding a white rose handed to them by a white-gloved, tuxedoed teenager stationed at the front door. There was definitely a theme here. Who themed a memorial service? Was this the latest trend?

I tried to remember how to get downstairs to Hugh's office. It had been a long time since I'd been here, and anxiety about how I was going to get Hugh's files buzzed in my gut. A silver-haired woman in a white dress stepped to the music stand. Richard, Paul and I hurriedly took roses and found seats.

"That's Maria," Richard whispered.

"Thank you for coming." Her voice was melodious and soft, like listening to Madeleine Peyroux sing "Summer Wind." She was also beautiful. The dress, a fitted woolen sheath, fell just to her knees, accentuating her trim figure and muscular legs. With blue eyes and silver hair almost to her waist, she looked like a gracefully aging Snow White.

"I want to keep this pretty casual," she continued. "I see so many people who knew Hugh well. I have a few words to say, but then anyone who wants to talk may. I don't want to keep you here all afternoon, so if each person could limit their thoughts to a minute or so, I would be grateful." She paused and seemed to pull some energy from the packed room.

"Hugh loved this town. He loved the people; he loved the place itself. That someone here brutally murdered him is an outrage I'm having difficulty comprehending. Most of you know Hugh and I loved each other deeply, but chose to live apart. While I don't regret that decision, I do regret I was not here for him the night he was killed. People say you can't second-guess life, but I will always second-guess Hugh's death. If the killer is in this room, I want you to know that I won't let the police rest until you're behind bars forever."

I looked at Richard and Paul, a little shocked. Is this how people behaved at society funerals these days? Maybe I wasn't the only one who was out of sync. Paul raised an eyebrow at me and Richard gave a little head shake. Surreptitiously, or at least as surreptitiously as I could, I looked around the room to see who might be counted among the suspects. Everyone else was looking around, too.

Hetty cowered in her chair at the end of a row, her clogs caked with mud. Andrew and Mary Ellen Winters sat two rows from the front with Andrew's wife, Jennifer, a blonde with the kind of perfect face only achieved under the surgeon's knife. A senior lawyer at Bailey's firm, William Morgan, and his wife, sat in the front row with Nat and Beulah Mueller. Winken, Drinken, and Nod, as I'd nicknamed them, three of my new Women's League buddies, had settled a couple rows up from the mayor. Winken, I had learned from Paul, was having an affair with her podiatrist, Drinken smelled of gin, and Nod was in serious danger of overdosing on decaf coffee. She must have had eight cups at our two-hour Women's League meeting. Their real names were Wendy, Darcy, and Nancy, but it was much easier to remember them this way. I knew most of the other people by sight, but my recent self-imposed exile had caused their names to vanish.

Every one of them looked a little sick. Why would any of them want Hugh dead? What could Hugh possibly have done to anger anyone? The man I remembered was kind, even when he was skewering one's self-delusions. I shook my head, wondering how I would escape all this to find the file.

Maria paused for a moment of silence, then took the rose from her hair and laid it in front of Hugh's framed picture. "Would anyone like to speak?"

Andrew waved his rose in the air. Of course.

"We all loved Hugh," he began, as he made his way to the front of the room, and I wondered if he was making that up or knew it to be true. "When we attended Chumley Academy, we were close, close friends." I saw Richard give Paul a look. Winters then recited a story about some prank he claimed he and Hugh had pulled involving a goat from a nearby farm and a French teacher. Hetty looked incensed. "Hugh would never have hurt anyone," Andrew wrapped up. "I, also, will do whatever I can to see that justice is served."

Ah—the campaign pitch. He laid his rose in front of Hugh's picture and returned to his seat. After him came a long line of women, including Winken, Drinken, and Nod, testifying weepily to Hugh's amazing skill as a therapist.

I whispered, "Is every woman in this town in therapy?" Was it even possible that Hugh had that many patients?

Richard answered. "Pretty much."

"Seriously?"

"You grew up here; you should be able to answer that."

"It wasn't *that* bad."

"That's why you left?"

The afternoon had gradually dimmed, and now at quarter to five, the room was nearly dark. Maria gestured and a girl started lighting the silver and white candles strategically placed around the room's perimeter. Everyone watched the flames slowly create a sinister glow. Flashes from my dream in the police station flickered across my mind, and panic knotted my intestines. Someone was going to knock one of those candelabras over onto the white carpet; it would ignite and we'd be caught in the inferno, trampling each other in our efforts to get out. I started to rise, but Richard pulled me down.

Mother had appeared to a collective gasp.

She wore a white wool suit with a cream shell underneath, and her blonde hair was swept up into a chignon. Wasn't she in jail? Why would they let her out? I looked around for Chief DuPont or a police escort.

Mother was speaking. "My daughter and I have many things to be grateful for. Hugh is one of them. He guided me through some of my lowest points and kept me functioning so that I could be a mother to Clara."

Well, that was startling. We obviously had different perspectives on what mothering was. "Hugh was my closest friend, and he told me everything. He told me who his enemies were. He told me what he was planning." She paused. "*I know who you are,*" she hissed. "*And I'm going to get you.*"

The room went deadly still. The afternoon light had completely gone, and only candles illuminated the room, wavering as if they were on the Phantom's pipe organ. I felt Richard tense just as a sudden crash sent the room into chaos. At the end of the row, Winken, in her sudden haste to leave, had knocked over her chair, which fell into one of the candelabras.

I watched, locked in a panicked dream of a fiery explosion, as it wobbled over that pristine and flammable rug.

At the last moment, Nod stabilized it before the candles loosened in their holders. Meanwhile, Winken clutched the scarf at her neck and skittered toward the foyer, her heels catching on the carpet so she stumbled every couple of steps. People kept reaching for her, then pulling back as she righted herself. Others twisted in their chairs and whispered to their neighbors. The man I assumed was her husband half rose, but then subsided, as if weary of such scenes. I heard Hetty squeaking with a sort of mouse-like glee. Seconds later, the front door banged shut. The startled crowd rose as one, as if to sing a final hymn. When I looked for my mother, she had disappeared in the melee.

My mother, the fugitive. Wouldn't that be a pretty story on the front page of the local paper?

Maria got our attention by banging a baton on the music stand. "Thank you for your kind words. The reception is out the door and to your right." The crowd, responding like Hetty's sheep, tried to cram through the doorway, everyone at the same time. This was my chance.

"Why the hell isn't she in a psychiatric institution?" Paul derailed me.

"How the hell did she get out of jail?" I said.

"Who the hell are we talking about?" Richard said.

"That woman that just ran out of here, hysterical and drugged to the gills," Paul said.

"No, my mother," I said.

"I see," Richard said. "That is an interesting question to ask about your mother."

"That would be my doing," a wry voice said behind me. I turned to face the luscious Kyle DuPont. "Now I've got to find her."

An image rose behind my eyes. "Master bedroom."

The chief cocked his head.

I shrugged. "I just know that's where she is."

He turned without a word and made his way through the crowd. A few minutes later, when everyone had squished into the kitchen, he came back, towing her. He looked furious.

She had that way about her.

He nodded at Paul and Richard. "Would you gentlemen excuse us?"

Richard touched my shoulder. "We'll be near the food." I hoped it lasted long enough for me to get into Hugh's office. With that crowd ravaging the buffet table, I might not have more than fifteen minutes, and I didn't know how long it would take me to find what I was looking for. I couldn't do many more sleepless nights, or nights where I drank enough to keep the dreams at bay. I had started to feel the darkness pressing at the edges of me.

The chief told my mother to sit and she did. "Your mother has something to say," he growled.

Mother didn't look the least bit cowed, but she didn't like his anger, as if she found it an excess of emotion under the circumstances. She looked at him for a moment to indicate that she was speaking of her own free will. The chief was unfazed. Maybe she'd met her match. Wouldn't that be fun to watch?

"Clara, Chief DuPont was kind enough to allow me to come this afternoon to say goodbye to Hugh, but it seems he frowns on my using myself as bait to catch a killer."

I looked at the chief. "Which means what?"

"Your mother's lawyer was attempting to negotiate bail, but her performance just now puts an end to that."

"Do you really know who did it?" I said to my mother. "Why don't you just tell them?"

"Stay out of this, Clara. You're making it worse."

"She doesn't know," Kyle said.

"But—"

"I know what she implied. Your mother has been telling us a great deal." He held up his hand to stop her from interrupting. "Whether it's unfounded accusations and supposition, or not, we are investigating."

"Who does she think murdered Hugh?" I was incredulous. This was so like my mother.

"That's between your mother and the police."

"You shouldn't talk about me in third person," my mother said. "It's impolite."

If the chief had been a teakettle, the whistle would have screeched. He took her arm, forced her to stand. She managed it gracefully—almost. He said to me, "If someone thinks your mother knows something, they may also think she's told you. Lock all your doors, set your alarm, buy a dog, whatever. You might even stay with friends for a while."

He tossed all this off rather casually as I followed them to the foyer. He pulled my mother's coat off the rack and handed it to her. Without waiting for her to put it on, he escorted her out the door into a silver and white winter afternoon that didn't have a chance of dousing the fire started here.

CHAPTER 7

omehow I made it into the kitchen and found Richard in the press of people while managing to avoid Hetty, Drinken—who appeared to be on her second glass of wine already—Nod, and a half dozen others who wanted to be the first to know what Mother knew.

He shoved a plate of food into my hand and whispered, "What happened? You look like shit."

"The chief was tactful but said she was blowing smoke up our asses."

"What do you think? Does she know anything?"

I took a bite of shrimp. It tasted bitter and metallic, and I put it back on the plate. "How would I know?"

I'd said that phrase more in the past week than I'd said it in my entire life. "The chief thinks it may make whoever did do it come after me. He told me to get a dog. I hadn't counted on being a target."

Richard drew me over the window and put his arm around my shoulders. "Let's see if we can find a bathroom, maybe get you feeling a little better, a little more in control," he said. "You don't look so good."

In the window's reflection, his dark hair and black turtleneck disappeared into the darkness outside, leaving his pale face floating like something barely glimpsed under a wash of dark water.

"Are you sure? I mean, Paul..."

"I'll stand watch," he said.

I looked around for Paul, but he was listening to Drinken warble on about some party she'd been to last night. The next thing I knew we'd ducked under the police tape downstairs. Richard pulled his leather driving gloves out of his pocket and handed them to me. "I'll wait here," he said. "If I hear someone coming, I'll get you out."

I slid the door shut behind me. Hugh's therapy suite was lit only by the displays from the digital clocks on various pieces of equipment, as well as the glow from a switch on a power strip. Light from the outdoor spots shone through the glass doors that led to a small patio. I allowed my eyes to adjust and tried not to feel creeped out by the slightly green cast these lights gave to the room.

Jammed bookcases shadowed the walls around the fireplace. I didn't want to get too close to that part of the room anyway. I wondered if Maria had had the carpet cleaned yet, or if Hugh's blood still stained it. I shuddered, looked away, tried not to conjure an image of Hugh with his head cracked open. Was that odd smell his blood—or was I imagining it?

His desk faced the windows, no computer. I suspected it was probably being abused by a computer forensics expert. I couldn't see any filing cabinets, but he had to have paper notes, right? Doors opened to a bathroom, a hallway, and a small room with a copier, supplies, and file cabinets whose edges glinted like cat's eyes. I pulled the door to the supply room shut behind me, hoping I would hear Richard if he sent a warning, and turned on the light.

My heart pounding, I pulled open the top drawer of the first cabinet. Perfect. Patient files. The third drawer down held the M's. While the copier next to me suggested an alternative to "borrowing," Mother's file was too fat to copy, and someone would notice if I walked out with a huge envelope in my purse. Could I take part of it? What part would be most useful?

I suddenly felt seedy. How would I feel if someone read my file from that Swiss hospital? Even if their intention was to help me, I wouldn't understand and neither would Mother. I stood paralyzed, then set the file down to check out the second file cabinet. It held a second set of patient files. I pulled out another file with Mother's name on it and, puzzled, flipped the covers back to compare the contents.

The first file contained DSM diagnostic codes, session notes, a list of pre-scribed medications, behavioral changes and so on. The second contained pages of prose. Its dates corresponded with the first file. Why would there be two? Quickly, I put the first one back and kept the second. I'd deal with my ethics later. I shut the drawers, grabbed an envelope from the stacks of office supplies and shoved the file in. I snapped out the light and cracked open the door only to hear Richard say, "I was curious, Officer, but I haven't touched anything. I didn't even know the police had posted a guard. Is that only for the party?"

The cop's response was muffled, but Richard's message was clear. I tiptoed to the glass doors. Installed with metal tracks, they might scrape open, but I had to risk it or sleep where Hugh was killed, and I was already freaked out enough.

Richard, bless him, was still chatting up the guard. I clicked the lock open and pulled slowly. No luck. The door squawked. I yanked it and ran, my heels slipping on the snow-covered slate. I fell to one knee, the file skittering out of my hands. Behind me, I heard the inner door slam open and the guard shout.

I scrambled up, grabbed the file, and skidded around to the front of the house as a group of people came out the front door. I inserted myself into their posse as if I'd walked out with them, brushing at the snow on my hands. Richard appeared magically behind me carrying my coat, which he casually draped over the envelope in my arms. "I'll call Paul later," he muttered, shepherding me toward the car. He had just turned the key in the ignition when the back door opened and Paul got in. "Leaving me behind?"

"Shut the door," Richard growled. The cop was headed down the path toward us, waving his flashlight like a baton. "Stop the car," he yelled.

Richard pretended not to hear him, but he couldn't go anywhere until the Mercedes in front of us moved, and the Mercedes couldn't move until the Lincoln Navigator in front of it finished maneuvering out of its parking space. The officer started to run. He shouted, "I've got your license plate number."

"Did you steal her file?" demanded Paul, peering over the front seat at the envelope. "Hand it over."

"That cop can't see me giving you anything."

"Put it around the seat. Hurry!"

I slipped the envelope between the door and the front seat. Paul yanked it through.

"What are you doing!"

"Pretending to be the therapist I am." He pulled the file out and started flipping pages. "You've taken his shadow notes."

"Shadow notes?"

"Process notes for his use only. Stuff that he's kept out of the public record."

The officer tapped on my window.

"We're busted. Chief DuPont is going to kill me," I whispered.

Paul lowered the back window. "Yes, officer? Can I help you?"

"Step out of the car. All of you."

"Whatever for?"

The cop looked at me. "Ms. Montague knows what for."

"Clara?" Paul looked shocked. "Really, officer. She just lost a close family friend. Can't it wait?"

"Step out of the car, folks."

Richard put the car in park, opened the door and stepped out. He'd managed to swing it partly into traffic behind the Mercedes, which now could accelerate away, since the Lincoln had finally gotten itself extricated. The BMW behind us honked, trying to edge by. Richard had pulled out just far enough to block him. A long line of cars joined the chorus. The officer looked exasperated. "Sir, you'll have to move your car, so traffic can move."

"You told me to step out of the car."

"Don't be difficult, sir."

The officer, McNulty according to his name tag, extended his hand to Paul. "I'll take that file, thanks."

"These are confidential notes on a therapy patient."

"I believe Ms. Montague took them from Dr. Woodward's files downstairs."

"Do you have proof of that?"

"I have enough. You'll need to come down to the station and tell Chief DuPont why you were rooting around in Dr. Woodward's confidential files in a crime scene." The chorus of horns sounded like a symphony of coked-up ducks. "Ms. Montague can ride with me, and you can follow behind."

———

I felt sick. The chief listened to Officer McNulty's story and put me in a cell across the aisle from Mother. Bailey reassured me it would take a couple hours at most to get me out, but I felt as trapped as I had when I lived at home, before father died. Why was it so easy for me to slip back into that feeling—as if coming home immediately shaved off adulthood and left me an awkward and desperate ten-year-old trying to figure it all out. Sometimes, I felt as though I were a blank space in the room. Mother could see everyone else, hear them, interact with them, but I was the margins at the edge of the page, the spaces between the type, the negative shape in the painting: there but not; there but only if you knew how to look.

She only saw me, it seemed, when she was angry, and she was angry now. Although she held back everything else, she never held back her anger. As a child, it took me days to get back into her good graces. Transgressions as minor as wearing the wrong clothes or addressing a maid in the wrong tone of voice would set her off. I wondered now about the benefit of those good graces. It never seemed to soften the critical spotlight she aimed in my direction, harshly illuminating every flaw she could find, as if pointing them out might make me become what she wanted.

She gripped the bars across the way, holding herself rigidly upright, and let fly: "Really, Clara. What did you think you were doing?" Each word had an exclamation point after it.

Sitting in the cell's one wooden chair, I spoke past the knots in my stomach. "You refuse to talk to me."

"Don't think that's going to change—not with impulsive behavior like this from you." It was a relatively minor hit, given Mother's capabilities.

I snapped back. "Unlike you getting up at a memorial service and claiming you knew who the killer was? Making us both targets? I'm sure you thought through the consequences of that carefully, especially since I was the one exposed, while you're cozy in your safe little cell." I'd learned from the best.

The edges of her anger softened, surprising me. "Oh, Clara. This won't do us any good. Why did you come home? Why now, after all this time?"

I bit my lip and went for it. "I'm having dreams. About you. Just like the ones I had about father."

She turned her face away. "Not this again. Clara, dreams don't mean anything. They're the body's way of warming the mind up for the day. Look it up. *The New York Times* "Science" section did an article on it a year or so ago."

"I know you don't believe that. Why would you have me talk to Paul about fire?"

She unhooked one hand from the bars and rubbed her forehead, as if erasing a headache.

I said, "There's something wrong. You need to let me help."

"Why do you think you, of all people, can solve it?"

I felt myself redden, as if I were a fifteen-year-old being dressed down by the principal for skipping classes. "I won't know until you tell me the problem."

Agitated, she started to pace, then seemed to think better of it. "Why would I want to be helped by someone who has shown so little interest in me over the past fifteen years that she couldn't even bother to remember my birthday? Who hasn't come home to see me once, even though she's been in town to see her friends?"

She must have seen something on my face. "Oh, yes. You thought I didn't know? This is a small town. Everybody talks, and the people who don't like me talk the loudest. Just leave. Go back to Spain and that cyclist husband of yours, and try to make it work."

"How did you—"

She waved her hand in disdain. "Don't kid yourself. So he wants to ride bicycles. So what? You said 'for better or for worse,' and this is the 'for worse' part—and it's nothing, as far as 'for worses' go. I don't need you here, and your being here is only making things more complicated."

Good to know the same reliable woman who could bite my heart from my chest and spit it out in pieces was still there. I tried to calm myself by concentrating on my breathing, like the Berne therapist had taught me. Mother went to the cell door and rattled it. "Guard!"

He ambled over. "You need something, Mrs. Montague?"

"My daughter's done here. You can let her out."

"No, ma'am. Chief DuPont says she's in for the night."

"For the night!" I stood. "You're kidding. He can't hold me overnight. There aren't any charges."

"Sorry, ma'am." He strolled away before we could protest further, his boots clicking down the concrete hallway.

I looked around the cell. No doubt Mother's was identical. Decorators would call this grey on grey: grey walls, grey floors, grey blankets on grey bunks. No reading material, no make-up, no clean underwear, nothing to do but stare at the walls or talk. Maybe the latter was what the chief had in mind, but he didn't know Mother. She had practiced the great shut-out for all thirty-four years of my life, and that's what she did now. I waited until I could hear her gentle snores from across the corridor before I let myself cry.

In the morning, Chief DuPont himself unlocked the cell, Bailey trailing behind like a slug on a leaf. *Have you out in a couple of hours. Yeah, right.*

I'm not at my best in the morning.

I'd had a mostly sleepless night. Falling asleep too deeply meant I might have the dream and cry out in my sleep, so this morning, everything seemed unfocused and hard to understand. Noises were too loud, and colors, even the grey, too bright.

The chief grabbed my arm and steered me down the hall toward the door. Bailey stayed to talk to Mother. He said, "Be grateful there are no charges pending, Ms. Montague. And go home, lock your doors and stay there. Do not leave, do not pass go, do not collect two hundred dollars. Are we clear?"

I stared at him. "What are you talking about?"

"Did she tell you anything about Hugh or what happened that night?"

"She *never* tells me anything. I don't know what you thought you could accomplish with that little stunt, but getting her to talk to me isn't possible."

"I was actually hoping it would be the other way around, that she'd talk some sense into you. Leave the investigation to the professionals. I'll say this slowly so you get it. *It is a felony to suppress, by an act of concealment, alteration or destruction, any physical evidence which might aid in the discovery or apprehension of a criminal.* Got it?"

After a night of Mother scraping at me like a vegetable peeler, I had no stamina left. I'll tolerate that tone of voice from Mother, but I didn't have to take it from anyone else. I turned around and walked out.

I drove home fuming. Everyone seemed to think they knew what was best for me: Lock myself in tight to avoid the bogeyman; stop asking questions; don't read the file that could provide me with answers; go back to Spain and patch it up with my husband. No one seemed to think I had a brain or valid reasons for my choices. The only person on my side was Richard; when I finally got my phone back, he'd left five messages. I left a reply on his voicemail.

I walked upstairs to my mother's bedroom, her sanctuary. The bed was draped with lush, heavy silks; gold and cream pillows banked the wall, and a heavy hand-woven cotton blanket adorned the foot. Ornate Georgian armoires on the bisque-colored carpet held her sweaters and lingerie while dark-paneled closet doors hid acres of beautiful clothes and shoes. A reading chair in crushed red velvet looked out the long window. A small table by its side held a stack of my mother's books. I scanned the titles: Instead of the mysteries she'd read when I was a child, the headings now ran to things like: *Waking the Tiger: Healing Trauma: The Innate Capacity to Transform Overwhelming Experience;* and *Silencing the Self: Women and Depression.* They barely registered. I was so tired from not sleeping all night.

I sat on the bed, took off my shoes, and pulled the covers over me. I sank into the pillows and closed my eyes. The monsters of darkness rose up to greet me. I was running through the field, that endless green field with the black, roiling cloud at my back, running for Mother. Only she wasn't there, and the cloud was coming for me, and the blackness wasn't black at all, it was blood and the blood rained on me, covering me in its slick and greasy dampness. It fell on my shoulders, slithered down my back, coated my legs, made the ground slippery, and I fell to my knees as it pressed down closer and closer over me. Light as a whisper, it drifted across my cheek, first one cheek and then the other, as if it were a finger tracing the line of a bone.

I woke, screaming. When I turned over to catch my breath, I found two small cloth dolls, crudely made and dressed in a patchwork of fabrics, beside me on the pillow. Pasted on the boy doll was a picture of Hugh; pasted on the tiny face of the girl was a picture of me. Punched through their tiny hearts were two large hat pins.

CHAPTER 8

 slithered out of bed carefully so as not to disturb the dolls, called the police and dressed quickly. Even though it was well past winter sunset, I made a double espresso while I waited for the patrol car.

How had someone snuck into the house? What had he wanted, other than leaving the dolls? Why did he leave the dolls and what did they mean? Was it really as obvious as it seemed, that I was next on his list? If I was, why hadn't he taken his chance? What advantage did I have to him alive? I remembered the whispering blood on my cheek, and shivered.

The caffeine or my heightened anxiety or both made me suddenly aware of the house's noises. Every creak from the cold startled me. Birds fluttered at the feeder just outside the kitchen window, and tree branches cracked in the December breeze. Each sounded like a footstep or a door opening. I slid a knife from the countertop block and sat with my back to the kitchen wall, as the questions kept coming.

How could he know I would be sleeping? Was it a he? Was it a she? Were the dolls meant for me or Mother? Or—had the dolls been there all along and I'd been so exhausted I hadn't seen them? No, someone had snuck in, I was sure of it. Had he—or she—left anything, maybe something to incriminate Mother? I realized I had to search before the police arrived.

Back upstairs, I started with her closet, which held only Chanel and Lagerfeld, jewelry, cash, and my father's gun in a wall safe. She'd told me about the safe years ago—"just in case."

"Just in case what?"

She hadn't answered.

I panned the room, knife in hand. Nothing on the tables, the bed, the windowsill, the carpet. Nothing except the dolls. The books snagged my eye again, and I wondered why she would have them.

I skimmed the top one, *Silencing the Self,* and noticed she had underlined and made notes in the margins. One highlighted section read, *Identifying with the male gaze is a gender-specific form of what psychoanalytic writers have called 'identification with the aggressor,' and this phenomenon explains the fundamental*

*aggression against the self—the acts of self-alteration and hostile self-judgment—
described by depressed women.* Incomprehensible to anyone who hadn't majored
in self-help.

Other passages talked about the "immobility response," like the rabbit still-
ing itself so the fox won't notice, or "stuck energy" or "rebuilding connection"
or "setting limits and boundaries." Mother was queen at that last one—and
she hadn't learned it from a book. Had she experienced some kind of trauma?
But *what*? And when?

Maybe Paul was right that I wasn't ready for what I would find in Hugh's
shadow notes. She'd never talked about anything happening... not that she
would have. It explained all the therapy with Hugh, but *everyone* was in therapy
with Hugh. They compared neuroses over martinis at the club.

I flipped open the cover of *Waking the Tiger*. A small envelope taped inside
contained a key. Nothing indicated what it opened. I checked the other books,
and one had a lightly penciled address which seemed vaguely familiar. It wasn't
a very promising lead. I dropped the books, just as the doorbell rang.

Chief DuPont did not look pleased. "What happened?"

I hadn't expected him to come, and something about his demeanor made
me feel I'd overreacted until I took him upstairs and showed him.

"Did you touch these?" He indicated the dolls.

"No."

"They weren't there when you fell asleep?"

"What kind of idiot do you take me for?"

"Did you arm your security system?"

"No."

"That kind of idiot. Do you ever listen to anyone?"

"Yes."

His exasperated look said he didn't believe me.

"I listened, but I was so angry.... I won't do it again. That picture of me—
that's from this trip. I mean, it's been taken since I got home."

He pulled his radio out and called for his detective. "Did you touch anything else in the room?"

"I been looking through my mother's things for the last couple of days
trying to figure out....yes, my fingerprints will be everywhere."

He sighed. "We'll need to take them for elimination."

Downstairs, he examined the doors for scratches. "Who else has house
keys?"

I shrugged helplessly. "I've only been home two weeks."

"Guess."

"Mother and me, obviously; the maid, maybe some service people? I really don't know. Why would someone do this?"

We moved to the kitchen, and he turned down an espresso. I made another one for myself. Probably not the best idea.

"Who has it out for you and your family, Miz Montague?" We were back to formal address.

"The only enemies I know about are the Winters, and that's just a society thing, some slight from school that Mary Ellen and my mother have never let die."

"You think the Winters did this?"

"Of course not!"

"Then who? Who doesn't like you?"

I didn't want to suspect the people around me. I had so few friends left as it was.

"You heard Hetty the other night." I shrugged. "She's obviously angry with me. Mother's lawyer, Bailey Womack, used to be a friend, but I'm not sure any more. Paul Love is a friend, but he's not happy with me at the moment. But I can't imagine any of them being this...sadistic."

He studied me with a bemused expression. "Do you have any friends left that you could stay with for a while?"

"I'm not letting someone drive me from my home! Anyway, at least it's clear now that my mother didn't kill Hugh, so you can let her out. She couldn't have snuck into the house today, nor would she make voodoo dolls."

"You sound just like her."

Did a sense of humor lurk under that expensive suit?

"However," he continued, "that doesn't mean that you're right. *We* will release your mother when we are satisfied there is no further reason to hold her. *We* will investigate the dolls' possible relationship to Dr. Woodward's death. In the meantime, *we* would prefer you didn't do anything rash."

If only he weren't so damn good-looking.

The next morning, I called Bailey. I was the one writing the checks until Mother got out, which might buy me some answers. Plus, I could figure out if any of my friends were trying to scare me half to death.

But Bailey had a different agenda.

"Aren't you supposed to be at the Winters campaign offices?"

Shoot. I'd forgotten. "I'm going to be late."

"Get your butt over here. I'm supposed to show you the ropes, and I have to be in court in an hour."

———————

In town, the streets were filling with an assault of early shoppers. Stores strove to outdo each other with festive displays, their red, green and gold spilling into vaguely menacing elf and Santa statues on the sidewalk. The hat on one had slipped down over his eye, turning him into a Santa cat burglar.

The headquarters consisted of two ugly, mint-green rooms on the second floor of a brick office building across from the train station. Nowhere in this town qualified as "the other side of the tracks," even the other side of the tracks, which was filled with chic coffeehouses, done-in-a-day dry cleaners, shoe repair, and gourmet take-out for New York commuters.

When I pulled the door open, the office was in full swing—or at least as in full swing as four people can be. Maybe more were hiding out "in the field," like spies. Mary Ellen, wearing a black suit and cream silk blouse so lustrous it glowed from across the room, was talking on her cell phone. So much for Uggs. Jennifer Winters, Andrew's wife, in jeans and a red L.L. Bean sweater, stood at the copier. Andrew himself talked into the office phone, while a young woman of about twenty-two hovered next to him holding a stack of file folders. No one paid me any attention.

"Sometime today are you going to move into the room and do something?"

I turned. Bailey Womack flipped her briefcase onto the closest desk and gestured to a chair. "It's about time. How'd you fall into this nest of vipers anyway?" She grinned.

"Nice way to talk about your boss."

"All political campaigns are nests of vipers. Winters might make a good congressman, even if he's somewhat, uh, personally distasteful. Besides, my firm assigned me, and I'm oh-so-close to making partner." She pinched two fingers together. "Then, no more scut work, like babysitting the campaign while the election law partner skis for two weeks in Vail."

"Convincing. I hope you're not making fundraising phone calls."

I sat down. She looked as if she were gauging my sincerity, then burst out laughing. "Damn, Clara. I forgot how much I missed you."

It was hard to imagine her sneaking into my house with voodoo dolls. "How about a drink after work tonight to catch up?"

"We do have some history to review," she said, "like your stealing Ethan Olsen from me sophomore year."

"You're not still pining after Ethan, are you? Well, then, I owe you a drink for sure." Maybe she'd know if someone else in town held a grudge.

She hesitated. "It'll depend on work, Clara. I'll let you know at the end of the day?"

It seemed like an excuse, but I couldn't force her. "What do you do here, anyway?"

"Make sure they file everything by deadline and play by the rules, blah, blah." She waved her hand, dismissing the work as inconsequential. "The most important thing a candidate has to do is raise money. Andrew wants you to arrange a bunch of fundraisers. You have event-planning experience?"

I nodded.

"I thought you grew up to be a gardener like your dad and Ernie."

"Some of that, too."

She swung her skinny hip onto a corner of the desk and lowered her voice. "You probably should have stayed with that. You don't want to associate with this side of town, you know what I mean?"

"I thought he was a popular candidate."

"That doesn't mean people like him. Why are you here anyway?"

She leaned in and I felt myself pull back. "I needed something to do."

"Last I knew, you weren't a Republican."

"Still true."

"So..."

"Is there a problem?" Why was she giving me the third degree? Was she trying to help me or scare me off?

"Are you the best fit for this campaign, given your circumstances?"

"I should stay home?"

"You could tell them your situation demands more time than you anticipated."

"Having a mother in jail is the reason I'm here." I kept my voice low to match hers. Maybe she would get the message behind my words. While she appeared completely relaxed, something underneath was coiled. I reached out to touch her, to reassure her, but as I did, I got a jolt, and tasted blood at the back of my throat. I felt a sudden frisson of fear. Where had that come from?

Bailey said, "You will not interfere with either this campaign or the investigation into Hugh's murder. You don't know this family, Clara, so stay out of it, okay?" She paused. "Please."

I set my bag on the desk. "I have to do whatever I can to help Mother."

"Suit yourself." She raised her voice. "So Mary Ellen and Andrew thought an auction—art, bachelors, whatever—and another concert and dinner event. Both would appeal to the local demographic, and maybe even draw in younger people. What do you think?"

"I think training me seems more appropriate to a campaign aide than a lawyer."

"And you would be right."

I held my hands up in surrender.

"Great. Let's get started." She showed me the donor files, suggesting I familiarize myself with my audience, as if I didn't know this town. Big money donors, she reminded me, earned the right to big name entertainment and luxurious venues. The common man mingled with the candidate over hot dogs at the beach. "You can find their income and contribution levels in the database," she said.

She showed me the files of caterers, musicians, event locations, florists, rental companies and gift shops. She named the dates already set aside for fundraisers. I tried not to hyperventilate or to wonder how I would find time to talk to mother's friends about her past if I did this much actual work, never mind that it would help the wrong candidate. Somehow, I had conceived of this as a lark—chatting on the phone, maybe, or talking up donors at a party while slipping in my own questions, but Bailey set me up at a desk with a phone, then stalked off to court, promising me that we would have it out later. I hoped that meant over drinks.

I still wasn't sure if she was friend or foe.

I sighed and started calling venues while reviewing the files for the appropriate people to invite to each event. Each contained the name, address, phone number, email address, and rough net worth of the donor. I wondered which of Andrew's friends had provided that information or if it was a guesstimate based on a lifetime of acquaintance. In addition, files listed the number, frequency, and amount of donations to the campaign, as well as favored foods, wines, and restaurants; schools they and their children had attended; club memberships; employers (and if they did matching donations); number of cars and makes; spouse's and children's names and occupations, if any, with notations to check separate files if they, too, had become donors; and any specialized interests, like golf or rock collecting. The notations varied in handwriting and pen color. A real long-term approach to winning friends and influencing people.

About halfway through the stack, I stumbled across Winken's file. She and her husband had contributed the maximum amounts to both the campaign and several PACs for at least ten years. They owned a modest home in a less expensive neighborhood and they both drove Hondas; his was seven years old; hers, six. Strangely, her two children had attended public schools and the University of Connecticut. I expected expensive private schools. If money was tight, why the huge donations? Maybe they were so passionate about politics that they sacrificed?

I slogged through several more calls to venues and caterers for quotes, and surveyed about ten more donor files before I hit lunch hour. By this time, the room had cleared. The twenty-two-year-old hadn't stopped hovering over Andrew all morning. He'd probably taken her for lunch, to give her some insight into the workings of Great Political Minds. I wished her luck and freedom from straying hands.

Through all the phoning, my mind kept straying back to the files. I trawled through several others but didn't find the same discrepancies, as in Winken's. However, some files had a notation in tiny letters on the lower right of the last page. Winken's read BSA. Boy Scouts of America? Her husband's read BRE. Bare? Bore? Broke? None of my guesses made any sense.

And none of it was useful for me, or Mother.

CHAPTER 9

 ordered a crab salad sandwich at the deli across the street and grabbed a seat to eat and think. I'd come home because my dreams said Mother was in trouble. How did Hugh's murder, Mother's performance at Hugh's funeral, and the dolls on my pillow fit together? Was my meddling making things better or worse? Was I the one actually putting Mother into danger? Why the hell was I working for Andrew Winters? How would I face Mother when she found out?

Funny about that anger: She never locked me in my room or cut off privileges. She didn't isolate me from my friends, or tell me I couldn't talk to them. But if I did the wrong thing, she cut me out.

Mother dreamed like I did; I knew it, even if she wouldn't admit it. That meant she understood something about me, something primal and scary and outside normal human interaction. If I lost my connection to her, I would be alone in the world, especially given the rate at which I seemed to be alienating my old friends.

I felt myself tear up. *Great.* Crying in the local deli. As I dug a tissue from my purse, I mused that Winken, who was close to my mother's age, might know a lot about her past. If I could get Winken talking, at the very least, she might know why my mother and Mary Ellen hated each other, giving me some leverage with Mary Ellen.

I dumped the remainder of my sandwich, and trudged back to the campaign to make more phone calls and surreptitious notes. At five o'clock, when Bailey rang to say she could meet for drinks after all, I nearly danced a jig. Could I ask her what the notations in Mother's books meant? Would she have heard gossip—would she know what had traumatized Mother?

I stuffed a rubber-banded packet of discarded envelopes with notes on them into a pocket in my purse. Bailey came upstairs to fetch me, and I followed her silver-blue Porsche through the glimmery early evening cold. Down by the water, where rows of pretty little shops offered useless imported goods to people with excess cash and space to display them, we snagged parking spots and went into a bistro with a bar strung across its right wall. Terracotta colored walls, low lights, and cream and brass fixtures signaled the high prices. Bailey ordered us martinis and slid onto a bar stool, shrugging off her cashmere coat.

"So, Clara. What have you been up to for the past fifteen years?"

The bartender flipped down cocktail napkins. Neutral and cool, Bailey adjusted hers a millimeter to the right.

I aimed for a light tone. "Mmm. A husband, six jobs, huge stretches of boredom. You?"

She laughed. "No husbands, lots of school and two jobs. Huge stretches of boredom. Not so dissimilar."

"Two?"

"I did a stint with the DA, then switched sides to criminal law. How'd we lose touch, anyway?"

"This morning you claimed Ethan Olsen broke us up."

"Oh, poor Ethan."

I shook my head, not sure why I disagreed with her assessment. "I can't remember why we both wanted him. Was he smart? Good-looking? Or did I just want him because you wanted him, and you wanted him because I did?"

"I really did want him. He had that scruffy musician charm, you know? Didn't his band play at one of the school dances?"

The bartender placed two chilled glasses with olives on the bar, and, with a great flourish, opened the martini shaker and poured. Bailey thanked him gravely, then lifted her glass in a toast: "To old friendships. May they live long and prosper." Then she frowned, shook her head, and clinked glasses with me. The bartender set out a tripartite bowl of snacks: olives, nuts, pretzels.

I said, "Ethan designed t-shirts, too, didn't he? I seem to remember buying one and being so proud that I'd gotten it before you."

"That black thing with the band's name in silver script and a skull, right? I might have one of those in my bottom drawer."

"You dirty sneak." I took a sip of my drink and let the gin linger on my tongue, while I figured out how to proceed. "Bailey, I had a strange run-in with Hetty the other day."

Determine friend or foe by seeing if she would dish on someone else.

"You and the rest of town."

"She intimated we were nasty to her in school. Do you have any memory of that? She still seemed pissed about it."

"That's not hard to believe." The statement had multiple sharp edges. "It was Ethan Olsen."

"You're making that up."

"No, I'm not." She leaned forward, eager. "Remember that dance his band played? Hetty came in that awful red dress with the flower on the shoulder."

A picture formed of the dress, the evening. "She was sweet on Ethan. You and I showed up in designer jeans and spiky boots."

"Right. Every time the band took a break, we swooped in on Ethan. Hetty tried to be part of it—stayed close to the stage, waved at him, danced near him, and she came with us once on a smoke break. She even volunteered to supply us with a bottle of something or buy cigarettes, didn't she?"

"Sort of pathetic."

"We were dumb and self-absorbed."

"Cruel, too," I said. "I distinctly remember making fun of that shoulder flower."

Bailey grimaced. "You said it looked like Sears put chiffon through a blender."

"I can't believe you remember that."

"Your shame blocked it out." She reached for her drink, then hesitated. "I do remember thinking, though, that it was you she wanted, not Ethan." She sipped and tipped her head back in pleasure. "If I had an addictive personality, I would surely be a martini alcoholic."

"Hetty had a crush on me?"

"That never occurred to you? It would explain why she still hates your guts."

"No, it never occurred to me. Why did it occur to you?"

"Something about the way she looked at you. I don't know. Why does anyone ever intuit this kind of stuff? That's your arena—intuiting things. I have no idea. I just remember thinking it."

"If it's true, it makes me feel even worse for her."

"Gives a whole new spin to a woman scorned, doesn't it?"

I snorted. "You are so full of yourself!"

She laughed. "I am, aren't I? Good thing you've returned to keep me on the straight and narrow."

Friend or foe. Now was the moment. "Bailey, someone broke into the house last night, left a couple of voodoo dolls."

Her shock seemed genuine. "You're okay? The house?"

"Everything's fine. I'm just creeped out."

"Who would do something like that? Is that why you're asking about Hetty? She's nuts, but I don't think she's that crazy. How would she have gotten in?"

She paused for another sip of her drink. "I know people say she's into witchcraft or maybe black magic, but I don't think she picks locks."

"I'm not sure I locked the house. I thought I did, and that's what I told Chief DuPont, but..."

She raised her eyebrows at me, and something started clicking away behind her eyes. "Any other suspects? Like me, for example?"

I fished an olive from its gin bath. "It's the kind of prank you loved as a kid, but we're not kids any more. Besides, the other doll had Hugh's picture on it. That's cruel, and I've never known you to be cruel."

I paused, gave her room to respond. She adjusted the cocktail napkin another millimeter.

"So who then?" she asked.

"It has to be related to Mother's arrest and Hugh's death. Someone warning me off?" I shrugged, shook my head.

"Your mother has made a fair number of enemies over the years."

That was news. "Like who?"

"You want me to email you a list?"

"Would you?" I said, unable to keep the sarcasm out of my voice.

"Ouch," she said, adjusting the cocktail napkin another millimeter to the right.

I couldn't get a read on her. Was she serious? Or were we just old friends trading bitchy comments? I changed the subject. "Speaking of my mother, I found an address in one of her books." I recited it.

The red nail started picking at the napkin. Little bits littered the bar top. "It's a stable. You should know that place. Hetty's mom owns it. Loretta, remember her? She's married to your Dad's partner Ernie."

"Mrs. Gardner married Ernie Brown?" No wonder the name and address seemed familiar. "Why don't I know this?"

She sipped her drink.

"Don't answer that."

She watched me carefully, as if the answer to her next question would determine something for her. "You going to check it out?"

"It was penciled into a book on psychological trauma. I thought it might be important. Want to come?"

She nodded once, seemed satisfied, drained her glass. "Your mom's trial, you know there's no guarantee she'll get a not guilty verdict."

"She's not a murderer, Bailey."

"Everyone is capable, even us." The red nail drew a line in the air connecting us. "My point is that anything helpful, well, I need it, and the sooner the better. She has no alibi, and there's a fair amount of circumstantial evidence pointing to motive. You might try to persuade her it's in her best interests to talk."

"She doesn't listen to me." Just saying it made me feel desperate.

Bailey just shook her head. "Well, right now, I want some dinner. You in?" She threw a couple of bills on the bar, told the bartender it was all his, and we went to eat large hunks of meat and drink a bottle of red wine, like real men and real lawyers.

The next morning, with another hangover—I had to stop drinking so much—and earlier than any sane person would choose to rise, I drove to the stables with Mother's key in my pocket.

Bailey's unsettling comments about Mother's enemies had fueled a restless night. The dreams had woken me every hour. While they still showed me with blood on my hands, they kept pausing with that whisper touch on my cheek, as if my dreams were a record that skipped to the beginning every time it hit that mark. Maybe I hadn't noticed something critical about the image. Maybe it was my fear that the touch had been made by a real human hand—the intersection of the dream world and the real world—that kept waking me.

Even now I could feel it creeping along my cheek like a spider.

Looking for something to distract me, I focused on the bright, sunny morning. An inch of snow had fallen overnight, just enough to make the landscape sparkle. Old stone fences rambled along the road's edges, competing with manicured hedges and the creep of bramble. Even sleep-deprived and half-frightened, I still appreciated Connecticut's beauty. The Land Rover easily climbed the long slope of Sunset Hill Road, and just before eight o'clock, I pulled into the graveled drive and found a spot to park.

I figured visiting the stables would net me only a footlocker of riding gear. But Hetty's mother and mine had been close once; maybe she would know why Constance was in danger, why someone would want her dead or locked up. The clock was ticking. Once the judge set a trial date, it would tick even faster.

I remembered from my own riding days that horse people were up early. Sure enough, people were bustling around with buckets, tack, shovels, pitchforks, and were walking large steaming animals. My adolescent riding lessons lurked far enough in the past that I'd almost forgotten the names for all the accoutrements, but the smell of manure started to bring it back.

I decided to arrange a ride while I was home. I asked a person with a bucket how to find Loretta, and she pointed me across a gravel drive to a white house with dark blue shutters. Muddy prints from stable boots tracked back and forth along the path. I knocked, heard a call from within and twisted the knob, rubbing the key in my pocket, as if for luck.

The door opened into a spacious country kitchen with an office to one side. Several pans emitting mouthwatering odors simmered on a large gas range. A full coffee pot sat on the counter next to a jug of milk and a sugar jar. Pots and dried herbs hung from a rack over a work table in the center of the room. On the left side of the room, near a comfortable-looking red and white patterned sofa, and a large French country desk, stood a tall, rangy woman in a grey Henley and Levis. Her hair showed streaks of silver, and her well-weathered skin spoke of a life outdoors rather than in the plastic surgeon's waiting room. Her deep blue eyes were still sharp, and she looked surprised to see me.

"Why, Clara. How nice of you to stop by."

I adjusted the image I'd carried all these years to the one I saw now. We step back into the time frame as if we'd never left, as if nothing had changed while we'd been gone. But everything had changed, including the woman before me.

"Mrs. Gardner?"

Hetty's mother nodded. "It's Mrs. Brown now, but call me Loretta. You're old enough."

"Your place is beautiful."

"Would you like coffee?" She strode toward the pot.

"That would be great." I accepted the filled mug and added cream and sugar. "I ran into Hetty the other night. She seems to be doing well for herself."

Loretta paused. "How surprising that you came to talk about Hetty. I never got the impression the two of you were close." She sat down in her desk chair, a comfortably padded tweed model.

I figured I'd better own up to my purpose. "Actually, I came because Mother asked me to get some of her things. She said all I needed to do was show you the key, and you'd point me in the right direction." I pulled it from my pocket and set it on the desk.

She stilled. "Really." I could feel her searching under my skin for the truth. I put up a neutral wall, something I'd learned to do well when Mother dismissed my dreams.

Finally, she relented, but not because she was sure of me. "I'm glad that things are better between you and Constance. She always told me how sad she was about the distance between you, wished she knew how to talk to you." The statements were questions, testing me.

I laughed. "Talking to me at all might have helped."

She gave me a funny look. "But she's told you about the cottage?"

I shrugged to keep myself from yelling "What cottage!" and held my breath, hoping she fell for it. "She doesn't have a lot of options at the moment."

"Why didn't you let yourself in?"

"I didn't want to tramp around on your property. Besides, Mother's directions weren't the clearest."

"Constance? Imprecise?" She gave the look all mothers have perfected: the one they give when their child tells an outright lie.

I kept the neutrality in place and brazened it out. "As I said, she needs some of her things."

"In jail?" Her disbelief grew.

I faltered. Mother might only have riding gear here. But she had hidden that key and address, almost as if she was anticipating trouble. That meant she might have hidden something here that would help me figure out the kind of trouble she was in. "Please," I said. "I'm just trying to help her."

"Well, then." Her face softened, and she gestured for me to follow. She led me through the house and out the back door, pointing to the right. "If you need to come back, a little path comes around the house."

We walked across the yard, following a large boxwood hedge, until Loretta pushed through a thin slot. I flailed through the snow-draped branches while trying not to get any down the neck of my coat, then emerged into the sweetest little space I had ever seen. The high shrubs circled a tiny cottage—a doll's house. Like the main house, it, too, was painted white, but with green shutters, a little green door and a porch with a snow-covered rocking chair. Two tiny windows peeped from either side of the door.

"You are the fourth person to know of this place," she said. "Ernie's agreed to rent it to your mother for as long as she wants it, and while she's renting it, no one else is to know it exists or enter it." She looked at me. "No one can know it's here. I assume your mother told you that, but I want to reinforce it, just in case." *Just in case she has no idea you're here.* With that, she vanished back through the hedge and left me in the perfect silence of the circle.

The snow between the hedge and the porch was unmarred by footprints. I crossed carefully, as if by putting my feet lightly enough, I too wouldn't leave a mark. Winter wind had blown the porch floor almost clean. Feeling a little dizzy, probably from all my sleepless nights, I wiped off the rocking chair and sat. How many more questions about my mother could I possibly find? Now I had to add *why did Ernie rent this space to my mother?* and *why wasn't anyone allowed to know it was here?* to the list that included wanting to know why she and Mary Ellen Winters were enemies, what the trauma was, whether she'd been having an affair with Hugh Woodward and killed him, and who left the voodoo dolls on my pillow. That was too many questions for a girl of no talent, such as myself.

I pulled the key from my pocket and rubbed it with my mittened thumb. I wondered how many times she'd sat here and done the same thing. Rising, I stuck the key in the lock and twisted, praying that I wanted to know whatever I found inside.

CHAPTER 10

arkness greeted me. I stood for a moment, orienting myself. I felt absolute stillness, as if the energy here knew how to curl into a ball and purr. I fumbled around by the door and finally found the light switch.

The bare walls were painted white. Heavy white velvet drapes covered the windows. A turquoise ceiling echoed more than twenty turquoise cushions of various sizes and color intensities that littered the white carpet and leaned against the walls. A white chair-and-a-half, with a matching ottoman, graced the far corner, draped in a turquoise cashmere blanket. Mother took care of her creature comforts. All outside sound was muffled by the hedge and the walls. I wondered if it was soundproofed.

Two doors led off this room. I twisted the knob to the first and discovered a slate-floored kitchen furnished with a small table and chair. Randomly, I opened cabinets and drawers. They were stocked with tea and sugar, dishes and cutlery, linens and canned goods. One of the cupboards held books similar to the collection I'd found in her bedroom. In a sudden flash, I saw Mother eating meals here, a solitary glass of wine and white china dish centered before her in silence. Tears streamed down her face, and it was a long time before she picked up the fork. Was this was a refuge for her? Or solitary confinement?

Behind the other door was a bathroom. Again, I opened all the drawers and cabinets. One drawer was locked, but the key to the house opened this drawer as well. In it rested one thin file folder. I flipped it open and saw a list of what appeared to be injuries and repairs: lacerations, tears, scrapes, stitches, and antibiotics. It looked as if Mother had taken a bad fall off a horse, a long time ago, before I was born. Why keep a description of it in a locked drawer in a house no one was supposed to know about?

I stuck the file in my purse. I was becoming an accomplished file thief. Maybe the information would add up to some meaning, especially if I could ever convince Paul to return the file I'd taken from Hugh's cabinet. In the main room, I sat in the chair and pulled the blanket around my shoulders. What was this place? I let the silence soak into me. For the first time, it felt good.

At home, we had far more rooms than we needed; half the bedrooms were for "guests." Why wouldn't Mother simply use one of those for a retreat? What required so much privacy? Had she met Hugh—or others—here for trysts?

If I believed what Loretta said, Hugh hadn't known about this place...

Unless.

Unless I was right and Mother had the same gifts I had. This would be a perfect meditation space.

But only one person could answer these questions. I threw off the blanket and collected my purse with its stolen file.

Time to get some answers.

⸻

I seated myself across from Mother at the utilitarian jail table and practiced breathing slowly to calm myself. Same room, same ugly walls. Bailey was right. I had to get her to cooperate with me, one way or another.

"Clara."

"I hear you're going to trial." Bailey had called me in the car with the news.

"Stay out of it, Clara."

"Too late." I slid the key between us. She looked at it, then at me.

"You've gone through my things."

"I know what it opens."

She gestured to the corner of the ceiling. "We're being taped."

I didn't bother to look at the camera. "So?"

"You never know who has access to those tapes, who might hear what we're talking about."

"Are you afraid of someone?"

"Why won't you stay out of this?"

"Because you're in trouble. Why won't you let me help you? Yes, I've been gone for fifteen years, and we both know why. But I came home because *you* called to me in a dream. Why are you shutting me out?"

She looked resigned. "I shouldn't have done that." She slid the key in a circle, thinking, then pushed it back toward me. "Did you talk to Paul about fire?" she finally asked.

Seriously? How would she know about my police station dream? I hadn't told her anything. She could only know if she had them herself and god forbid she tell me that. "Not yet."

Paul might not even be speaking to me. He'd persuaded Chief DuPont that he would make a worthy custodian of Hugh's file on Mother—which still offered me a fighting chance of getting my hands on it. But he was still furious I'd taken it.

"Get him to teach you to meditate," she said. "It's calming and centering, and it provides such valuable and informative insights into situations."

"So that's a medita—"

"Clara! The tape!"

I stared at her. "Couldn't you, for once in your life, be direct and tell me what I need to know?"

"You and I share some gifts, but you haven't yet learned how dangerous they are to use." She shook her head. "I've tried to explain."

My anger found its way through a crevice in my control. "I lost my father because I didn't trust my gift. If you had only been willing to help me—"

"Clara!" The full-on command voice. "You must never tell anyone about what you've found. You will need a safe space. Do you understand?"

"No. I don't understand anything, because you usually make things more confusing."

"That's how learning works," she said piously. "You get a whole lot of information and you don't know how any of the pieces fit together. Then, something clicks and you see the whole thing. I'm giving you as much as I can, but you need to see the whole picture yourself. I can't provide that for you."

"Did you kill Hugh?"

"Don't be ridiculous."

The guard poked his head in. "Two minutes," he said.

"Do you need anything?" I asked her. "Cigarettes to trade, chocolate cake, your favorite sweater?" Her look of disdain was so pure, so very her, that I was startled it didn't provoke the usual sense of guilt.

Maybe being angry gave me some kind of shield.

Instead, a laugh bubbled up from the place that recognized the absurdity of the situation—from her incarceration, to her calm acceptance of my snooping, to her cloak-and-dagger hints. Her irritation dissolved, and she started to laugh, too.

That's how the guard found us—dissolved in helpless giggles over the ugly table, our hands clasped in recognition that we were, at least, family.

The next morning, I walked into the Winters campaign office an hour-and-a-half late to find the place deserted. There was a note for me on the desk on top of a stack of folders, signed by Andrew himself:

Clara:

I'm so glad you've chosen flexible hours. Your presence, in formal dress, is required at our fundraiser this evening. 8:00 p.m. at Mary Ellen's. Bailey has directions, should you need them.

A.W.

A.W., my ass. I resigned myself to a long afternoon and evening of tedium, but when I crumpled the note to throw it away, it burned my fingers.

———

At 7:45, Bailey tooted her horn. Andrew's snide note and the burning tingle it had left along my fingertips bothered me all afternoon, along with Hugh's murder and my own helpless banging about in search of answers. The last place I wanted to be was anywhere near Andrew Winters. But I'd dragged myself through a shower and into a Dolce and Gabbana evening gown I'd discovered buried at the back of Mother's closet.

"Ooooh, vintage!" Bailey cooed when I got into the car.

"Ha—which only means dresses several years out of fashion are still okay to wear because they cost megabucks."

She grinned. "You haven't forgotten the valuable lessons I taught you."

She put the Porsche in gear and whirled out of the driveway. The sun roof was open and I could see the sky, seasoned with clouds and brightly lit by the moon. Patches of stars, like little spills of salt crystals, showed between them. Cold air blew in over my shoulders, warring with the heat pouring across my feet: luxury.

"I don't even know why I'm going to this thing. All I want is to be home in bed with a book and a glass of wine. Why does Winters want me there? I sort of figured that by now you would have convinced him I was bad PR to have around."

"I tried. He thinks it's funny that Constance's daughter is working for him."

"Like funny-ha-ha?"

"More like funny-ironic. Like he's secretly pleased you're there, especially because it will drive your mother nuts. There's some weird dynamic there... whatever history is between them all runs deep. He actually laughed when I suggested he let you go. "

"Do you think he's a good guy?" I asked it without thinking, as if I could still ask her anything.

She glanced away from the road for a moment, as the car swerved around a corner. "Why?" She seemed wary, but it was hard to tell at this speed.

I had to decide in a split second if I believed she was on my side or not, if she was still the Bailey I knew from high school, before things got tricky. She was working for a family that was not only politically opposite to what used to be her own views, but was also one of the more powerful and wealthy in our town and state. Would she be able to put aside her own ambitions to support me?

The only thing I could do was to take the risk. "I'm not sure. I keep getting strange feelings around him—like white noise with a black line through it—like he's exuding a whole lot of energy to control or hide something." I paused. "Sounds insane, but I don't know how else to explain it."

The car filled up with quiet. I bit my lip, hoping, resolutely watching the road.

Bailey said, "Yeah, but you've always had really strong, *accurate* feelings about people."

I stopped chewing my lip. She inhaled sharply, as if for courage. "Clara, I remembered about Ethan Olsen. You made fun of Hetty's flower." Her hands glowed green from the dash lights.

"You reminded me last night."

She stared at the road. "When just you and I and Ethan were hanging out, you were fine, laughing and teasing Ethan about being the only musician in the band who hadn't gotten laid—like you wanted to be the one. But when Hetty came up, you completely changed. Those comments about the flower were intended to drive her away, and that flip-out you did on Ethan, telling him he was a sex-crazed fiend..."

The green dashboard light wriggled along a strand of her hair. "You didn't want Ethan for yourself; you wanted to protect Hetty. When we fought about it later, you told me you'd seen something in his eyes, like Hetty was an easy target; he could do whatever he wanted with her and get away with it. I didn't believe you. I thought you were trying to keep him away from me."

Dimly, through all the barriers I'd erected to separate myself from my adolescence, the scene Bailey painted emerged. I remembered I touched Ethan's arm when Hetty joined us and got shocked with a vision of her dress floating in the water, the full skirt ballooned up with trapped air, and Hetty herself half-naked, blood streaming down the inside of her thighs.

I'd done the only thing a teenaged girl knew to do. I'd humiliated her to drive her away, keep her safe. The sensation I'd had earlier with Bailey, blood at the back of the throat, returned.

Bailey's confession continued to spill into the dark spaces in the Porsche. "Later that night, I saw Ethan with Dara Oakford going at it like bunny rabbits. We all knew she was a slut, so I didn't think much of it, until I got a little closer and heard Dara hitting him and telling him to stop. He didn't, and she stayed home from school for a week after that. I couldn't tell you after our huge fight. Nothing ever happened to Ethan. Dara didn't press charges. I think she's part of the reason I became a lawyer."

She downshifted and slid into a parking spot in front of Mary Ellen's house. When the car stilled, she twisted toward me in the dimness. "I'm so sorry, Clara. Can you forgive me?"

It was as though an overstuffed bag split open. Memory upon memory tumbled out: decisions I'd had to make like the one about Hetty and Ethan. Most people weren't ready to hear what I told them. They got angry or frightened, told me to mind my own business, told me I was weird.

I had learned early how to drive someone away to protect her. But if these were gifts my mother and I shared, why hadn't she guided me instead of denying what I saw?

"Clara?" Bailey was fumbling in her evening clutch. "Oh god, I'm so sorry. I didn't mean to make you cry. What did I say?" She held out a monogrammed lace handkerchief. I grabbed her hand and squeezed hard.

"Thank you," I managed to get out between hiccups and decorating the lovely lace with mascara. "You always believed in me. After my father died, I felt so overwhelmed by my failure to save him. I couldn't tell anyone. I felt so lonely without you."

"I'm sorry. I wanted Ethan with the full blast of my sixteen-year-old hormones. I couldn't see past that to my friend. If it counts, I've been lonely for you, too." We hugged awkwardly across the gear shift. I rested my head on her shoulder, savoring the closeness I wished I'd had all along, the same closeness and nurturing I longed for with my mother.

As we pulled apart she said, "You asked if Winters was a good man, then said you were getting weird energy. If you think he's hiding something, I need to know."

I shook my head, blew my nose. "I haven't seen him enough."

"Maybe you could test it tonight. Get close and see what comes up."

"That's dangerous, Bailey. I'm not... I'm not really sure enough of myself." Something had always held me back from *asking* for a vision.

"More dangerous than letting him get elected? What if what he's hiding could damage a whole lot of people? I don't want you to do anything that makes you uncomfortable, but your visions were usually on target..." She shook her head. "It's important, Clara."

I hedged. "I need more training. Mother's insisting I talk to Paul, but Paul's mad at me..." I couldn't tell her I'd stolen a file from Hugh's house. "Anyway, the impressions just come when they come."

"At least try. For me? Please?"

The last thing I wanted to do was test myself out on Andrew Winters. I'd met his type all over the world. But Mother was right; I should have had Paul working with me. I should have asked about fire, for lessons in meditation, for something to prepare me. I sighed, shook off my reservations, and climbed from the car. At least it gave me a purpose for being here.

As I slammed the Porsche's door shut, Bailey hissed, "Clara, look! Speak of the devil!"

Hetty stood by the front door, talking to Detective Samuels. She leaned in close, her hand on his arm. I couldn't imagine what Hetty and Samuels would have in common, but Hetty had often pretended intimacy where there was none.

She turned abruptly when she heard the car door, then disappeared inside. Samuels nodded and smiled as we walked past, but didn't speak. Despite the smile, he seemed to look through rather than at me, something chilled and dim in his eyes. Maybe all detectives looked like that; maybe coldness and reserve were hazards of the job. He appeared to be working security, since he was armed and had a walkie-talkie clipped to his belt.

Mary Ellen's foyer boasted a curved staircase to the second floor. Off the foyer, a library opened to the left and a drawing room to the right. French doors led to patios, their chaises and tables demurely blanketed with snow. Despite these romantic notes, Mary Ellen had furnished the interior in starkly minimalist pieces, as if one of those steel and granite kitchens had invaded and conquered all the other rooms.

When I handed my wrap to the coat-check girl just inside the front door, she touched, ever-so-briefly, her own deeply kohl-rimmed eyes, and pointed to a door past the library. Grateful, I touched up my make-up in a bathroom large enough to house a family of five. In the mirror, my ravaged face reflected my mother's fears about my gift. Her message, hidden under the dismissals, had always been that the dreams would endanger me because others would want my power for themselves. Never once had she suggested it was okay to use it. But who or what was she afraid of? No one had ever *threatened* me, not until I'd arrived home. I wasn't even sure those voodoo dolls were meant for me.

Face repaired, I joined Bailey at the bar. She handed me a martini and pulled me into the crowd. I followed, nearly ramming a waiter passing a tray of steaming shrimp skewers. Why were the only black faces in the room on the guys carrying the hors d'oeuvres? When the throng parted, I found myself face-to-face with a beautiful white-haired woman.

Bailey said, "Maria, this is Clara Montague. Clara, Hugh's wife, Maria Leiber." To me, she whispered, "I'll talk to Richard." She winked and headed off on her own, the rat.

Maria took my hand and looked at me for so long it felt offensive. "I have heard so much about you over the years. And I'm so sorry Constance is jailed for Hugh's murder." She pressed my hand. "I don't believe she did it."

"Thank you."

Her grip was almost painful. "I have reasons." She drew me off to face a small glass table with a smooth white rock on it. Above it hung an all-black painting. "You always were a very insightful girl. I hear you've been asking questions about Hetty."

"Actually, Hetty—"

"That's smart." She barreled on as if she hadn't heard me. "My husband had a lot of questions about Hetty. Did you know she gives readings?"

"What kind of readings? Poetry readings? Psychic readings? Aura readings?"

Maria's face flushed and the palm that rested on my arm seemed sweaty. "Psychic readings. She apparently has a blue and white room in her house where she conducts her *interviews*." She said the word as if it tasted like a mouthful of bug spray. "At least that's what I hear."

I stared at her. Had Mother told Hugh about the cottage after all? Had Hetty snuck into the cottage? How would she know what it was used for, unless...she'd spied on Mother? She'd been a kid, and there was a cool little cottage on her parents' property, and she'd be bored and curious and do what any kid would do.

But why would she think she was psychic?

Maria wasn't finished. She lowered her voice to a rumble, like a subway train running underneath the sidewalk. "Some of Hugh's patients consulted Hetty as well. He was convinced Hetty was...a fraud. He confronted her about it."

"You think Hetty killed Hugh?"

"I don't know who killed my husband, but I intend to find out. I imagine you're as motivated as I am." She turned abruptly away and left me staring at the painting. Its blackness wasn't uniform; the artist had woven in shimmers of color—a wash of red-black or blue-black or green-black; it looked like a bruise a long time after the wounding.

"Clara! So glad you could make it." Andrew's voice startled me and I nearly crashed my drink into his sister's precious side table. He slithered his arm across my shoulder. "What do you think of my sister's taste in art? Hideous, isn't it?" He went on without waiting for my answer. "Listen, I need you to go make nice to that elderly gentleman over there in the corner."

He gestured with his head. I craned to see. "Melton Honey?"

"Ah, good. You know him. See if you can talk him out of a sizeable donation."

I frowned at him, but he just smiled. He was dressed tonight as the hard-working candidate: light wool dress slacks, white cotton shirt with its sleeves rolled up, red silk tie with little blue boats on it. Serious colors, but a touch of whimsy to show he was a regular guy. But no polyester had ever sneezed within thirty miles of Andrew Winters.

Now would be the moment to do as Bailey wished. I reached for his arm as he turned away, but then he turned back. I dropped my hand, relieved.

"Mary Ellen says you know things."

White noise exploded in my ears. I took a step back. "I know a fair amount about landscape architecture, and flight times in and out of Paris."

He granted me a small, nasty smile, acknowledging my dodge. "I've known your mother a long time, Clara." He moved closer and I could barely hear him over the ringing in my ears. "You will answer my question. Maybe not now, but you will."

I didn't need to touch him to be flooded with his malice. "Hetty does readings."

His eyes, already dark, darkened further. "What do you know about that?"

"Why do you believe in psychic phenomena, Mr. Winters? A rational man like you."

"Your mother used to talk to me, years ago. Once, she told me that the darkness would burn me unless I conquered it. I have spent my life, Ms. Montague, striving to bring light to people, to create laws that would create justice and fair play. So yes, I listen."

"My mother doesn't think you or Mary Ellen have much to recommend you."

"And yet, you're here," he sneered. "Now," he shoved his chin in Melton Honey's direction, "go do your job."

Maybe Mother was right that I didn't know what I was getting into, but I bit my tongue. As I turned, he patted me a little too close to my ass. I cursed him out with a string of expletives, carefully chosen and absolutely silent.

Melton was a dear, told me about how the government almost put him out of business except, wink-wink, for a friend who helped him out, drank down a couple of Manhattans, and wrote out a check as if he were giving away promotional cologne samples in Neiman Marcus. He twinkled as he handed it to me. "You tell that rascal Winters I've got his number. You couldn't have been a more charming companion, my dear, and I have thoroughly enjoyed the evening. Now, I'm an old man, and I'm going home." I helped him find his coat and the parking valet.

All the while, I heard the buzz of white noise in my ears, but I couldn't tell if that was because I'd raised money to help a Republican get elected, if I was still getting a vibe off Winters, or if it was the room full of Stepford-perfect people. I gave the check to Mary Ellen and tried to escape, but Andrew found me and sent me off to charm a few more donors. Melton remained my high water mark, but by the end of the evening, I had significantly enriched the campaign coffers.

Even Mary Ellen found it in her cold little heart to compliment me. "You're a natural, dear. Who knew?"

Tomorrow, I would have to write a very large check to the Democratic contender. I might even have to talk some of my friends into contributing.

By one in the morning, all the "marks" had left, and Bailey and I retreated to the Porsche.

"So, anything?" she asked.

"Nothing except white noise," I said.

She shrugged, as if it hadn't mattered after all. Exhausted, I shut and bolted the front door, stripped off the gown in Mother's bedroom and headed immediately for the shower, as if scrubbing could wash off my disgust and confusion.

When I stepped from the shower with only a towel wrapped around my body, a man stood in my bedroom.

CHAPTER 11

lack balaclava'd face, black leather jacket, black jeans, black engineer boots. Dark brown eyes. A long hunting knife in black leather-gloved hands.

Dammit, dammit, dammit. I hadn't set the alarm.

I shrieked. Turns out I was good at it. The cops probably heard me three counties away.

"Shut up."

Instantly, the Montague asserted itself. "Don't tell me to shut up in my own house."

He advanced toward me, the knife point glistening in the half-light spilling from the bathroom door. The bedroom was dim, but I tried to see and memorize the details of him: Oval face under the mask? Wide shoulders under the jacket? Or were they padded? Long lean legs in the jeans, large feet in damp, snow crusted boots. He couldn't have been indoors very long.

"What's that for?" I took a step back and pointed at the knife with the hand that wasn't clutching the towel closed above my breasts.

"To make sure you listen."

"Fine. You've got my attention. What is it you want?"

"Your mother killed Hugh. Let it go." The knife seemed to sharpen as it moved closer. A hunting knife, not a kitchen knife, it curved into a notch near the handle. I wondered what the notch was for, and then figured I didn't really want to know.

I wondered why now, of all times, the intuition had gone dark. *Useless gift.* Idly, I noticed his jacket had fringe on the sleeves, like a biker jacket. For some reason, this suddenly made me furious.

Why was everyone wound up about me? *I* hadn't killed anyone. *I* hadn't even been here for the past decade and a half. Why wouldn't they leave me alone? Why did they think they could waltz into my house whenever they wanted and leave dolls and threaten me with knives?

"I know nothing! How many times do I have to say that!" Still damp from the shower, I felt myself start to shake.

"You know more than you should, and my employer is willing to send me again with a stronger message, if necessary." He lunged at me, the knife wounding the air by my cheek. I leapt back, lost my balance and landed on the floor with the towel open to expose my thighs, my waist, my vagina. Before I could cover myself, he got himself a long look. He raised his eyes to mine, and laughed, low, dirty, and mean. Then he turned and disappeared out the door.

I scrambled to the bedside phone, hugging the towel tightly and trying not to cry. I called the police. Fifteen minutes later, Chief DuPont strode through my front door. I had dressed, but my hair still hung wet, and I couldn't stop shaking. I hadn't, in all my travels—not even in that Swiss asylum bed—felt so exposed and vulnerable.

The chief called to the officer who had accompanied him. "Get her a blanket, would you?" He turned to me. "Where's the kitchen?" I pointed, my finger wobbling through the air like a drunken bird.

He made me sit at the kitchen table while he fixed hot chocolate—lots of sugar, caffeine, protein. Things to calm the shock. The officer, Joe Munson, found a towel to wrap my damp hair and draped a chenille blanket from our living room sofa over my shoulders. Its weight and warmth comforted me.

The chief plopped a large mug in front of me. "Take me through it."

I did.

"Fringe? A hunting knife?" he asked, when I'd finished.

"Why would I make that up?" Anger felt reassuring. This was an emotion I was well acquainted with.

"Not questioning your memory. Just confirming." He shot Munson a look, and Munson disappeared.

"Did he have a scent? Garlic? Cigarette smoke? Anything?"

I closed my eyes to remember, but instead of an image of the intruder, I saw the chief on patrol, surrounded by mud and debris, a dark speck in the middle of a shining disaster. Now I got a vision? Seriously? I opened my eyes. "You from New Orleans?"

"Good guess," he said, bemused, "but that doesn't answer my question."

"He smelled like talcum powder and shampoo, like he'd cleaned up to come scare me. It was creepy. I mean, what kind of criminal does that? Is it like taking a bath before you go to work or something?" I put my face in my hands, trying to keep the shakes from starting again. I could feel them circling in my gut.

He nudged the chocolate closer. "Drink this." I picked it up as he looked around at the vast kitchen. Mother had redone it a couple years ago in green granite and cherry cabinets, with a stainless steel Sub-Zero refrigerator and a six-burner gas range with a grill. *Who cooked in here?* Not her and not me. Caterers probably appreciated the equipment when they prepared for her parties. Even so, after six years, it was probably due for an update.

He said, "Is there someone you can stay with tonight?"

"Oh, please, can't you just stay?" I blurted it without thinking, felt my face get deep red hot.

"Well," he drawled, amused, "while I might certainly be interested in that offer on some other occasion, as the Chief of Police investigating your mother as a murder suspect, I can't see it doing my reputation in this town a whole lot of good, and since I'm new, I need that reputation. If you haven't noticed, I don't exactly look the same as most of the people around here."

"I know I know I know. I'm sorry. I'm just so... so... " I didn't know how to finish the sentence. "I'd really rather not rouse one of my friends. What time is it, anyway?"

He looked at his watch, a rather expensive and very thin Movado. *How did a police chief afford that?* "Quarter to three."

"The night is nearly done. I'll be fine. He's delivered his message, and he won't be back until he—they—whoever—figures out that I'm going to ignore it." *There.* I'd made a commitment to stay the course, and I'd done it in clichés. Bravo for me.

"You can't do that." His face lost its indulgent look.

"Montagues don't negotiate with thugs. And you wouldn't back down if it were your family." There it was again, the proud gene, Constance by another name. I wish I didn't feel so scared saying it.

"Yeah, you and the American government and your mother, whom you seem to be channeling again. As for the other part, I'm a trained police officer, and I grew up fighting the bigger kids on the streets in New Orleans. You are... what are ya'll, anyway? Do you work?" His sudden descent into drawl made me suspicious.

"I'm working for Andrew Winters, remember?" I summoned my tattered dignity and sipped hot chocolate, but the cup was empty and I sucked air.

"I meant for money."

"I don't need money." Between my father's business and my inheritance from him, I had more than enough.

"Of course you don't. My mistake." Frustrated, he ran his hand across a scrim of dark hair as thin as a ruler.

"You're awfully antagonistic."

He pushed back his chair and stood up. "It's late, Miz Montague. I recommend sleep, and in the morning, assuming your other commitments aren't too pressing, if you could come to the station and sign a statement, the police force would be eternally grateful. That way, the police department can investigate this incident instead of leaving it to your superior investigative skills. Please set the alarm after I leave, so I don't have to get up again in the middle of the night and waste my time coming out here to help someone who obviously doesn't want my help."

The next morning, even though His Grouchiness wasn't there to take it, I gave the police my statement. I had to make do with Pete Samuels and his dark charm.

"You Montague ladies sure are asking for trouble." Pete crossed his forearms on his desk and leaned toward me with a sympathetic look that didn't quite fit his features. "Must be tough having your Mom jailed and then finding someone in your bedroom in the middle of the night. You okay?"

"Life's a challenge." I just wanted to give my statement and get out of there.

"Sounds like a bit more than a challenge." He tipped his chair back and looked over my shoulder into the bullpen. "If I took you for dinner some night, I could fill in some gaps our charming new police chief might not be willing to share." He looked back at me and rolled his eyes.

"That's so nice of you," flew out of my mouth before I could censor it—or wonder what his problem was with the chief. Pete would give me only the information he wanted to, but maybe he would slip up if I asked the right questions.

"Great." He patted my hand, let it linger a little too long. "How about tonight? I know a great place north of the parkway."

I nodded my assent, signed my name to my statement, and stood up.

His chair smacked to the floor like a whip-crack. "I'll pick you up at 8:30."

I arrived at the campaign barely on time and feeling shaky, but being there was a routine, and routine was good. As I pulled up the campaign donor data I'd been reviewing yesterday, Andrew walked in, Jennifer trailing him like a bedraggled puppy. Her hair was pulled back in a scrunchie, and she wore blue jeans with the right knee ripped out and a t-shirt with what looked like a blueberry stain on it.

I forced a smile as she crossed next to my desk. "Morning."

She looked at me as if she'd never seen me before. Maybe she hadn't. She was that sort of woman. "Who did you say you were again?" Andrew had disappeared into his office.

"Clara Montague. Constance's daughter."

She blanched. "You-you're, um... What are you doing at our computers?"

Brain dead. The bleach must be working on more than her hair. "I work for your husband. I've been in the office for several days, and I attended Mary Ellen's fundraiser last night."

"He told me he'd hired someone. I—I... I didn't put it together."

"Is there a problem?" Why would it matter if it were me or the man in the moon?

"Uh, no. Of course not." She straightened her WASP backbone and waved her hand vaguely in the air. "I just didn't expect, um, anyone to be here when we came in." She wandered off unsteadily.

What was that about? My stomach started flip-flopping, and I dropped my coffee in the trash.

———

So someone wanted me to back off asking questions about Mother's problems. Who? If they thought they could scare me off, they didn't understand my resistant personality. My soon-to-be-ex-husband understood that now. My lawyer had gotten her claws into him, and he was whining at me from the answering machine, calls I deleted every afternoon when I came home. I knew I'd have to deal with him eventually, but I couldn't face him yet. One crisis at a time. I started listing questions:

1. Did last night's intruder also leave the voodoo dolls?

2. Why did someone want me to stop asking questions? Did that mean Mother was innocent?

3. Who killed Hugh and why?

4. What was Mother's trauma? Did the medical report from the cottage relate to it? Who could I ask to review it with me?

5. Who were the suspects?

Mary Ellen and Mother had a long history, but would she risk Andrew's candidacy? Hetty had a grudge against me, but why would that make her kill Hugh and frame Mother? Maria seemed innocent, but the common wisdom said to look to the spouse. Did she have a motive? Why had Winken freaked out when Mother said she knew who the murderer was?

Hugh would know where the bodies were buried, but Hugh was gone, which took me back to Mother's file. Maybe I could persuade Paul to give it me. Or maybe I should just go back to Plan A: chat up some of Mother's friends. I wondered if Ernie Brown would tell me when and why Mother rented the cottage. The complicating factor was that I'd inherited my father's half of their landscape architecture business, and a conversation about my role in the business was on the longish list of things I'd avoided for fifteen years.

Round and round the questions spun in my head. Who would give me a hook to pry open this Pandora's box?

Late in the day, Mary Ellen arrived, dressed again in black Prada and spiky boots. She sidled my way and planted her tiny butt on the edge of my desk. "Working on anything interesting?"

"What's up, Mary Ellen?" I could see why my mother had lost patience with this woman a long time ago.

"Just curious about how you're getting along."

I wondered idly if she saw herself as guileless. "Since you've known my mother for such a long time, maybe you can tell me about the major trauma in her life." Going on the offensive made me feel I was getting off the merry-go-round in my brain.

Mary Ellen went still, like a lizard, but it took her only a moment to regroup: "I have no idea what that might be." She stood, brushing off her skirt, as if my desk had sullied her designer wear. "I can't answer vague questions like that, despite our agreement."

So she did know.

She and her boots clacked their way to the door marked "Private." It led to Andrew's office, which he rarely used and which no one treated as private. He'd left hours ago for a meet and greet. She picked up the phone and turned her back even though I was too far away to overhear her conversation.

As I closed out the files, I noticed one from the first fundraiser I'd attended, where I'd seen Mayor Nat. Nat had been kind to me that evening and had said he would help. Mayors were public servants, right? That meant they always worked late...

Maybe I could catch him before he left for the day. I had plenty of time before I had to meet Pete at 8:30. I shouted a loud goodbye and hustled out. The cold December afternoon had added wind to its icy package, and ribbons of it wound up through my sleeves and around my neck. I scooted along the sidewalk, noticing that the windows were decorated festively with red and green velvet and those cutesy little caroling dolls that people collected and displayed in cloying groups. Too bad they didn't do something useful, like actually carol rather than just spewing tinny recorded music from their tiny mouths.

The door to the town hall was open; I was in luck. The security guard—a token addition after 9/11 (what terrorist would bomb our town?)—lazily checked my bag and waved me through. Mueller's office, he said, was on the third floor, elevator to my right. I rode up alone, marveling that buildings in this world still contained fake paneling and green indoor/outdoor carpet. Stepping into the hall, I recognized Lyle Lovett's album *It's Not Big It's Large* working its way under a 1950s frosted glass door. "All Downhill" was the tune playing.

I knocked and heard a growled "What is it now?"

I turned the knob and went in.

He was huddled behind a desk piled high with papers. A large 7-11 cup rested precariously on a stack of books about campaign finance. Two green leather chairs faced him, one with duct tape patching its torn seat.

He grunted. "Wondered when you'd show up." He waved at the chairs, and I sat.

"What do you mean?"

"I shouldn't have brought up the dancing." He brushed his hand across his face, and I had a sudden image of him grey-faced and gasping for breath.

The image disquieted me. "When did you last get some exercise?"

Surprised, he pulled at an eyebrow. "Exercise? In this job? That consists of walking to the podium."

"You should make time for it," I said, insistence perhaps too evident in my tone.

"You shouldn't—" He faltered, then gave me a thoughtful look. "I'll try. Now, what can I do for you so I can go home?"

"Do you know anything about Mother suffering a trauma? Does it, would it... have anything to do with Hugh's murder?" I unwound my scarf, suddenly warm.

He fiddled with some documents on his desk. "If she did suffer some trauma way back when, Clara, why bring it up now? Wouldn't that hurt your mom's case more than help her?" He leaned back in his chair so far that he could have toppled through the window behind him if it were open.

"Only if it connects with Hugh's death. Does it give her a motive? They've been friends all these years. Why would she want him dead now?"

He looked a little shocked. "You're jumping to conclusions, Clara. Your mother's not a killer."

"I need to know what happened if I'm going to help her clear her name."

He cracked his neck first on the left and then on the right, toyed with his wedding band. A lot of tics to decide if he should tell me. "You should talk to your mother," he finally said.

"She won't talk to me. Someone broke into the house last night and threatened me with a knife. I need to know—I'm involved now."

"It's her story," he insisted. "I can't tell it for her. Anyway, she didn't tell me everything." He turned his head away.

"What's your relationship with her like?" The leather creaked as I leaned forward.

He smiled a little, breaking the tension. "Your mother was my first kiss."

"Really?" I laughed. "That's great!" I settled back, feeling my body unkink a smidgen. Finally, something benign and a little racy about her, the upstanding model citizen.

He looked a little surprised. "She never told you?"

I shook my head. "She hasn't told me a lot of things."

He shrugged. "We were eleven or twelve, I don't remember exactly, at a party, some birthday for a friend who moved away a couple years later. We were drunk on cake and ginger ale, running around in the hot sun, jumping in and out of this guy's pool. Your mother was beautiful, even then. She was tall early, long and slender and with legs like that Arabian she always wanted your grandfather to buy her. Anyway," he paused and ran his hand over his head. The streetlight through the window gleamed off the damp sheen his hand left behind. "I persuaded her an amazing bug was lurking behind a big bush in the garden. I took her hand and pulled her over there with me, although I didn't have to pull too hard. She'd just come out of the pool, and her body was sleek with water. She smelled like chlorine and sunshine, and her hand was cool and a little sticky.

"When we got around behind the bush, where no one could see us, I realized I didn't have a plan. What was I going to do if she didn't want to kiss me? What if she screamed and ran?" He smiled. "People would still remember it and be asking me, 'Nat, what were you doing with that girl in the bushes!'

"Lucky for me, your mother knew exactly what she wanted. We got into that dark, cool corner—there was even a little bench—and she sat me down, took my face in her hands, and kissed me smack on the mouth. Then she sat back and looked at me with those green eyes. I told her I loved her, and she said she knew, and then she kissed me again. I thought I was going to die right there. I'd closed my eyes, and by the time I opened them again, she was gone."

I laughed. "That's a great story, Nat."

"Yeah, she always knew exactly what she wanted, even if she didn't get it."

"Didn't get it?"

"We've been friends a long time." He wiped his hand over his bald spot again. "Your mother's a good woman, Clara. She doesn't understand that her actions don't always come across the way she wants them to. I know you feel she abandoned you, left you to figure out how to grow up on your own because she was in emotional cold storage. She's told me you feel that way. But she did the best she could."

He was the second person to tell me that. It would have been nicer if she'd told me. "You know a lot."

He nodded. "I know more than I should. My wife's been pretty tolerant all these years. Knew that I loved her first and foremost, but that I had a responsibility to Constance she couldn't stand in the way of."

"Responsibility?"

"I should have stopped what happened. I offered to stay with her that afternoon, and she waved me off."

"What afternoon, Nat? What's the trauma?" *Now.* He would tell me now, and I would know why my mother had shut me out all those years. I hunched forward, waiting.

He crashed the front wheels of the chair to the floor and abruptly stood. "I'm sorry, Clara, I can't. When you see Constance, you tell her I said it was time. She's creating a monster for all of us if she doesn't set the record straight."

CHAPTER 12

rustrated, I stood on the street outside Nat's office in the late afternoon dark. *Why wouldn't anyone talk to me?* At least I had confirmation of a trauma, but what did it have to do with Hugh's murder? I was getting blocked at every turn, and I had to find out fast, because the minute Mr. Black Leather or his employer found out I was asking questions again, they would come back. And Mother was still in jail.

Nat was right. Everyone was right. Going to Mother would be the easiest, most direct route, but every time I asked for answers, she suggested I meditate. I didn't have time for that. While I was meditating, someone out there was plotting to kill me and lock her away for twenty-five-to-life.

Cars moved slowly through the icy air, navigating the clutter of Christmas shoppers and traffic. I stepped under the streetlight and rummaged through my bag, extricating the envelopes with the notes on Andrew's campaign donors. I flipped through them like a pack of cards, wondering who could be useful. Mother had lived in this town all her life. Someone here had to know what had happened to her.

My eye caught on a name. Maybe Winken, who'd had a meltdown at the memorial service and knew me from the Women's League, would talk. Something in that file indicated she had a secret—the penciled notations, the financial oddities. All I had to do was find her.

I hurried back to the campaign office. The second security guard, the one who came on at three o'clock, sat at the desk. A lanky black man with cropped hair, he'd told me he commuted in from the next town—the one where they had housing projects—and supported his aging mother and young son. This gig was his second job. His first was as a breakfast cook in one of Stamford's fancy hotels.

"Hey, Horatio. I've left some papers in the office. Is anyone still up there?"

He shook his head. "They've all gone."

"Oh shoot. I really need them tonight. Could you let me in?" I wasn't supposed to be there during off-hours, unless the candidate authorized it. Campaign strategy was all very hush-hush.

"Sure, Ms. Montague." He reached into his desk for a ring of keys, then led the way up the stairs. "You want me to wait?"

"That would be fine," I said. "I'll only be a moment." Enough light came from the streetlights that I could grab the file without turning on the overheads. I would return it in the morning, with no one the wiser. I stuffed it in my purse and walked back to the door, which Horatio locked behind me.

"You're a real member of the team now," he said. "They should get you your own key."

"It's early days," I said. "You never know how people are going to work out, and even though I'm trying my best"—I was laying it on thick here—"it just might not be the right fit with Mr. Winters."

"I'm sure Mr. Winters will see your good work. He's a good man."

"Do you think so?" I asked, interested in how he perceived the candidate.

"He always thanks me at the end of the day for the good work I'm doing, and tells me if anything unusual happens, like, for example, you coming back to the office tonight, I should let him know and he'll take care of me. I did that last month when I noticed that lamb farmer girl"

"Hetty Gardner?"

"Yes, ma'am, her, she came by at ten o'clock to drop off an envelope, and he gave me a hundred dollar bonus."

I panicked. Winters would prosecute me if he found out I was "borrowing" campaign files. Getting locked up wouldn't help Mother. "That is really nice of him, Horatio, but you won't mention my little visit, will you? I was supposed to be further along on this project than I am, and I'll get into trouble if he realizes I'm not finished yet."

"It's okay, miss. We new people have to stick together. I won't mention it." He winked. I wondered if Horatio saw me, a white woman working for a white politician, as someone with potential power, someone to cultivate. He'd seen how the old-boys-network functioned, and I'd always felt the disenfranchised knew more about the powerful than the powerful knew about themselves. Maybe he figured he was better off with me in his debt. My town, despite its liberal bias, put relatively few of those liberal ideals into action. Better to do that the next town over, where those other people lived.

When I reached the car, I turned on the heater and took a few minutes to peruse Gary Hankin's file. Winken's doctor husband had started his women's health practice when my mother was about twelve or thirteen. Four years later, he'd moved into New York City, where he'd formed a larger practice affiliated with Columbia University. It looked as though he was the principal in this practice, which had grown to ten doctors.

Past traditional retirement age, he appeared to be mostly teaching and seeing a few select patients. He had made a lot of money over the years, not only through his practice and teaching, but through specialized obstetrical surgery, and some invention related to it. Strangely, he lived in a modest part of town. I scanned the list of his favorite hangouts. They were all in the city with one exception: the local country club.

Of course he needed the golf course.

I sighed, wondering if Mother had kept up her membership.

———

A half-hour and a shower later, in a pair of tight black pants I should have thrown out one size ago and a bright pink cashmere sweater with a deep V-neck, I arrived at the club. At the front entrance, a butler asked my name. I gave it to him, explained that the membership was my mother's. He made a mark in his book and took my coat with an only slightly disapproving look at the pants. Mother would never have shown up dressed like this.

I headed for the bar. It was done up in brothel-red velvet and dark wood paneling, the original gentleman's club décor. It was 6:30; the commuters had just arrived from their daily grind, ready to let off steam. The wives, who'd left the children with the nanny, dribbled in wearing appropriately fitting black pants and high heeled boots. Everyone seemed to have a martini. I ordered chardonnay, needing a clear head. A better idea would be to stop drinking, because I kept waking up with a hangover. But the wine kept the nightmares in check, and that was a very large advantage.

The country club, a fishbowl, was filled with gossips. That gossip was sure to quickly reach the ears of whoever didn't want me poking around. I had to make what I found out count, and then act on it fast. I surveyed the room. As the only single woman, I was getting more dagger looks during my first two sips of wine than I had in the past ten years. I needed to make friends, so I started with the bartender. Bartenders were good for information, and they made you feel wanted.

"Everything okay with your wine?" he asked when I smiled at his combination of blue eyes, blond hair and broad shoulders.

"What's the label?"

He told me.

"Ah. That explains its little edge."

He grimaced. "Yeah, I can't talk my boss into stocking good wines by the glass. He's too worried about roof leaks and stuff."

"I bet it costs a lot to keep this place up. How old is the building?"

"1891. Built by the last son of a shipbuilding family, who imported all the stone from France. They didn't mention *that* much around here after 9/11." He shook his head a little at the hypocrisy.

I raised my eyebrows.

"Remember Freedom Fries?"

Comprehension dawned. "Right. Personally, I'm glad to have French fries back on the menu." *And I would really love to be in Paris right now.*

He grinned, conspiratorial.

Good. I'd gotten him on my side. "Been working here long?"

"About three months. I took a year off school that turned into four years of bumming around the world. This job is pretty boring and," he leaned over the bar, "waiting on rich *married* women is even more boring. They're too easy." He grinned. "It's time to go back to college."

"Have you applied?"

"Got accepted at Gettysburg last spring—deferred it, since I had to earn enough money to get home from Thailand. I start in September."

"Good school. What will you study?"

"International business, I thought, but looking at these guys, I don't know. I was thinking maybe wood science or philosophy." He said it with a straight face.

"Wood science, huh? Gettysburg got a big program in that?"

"They've got a good philosophy program. Anyway, it's all about learning to think like the plants, right? I figure I'm golden."

"Good thinking." I raised my glass to him. "May your future open to you like a spring full of flowers."

He snickered, but straightened quickly when a man with a bristly red mustache beckoned imperiously from the other end of the bar. "Be right back," he muttered.

It gave me a minute to check out how the composition of the room had changed. More of the wives had arrived, creating a sea of blonde hair interspersed with little bald-head boats, and fewer were shooting me daggers, since I was obviously flirting with the bartender. I still didn't see Winken.

The bartender returned. "Find who you're looking for?"

"What's your name?"

"Bret."

Of course it was. "I'm Clara. Do you know the Hankins?"

"Oh sure! Dr. Hankin is great. They're around the corner." He pointed.

"Think I'll go say 'hi.'"

"Don't forget to say goodbye before you go." Bret winked, which was very good for my confidence.

I crossed the room thinking about how Hugh's murder, Mother's public confession, my dreams, the claustrophobic feeling of this town, and the unwillingness of its residents to talk to me had convinced me that someone wanted Mother behind bars—or worse. Chief DuPont's attitude hadn't calmed me down either. What could Mother know that would hurt someone? And what did Hugh have to do with anything? All of it made me feel rather protective of Mother. Sure, we hadn't gotten along. Ever. Sure, we didn't really know each other. But we were blood, and no one would harm her if I could help it, especially since I had questions I needed to ask her first.Snatches of conversation started to register. "...Constance's daughter... in jail, you know... a little strange... fifteen? ...gone a long time..." I ignored them. I'd located my quarry.

"Wendy!" I'd almost called her Winken.

She was decked out like a Christmas tree in head-to-toe Burberry. "The bartender told me you were over here. Do you mind?" I pulled out a chair and sat. She grimaced polite acquiescence, although obviously she wanted nothing to do with me.

"How are you, Clara? You remember my husband Gary?"

The man sitting catty-corner to her at the table was pushing seventy, but looked ten years younger, even with a full head of silver hair. A heavy tan seemed to be his only affectation. He wore a simple, well-cut suit, its jacket tossed over the back of the chair next to him, a gold Rolex, and his wedding ring. I vaguely remembered him from Hugh's memorial service.

I reached across the table to shake his hand, maneuvering around their forest of martini glasses. They'd already gone two rounds and were working on their third. The waitress appeared at my elbow.

"Can I get you a drink?"

I held up my wine. "Good for the moment. Thanks."

She nodded and disappeared.

"I was just telling the bartender about the great Women's League projects we're doing. That's how your name came up." Winken looked a little glazed. "What do you do, Gary?" Always ask what you already know. Lawyer trick. Socialite trick.

"I'm a doctor."

"Do you practice here in town? I'm newly back and looking for a good one."

"Uh, no." He appeared somewhat alarmed. "I practice in the city, and, actually, my practice isn't taking any new patients."

Tiny frown lines formed between Winken's eyebrows. She didn't say anything, just smiled vacantly and picked up her glass. It was empty, so she fished out the olive and started to suck on it, somewhat noisily. Gary's "my dear" could have iced over a California wildfire. Winken quieted immediately, like a well-disciplined child. I asked, "Did you ever practice here in town?"

Winken started, rattling the table.

"Early in my career." He covered for her smoothly. "I soon realized, though, that the city offered more. I got a great opportunity and took it. I've never looked back."

"When did you move?"

"Over thirty years ago," he said with pride.

That made the timing about right.

"Did you ever see my mother as a patient? When she was growing up?" I left it vague, hoping to provoke him. I wanted to ask about finances and the BRK notations in the files, but I couldn't with all these people around.

"I don't recall. It's been quite a long time." Winken got paler and paler. I wondered if she would pass out. Gary patted Winken's hand. "Are you okay, my dear? You look a bit unwell. Maybe we should head into dinner."

She nodded mutely.

"Clara, it has been lovely speaking with you. I'm sure we will see you here occasionally. Do give your mother our best in these difficult times. If there's anything we can do to help..." He let it drift off.

"Actually, there is something," I said.

He paused while shrugging his jacket straight. Winken remained seated. Maybe she was nailed to her chair. Maybe she was hammered.

"I came across a medical report among my mother's things. Could you review it, confidentially of course, and tell me what it means, before I turn it over to our lawyer?"

"Your mother's doctor and lawyer should handle this, if it's germane to the case."

"She's given me power of attorney to handle her affairs while she's unavailable," I lied. "I'm trying to sort out what's important. Anyway, it's from some time ago."

He went still for a fraction of a second, then recovered so quickly that I wondered if I'd imagined it. He shrugged. "Make an appointment with my secretary." He extracted a card from his wallet and handed it to me. "Darling?" He extended his hand to his wife. She grabbed at it and pulled herself up, knocking the table again and making an orchestra of the glasses one last time. People turned to look, and she went from pale to bright red. She started to breathe in short, panicky breaths.

I grabbed her arm to steady her, but she pulled back. "Get away," she hissed. "Get away."

Gary shook his head. "She'll be all right. I'll just take her home. Too many martinis after a long, empty day." He smiled sadly. "Come along, dear."

I watched him navigate her through the room and out toward the lobby. It seemed kind and loving, except for his iron grip on her arm and the fierceness with which he kept her on course. I wondered if she would have bruises tomorrow. I wondered why he was suddenly so tight and controlled, and why Winken was so frightened. What had I said?

I collected my wine and headed back to the bar to confer with Bret. The Red Sea parted for me all the way across the room, and, shortly after that, Bret and I had the place to ourselves as they all made their way into dinner.

"You're as good as the threat of the anthrax virus," he said. "You'd better be a really good tipper to make up for it."

"You don't get tips at the club."

He leaned over the bar, bringing his grinning face close to mine. "I don't turn them down, either."

I left a really big tip.

―――――――

I only had a half hour before I had to meet Pete Samuels. I didn't even have to time to process the Hankins' reactions. from Hankin and Winken. Had something I'd said frightened Winken? Was her husband abusive and controlling or was gripping her arm like that how he showed his fear? Was it simply that they thought it unseemly to talk about Mother while she was in jail? The rest of the room had pressed its irritated community lips together. I would have to take Hankin up on his offer of an appointment, see what came of it. Maybe he would help me after all.

I sped home to change into something more decorous. I didn't want to give Pete Samuels the wrong idea, so I chose a long, straight wool skirt with riding boots, and a thick hand-knit sweater over a silk t-shirt. I didn't even know why I was going out with him. Some part of me kept insisting I shouldn't trust him—even though I hoped he would tell me about the investigation into my mother. I was a walking bundle of contradictions.

Pete arrived promptly, wearing black jeans and a black leather jacket over a brilliant blue shirt that highlighted his eyes. He shook his long dark bangs from his eyes, like a small boy getting ready to pitch a baseball, and gestured toward the car, a new-looking Range Rover. How could he afford that on a cop's salary?

"Been saving for it for six years," he said. "Drove a clunker the chief kept telling me to get rid of, because he was never sure if I was going to make it to work or not." He grinned, opened the door for me. The interior still smelled of new leather.

We made small talk for the twenty minutes it took to drive to the restaurant and get a table. Despite the lateness of the hour on a weeknight, the place was packed with people who hadn't yet figured out that they lived in the suburbs. The maître d' put us near the fireplace. I shrugged out of the sweater, too warm in the close room.

We ordered salads, beef bourguignon, and a bottle of wine, a cozy late dinner. Pete settled back in his chair, and I noticed how his shoulders muscled out the seams on that blue shirt, even if his eyes were cold. "So Clara. Tell me about you. I only know what I've read in the police reports."

That was unsettling. "What do you already know? I wouldn't want to repeat anything."

"It's more interesting hearing it from you."

I decided to go all intellectual on him. "Pierre Bonnard, the artist, said that the precision of naming takes away from the uniqueness of seeing."

"Pierre who?"

"Bonnard. He did glorious impressionist paintings, many of them with garden elements."

"Ah, that's the connection. Do you have favorites?"

"Artists?"

"If you wish. I meant gardens."

I nodded and raved about the plum trees at the Kairakuen garden in Japan and the formal Drummond Castle Gardens in Scotland through the salad course. He let me do it, and I could feel the letting, like he was feeding out rope.

After the waiter served the main course, he took my hand. "I'm more interested in the real you. Like for instance, if you're going to listen to the warning that guy gave you the other night." He ran his thumb run slowly up and down the back of my hand. My inner voice yelled loudly. I gently pulled away. In the next moment, I got a sharp pain in my arm, as if I'd twisted it.

"The real me wants to know why you all think my mother is a murderer."

"You all? You mean all us cops? Or our new King of the Jungle?"

I looked at him, slightly shocked. He raised his eyebrows at me. "Oh don't get all hoity-toity on me. I don't mean anything racist, but I don't know why your mother felt she had to go out of state to find a new chief." Petulance didn't suit him.

"I don't know anything about that."

He held up the rejected hand and counted off on his fingers. "Motive: She and Hugh recently broke up. Hugh took it hard. Means: Anyone could have picked up that poker, but she'd used it before. Opportunity: She had keys to his house and/or," he switched up a new finger, "he would open the door to her, ex cetera, ex cetera."

I resisted correcting his Latin. "All circumstantial."

"DNA will prove it."

"Where'd you get DNA?" My arm throbbed again and I rubbed it.

He looked the tiniest bit smug, but softened it by cocking his head. "Skin under his fingernails. Results should be back this week."

"Mother and Hugh were having an affair. There are all sorts of reasons for her DNA to be on him."

"Maybe," he said, "but they'd already broken up. That means he scratched his killer."

"Did Mother have scratches on her?"

He shook his head. "I can't talk about that."

"People have sex after they're broken up. Sometimes it's rough."

His eyes flicked over the V in my silk shirt. "Mrs. Montague told Chief DuPont she'd met someone new—and unmarried—wanted a different kind of relationship."

"She's got a new boyfriend? Who?" Why hadn't she told me?

He picked up his fork and speared a cube of beef. "She won't say. The chief's going ballistic, as you might imagine." He looked sideways at me.

I pretended Kyle was just another man. "Oh, I can imagine all right. But if she had moved on, why kill Hugh?"

"He was hanging on to her, messing things up."

"That doesn't sound like Hugh. Or my mother."

Pete shrugged. "Doesn't matter. We've got enough to make our case."

Pete's confidence, like a curtain of ice, descended between me and the future. Had Mother really killed Hugh? If she had, why would someone be worried about my checking into her past? The pain in my arm migrated up to my shoulder.

"Enough about your mom," Pete said. "Just reassure me you're not going to poke your nose in any further. Stay safe, Clara. You're better off leaving it to us to handle."

I couldn't do that. My little voice was muttering something I couldn't quite hear, something ornery and contradictory, something that refused to believe Mother was a murderer.

So I rallied, because that's what good Connecticut girls did, and we drifted into small talk about weather and politics. Pete, a die-hard Republican, supported Andrew Winters. As we drove home through the dark, I heard how Winters could get people jobs—the right people, of course, not those illegal immigrants—and help us keep our hard-earned money, if we would only elect him to the Senate. I wasn't sure if the evening had been worth it or what I'd learned, but I figured I was pretty safe from another date with Pete Samuels, especially since, the moment he dropped me off, my arm felt fine.

CHAPTER 13

 called Gary Hankin's office the next morning to make an appointment. I had to find out what the notations in Mother's medical file meant. At first, his receptionist refused to schedule me, claiming the doctor wasn't taking new patients. After I explained what I wanted and waited for seventeen minutes on hold, she gave me an appointment five weeks out. Feeling desperate, I thought about what I needed to know and who could help me. At the core of it all was still my ignorance of Mother's trauma. If I could understand that, understand her, I might understand why she refused to talk to me, why she refused to talk at all.

Why did other people get to know more about my mother than I did? And why hadn't their knowledge seeped out into gossip? Surely, some kid in school should have heard adults gossiping and made up some miserable name to call me like WitchyPoo or LoserMama's Baby. Or Paul and Richard would have heard and told me, right? Then again, maybe only a few knew: Mary Ellen, Mayor Nat, and the Hankins, perhaps.

Mother had said I should learn to meditate. Last night's arm pain was my body's way of trying to warn me, but about what? Maybe learning to meditate would help me figure it out. Maybe the meditation would help me figure out how to get Dr. Hankin to talk in sooner than five weeks. *Yeah, sure.*

I called Paul. His receptionist gave me an appointment in thirty seconds for five o'clock that afternoon. I wondered if I could persuade him to give me the file we'd stolen at Hugh's funeral... or at least tell me what was in it.

At ten o'clock, I left to work at the campaign office. The day passed in the usual tedium as I surreptitiously wrote a stream of notes in a tiny notebook I'd secreted in my purse. I'd created a spreadsheet on my laptop, and started entering the data I was collecting from the campaign and from my conversations, hoping a pattern would emerge. Eventually, some little item would appear, and when I typed it into my list, all the seemingly random items might make sense.

Around noon, the office registered that their Democratic competition had gained in the polls. Claims about Winters integrity were getting airplay, stories about city contracts and trading favors during his time on the city council.

Suddenly, everyone wanted updates on everything, including my progress. I had long experience placating an exacting taskmaster, and reassured Mary Ellen at least seven times that I was "on it." At 4:45, I collected my coat and left.

Paul's ground-floor office was located in an old Victorian house two blocks off the main street, and abutted a backyard garden where he grew medicinal herbs. He was always researching the best herbal combinations to treat his patients, and had begun corresponding with ethnobotanists about possible traditional medicines that could treat HIV. We didn't talk about it much, but I knew that his helplessness in the face of Richard's disease ached in him, like a swirl of red locked inside a glass bird. The office was decorated in a mono-chromatic palette of greens: deep on the carpet, medium on the chairs, pale on the walls. His receptionist had left for the day and his door was closed, so I sat and tried to calm down by practicing a few of the breathing exercises I'd learned in Switzerland. They were only marginally successful. In a few minutes, Paul walked out with Maria Leiber.

"Clara." She came immediately to me, holding out her hands. "How are you holding up?"

I took them into my own. "I'm fine, thanks. Mother seems to be doing well, even if she's trying the patience of the detectives working her case. And you? How are you managing?"

"It's so much to absorb. Finding referrals for Hugh's patients, settling the estate, selling the house, it seems as though I'm going to be stuck here forever." She laughed, rueful. "I know you all love it, but I miss my Montana skies."

"I hope it goes quicker than you think." I smiled. "If there's anything I can do..." I could use that drift off as well as anyone.

"Of course." She leaned forward to kiss my cheek, whispering in my ear, "We should have lunch before I leave town, talk about, well... you know." She gave me a dark look. I'd almost forgotten her comments about Hetty.

I let go of her hands. "Whenever you like."

She collected her coat and closed the door ever-so-softly behind her.

"She's good people," Paul said. "You shouldn't take her for granted like that."

"What do you mean? What did I do?"

"She offered to help. I know you, Clara. You didn't mean a word you said."

"The last thing I need is a second mother," I huffed. "I can feel her wanting to involve me, like octopus tentacles wiggling through the water. I feel every single person is looking at me and they all know something I don't. The fact that I don't know it is going to sink me, but no one will freaking tell me what it is."

He just raised an eyebrow and gestured toward his office. "What's up?"

"I need my mother's file."

"Not yet."

"Why not?" I flopped into my favorite comfy velvet chair, my stomach churning.

"You're not ready." He sat, crossing his legs, and waited.

"You haven't forgiven me yet."

"For what?" he said. "Stealing the file?"

I nodded.

"I'm working on it." He smiled to take the sting from his words. "Is that why you made an appointment? To collect the file and find out if I was still upset? You could have stopped by the house."

I made myself sit up straight, like a grown up. "Mother has decreed I should learn to meditate." I squared my shoulders.

"Do you want to?"

I shrugged, reverting to grumpy teenager. "It's why I made the appointment." *At least partly.* I was behaving like an idiot, but it bugged me that Paul felt he could chastise me about Maria Leiber, never mind about the file. I had left because this place was beyond claustrophobic. When there was a secret, it sucked up all the air and no one could breathe. Acquiescing to my mother's demands about meditation and whatever else she dreamed up used up more air—air I needed, thank you very much.

"Why does she want you to learn?"

"You think she's told me?!" I nearly exploded out of the chair. Paul squashed against his upholstery in surprise. I began to pace. "She doesn't tell me a damn thing. She speaks in riddles, like a Jungian therapist. 'Beware of fire.' 'Learn to meditate.' What in *the hell* am I supposed to do with messages like that?" I put my hands on my hips. "And no one else will help me or tell me anything either!"

Paul said mildly, "Meditation might help."

"Will it teach me to read her mind?"

"No. It will teach you to read your own. Since you and she are genetically connected, you might access the information she wants you to access simply because your brains are wired the same way."

"Why can't she talk to me like a normal person?"

"Which one of you is normal?" He smiled again.

I felt the heat of my anger leave me. I sat down again, put my head in my hands. "I don't want to be wired like her."

I felt his hand on my shoulder. "Not true. What you don't want is her coldness—and you don't have it. I'm not even sure that coldness is her true self...." He paused.

I looked up. "I've had a perfectly good life for fifteen years without any of this."

"No family connection? A failed marriage? A series of jobs you couldn't care less about? Every time we've visited over the last fifteen years, you've been miserable."

"You're wearing me out."

"Listen to me: Learning to meditate might help. It calms the mind. Doesn't that sound good?"

I looked around. The office felt cozy and warm with its plush cushions and lacy jacaranda tree. Paul had brought the seeds back from California. Since the little tree would never survive the bitter northeast winters, he grew it indoors. Against its fetching greenery were three neon pink geraniums he'd turned into perennials. Behind them, two windows offered views of the garden. At this hour I could see nothing but blackness.

"Meditation feels like chaos, but if it will help Mother, I'll do it."

"It's for you, Clara, not your mother."

"Fine. Whatever."

"Then let's get down to business."

He had me shut my eyes and took me through the process of relaxation, one muscle group at a time—tense and relax, tense and relax—until my body melted like honey in hot tea. I lost track of time, sinking into an emptiness filled at first only with the senses, almost as if the senses were heightened by the calming of my mind. Even the part of me that stood apart and mocked and worried was lulled into quiescence. I heard the clock tapping the minutes out, the wind batting leaves against the windows, Paul's breathing. Thoughts about Mother and Hugh and my divorce drifted through, but Paul counseled me to let them float by, as if I were watching clouds from the comfort of warm sand on a summer afternoon.

After a while, he suggested I imagine a safe place, either somewhere I loved or a retreat I created. My mind conjured up my mother's little house at the stable. I walked through it, room by room, claiming it as my own, changing the pillows from turquoise to peach, painting the walls a delicate taupe, filling the kitchen with Tippy Assam tea and the chocolate chip cookies my father used to bake.

When I was comfortable, he said, "Ask for an animal to guide you, to nose out the deceit." For a moment, nothing came. Then I looked out the window of the little house and saw a grey wolf, his head turned toward me, as if in invitation. I could see his damp black nose surrounded by white, caramel and grey fur, his hazel eyes a match for his thick coat. While I watched, he howled, long and plaintive. Within moments, as if they had fashioned themselves from air, other wolves drifted from the trees, adding their voices to the chorus. The cabin was surrounded, wolf pack upon wolf pack howling into the moonlit sky.

I felt loved and protected for the first time in a long time.

Paul and Richard fed me dinner that night. Paul and I had talked about the wolves and what they meant in the office, but we didn't agree. Richard took one look at us and opened a bottle of wine.

"I can see that my day at work was cake, compared to yours," he said. "I'm making *coq au vin* for dinner. Clara, can you get the chicken and mushrooms out of the fridge? Paul, could you set the table?" Richard removed the Baccarat from the walnut cabinet in the dining room and poured generous glasses. Paul gave him a funny look, but didn't comment.

They'd bought those glasses a couple of months after Richard's diagnosis. The pattern was called *Perfection*—a simple, thin, crystal design. They'd been in hysterics in the Madison Avenue boutique, joking about the dark irony of claiming *perfection* as their own, a magic wand to clean up their messy and complicated lives.

I'd tried to talk them into Massena, a heavier, dramatic design with deep cuts in the crystal base, but they said it was named after a fortified city, and they didn't want to think about war when they were drinking wine. I told them that was Masada, not Massena, and that the design was actually named after a French general, but they said that was the same thing, and dissolved into another round of giggles—an act of hope against the dark.

Richard raised his glass in a toast. "To us," he said. "To good friends who will see you through." Our glasses clinked and the wine trailed its warming way down my throat. He set his glass on the counter. "Okay, Clara. You're in charge of wiping mushrooms and finding the tomatoes in the pantry. I'll chop onions. Paul, your job—should you choose to accept it—is to keep Clara plied with wine." He slid the papery skin off the first onion and attacked the root with a small paring knife. "So my day was pretty much the same as usual: do more work than everyone else while being avoided. You?"

I glanced at Paul, but he was getting napkins from a drawer, his back to me.

"Paul took me through a meditation today." I shrugged. "Mother wants me to learn."

"What did you think?"

"Relaxing at first."

He slid the skin off a second onion.

"I saw a pack of wolves surrounding my mother's little meditation house." I stopped, realizing I hadn't told them about the little house. They were my best friends. Paul was a therapist. How could I not tell them—and anyway, I'd already let it slip. "At least, I think that's what it is," I amended lamely. "Over at Loretta's farm."

Richard raised an eyebrow, letting my confession slide. "That imagery isn't too hard to interpret."

"Yeah, except I felt at one with them."

"Ah."

"Am I really the same as the rest of them, just wanting to dissect her?" I shook my head. "I don't even know my own motivations anymore."

"Maybe that's not what the wolves meant." Richard turned on the flame and began to brown the chicken. "You're trying to heal things, right? Isn't a wolf a symbol for a guardian, Paul?"

"Yup."

"So maybe the wolves are trying to keep her safe. Maybe that's your role—fierce guardian—and why you felt so at home."

"Yeah, that's what Paul said."

Paul flipped a chair around and sat down, leaning his arms on the back. "Maybe you need to walk away from this for a little bit. Get some perspective."

"I thought you told me, not two hours ago, that walking away was bad." I turned, exasperated. "I just want the truth. If I'm going to help her, then I need her to be honest with me."

"And you need to be honest with her."

"About what?"

"What you need from her."

"I don't need anything from her."

"You need her to tell you who you are. Isn't that what all this is about? If you know who she is, then you can know yourself."

"Argh!" I slapped down the knife and walked into their pantry, essentially a small closet off the kitchen, to search for the tomatoes. For a moment, I didn't turn on the overhead light, enjoying the warmth and darkness like a shield between me and Paul's probing questions and therapy-speak. He was right, of course. All the visions I'd had over the years, from poor Timmy in the schoolyard to my painful arm the night before, made me want to know how the gift worked. I wanted to know if all the women in my family had it. I wanted to know what it had told Mother over the years. Maybe if she would acknowledge its usefulness, I would have permission to be who I was.

I yanked on the overhead chain. The tomatoes were staring me in the face. Grabbing the can, I flicked off the light and walked back into the kitchen, catching Paul and Richard in an embrace.

"Cut it out, you lovebirds. This is all about me."

Richard ran his hand down Paul's cheek and gave him another kiss. "Open the tomatoes and quit your whining," Richard said.

I handed the opened can to Richard, who dumped it into the pot over the onions, mushrooms and chicken. He poured in some wine, stirred it once, and popped on the lid. With some pâté, a basket of crackers and our drinks, we trailed into the living room, where Paul used a long match to light the fire.

Richard eased into his maroon recliner with a slowness I found worrisome. "Are you okay?"

He nodded. "I think I need to slow down a little. My joints are stiff and painful. Sometimes I feel a bit weak."

"Weak? What kind of weak?"

"Like my legs won't hold me up, and sort of like the flu, but without the chest and head part."

A thought flashed, a brief bit of lightning. "How long?"

"A week, ten days. Not long. I keep thinking it'll go away."

I rested my hand on his arm to double-check, got the same answer. "Dad had Lyme Disease once," I said. "Those sound like his symptoms." My knowledge felt as sure and real as Richard's chair.

He looked surprised. "It's the middle of winter."

"Lots of deer around here, and you have a woodpile." I nodded at the crackling logs.

Paul expelled a breath and Richard's shoulders dropped about an inch. He said, "Here I am thinking the worst. I'll make an appointment tomorrow. Thanks, Clara."

"Will it make things worse for you?"

"Probably. Anything that compromises my immune system makes it worse."

Paul said, "I'll do some research, see what I can find."

Richard just nodded. I realized they had this conversation often and dwelling on it wouldn't help. I smeared pâté on a cracker and settled into the overstuffed couch. It was a big, dark piece for the room, but somehow Paul made it work. A small Christmas tree glimmered in the front window, surrounded by small, gaily wrapped boxes.

"Am I invited for Christmas? That is, assuming Mother's still in jail."

"You're always invited for Christmas, and she can come too, if she gets out. We're having a Christmas Eve party, champagne, lots of hors d'oeuvres, and roast beef. Christmas Day we'll roast a turkey. Come whenever you want—Sondra and Joellen, and Alcott and Morrie are joining us. You could even bring a date."

"Uh, no date." I recounted my dinner with Pete Samuels, including the painful arm.

Paul looked into the fire, silent.

Richard said, "That yummy Kyle DuPont is our pick for you."

"That feels—complicated."

Richard shook his head and shot a look at Paul, but neither said anything further.

I changed the subject. "Are you going to midnight service?"

"We might. It depends on how Richard feels." Paul stretched out in his chair, finally relaxing. We chatted about the little details of our days and workmates, the same old gripes we had rehashed a hundred times. It felt reassuring, somehow, as if we could put aside, at least for the moment, our difficulties, and as if, here if nowhere else, I was loved for myself.

After some negotiation about the festivities, we agreed I would bring wine to both events, and that I would ask Bailey to join us, and, if I got my courage up, I might ask the chief—as a friend. I had to submit to some intensive teasing, which, I pointed out, did plenty for my courage.

The fire crackled in the fireplace, its cheering flames reflecting off the hearth's open glass doors and the faces of my two dear friends. The play of light and shadow smoothed the lines that were starting to form on their faces from worry, exhaustion, the stresses of living. I kicked off my shoes and tucked my feet up underneath me.

"I love you guys. You know that, right?"

They looked at each other first, then at me. Richard reached for my hand. "We love you, too, Clara."

CHAPTER 14

ater that night, the dreams were different. The field still opened in front of me, and Mother and I were still running, the bloody cloud hovering over us. But this time, out of the clouds materialized, almost like ghosts, a group of sentinel wolves. One by one, they appeared, and as they appeared, the cloud receded, until it was only Mother and I, in the middle of the field, in the middle of a pack of wolves, their yellow eyes glimmering in the dusky light.

I woke, my heart pounding. Sun streamed through the curtains of my mother's bedroom. My meditation and my dreams had merged. What did *that* mean? I threw off the covers, and sat up, and then had to brace myself, my hands planted on the mattress, against a sudden wave of dizziness. I felt as though I might topple, but not from exhaustion. I shook my head, hoping to bring clarity, but it only made me feel as if a giant slug was sliming a trail inside my skull. I'd had only a couple glasses of wine at Richard and Paul's. What was making me feel this way?

Since I'd left home, I had noticed when the message the dreams sent was particularly important, I would be affected physically: nausea, headaches, body aches—like the sharp pain in my arm the other night. At first, I hadn't recognized the warning signs. I thought I'd injured myself accidentally, slept funny, or eaten something that disagreed with me. Slowly, I grasped that the physical pain increased when the danger was greatest. The blinding pain I'd felt around my heart before my father died wasn't panic or grief from the dream, but a warning of what he would feel if I didn't act. Of what he did feel because I didn't act. It was a sense memory I'd never forgotten.

Now I was trying to do the right thing. I was respecting the dreams by listening to them. I'd come home, for god's sake. I was learning to meditate, as Mother wanted. And while I was doing all sorts of things Mother probably wouldn't want, the dreams weren't synonymous with Mother's needs and desires. They belonged to me. Mother must understand that one couldn't control an intuition. She would forgive my prying because she would know I had to honor what the intuitions gave me, right? But it didn't make sense that my dreams were still waking me. What was I missing? What was I supposed to be doing that I wasn't?

Tentatively, I reached my toes toward the floor and stood, hanging onto the bedpost. The room swayed, then righted itself. *Oh, good.* I sat down again, assured I could stand when I wanted to. Not that I wanted to. Not yet.

A long time ago, Paul said it wasn't necessarily the images that were important, but how I felt in the dream. My heart had pounded, but it occurred to me, it wasn't from fear but from excitement: my people had come to rescue us. That was all well and good in a dream, but who were my "people" in real life? I didn't see any white knights on horses. These days, a girl was in charge of her own rescuing. I moved my head slightly. The slug had calmed down. Maybe I could walk across the room. I stood again and tottered into Mother's bathroom. I was still sleeping in her room, wearing her clothes. Weirdly, I hoped it would get me inside her head.

Fifteen minutes later, after a hot shower and raiding her make-up and closet, I padded back to my own bedroom and stood in front of the mirror. I'd created a hybrid image, a combination of Mother and me. If sleeping in her bed didn't get me inside her head, maybe wearing her Calvin Klein suit would.

But Mother's behavior worried me: why wouldn't she tell the chief what she knew? Why had she torpedoed her chance at bail with that stunt at Hugh's memorial service? What was she getting protection from? Or what was she protecting *me* from? I stared at myself, the image in the mirror warping and slithering in the glass, and tried to think what to do next.

Wolves... beautiful gray and white hair... my people... wolves and sheep... the cottage... the Christmas fête...sheep... Hetty...

Hugh and I had sat across from Hetty at the Christmas fête, and all during dinner, she'd watched us as if she were a jealous wife. I couldn't imagine Hetty and Hugh involved with each other, but perhaps they hadn't been and that was the problem. Maybe Hetty had a thing for Hugh, and I'd gotten in the way, just as I'd gotten in the way with Ethan all those years ago.

After I'd chased Hetty away from Ethan, she came after me with a vengeance. It started with notes taped to my locker accusing me of sleeping with the football team or cheating on an exam. When I didn't react, the notes went to the school newspaper, teachers, and principal. When a letter to the editor appeared in the local newspaper about the children of the rich getting away with cheating—Hetty all but named names—my father called Loretta, and then, with her blessing, called his lawyer. Hetty, threatened with a libel lawsuit, backed off.

Could Hetty have killed Hugh? Maybe that's why the DNA tested female. But why would she *still* be coming after Mother and me? Balaclava Guy hadn't sounded or looked female, but maybe that was more what I expected than what I'd seen. And I'd nearly forgotten: Maria had suggested I check out Hetty's psychic side business because of Hugh's attempts to shut her down.

I changed out of my mother's suit and pulled on flannel-lined jeans, a cashmere turtleneck, and thick socks. I breakfasted on espresso and an English muffin while checking out Hetty's property on Google maps. The aerial photo showed three structures: the barn, the house, and a smaller building off to the west, at the edge of the woods. A path wandered alongside the fence, and a second drive came straight to that cabin or shed. Maria had said Hetty used a room in her house for her readings, but if I knew Hetty, that cabin was a re-creation of the one at her mother's farm, the one that my mother used. I printed the image and the map, then put on my sheepskin coat and shoved my feet into quilted boots, all the while careful of the slug in my head, who was slowly, slowly shrinking. I checked my watch: eight-thirty. How long did a farmer need for morning chores?

The drive took me north, into the greenest part of town, with its generous land parcels. Charming split rail fences and stone walls acted as boundaries between snow-covered meadows. Christmas traffic was concentrated downtown and at the malls in Stamford, so I had the roads mostly to myself. Twenty minutes later, I pulled off near the driveway for Rising Moon Farm. I double-checked the map, then swung out, drove a quarter mile down and turned right into a narrow, unmarked drive.

The trees folded over me, heavy with ice and snow. Little sunlight penetrated here, and the ground remained frozen. The driveway wasn't well maintained. Perhaps Hetty didn't see clients in the winter, or maybe this was a test: if they braved this road in their precious cars, they were worthy of her attentions. I slowed the Land Rover to a crawl, hoping Hetty, wherever she was, wouldn't hear the engine.

Finally, I saw the faint frame of the house through the trees. Small and white, it huddled under the pines like the gingerbread house in the fairytale, but without all the sugary enticements. It stood like a ghost house against the dark evergreens. One concrete step led to a door, in front of which sat a metal pail. A path had been shoveled to the door and the little stoop was brushed clean of snow, so even without clients, it appeared someone maintained it. I backed the car around so it faced back down the drive and got out.

I climbed the steps. The pail was filled with sand and cigarette butts. Next to it sat a bag of half-frozen garbage. I tried the knob. It was locked. Of course it was. Had I thought she would leave it open for me?

I looked around, as if for a weapon, then stopped myself. I couldn't break into Hetty's cottage. I leaned off the stoop toward the nearest window, feeling the dizziness press at me. I grabbed the porch railing and checked out the heavy white curtains blocking my view. There wasn't even a slit between them. I sighed. The snow and I had a date.

I stepped carefully off the stoop and into the drifts that surrounded the house. If I was lucky, it would snow again and Hetty wouldn't know someone had snooped. If I was unlucky, she'd show up, wondering why a strange car was at her cottage. If she found me here, she would call the police, which would put me in the sights of the police chief yet again—and neither he nor I would be happy about that.

I felt too wobbly to move very fast; the snow was mid-calf deep and had drifted against the house. Most of the windows were curtained, but, in the back, one opened to the interior. I struggled through the drift, my feet sinking deeply into the banks. Snow snuck over the tops of my boots and melted into my socks. It clung to my jeans, freezing them crisp. My breath fogged the glass as I hugged my hands around my face to see inside.

I was looking at a tiny kitchen, a near replica of the one in Mother's cottage. Through the open door to the main room, I saw a turquoise rug and walls, a white chair and white cushions. A small table by the front door was cluttered with objects, but I couldn't see clearly enough to determine what they were. Damn. So close...

Almost without thinking, I pushed on the window. It opened. I shoved it up as far as it would go and slithered through the gap. I was covered with enough ice to slide through just about any opening. Hastily, I pulled the window down behind me and crouched out of view. Going head first hadn't been a good idea. The room spun around me and I tried to stabilize myself by hanging on to the windowsill. I had to look fast. Hetty might be coming through the woods to check out the engine noise.

The kitchen was half the size of Mother's. A tea kettle rested on a two-burner stove. Ripe garbage was piled near a dorm-room sized refrigerator. I crabbed through the doorway into the main room and stood up once I had a wall to hide me from view and use for support. The clutter on the table turned out to be a pack of Tarot cards and an upmarket digital camera, a couple of memory cards and a package of batteries. A half-burnt candle sat in a puddle of its own wax. When I turned to face the wall behind me, I almost cried out. That's why the curtains were drawn so tight. I lunged for the nearest chair and sat down fast.

Pinned on the wall was a photo gallery: Hugh, me, Mary Ellen, others. I didn't have time to look at them all closely. Hugh, Mary Ellen and I each had our own section, and we'd been captured in a variety of places, with others and alone. My photos had all been taken since I'd gotten home, but Hugh's and Mary Ellen's spanned several years. Hugh's hair greyed and his weight fluctuated, while Mary Ellen progressed from thin to thinner, from Prada to Jean Paul Gaultier and back again. On the wall to the right, a new gallery displayed photos of Pete Samuels with a snarl on his face. I wondered who he'd been looking at.

What did any of these people have in common?

Even more disturbing than the photographs were the dolls attached to the pictures. Mary Ellen, Hugh and Pete all had red dolls. My doll—green for gardens?—had about thirty pins stuck through it. Just looking at it made me feel prickly. *Hetty* left the voodoo doll on my pillow? How had she gotten in and out of my house?

And there was something else. What was there? What was I seeing but not recognizing?

I grabbed my phone from my jacket pocket and photographed each of the walls, then took pictures of the rest of the room, a couple of the kitchen and the garbage, and the table with the Tarot cards. Something crashed outside.

I ran to the back window, shoved it up, and clambered out. Pulling it closed behind me, I slogged as quickly as I could to the front. A quick look from the edge of the cabin showed the coast clear, so I jogged to the Land Rover, jammed the key in the ignition and high-tailed it out of there. I thought I heard someone yelling, but that could just have been the sound of the ice beneath my tires. I didn't see anyone in the rearview mirror, and no one chased me down the drive. Maybe I was in the clear.

I had to take the pictures to Kyle, but I couldn't tell him I'd broken into Hetty's cabin. Plus, I needed a shot of the outside right after all the interior pictures I'd shot. My phone would register the time and location link. That wasn't evidence Kyle could actually use, but maybe it would get him a search warrant. Then I thought about that bag of garbage sitting on her step next to the bucket of cigarette butts. Garbage was fair game, right? At least it was in all those TV detective shows. But that meant going back and risking that Hetty had returned in the meantime. *Damn.*

I drove to the end of the lane and pulled the Land Rover as far off the main road as I could. The only way I could see to be a little covert would be to go back on foot and hope I didn't meet Hetty coming through the woods. At least the ten or so minutes it would take me to walk down the driveway would also give me time to make sure no one else was there.

The frozen denim had melted a bit in the car, but as I stepped back into the chill, the wind whistled through the fabric as if I were wearing lace and chiffon. I hustled as fast as I could; the drive crunched underfoot, and my jeans stuck to my legs, icy cold. My head pounded and everything remained blurry at the edges. In the distance, I heard the occasional car and a metal banging, like a screen door against its frame.

When I neared the clearing, I paused in the shadow of a spruce, inhaling its resiny scent, to see if Hetty had arrived. From where I stood, I thought I saw only my tire tracks and footprints, but to be sure, I moved along the edge of the clearing, from tree to tree, hoping that if Hetty had gone inside, she was too busy worrying about what I'd found to look out and see me.

I pulled my phone out, yanked off my gloves and opened the photo app. I took two pictures of the house, one with a close-up of the garbage bag, then shoved the phone away again, and ran across the clearing to the steps, scooped up the bag and hightailed it, slipping and sliding, down the drive. The slug had to deal.

In the car safely headed for home, I turned the heater up high and deep-sixed my idea of visiting Hetty. Not with that wall of photos. Instead, I burned up road back to Mother's, divested myself of my wet clothes and made myself a large cup of hot chocolate with marshmallows in it. Next, I spread newspapers on the floor in the mudroom and starting sifting through the garbage. For all her organic farming ways, Hetty seemed to survive on beef jerky and chocolate cookies. Mixed in with those wrappers were rejected photo prints and memory cards. Two, to be exact.

That's when I realized I didn't have a memory card reader. I usually hooked the camera up to the computer. I put my coat back on and wasted another hour and a half going to an office supply store, getting help finding the right card reader, standing in the endless Christmas line, and coming home again.

By the time I reheated the chocolate and made myself a peanut butter and jelly sandwich to go along with it, I realized the slug was mostly gone. Comfort food, sifting through garbage, and long waits at Christmas cash registers were apparently good for recovering from bad dreams. I got the card reader set up and scrolled back through Hetty's photos. The pictures of Pete Samuels were there, along with ones of me and Pete at dinner, taken through the window of the restaurant. She'd stood outside in the cold and the dark to take them. I shivered. The few photos of Pete taken prior to the ones of us together looked posed. He stared straight into the camera, with a challenging glare.

Why was she taking pictures of Mary Ellen, Pete, Hugh and me? And why had she left those voodoo dolls?

Okay, photos of two men and two women. Of the two men, one had been a psychologist; the other, a police detective. Had they known each other, other than superficially? Mary Ellen certainly knew Hugh, but something about the photographs of Mary Ellen felt different to me. They were mostly of her alone, in a location I couldn't identify.

Hetty had tried to get as close as possible to Hugh to take photos. There were shots of him in his office, taken through the patio sliding doors, as if she'd perched behind the rocks on his property with a zoom lens. One shot apparently had gone wrong; it looked as if a blonde ghost was streaking across the camera lens. Other shots caught him at dinner downtown and at parties or with Mother and a handsome, silver-haired man. Who was that guy, anyway? Was that the new boyfriend Pete had mentioned?

I copied all the photos onto my laptop, printed them, and stuck the pictures in an envelope with a note that explained where they had come from. I labeled it with Chief DuPont's name and took it to the police station, where I left it with the desk sergeant. The desk sergeant knew me, glanced at the envelope with interest, told me Mother was in with her lawyer and couldn't see me just then. I'd been so absorbed in my own quest, I hadn't even thought about asking after her. *Bad, Clara.*

As for the pictures, I'd have to take my chances with the breaking and entering—and if I were lucky, no one would ever know. If Hetty was stalking me and two other living people, I needed to know why, and I wanted the cops to know, too—just in case.

As I drove home again, I mulled over possibilities. What—if anything—was Hetty's relationship with Balaclava Guy? Maybe she'd snapped the pictures, constructed the dolls, and had balaclava guy deliver them to my pillow. Why? Just to scare me? Why scare me? Revenge for things that happened in high school?

Why would Hetty care about Mother's innocence or guilt? One possibility was that Hetty had killed Hugh and set Mother up. What had Mother done to cause Hetty to choose her as the fall guy? As far as I could tell, Hetty loathed me, not Mother. But Hetty's cottage, a miniature of Mother's—what was that all about?

Maybe Hetty's photographs were a lover's obsession, although that appeared unlikely. Didn't stalkers shadow one target at a time? I mean, who could handle Hugh, Pete, Mary Ellen and me all at once?

I pulled into the garage. Whatever Hetty's obsessions, they were distracting me from figuring out Mother's trauma, and I was more than ever convinced her trauma lay at the heart of everything. I could feel it in my gut, even if nothing I had found so far confirmed it.

My watch read three o'clock. Time enough to head back to campaign headquarters and use my newly found leverage. I ran into the house to print a couple copies of the photographs, just in case.

CHAPTER 15

arrived about three-thirty, which I could justify since I needed to attend another command performance fundraiser that evening. I opened my bottom drawer and dropped in my purse and its curious photographs, then turned to toss my coat over the back of the visitor's chair next to the desk. Someone was sitting in that visitor's chair. I gave a little cry and stepped back. The slug protested. It didn't need any more drama today.

He grinned. "Sorry. Didn't mean to scare you."

I felt my face grow furnace hot. "Jeez. Don't sneak up on a person." I set down my coat, hoping my flush would disappear by the time I turned back. No such luck. His long legs stretched out in front of him, draped in fine-gauge navy wool. The suit jacket had apparently been abandoned elsewhere, since his pale green shirt and dark green tie were unadorned. Blond hair, blue eyes, a slightly crooked nose—a freakish lacrosse or skiing accident, no doubt—topped a square chin, and thin patrician lips.

He held out his hand without getting up. "Andrew Winters, Junior." My face must have betrayed surprise, because he leaned in, pulling me toward him and whispered, "Right. You didn't think my mother was capable of doing anything as messy as reproducing?" He rubbed his thumb across my hand, then released me. What was it with guys and that move?

I sat down abruptly, surprised my head still sat on my shoulders, given the thumping going on between my ears. "I, uh, they don't talk about you. In fact, they don't talk about any of their children. I didn't even remember they had children."

"I'm the bad seed. Law school, yes, but I'm headed for the public defender's office."

"A noble goal, if a tiring one. Or so I've heard." My skirt slid up slightly as I crossed my legs. His eyes rested there a moment before returning to my face. He'd inherited some things from his father. I pulled it down again. "You're home for the holidays?"

He nodded, talking about his law career as if I hadn't mentioned another topic. Typical—of men, I could say, but it was also a Winters trait. I found men obsessed with themselves interesting—for a time. Men like my soon-to-be-ex, for instance.

"It's the wrong side of the tracks. I'm supposed to join my father's firm this summer, become a partner, buy a house in town, raise blond children. You're not available for that, are you?"

I put my chin in my hand—it would steady things, yes?—and studied him, my eyebrows raised. He was funny. I liked that. "Raising blond children? Not at the moment. Thanks, though. I appreciate being considered for a part in your truly meteoric rise."

Out of the corner of my eye, I saw Mary Ellen step into Andrew's office. Ah, my quarry—dressed in what appeared to be Carolina Herrera, the softest look I'd yet seen her wear.

He gave an exaggerated sigh. "I thought if I could find the right woman, it might make Dad's plan palatable."

I shook my head. "How old are you anyway?"

"Twenty-seven. Why? Am I too young?"

"I'd have to know a bit more about you than your career plans."

"Great. It's settled then." He stood up, pulling the secretive suit jacket from the floor where it had dropped behind the chair. Armani. On the floor. No wonder he was the bad seed.

"What is?"

"Dinner. With me. Tonight. Eight o'clock. I'll pick you up."

"Can't. I've got your Dad's fundraiser." Never mind that I couldn't comprehend remaining awake that long.

But, the snake in the Garden of Eden whispered, *he might know why Mother and Mary Ellen hated each other, which might tell me about my mother's trauma, which might give me a way to get her out of jail.* The slug was on a roll.

"Blow it off," he said.

"Not possible. I'm sure you know a bit about that." Mary Ellen stepped out of Andrew's office and glanced at us. I tried to smile perkily at her, but it came out like a grimace. She raised an eyebrow at me, got her coat and sashayed out the door, along with my opportunity to question her.

"We'll go after the fundraiser's over. It can't last longer than ten, right?"

I tried to refocus on Junior. "You think you can find a restaurant in this town still serving at ten?"

"No problem." He grinned again, swung the jacket over his shoulder and sauntered off toward his father's office.

As I flicked on my computer and pulled up the file I needed, I felt a little knot in my stomach, a warning. Handsome yes, but he was a Winters. And for god's sake, I was divorcing my husband. Since when did I date guys to get information? I twitched around a little in my chair, trying to get comfortable as I thought about why Junior bothered me. I was beginning to listen to myself, but knowing when my intuition spoke and when my imagination spoke still wasn't clear.

Why would Junior home in on me? Maybe he liked flirting, or he was sent by his father or Mary Ellen. *Do your part, son: wine and dine the new girl.* Maybe that's what the knot was warning me about.

———————

Later that evening, I stepped outside the latest palatial mansion used to persuade the party adherents into giving up their cash, and found Junior standing by a black stretch limousine. Light from the portico glimmered off the high-gloss paint and reflected off the smoked windows. I could barely see the dim outline of a driver. The car was running, the exhaust pipe steaming into the bitter December air. Junior, unfazed by the temperature, waited sans gloves or coat, his thin-soled loafers soaking up the chill from the graveled drive. I'd draped Mother's mink wrap across my shoulders.

"Bit of overkill, no?" I gestured at the limo.

He rolled his eyes. "Just get in," he said.

Mary Ellen had been far too busy that evening to corner for a chat about Hetty's photos. She even seemed to avoid me, which meant cajoling whatever Junior knew out of him was my next best option. Thankfully, the slug had shrunk so I could function, although my general wooziness remained, and I'd felt flashes of pain in my arms and back and forehead all through the party. That meant time was running short. I needed answers quickly, or the hallucinations would begin. As I speculated on the lengths I might be willing to go to get information from Junior, I heard the door open behind me.

I turned to see the chief. His cop eyes flickered over the limousine, my figure in Mother's clingy gold lace dress, young Winters. His cop eyes said, *Don't get in that car.*

I smiled. "Chief DuPont, have you met Andrew Winters, Junior?" He smiled back but it didn't get past his mouth. Stepping forward, he held out his hand. Junior reeled a bit from the ice in the chief's gaze, but shook anyway, as a good upper-class boy should.

"Mr. DuPont is our new chief of police."

Junior stilled like a rabbit in the grass when it hears the hawk screech, then managed to nod.

"Y'all goin' out?" The chief thickened his southern accent to pure syrup.

"To dinner, yes."

The chief slung his arm around me, as if somehow we were an item. For a few brief seconds, it felt like home and the pains receded. "I like this girl, so you take good care of her." I wasn't even sure this was a date, but I guess it looked like one. I'd dressed for the fundraiser, not dinner, but the chief wouldn't know that. I sighed. Maybe I should have taken more than one night off between dinners with strange men to think things through.

"Yes, sir." Winters opened the limo door. "We have a reservation, Clara."

I slid gently from DuPont's hold. His fingers grabbed my arm. Something else lingered in his eyes, but I didn't know how to read it. I patted his hand and stepped into the car. He stood there until we drove out of sight.

I looked around the car. A little brass nameplate screwed into the back of the driver's seat spelled out the name of the Winters law firm. A bottle of champagne chilled in its own built-in cooler; Junior poured me a glass as the driver pulled the car onto the Merritt Parkway.

"Where are we going?"

"That's for me to know and you to find out."

"What is this, twenty questions?"

"If you like." He touched his glass to mine. "A toast: to meeting the most beautiful woman in town and capturing her on the first day."

Capturing?

"We have reservations for two at ten-thirty," Junior said. "Drink up."

The restaurant he'd chosen, an intimate space off lower Park Avenue, served overpriced, undersized portions of the latest fad in haute cuisine. The waiters treated me as if I didn't deserve what I was getting, but Junior, of course, they treated with great, if icy, respect; I imagine they assumed he carried the cash.

My unease persisted. Junior himself entertained cleverly, telling me stories of his nightmares in law school: professors who assigned impossible reading loads, forgetting an exam, the competition for editor of the law review and for summer internships.

Through it all, he conveyed his high ambitions, but in a sufficiently self-deprecating way that expressed his own self-aware judgment of those ambitions as superficial at worst and as earnest at best. Even the public defender's office

was held up to a certain ridicule as a path to district attorney or a successful criminal practice. And throughout his discourse, he ignored the luscious
parade of young women on the arms of gray-haired financiers, an admirable
show of fortitude.

Sure, he came on to me, which surprised me given the difference in our
ages, but it felt half-hearted. Some dark, snaky part of me wondered if his father
had put him up to it, although what Senior would want from the interaction
stumped me. I was just his employee and only in town for as long as it took
to sort out my mother before hightailing it out of here again. Paris was calling. Insistently. I'd even dreamed briefly—a pleasant dream for once—about
wandering lost in the Musée D'Orsay.

"What are you thinking about?" Junior picked up his wine glass and drank
off what remained, gesturing to the waiter for a refill. The waiter complied,
and then delivered elegantly composed salads of five slices of endive centered
on three perfect raspberries.

"*Romeo and Juliet.* You know, Mary Ellen and my mother have been feud-
ing since before you were born."

"Yeah. Which makes me wonder why you're working on Dad's campaign.
You're not a mole, are you?" He smiled, but I knew we'd reached the reason
for the evening. Then, I remembered the dip in Winters's poll numbers. What
kind of father would send his son on this kind of dirty mission? What kind
of son would accept it?

I said, "Just trying to rattle things at home. Do you know what Mary Ellen
and Constance have against each other? Mother never told me."

He shrugged. "Something your mother owned that she wouldn't give Dad.
Something that belonged to him, he says. I don't know what."

Then he continued telling me about his ambitions almost as if his only goal
in asking about my motives was to be able to report that he'd done it. He didn't
seem to care about my answer. "I can live without Dad's kind of ambition. I
know I just said I'm interested in being D.A., and that's no small ambition,
but if I never get there, that's fine. I'd rather have fun and make a difference in
the world." He came in close and lowered his voice. "Dad told me once that
he wants to be President. I think he'd give up almost anything for that."

I flashed on rumpled, freaked-out Jennifer. "What does your Mom think?"

The waiter cleared the salad plates, brought out entrees.

"Mom doesn't think. She does what Dad tells her." He slouched against the
banquette, flipping his coffee spoon back and forth on the table top. "I wish

she'd stand up to him, you know, make a life for herself or something, rather than running around after him."

"Maybe that's all she wants." My wariness meter inched toward the red zone, and the slug started to wake up. *Why would Junior trust me with such intimate information mere hours after I'd met him?* I remembered from some distant psychology course the basic premise of self-disclosure: I tell you something and you tell me something of equal importance and meaning. As we trust each other more, we begin to reveal things of greater and greater meaning. I barely knew this guy and already he was revealing family secrets?

Paul's words floated through my brain: *Maybe you should just ask.* "Why are you telling me this? Isn't it confidential?"

"Nah." He waved his hand dispiritedly. "It's an open secret." The waiter, thinking his gesture meant he wanted something, slid up to the table. Junior flicked a finger and he went away.

"Why is it important now? You're grown up, living away from home."

"I'm not sure I can vote for him. I know him too well."

"You're his son. Surely, there's room for forgiveness?"

It was as if he suddenly saw me. He turned his body toward me, his knees touching mine under the table, his shoulder pressed into the banquette. His hand brushed my fingers and it felt like fire. I almost thought he'd blistered my skin. Then came an image of an inferno so powerful and hot I nearly shouted for people to run from the restaurant. The minute the image passed, I had another, puzzling and brief: Winters Senior, standing legs apart, arms crossed, staring at me. It was as if I could see into his mind, and he was puzzling over me.

"Clara!" Junior jarred me back to the present. "Are you okay?"

I became abruptly aware that I had pressed back against my seat panting. I slowed my breathing, made myself relax. "Sorry. I didn't mean to react that way. You...did nothing."

"Yeah," he said. "I know." He had a funny look on his face, the kind I'd seen before when men feel women have wronged them. I couldn't tell him what I'd seen. He would think I was crazy. "You were telling me why you couldn't vote for your father."

He hesitated, unsure of me, then responded. "He's a liar," he said. "He promises things all the time, and they never happened. He said we would see Greece, Machu Picchu, Hawaii, and every single trip was cancelled, and we spent the summer in the moldy old house on Nantucket his relatives have owned since, like, 1776."

The waiter silently removed our empty plates, offered desert menus. Junior ordered us coffee.

"So he broke a few vacation plans. He had good reasons, no? What about the serious stuff, like paying for your college education or making sure you had a car or food on the table?"

"You don't get it. We *never* saw him. He worked seven days a week, three-hundred-sixty-one days a year."

I giggled. "Three-hundred-sixty-one?"

He looked wry. "He takes off Christmas, New Year's, Thanksgiving and the Fourth of July. The office is locked down tight those days."

"He must have a key. He owns the firm."

Junior shrugged. "Those trips, that was time for him to get to know us, me and my little sisters. He didn't want to, I guess. He never came to my lacrosse matches; he didn't even attend my graduation from Harvard. It was just Mom and Mary Ellen. It's always just Mom and Mary Ellen. Sometimes, I think they're our parents." He paused. "Your Dad died, right?"

"He's been gone fifteen years now, hard to believe it's that long." My guilt corroded a hollow under my ribcage.

"He owned a landscape design firm?"

"Yes, landscape architecture, actually. He travelled all over for work. He brought pictures home to show us his gardens and the cities they lived in. He had clients as far away as Vancouver. I remember thinking that must be a magical place when I was a child."

"Did you travel with him?"

"When I was little, we occasionally met him for long weekends when the job lasted more than a couple of weeks. In my early teens, Mother let me go alone once or twice. He took me to dinner like an adult, all dressed up, somewhere serious. During the day, we'd tour gardens." I sipped the last of the espresso in my cup. "It was always better with me and Dad."

A look of longing crossed his face. He said abruptly, as though he couldn't bear to hear about my father anymore, "Mary Ellen says you know things."

A living, breathing jolt ran through me. "What things?" It was the same question his father had asked.

"Like about people. Was that what happened when I touched you? Did you see something?"

Suddenly, I knew I couldn't trust him. I didn't know if he himself was untrustworthy, or if Mary Ellen had prepared him—or if it was because my images of him had been fiery like the ones Mother had warned me about. This knowledge saddened me, as I felt a kinship with him over the loneliness that came from being abandoned by a living parent.

I thought briefly of Chief Dupont's cop eyes and deflected Junior. "You startled me, that's all," I said. "Your aunt must have me confused with someone else, maybe Hetty. I know she does psychic readings."

He shook his head, but didn't press it. Shortly, he called for the check. The waiter appeared as if from a genie bottle and deposited the leather folder on the table. Junior inserted several one hundred dollar bills and handed it back. Within minutes, the limousine collected us and headed for Connecticut.

The next day, Mother summoned me to the jail.

CHAPTER 16

showed up at the jail in a grey, pinstriped pant suit with a neon pink chiffon scarf I'd borrowed from Mother's scarf drawer. I'm not sure what kind of statement I was making by parading her own clothes in front of her, but maybe provoking her would produce a chance to ask her about the photographs I'd found at Hetty's. Maybe she would know why Hugh was in them.

"Is that mine?"

"Isn't it pretty with this suit? I hope you don't mind. So many of my things are in storage." I planned to return to Paris, hadn't shipped all my things home.

She raised an eyebrow, a dark slash on pale skin. "You have *more?*" She hadn't lost any energy or fight.

"What do you need, Mother?" If I could get her talking...

"You dined with Andrew Winters, Junior, last night."

"Who told you that?"

She twitched a bony shoulder. "I have my sources, Clara. I'm not completely cut off from the world in here."

I waited.

She sighed. "Pete Samuels."

How disturbing. "Where's he getting his info?"

"He's a police officer, Clara."

"Why would he share anything with you?"

"Does this matter for some reason?"

"Don't you think it's curious?"

"I've known Pete since he was three, and he's doing something nice for me by keeping tabs on you while I can't."

Maybe that's why he'd taken me to dinner. "You need to keep tabs on me?"

"You're running around with Andrew Winters, Junior."

"So?" I didn't mention the squitchy feeling in my gut or the pain in my arm, but I did wonder why she trusted Pete. I didn't.

She leaned across the institutional gray table. "If the devil existed, that family would have sold their souls to him for power and money."

"Junior didn't try anything he shouldn't have, he paid for dinner, he dropped me home at a decent hour, and he was polite. What more should I want?" Besides, only Junior thought it was a date.

"You have flawed judgment when it comes to men, Clara. Speaking of which, how is that divorce of yours going?"

I was getting whiplash from her conversation shifts. "We're still negotiating."

"What's to negotiate? He keeps what he brought into the marriage and you keep what you brought in."

"Ah, yes, but he hasn't worked in a dog's age, so he thinks I should pay him alimony so he can continue to ride his bicycle: working would get in the way of training. My lawyer and I disagree with that; his lawyer is trying to talk some sense into him, but so far, Palmer's got his heels dug in. My lawyer will call when she has a tentative agreement in hand."

Just laying it out for her exhausted me.

"You're pretty cavalier about a man you said you'd love 'til death do you part.'"

"You would be, too, if you'd lived with him. He seemed perfect; he had charm, could make everyone in the room laugh at his jokes. Once you got beneath the charm, you realized he was nothing but a self-centered bastard who wanted whatever his greedy little self could lay its hands on."

"Sounds like Andrew Winters."

"Maybe the son isn't cut from the same cloth as the father. You're not always right, Mother."

"Oh, yes I am! I can't imagine why you consistently choose so badly; your father..." She stared at me. "He was such a good man."

"How very Freudian of you. Since we're discussing Freud, maybe it's *you* I inherited my man judgment from." She looked at me in shock. I'd never criticized her before. Not aloud. I held my breath, waiting for the lightning to wham through the cement block walls and ignite me.

"Clara—"

I plowed over her, hoping for thirty more seconds before spontaneous combustion. "Sneaking around with a married therapist for twenty years doesn't count as the greatest of role models for your daughter."

She drew herself up. "Hugh and I didn't 'sneak around.' Maria knew all about it and came often for dinner when she was in town." She sounded defensive, and the pink dusting her cheekbones turned an angry red.

My first piece of a real, hard fact. "When did this non-affair start?"

"After your father died." She asserted it, daring me to question her.

That part didn't matter as much as she might imagine. My father had given up expecting things from her a long time before he died.

"Not that it's any of your business," she said.

"Had it ended?"

"Six months ago. We remained good friends, but Hugh liked women, and I got tired of being one among many, even if he assured me I was the most important."

Something in me cracked open and dissolved in relief. She was talking. If I could just keep it going. "If everyone knew Hugh slept around, why did they attack you for it? And what about—?" I stopped. I couldn't ask her about the new boyfriend. Not yet.

Her face was slowly returning to its normal color. "Jealousy, I suppose. I hung onto him the longest. Besides, Mary Ellen had wanted him since god-knows-when, and anything I have that Mary Ellen doesn't is fair game. She spread the rumors, Clara. No one else cared enough to be vitriolic about it." She shook her head and muttered the next bit, scratching at something on the table surface with a manicured fingernail: "As if she hasn't taken everything from me." Then, while I was wondering not only what that meant but how she maintained a manicure in jail, she looked at me again. "That's why I don't want you hanging out with that family."

"Because Mary Ellen has taken everything from you, Mother? What has she taken?" I asked it quietly, as if I were coaxing a sparrow to take a seed from my hand. This was more important than the photographs, and for a moment, I thought she would tell me. Her face softened and she reached across to me. "Nothing. I have you, right? How could I blame her for anything when I have you?"

I almost couldn't breathe. *She had me?* That hadn't seemed to matter to her one iota all these years. But now, it almost felt as if she cared. In that moment, I would have given her anything.

Abruptly, she changed the subject. "How is your meditation training going with Paul?"

"My, uh, meditation training?"

She snapped, "You went a couple of days ago. Don't play with me, Clara. I don't have time for it."

So much for our moment of connection.

"Fine. Thanks for asking." She was going to have to pry it out of me.

"Did you see anything?"

Her look was feral, as if she would dissect my soul to get what she wanted from me. Rage welled up, like tears. "Nothing but a bunch of wolves," I snapped back. "I don't know why you're interested. You never listened when I needed you, when I was too young to understand the dreams and visions." I took a shaky breath. I wasn't ready to confront this. "When it mattered, you didn't care at all." Hot tears formed behind my eyelids and I blinked to keep them in place. "It's my fault that Father died, but you're culpable too."

"Wolves," she muttered to herself, as if she hadn't heard the rest. "That's very good."

"Mother." My voice sharpened with years of pent-up resentment.

She looked up from her meditation on the table. "I heard you, Clara, but I can't explain it now. Not here in jail with all these cameras and listeners. Persuade Kyle to let me out, since he won't listen to me, then we'll talk. I promise. Meanwhile, the wolves will protect you."

I shook my head, my body raging with pain and dizziness. I tried one last time. "Nat sent you a message. He says it's time to tell your story, or, and I quote, 'you're creating a monster.'"

She paled, but I saw her resolve harden. "You tell Nat I know what I'm doing."

On that cryptic note, she dismissed me, but not without one parting shot. She stopped the guard as he turned to lead her down the corridor, the harsh institutional light graying her face and etching lines in her skin: "I mean it, Clara. Stay away from the Winters. If you don't, you're risking everything."

On the way out, I ran into Chief DuPont. Well, okay, I took three deliberate wrong turns, climbed a set of stairs, and asked four people before I ended up casually outside his office. Mother had derailed me from asking about the photographs, but the chief might know something by now. I looked into his office, "Oh, hey. How are you? I seem to be lost."

He looked up from a stack of paperwork. "Ms. Montague, I've had three phone calls letting me know you were on the way."

I slumped against the door and laughed. "So much for subtlety."

"Perhaps you've come to explain those photographs you sent me?" His tone was cold, the warmth and humor I'd come to expect from him absent.

I sat on the edge of one of the faux-leather chairs, pulling my purse into my lap like a little old lady. "I was visiting my mother, thought I'd say hello."

"That woman is driving me insane."

"Welcome to my world." I grinned at him.

He glared at me. "I mean it. She's got my officers running errands for her. They've brought her a reading lamp, pillows, a duvet, take-out meals from the country club, and they've checked up on you in their off-hours. If I could catch them at it, I'd put a stop to it, but truthfully, there's not much I can do about their off-duty activity." He threw his pen down on the desk in disgust. "Not," he added, addressing his blotter, "that I think that keeping an eye on you is a bad idea, since apparently you've gotten yourself into trouble again."

"I thought the photographs would be helpful."

He pressed three fingers into the middle of his forehead as if locating the source of a headache. "Hetty is welcome to do whatever she likes in her own home. I haven't had a complaint from any of the people in the pictures. And I can't barge onto private property without reasonable suspicion or probable cause—and a warrant. You didn't even know she was taking pictures of you until you saw that wall. Catch her in the act of stalking you—if, in fact, that's what she's doing. She could be exercising her right to take a few long-distance photos of beautiful people."

At first, I thought it was a compliment, then he lifted his head, and I looked into the eyes of a bull just released into the *Plaza del Toros*.

"She took the photos on the voodoo dolls!"

"How am I going to prove that? There's a similar photograph on the memory card, but did Hetty take the picture? You can't prove the camera or the memory card belong to her. And if I had a good reason to question her, she'll want to know who broke into her house. Is that what you want?"

"Obviously not," I said, roundly chastised. "And anyway, I didn't break into her house." I crossed my fingers under my purse. "That memory card was in her garbage, and the garbage was sitting outside on her steps. Fair game. Can't you investigate? Check her out?" I leaned forward and the edge of the chair dug into my thighs.

"With what resources?" He waved his arm at the nearly empty squad room outside his door. "I'm up to my neck in Christmas mayhem. Some idiot decided it would be fun to break into houses and steal Christmas presents. Our good citizens are crashing into each other or the curb trying to fit into parking spaces too small for their SUVs. Yesterday, some guy ripped off The Open Toybox, stole a vanload of gift toys meant for the kids at the women's shelter. I think one of my officers is dirty, and then, I have your mother in my jail, creating havoc. What a nightmare."

I looked at his utilitarian office with its grey carpet and cream walls. The only bit of color was the green blotter centered precisely in the middle of his oak desk. A picture sat in the right corner, but it was turned away from me so I couldn't see its subject. I hardly knew this man, and he had little reason to trust me.

"Why don't I take her off your hands?" I suggested. No matter what I said, it couldn't get worse, right?

"You mean let her out of jail? I can only *imagine* what kind of trouble she could get into if she weren't in protective custody. Someone might kill her—maybe even me."

I laughed and sat back. "Give her to me; maybe I can arrange an assassination—" I made my voice gravelly like the Godfather—"in the family."

He stared at me as if I were the far wall, then sighed. "I had one of our computer techs take a look at the memory card. There's some deleted material on it that he's been able to resurrect."

"Material?" After all his grousing, it *had* been useful?

"I can't tell you what it is, but we can't hold your mother any longer. In fact, they seem more interested in you than her. No photographs of Constance," he mused, seeming to slip up. So what were the photographs of? And who was *they*? "However..." He paused for emphasis. "...your intruder has been careful to cover his tracks. You're still being vigilant, right?"

I nodded, thinking guiltily that I'd forgotten again to set the alarm.

"If he thinks we've given up, maybe he'll get sloppy and we'll catch him."

"Sounds like I'm bait. Do you know it's a he?"

"It could be a woman, although I'm having a hard time seeing Hetty as primary on this." He sat back in his chair, swung it to the side and put his feet on the desk. "Maybe having Constance around will keep you from dating unsuitable men like my officers and that Winters punk, and asking questions of innocent townspeople."

My eyebrows rode the escalator to my hairline along with my blush. "Winters 'punk'?"

He shrugged.

I pulled my purse off my shoulder and set it on the floor, sat back in my chair to mimic his relaxed pose. "Andrew Winters, Junior, is a funny, charming young man who knows how to treat a woman as if she is the only woman in the room."

"That family is dangerous."

"Are you and my mother conspiring?"

His feet hit the floor. "What did she say?"

"Avoid the Winters clan."

"She's right."

"Because? Maybe you can offer me something more substantive than my mother's airy-fairy warnings. *Maybe* someone around here could give me some facts about how wicked the Winters family is—for real, in this life, on the record."

I saw him trying to make up his mind, but before he could, an officer yelled across the room, and I heard footsteps behind me. "Chief! There's a fire on Adams Mill road. It's a barn on the Winters property. Mr. W. wants us out there, in case it's arson."

The chief stood, pulling his jacket off the back of his chair. "Officer Munson, Mrs. Montague is going home with her daughter. Can you see to her release?" I turned to find Joe standing in the doorway. The chief gave Joe a look that seemed to convey something other than his verbal instructions. Joe nodded, and I sent up a silent cheer that competed with the dread in my gut. Having Mother home meant I might be able to corner her and get some answers, since she could no longer use listening jailhouse ears as excuses. It also meant dealing with her disapproval every day. Despite all that, the pains seemed to recede, slightly.

The chief said, "I'll handle the arson investigation, if we need to do one."

Joe motioned for me to follow him, and within an hour, my mother and I were on our way home. She'd donated the reading lamp, cushy red pillows and duvet to the police department and had charmed a receipt out of them for tax purposes.

I looked over at her in the passenger seat of the Land Rover. She was staring out the window at the Christmas finery on the passing homes, her fine-boned hands resting in her lap.

They say that girls marry their fathers. I thought about Junior's casual assumption of my acquiescence to his plans. I thought about Pete's carefully controlled physical charisma. I thought about my cyclist ex, and his knack for choosing the best. I thought about Mother.

It wasn't my father that I found in my relationships.

CHAPTER 17

other getting out of jail and the fire at the Winters's barn were the the hot gossip the next morning. Everyone wanted to know if this meant she had been cleared of the charges. I fudged the truth and said yes: I didn't have the time or inclination to go into the details. Mary Ellen gave me a startled look and sailed into Andrew's office. Five minutes later, as we were all sharing horse stories, she came out and insisted I ride with her the next morning. The horses, she said, had been moved to Loretta Gardner's stables, and, anyway, we had never had that talk I wanted.

So much for avoiding the Winters clan. The slug had stuck around and wasn't happy, but my questions burned holes in my gut. Did Mary Ellen know about Hetty's peeping habit? Did Mary Ellen kill Hugh so Mother couldn't have him, as Mother had implied? What did Andrew think Mother had stolen from him? And why did Mary Ellen and Mother hate each other?

The morning broke with a twenty-degree temperature and spitting snow. Mary Ellen phoned a reminder before I'd even persuaded myself that getting out of bed was a good idea. "See you at eight o'clock," she said, and hung up before I could reply.

My mother, cloaked in a thick red robe, poked her head in to see who had called. When I told her, she cautioned me again. I pulled the covers over my head. "I hope you know what you're doing," she said. "I'll make coffee." The door shut gently.

She still refused to tell me anything, although I'd tried in the car on the way home from jail. "We have to talk at some point."

"I need more time, Clara."

"For what?"

"I'll tell you when we talk." Mother was talented at circles.

Half an hour after Mary Ellen's call, I parked at Loretta and Ernie's stables, and stepped from the car. Mary Ellen stood by the gate with the reins of two horses in her hands. She handed me a helmet with her other hand and cocked her head toward the horse nearest her. "This one is yours. His name is Horace." She handed me his reins, turned and glided up onto her horse, to whom I had not been introduced. She pointed him (let's name him Juvenal) toward the trail that ran off to the side of the paddock, and called over her shoulder, "C'mon, Clara, or we'll be late for work."

I thought *this* was my work for the day.

I clambered up on Horace, apologizing to him for my clumsiness, and whispering thanks to whatever gods might exist that I managed to get on him at all. The last time I'd been on horseback was in my teens. He didn't seem to care and amiably followed his buddy into the woods, where I immediately got nailed by a branch slapping back from Mary Ellen's passage.

"Oh, sorry. Didn't you see that coming?"

And wasn't *that* the theme song for my whole life at the moment.

"Isn't it beautiful out here?" she trilled, as if nothing had happened. I patted my cheek to locate the welt.

"Lovely," I ducked another branch. If it hadn't been twenty degrees, snowing, and Mary Ellen, the morning would have been enchanted. Snow frosted the evergreens, and the air had that silence it gets when cold tamps down all the sound. The trail wound along a little brook, and, when the horses paused, I could hear water tinkling under the ice and around the rocks in its path. We tapped our way along for almost ten minutes, and I remembered what I enjoyed about being out in the morning on a horse. A kind of solace grew between horse and rider, a total focus on the sensations of each other and the trail. Then Mary Ellen broke the quiet.

"So, Clara." I couldn't tell if I was supposed to answer or if she was thinking of what to say next. I didn't respond, engrossed as I was in my momentary sense of peace. She let me alone for two more swinging branches and a little ravine where I thought I would slide off the horse right down his neck and over his head, and then said again, "So, Clara."

"Do you have a point?" I asked, too annoyed that she'd interrupted my serenity to be politic.

"Tetchy, tetchy. Morning isn't your season, is it? Did you know your mother and I used to ride together—on this very trail?"

"Really? This *very trail*?" I didn't even try to avoid sarcasm.

She ignored me. Best practice, really. "She was a fine horsewoman, your mother." An original statement—right out of an English novel.

"*Was* a fine horsewoman?" I asked, but Mary Ellen didn't respond.

"We raced each other across the meadow, not too far ahead."

"What for?"

"No competitive spirit?"

I sighed again. I should have had a second cup of coffee and some food. "If there's something worth competing for."

"Like, say, your mother's life?"

Her statement jolted me to attention with all the wired-up electricity of an adrenalin surge. Prickling flashed around my heart. "What?"

"We all have our price."

"What's yours?" I snapped.

Mary Ellen had usurped the conversation. She laughed, a peal that rang out like the Tower of London's bells before a beheading. "None of your business. Now, do tell me all about that little cottage of your mother's that's hidden out there behind Loretta and Ernie's house. There must be a good story behind it."

How could she know about the cottage? Mrs. Gardner said no one knew except her, Ernie and my mother. But if she knew, then who else knew? "I only know about Hetty's cottage with all the photographs of you on the wall."

Her back stiffened, but she wasn't deterred. "Of course you know about your mother's cottage. You've even seen the inside. I'm not supposed to know, but I do, because I know how get people to do what I want." I thought about all the stable hands in Loretta's yard and the power of curiosity and money. "You haven't learned that yet, Clara, but I could help if you'd let me. It's almost like we're family, you know."

My laugh was a harsh, startled sound in the cold air. "Why? Because you and Mother were friends years ago?"

"I also know that your mother has had a key for years and years and that she never let anyone else in there. Your father didn't even know about it, but I've peered in the windows."

A squirrel scrabbled across the snow in front of us as if running for its life.

"It's very pretty inside, all that turquoise and white, like a Caribbean island. I'll tell you what she used it for—her trysts. You may think that Hugh was her only lover, but she had others before and after your father. Some lost their marriages. You know, she was the first girl to... have a boyfriend in high school. She has quite a reputation, our girl. This police investigation could be quite humiliating. You should watch yourself, too. Sounds like you're on your way to that sort of reputation also." She said it all in a very matter-of-fact voice, as if she were giving a freshman lecture on the basics of geology.

"Did something specific happen, Mary Ellen? Or are you telling tales to see what I'll do?"

She looked back at me briefly, a mistake, since when she looked forward again, a branch slapped her face. Glee welled up in me and I nearly laughed.

She didn't acknowledge the pain. "Your mother and I double-dated to the junior prom. We weren't juniors, but we were dating junior boys. I mean, your mother was, and she got me a date with his best friend. Roy and Ray."

"Make up better names, at least."

She snorted...or was it Horace?

"After the dance, Roy and Ray took us to a hotel where six of them had rented a suite and pirated in a bunch of alcohol. I don't remember what we drank, some combination of every liquor they could get their hands on, I imagine, with a little pineapple juice thrown in.

"Anyway, about three in the morning, I noticed Constance kept disappearing from the room, and each time she left, she left with a different girl's date. At the moment, my date was missing. About fifteen minutes later, she came back from the bedroom all disheveled looking and flushed, plopped herself down, and commanded another drink. Every boy there, even her own date, rushed to fill her cup. She was shameless, Clara. She is not a good woman or a moral one—but then, you already knew that."

If Mary Ellen had a grudge to play out, this ugly story would certainly be a good way to do it. I marveled a bit that I could remain so cool-headed, but Mother's statement about Mary Ellen's rumor-mongering stuck with me. I thought about my mother charming the entire police station to do her bidding, and I thought of the friends at her Christmas fête kissing the air around her cheeks in greeting. I thought about Nat and my mother's first kiss, and his gentle stories of her, about the chief's statement that the investigation hadn't really yielded anything.

Then, I remembered Mother's telling me at the lawyer's office after my father's funeral that everything was not as it seemed, which strangely echoed her warning about the Winters. I ducked another branch, and, when I looked up, the woods were ending and a snow-covered meadow opened before us, a few dried summer stalks of grass poking through the snow cover.

"And you, Mary Ellen? Are you a good woman? Or did you kill Hugh so Mother couldn't have him all to herself?"

Without warning, Mary Ellen let out a loud "HA!" provoking both her horse and mine into a gallop. Juvenal and Horace took off across the meadow at a rate of speed well beyond my capabilities. Snowflakes stung my face, even as I clung, low across Horace's neck, not only to the reins but to his mane, clamping my thighs to his sides, and occasionally peering between his ears to be sure he wasn't headed for something to jump, like a stone wall. Horace didn't seem to care that I was grabbing him as hard as I could, nor did he slow at my command; he was having too much fun running with his buddy, and Mary Ellen didn't intend to stop Juvenal.

We were approaching the edge of the meadow, and I could see that the ground dropped sharply away and back into woods. I hauled as hard as I could on the reins, feeling the muscles in my arms vibrate with the effort. Horace slowed an iota, but then Mary Ellen hauled on Juvenal's reins, bringing him to a shuddering halt. That stopped Horace in his tracks at the top of the trail.

"I won." She looked at me, sardonic and composed.

"Fuck you," I was breathing hard. I nudged Horace around her toward the path. Every limb was jelly, and I hoped I could affect an exit without falling off the horse.

She called after me. "Clara. I told you for your own good. I like you, and I don't want you to follow your mother's path. I wanted you to understand the rumors around town about your mother's affairs and the affair with Hugh. I wanted you to understand where the rumors came from."

I looked back at her. "Oh, I know where they come from," I said. "And I know that people don't forget when they are regularly reminded. I don't need to know every detail of my mother's history, real or imagined by you." I stopped, startled that what I had said was true, and that I'd said it before I knew it was true. Then the anger returned. "And what the hell do you mean by 'follow my mother's path'? Are you warning me off? I'm not good enough to date a Winters? For god's sake, Mary Ellen, it was dinner. I'm not engaged to Andrew, although, if you must know, he did ask me to marry him." I threw it at her, unthinking, fueled by the rage and fear she had provoked.

Her face went white as the steam from the horses' nostrils. "He *what*?" I studied her, calming down now that I had regained some control, however fabricated. I clucked to Horace and started down the trail, ignoring her question. I heard her move in behind me.

We rode in silence. I would have to explain that Junior was only flirting, or I could imagine the conversation that would take place around the dinner table that evening. I had his cell number; I would call and warn him after Mary Ellen clapped herself into her Beemer. I hoped I wasn't causing him a lot of grief; even if I didn't think I could trust him, I did like him. It wasn't his fault he was a Winters.

While she was on the defensive, I decided to spring my own questions on her about the photographs, but before I could get one formulated past the thickness in my brain, Mary Ellen started talking again, this time about her brother's campaign—or rather about his opponent. "It's a woman, you know. Leave it to the Democrats to find one. She's got decent credentials, if you don't count the fifteen years of raising her kids when she wasn't working at all, except in volunteer organizations, like the PTA or Big Sisters. She spouts all these liberal ideas about how to spend money—*our* money—that's your money, too, Clara, and you've got to protect it—if you want that business your father left you to grow."

I had a few ideas about that, ideas I would eventually need to talk to Ernie about, but I stayed silent, wondering where she was going with this lecture. She sounded as if she were reading off a campaign brochure.

"It's critically important we get Andrew elected. New business development, new outside investment, we need that capital if we're going to stay a premier community and continue to attract the right kind of people. Andrew believes in this community's values, its sense of itself, its view of the world, and he wants to maintain that."

And that view would be *what's ours is ours and keep the dirty rabble away from it*? Maybe I was too hard on him, but the speeches I'd heard Andrew Senior give had more to do with preserving Andrew's way of life than preserving anyone else's. Perhaps I was jaded. Perhaps I'd lived behind the high fences too long myself.

Mary Ellen didn't speak again until we had both dismounted and were walking our horses to the barn, and then she addressed my comment about marrying into the family. "Clara, I—It's not that you're not good enough to marry Andrew Junior, it's just—"

"He was flirting, Mary Ellen. We don't even know each other." Relief flooded her body. Were those tears at the corners of her eyes? I handed Horace's reins and my helmet to the barn attendant, a slightly chubby girl whose long blonde hair needed washing.

Mary Ellen followed suit. She waited until the girl and horses moved out of earshot then put her hand on my arm. Pain prickled through my muscles. The last thing I needed right now was an intuition. I wondered if Mother could control them. I removed Mary Ellen's hand. "I need to know—" Maybe all the power games earlier had been to psych herself up for this, whatever it was. "Could you ask your mother... or maybe you..." She looked into my eyes, as if she could read something there, the right thing, whatever it was she so desperately needed. "I know I've been cruel—today especially."

"Cruel doesn't even begin to cover it, Mary Ellen. Did you think that if you told me some titillating bit about my mother, I would do whatever you wanted? Or that your plea about your brother's campaign might make me feel sympathetic? If so, you need to rethink your methods. If you want something from my mother, ask her yourself. Our deal is officially off. I will not give you any more information, nor ask for anything further from you. Whatever your agenda, work it another way."

She reached for me again, but I stepped back. "I need to know about Andrew's campaign, I need to know what we should do to win. He has to win."

That was it? That was what she needed to know? Her exhausted, hollowed out face conveyed a desperation I found surprising and which almost raised a shred of pity in me if my gut hadn't been yelling so loudly about manipulation. Was the Democratic contender such a threat? Or was there something else? "I don't know what you think Mother can do for you, Mary Ellen."

"She... knows things." The third Winters to say that.

I ran my hands through my own unwashed hair, "What do you know about Hetty's photographs and her little blue cottage? What do you know about Hugh's death? I know you know something."

She stared at me, silent and white.

"Right." I paused so she would get that she didn't get something for nothing. "I'll tell Mother you want to speak to her, but I won't do anything else."

Her face twisted with spite and fear. "You do that. And tell her next time, I'll let you fall off the horse and break your neck." She pivoted and walked away to her car.

I watched her go. She was even more bitter and distorted than I'd thought. Never mind all the stories she'd told me about Mother's past. It was clear something had happened the night of the junior prom, but why would Mary Ellen lie and in such a flamboyant way? Roy and Ray—should they exist and not be clowns with Barnum and Bailey—were certainly trackable. Was she trying to shame me into giving her information about the cottage? Make me so off-balance that I would do what she wanted? Was something that happened at a high school dance supposed to explain how my mother acted toward me? Threatening my life was certainly calculated to unhinge me, but it only made me more determined to find the truth, especially since her fear made me think I was on the right track.

Mother was in the kitchen drinking coffee and reading the business section of the *Times* when I returned. "How was your ride?" Then she frowned, as if remembering who I rode with.

"I hate it when you're right," I said.

She responded with raised eyebrows.

I sighed. "Let me get some food, first." I opened the refrigerator and rummaged a bit before finding some relatively fresh English muffins. I put my breakfast together and brought it to the table. She'd moved on to the Arts pages.

"I have a message for you from Mary Ellen. She wants to talk to you." I bit into my muffin.

My mother shrugged. "I know."

"How do you know?"

"Nat told me when he visited me in jail."

"She told Nat?"

"Apparently."

"So you know she's worried about Andrew's campaign." I decided not to mention her threat to my life.

She started to raise her mug, then put it down. "Why don't you quit that job, Clara? I can't imagine it's giving you any satisfaction, and it gives me the willies thinking of you so intimately involved with that man's run for election. Do you really want to see him in office?"

"All politicians are the same, Mother. They want power, because they think they can do right or because they think they know what's right. Either way, it leads to hubris." I took another bite.

"No, Clara, all politicians are not the same." The intensity in her voice made me look up. She leaned forward to press home her point, the paper crackling as she crushed it. "Andrew Winters is a wicked man who must never be elected into any position where he has to put the interests of others before himself." She closed the paper and slapped it on the table. "Take a look at that," she said, "for examples of leaders who wrong their people. There are a lot of them, but plenty know how to do the right thing, or at least have integrity and their hearts in the right place, even if their decisions aren't perfect." She stood and picked up her cup. "I don't know what Mary Ellen thinks I would possibly ever do for her or her brother, but you can tell her that she needs to ask me herself."

She stalked from the kitchen before I could tell her Mary Ellen already knew that.

CHAPTER 18

 should have told Chief DuPont that Mary Ellen threatened me, but I thought I knew what he'd say. Instead, I decided to talk things over with Bailey, thinking her analytical lawyer brain might help me. I persuaded her to meet me after work over drinks. Large drinks. So much for abstinence and resolutions.

At least the alcohol was keeping the dreams away—not a good trade-off—but I needed the sleep. So badly, I needed the sleep. The slug had transformed into daytime hallucinations, which was exactly what I'd been trying to avoid. This afternoon at the office, I thought I saw my father standing there shaking his head at me. I blinked, and he was gone. My heart had started to pound. Had his expression been accusatory? What was I missing? What else should I do?

At about seven, after finishing up some projects at the campaign and putting a large check in the mail to the Democratic candidate, I walked to The Peak where Bailey waited at the bar. She signaled the bartender as I walked in, and, by the time I had unwrapped myself from my coat and scarf, a martini sat coyly at my place. Bailey was halfway through hers.

She leaned over and pecked my cheek. "What's up, sistah? You look glum."

I took a long drink from my glass. "You have no idea." I filled her in on Hetty's cottage as well as Mary Ellen and the killer horse ride. I was well into my second martini by the time I finished.

"I guess we'd better get some dinner. This is going to be a long talk." She signaled the bartender and we wound our way to a booth. She ordered a bottle of Tempranillo and a plate of fried calamari. "Hetty, a stalker? I suppose I could find out if any of the people she photographed have reported her. You'd think Pete Samuels, with all his cop radar, would notice someone lurking around taking pictures of him. Why didn't you just ask Kyle when you reported Mary Ellen? You know the man has the hots for you."

"I, uh..." A wave of guilt swept over me.

"You didn't report Mary Ellen? Are you crazy?"

"Kyle already gave me a lecture about breaking into Hetty's place. Plus, I can't believe Mary Ellen meant it. A murder threat would wreck her brother's campaign. Besides, she didn't say she tried to kill me this morning, only that if Mother didn't cooperate, she would next time. The chief would only berate me for going on the ride in the first place—and don't you start on me, too. Please. Everyone has told me to stay away from the Winters."

"Why bother listening to the people who care about you? You won't be in town long enough for a relationship anyway." She tossed it out with a little side glance, a fishing line with a baited hook the size of Cincinnati.

"I don't know yet whether I'm staying, but I've missed you, and I'm going to do my part to keep our friendship going this time."

She shook her head, dragging a loop of calamari through red sauce.

How did you persuade a person you meant what you said? Only action and time would do that job, and sometimes, even those weren't enough.

"How will finding out about wrong-doing in the Winters campaign clear your mother of Hugh's murder? That's your goal, right?"

"I came home because Mother was in danger. She keeps telling me to stay away from the Winters, ergo, to use lawyer-speak, I think they are connected. However, I have zero proof of anything fishy, only some strange notations in a couple of files. Maria pointed me toward Hetty. My theory, after seeing her photographs, is that Hetty had a crush on Hugh, which Hugh didn't return, and she killed him in a jealous rage."

She said, "That would fit with one theory, that it was a crime of passion, something to do with all Hugh's sexual affairs."

"But Hetty also photographed Mary Ellen, me, and Pete Samuels. If it's about crimes of passion, well, it's not like I'm having an affair with Hetty, and I can't imagine Pete or Mary Ellen having one either. Hugh and I are connected because the photos on Hetty's wall were the same as the voodoo doll photos. But what's the connection between the dolls and Hugh's murder? Did she leave the dolls or did someone else, like maybe Balaclava Guy? Did Balaclava Guy kill Hugh? Why would he do that? Why are he and Hetty partners? And if Hugh was a target, does that mean that Mary Ellen, Pete and I are too?" I paused to swipe the last calamari.

Bailey said, "Balaclava Guy and Mary Ellen both seem to have you in their sights, so maybe that question has already been answered, Clara."

I wiped my greasy fingers on a napkin. "Then there's the question of why Balaclava Guy warned me off my mother's past. What doesn't he want me to find? What does her past have to do with any of this and why won't she tell me about it?" I was babbling. I stopped.

The waiter cleared the calamari plate and deposited huge steaks nearly covered in piles of crisp French fries. He added small pots of ketchup and mustard to the collection of bottles and glasses on the table, and drifted away.

"Are there any... rumors about Mary Ellen's mental health? I'm telling you, Bailey, she was all-over-the-place-crazy today." Unlike me. "Between slurs against Mother, freak-outs about the campaign, and threats—a psychiatrist would have a field day. Maybe Hugh was trying to have her committed and she killed him to prevent it because she had to run her brother's election campaign."

Bailey laughed, full-throated and without reservation, the first time I'd heard it from her in a long time. It was a beautiful sound, and I smiled, glad I'd caused it. She said, "Your mother would know, wouldn't she? Seems like she could answer almost all of your questions."

I just shook my head and dunked a fry into the ketchup. Bailey understood. She sawed at her steak, then said, "I think we should tell Hetty about Ethan Olsen."

"Whatever for?" Talk about a change of subject.

"She needs to know we protected her all those years ago."

"Would you want to know twenty years later that you'd narrowly missed being raped? That people had to make fun of you to get you to back off? I would only feel more humiliated."

"I want her to know we're on her side."

"Are we? Do we need to be?"

"She doesn't have anyone."

"She has all her fluffy little lambs—until she makes them into lamb chops."

"Honestly, Clara. You could have a little compassion."

I rolled my eyes. "Okay, officially putting on My Compassionate Self. I still don't get it. She has family and she must have friends. She has her clients. And apparently, she has a little stalking business on the side. She might even be dabbling in murder."

"She's got Ernie and Loretta, but Ernie's not even her real father. Her real father died, years ago, like yours. She spun loose after that, remember? She's at every function in town, but that's just Hetty. She shows up whether people want her to or not, so they figure it's better to invite her. You know how people here think: *We might have a use for that woman someday*—like she's an old door hinge you store in the garage, just in case. You and I don't have to become her best friends, but we should make peace. And anyway, if you make nice, she might help you."

Bailey seemed determined to hook me into this town, but I didn't need to make peace with everyone here. "It hasn't exactly been gnawing at my conscience, and you've never had these scruples before. If you feel bad, apologize, but leave me out of it."

It wasn't me at my best. Bailey had a point, but I was already overwhelmed, never mind making up to a woman who had made her dislike of me apparent for longer than I could remember.

I would deal with it later, after the police arrested someone for Hugh's murder and I stopped having dreams about blood, and daylight hallucinations of my father. The last step before a trip to the loony bin.

Bailey slapped her knife onto the edge of the plate. "Those fifteen years might have given you a respite from dealing with all this stuff, but it never goes away. Eventually, even when you live your life as if you have no past, your past is underneath it all, influencing what you do."

"You think I've had a free ride all these years, while you slogged it out with the same old stuff and people we dealt with in high school?"

She sat back, twisting the cloth napkin in her fingers. "I have a past, too—some of it shared with you—and even if you don't feel guilty, I do, and I'd like to make amends. I have a lot invested in this town, and I don't want lingering negative vibes from anyone, if I can change them. I want to be central to this town's well-being and I can't be if I'm not promoting the well-being of one of its members."

I squinted at her. "That sounds suspiciously like a campaign speech."

She bit her lip, then shrugged. "So? Will you?"

"Clara!" Like the sudden explosion of a puffball mushroom, Hetty appeared at our table. Dressed in a red flannel shirt and jeans with heavy work boots and a long down coat, she looked like a dissolute Mrs. Claus. "I should report you for trespassing!"

"Hetty, honey, you're shouting," said Bailey. "Sit down a moment." She patted the seat next to her. The entire dining room had turned to stare.

"Yes, sit down. We wanted to talk to you."

She looked at me suspiciously, but slid in next to Bailey, who wrinkled her nose slightly. A moment later, sheep barn wafted at me. I pushed my plate away.

"You had no right," Hetty reiterated, almost pouting. "I've spent all afternoon with the police."

"Why were you photographing me, Hetty? Or Mary Ellen or Pete Samuels? I'm sure the police were particularly interested in the photographs of Hugh."

Hetty stared at me, furious, her hands crushing a fuzzy red beret. "I... I... took those for a friend."

"What friend?"

She folded her arms, the beret sticking out from under her arm like a tuft of hair. "I can take pictures of anyone I want to. Look at all those paparazzi."

"That's their profession, Hetty. This looks like stalking."

"I'm not a stalker!" Indignant now, like she'd never thought of it before.

"Of course you're not," Bailey patted her arm, perky smile glued in place. "So... there's something else we wanted to discuss with you. Clara has remembered the incident you mentioned."

I shot her a dagger look. I didn't want to talk about Ethan. I needed to find out about those photographs. And how come it was suddenly just me who was apologizing? "Actually, both Bailey and I feel badly. You're upset about Ethan Olsen, right?"

Hetty stared at me, stone-faced, like a Greek column. Okay, so she wasn't giving me any help, and I did remember what it was like to be humiliated. Who could forget how that felt? Here we were humiliating her again, by calling her out on the photographs. Bailey was right; we needed her as an ally.

I thought a moment about how to shape what I wanted to tell her, then said, "We were trying to protect you from Ethan, and because we were young and stupid and didn't know what else to do, we made fun of your pretty dress." I caught Bailey's expression from the corner of my eye. Never mind. She'd set me up for this, so she would have to deal with my exaggeration.

I leaned across and put my hand on Hetty's arm as reassurance, but the gesture backfired. My vision clouded and I saw the man who'd invaded my bedroom, still in his black balaclava, his arm around Hetty's throat, gun to her head. I flinched, pulled away, but Hetty's hand had flown to her throat, just where I'd seen the intruder's arm. She looked terrified. Even Bailey looked a little nervous, as she glanced back and forth.

"Sorry." I shook my head to clear it.

"What was that?" Hetty whispered. I wondered if she were intuitive after all. It would be terrible if she'd seen what I'd seen. Should I tell her? Would she believe me? I looked into her eyes, paralyzed by indecision. As I hesitated, I saw her anger crystallize like a sugary sweet she loved to suck on.

"I... nothing. Ethan was acting weird, all drunk and aggressive. It was a bad time for you to hang out with him, especially since, well, we're pretty sure he raped Dara Oakford that night."

Any color remaining drained from Hetty's face. "I don't believe you," she whispered. "Dara was absent for a week after that, remember? And she came back quiet. Not the same girl."

Bailey touched her hand. "We were trying to keep you from getting hurt."

"Why are you telling me this now?" The words stumbled past the dryness in Hetty's throat. Bailey pushed a glass of toward her. She sipped. Bailey's lipstick printed the glass's rim, but Hetty didn't notice.

"Bailey?" I said. "Why don't you tell her?" Revenge is sweet.

No reaction. All that court training came in handy. Finally, Bailey said, "We wanted to clear the air."

Hetty's hand shook as she sipped again. "You can't make up now for the fifteen, seventeen, whatever years of hurt you've caused." She was almost hissing, but tears glimmered in her eyes. The nearest diners looked over curiously.

"Hey guys! Imagine finding you here."

It hadn't seemed possible for Hetty to go any whiter, but Andrew Junior's appearance seemed destined to make her collapse. He slipped in next to me with a friendly kiss on the cheek. Bailey raised her eyebrows. I suggested Hetty needed something stronger than water, since she looked as bleached as new wool. Junior gestured to the waiter and ordered a round of brandies.

Yeah, great idea. More alcohol.

"How are you?" he asked me, after the drinks had arrived. He touched my hand briefly. "I had fun the other night."

"Me, too." I realized it wasn't a lie. Even if I did have reservations, I had that sense of being aligned with him.

"You feeling better, Hetty? Brandy always warms me up." He slid closer. Must have learned that move from his old man.

The alcohol hadn't improved Hetty. She appeared to be in a catatonic state of mute terror, only her eyes flicking rapidly between me and Junior, like some awake version of REM sleep.

"Hetty," I echoed, "are you okay?"

"You're friends?" She nodded at me and Junior.

"We met a couple of days ago."

"When did you get home, Andrew?" Bailey tried to smooth the conversational awkwardness.

"Just before Christmas. Figured I'd see the family until court starts up again after the new year." He looked at me, as if searching for something.

"You must get home a fair amount."

"For an overnight or dinner. I don't have a lot time available, but over the holidays nothing particular keeps me in the city—" at this, he glanced at me again—"so why not hang out here?"

Bailey said, "Are you helping with your dad's campaign?"

"No." He paused, then showed himself to be a politician cut from Winters cloth. "But Dad's got so many great people, really loyal..." this time, he looked at Hetty, "...and all the targeted campaign work is really paying off."

Hetty leapt from her seat. Junior grabbed at Hetty's brandy glass as it slid toward the edge of the table and nearly into mid-air.

"Hetty, be careful." I meant it on too many levels to articulate.

Oblivious, she scuttled across the dining room, yanked open the door, and practically threw herself out. Her pale face looked in on us for a split second before she disappeared into the night.

CHAPTER 19

fell asleep on the couch in the solarium and woke with a start from a dream about Hetty's attacker, with the smell of gunpowder in my nostrils. Mother stood over me. She'd turned on every lamp in the room. I sat up, shielding my eyes from the light. "What's the matter?"

She sniffed. "It's two in the morning and you were snoring like a common drunk. Couldn't you even make it to your bed?" She sat down in the chair across from me and surprised me by wringing her hands. "What's going on, Clara?"

I rubbed my face, trying to think clearly. The last thing I remembered was leaving Bailey at the restaurant. That wasn't good, since I'd obviously driven home and parked myself on the couch before passing out.

"I don't know what you mean." I stuck to my innocence in arguments with Mother, until I knew what the argument was about.

"I've been home for two days. I find your things in my bedroom and bath as if you're living in *my* room. You work for the Winters, date their son, and ride with Mary Ellen. You've asked Nat Mueller personal questions about me, and Wendy Hankin tells me you've badgered her husband for my medical information. Is that clear enough?"

Too much alcohol lingered in my blood for this conversation, so I picked the things in her litany I could actually disagree with. "You won't talk to me. Did you expect me to sit idly by while people accused you of killing Hugh? And I'm not 'dating' Andrew Junior. We went out for dinner. Once."

"You can't do that again, Clara." She said it without heat, not as if she were the mother of a recalcitrant teenager she was trying to control, but as if it were a given.

"Why should it matter? It's just something to perk me up while I deal with my divorce. I'm not going to marry him. He's too young for me anyway." I smiled and Mother grimaced. I'd had dinner with Junior only because I wanted information, but I wanted to see what reason she would give to dissuade me.

"No. I can't allow it."

As if she had power to stop me. Besides, it didn't matter. I would do what I wanted, anyway. The dreams had to stop, so I had no choice but to do what I thought was right, even going out with Junior again and peppering him with questions about Mary Ellen. I was not going back to that Zurich hospital.

"You'll do what if I go out with him again? Restrain me physically from walking out the door? Really, Mother. And I will do whatever is necessary to get answers. I'm not doing it for fun. I'm doing it because my dreams need to stop, and the moment they do, I'll be out of your hair again. So unless you're going to surround me with armed guards, you're out of luck."

Mother was made of armor. "Oh, I know I have no real power over you, but other ways exist to make sure you don't see him again. Anyway, you'll just not do it, and then we don't have to have this discussion anymore."

Ramping up the argument, as much as it might give me a perverted satisfaction, wouldn't gain me anything. Plus, I didn't have the mental stamina for it at the moment. "What do you really want, Mother?"

"Get away from the Winters family, all of them. Quit the campaign, stop seeing Mary Ellen and Andrew Junior."

"Why?"

"I've already told you why."

"Tell me again."

"No."

She'd done that when I was a kid, too. She'd tell me once, then refuse to repeat it or explain. If I didn't get it the first time, that was my problem, and it would be an even bigger problem if I didn't obey, whether I understood or not.

"Do you know why I'm involved with the Winters family?" I asked.

"To spite me, I imagine." She sounded resigned, stared at the wall past my shoulder.

I swung my feet to the floor. I really wasn't ready for this. "It started there." I stopped, started again. "No, that's not fair," I said as she looked at me. Her face was washed with incredible sadness and longing, as if none of her dreams had ever been hers to hold. "My motives aren't so easily read. Part of me wanted to pay you back for father. I believed that if you had allowed me to talk about the intuition, I could have told you I dreamed his death." She started to speak, but I held up a slightly shaky hand. "I know that's not true now. My own fear kept me silent."

"You were a child."

"I was a young woman, and now I need to make amends by helping you. You've been accused of murder. In this town, who better to know you than your oldest enemy? I didn't assume the information would come without bias, but I did assume there would be information and connections. Mary Ellen could get me in."

Wearily my mother said, "At what cost, Clara? I can only imagine what that woman has told you to turn you against me. Not that she would have needed to work very hard." She turned her head away, stroked the arm of the chair. "Has she succeeded?"

"You were a little wilder than I had imagined, if what she says is true, but I'm not here to judge you."

"You do judge me, Clara. You judge me harshly for all my failings. Especially for your father." She looked shrunken and tired in the chair, her bathrobe around her like an oversized blanket around a doll.

I stood up.

She looked wistful. "I'm sure you're tired."

"I'm beyond tired," I said. "If we're having this conversation, I need coffee. Are you coming?"

She nodded, trying to conceal her surprise. In the kitchen, I ground beans, rinsed the gold filter, measured water. Each second of ritual gave me more time to wake up. When the coffeemaker began its drip, I got out cups, sugar, spoons and milk. Mother suggested something to eat, but I shook my head, the surfeit of dinner still with me. When it was ready, I poured and sat opposite her at the table.

She spooned some sugar into her drink and stirred. When she began talking, she spoke toward the Subzero over my shoulder. "The intuition you have: all the women in the family inherit it. I have it, too, and so did your grandmother and great-grandmother."

"Why didn't you tell me?"

"No one in the family talked about it. My mother told me what it was and how I could use what I learned from the intuitions, but that was it. I wasn't to tell anyone, including other members of the family about the dreams and feelings.

"I didn't listen. I was young, and it was a time when we did tarot readings for each other and talked about intuition and ESP. We bared our souls to friends and complete strangers. We thought we were being open and trusting, and I thought my gift could be used for the greater good. So I told Mary Ellen—my best friend—and I told Loretta Gardner, and somehow it got back to my mother. She grounded me for a month: I couldn't call anyone, watch TV or listen to the radio, couldn't go anywhere. It was worse than just being grounded, it was house arrest, almost solitary confinement. She didn't speak to me for that entire month. Thank goodness I had school, or I would have lost my mind.

"At the end of the month, she informed me I would be attending a boarding school for the last two years of high school and if I told anyone there about my gift, I would be cut off from the family, no questions asked. The family would never help me again." I waited, shocked, as she blew across the top of the coffee and took a sip. How could a mother say that to a fifteen-year-old?

"What did you do?"

"You know the rest, Clara." She looked at me, perhaps because some part of what she was about to say was the lie. "I got pregnant with you, and that botched my mother's plans. You can imagine the scandal, but I finished high school—the GED, almost a sin in this town—and your father and I got married."

I couldn't tell which part was untrue.

"I adored you from the moment you were born, Clara. But you were a girl, and I knew you would inherit the gift, like all the other women in the family.

"Since it had led to such pain for me, I tried to train you out of it. Obviously, I failed, and, obviously, I hurt you in the process. I'm truly sorry for that, Clara. I believed not having the gift would be the greater good. After your father died, I changed my mind, but by then, I'd already lost you." She fell silent.

She cared that she'd lost me? Pain slit into my gut and made me nauseous. "What's the cottage?"

"Hugh brought me back to my intuition, encouraged me to find a 'safe' space to practice. Loretta suggested I fix up that little house. It's always been a very quiet arrangement."

"Hugh knew about your intuition, too?"

She nodded.

"Could that be why he was murdered?"

She looked startled. "Why would anyone care about Hugh's secrets? He'd taken an oath not to share them."

"And if, for some reason, he suddenly was willing to break his oath?"

"Are you asking me if I murdered Hugh?"

"It's a motive."

She picked up the cup, twisted it ninety degrees, put it down again. Nudged it with her finger. "Everyone knew anyway—Mary Ellen made certain of that." She looked up at me. "I didn't kill him. Do you really think I could?" That look of sadness re-inhabited her face.

"No," I said slowly. "Do you really know who did it, like you claimed at his memorial service?"

She shook her head. "I'd love to pin it on that despicable Winters clan, but I can't see any connection between them and Hugh."

I opened my mouth to ask her why she hated them so much, when the phone rang. My mother pushed herself up from the table with a frown. I glanced at the clock. It was five minutes past three. Her hand remained suspended over the receiver for two rings before she picked it up and greeted the caller with apprehension.

She listened a moment, said, "I understand. We'll be right there." She turned, her face suddenly drawn in on itself. "Hetty's been murdered."

We arrived at the stable at three-thirty on the longest, darkest night of the year. Only one or two stars glimmered between the sheets of cloud that covered the sky. "She was murdered here?" I asked as we pulled in.

"She was murdered near her farm. We're here for Loretta. I didn't want to leave her and Ernie alone tonight."

"Oh." I'd figured we were going to the murder scene, pictured a body bag with Chief DuPont supervising the action. Then, I could confess that I hadn't told Hetty about my vision, hadn't warned her to be careful. There, I could get absolution for my guilt. Instead, that guilt would further cloud my intuition, the only thing that might help.

An outside light shone by the front door. A dim glow emanated from the curtained window to its right. Ernie opened the door and waved us into the front room where Loretta sat, red-eyed and tense on a bright floral couch. She leapt up and ran to my mother. "Oh, Constance," she sobbed. Mother wrapped her arms firmly around Loretta and led her back to the couch, where she crumpled. Ernie suggested he and I make coffee in the kitchen.

"I'm so sorry." I stood near the sink, feeling useless.

He gave me an appraising look. "Thank you, Clara." His long, thin fingers swung open the coffeemaker's basket. "I know there was no love lost between the two of you."

"We tried to set that right tonight, Ernie." I breathed a prayer of thanks to Bailey. "It was a long time ago."

"I got the time, if you want to tell me the story."

So I told him about Hetty, only editing out my final vision of a man's arm across Hetty's throat. He listened, leaning against the counter.

Ernie reminded me of my father: gentle and kind, but no free pass either. He stood about six-foot-one, with broad shoulders and dark brown hair that, even in his early sixties, was just now thatching itself with silver. He wore loose jeans and a flannel shirt with the tails out. Thick wooly slippers kept his sockless feet warm on the tiled kitchen floor. A tiny diamond stud shot a spark from one ear.

When I finished, he said, "Something wasn't right with her recently. I don't know what, and she didn't confide in me. She and Loretta had been distant for several months. Maybe when the police are done with her farm, we'll find some answers." He shook his head. "She was a strange girl, even Loretta knew that. She never recovered from losing her dad." He saw my face. "Hetty didn't know how to be herself. She was too busy trying to impress someone, anyone, all the time, but she wasn't impressive, at least not in the way she wanted to be. I've never seen anyone with such an intuitive grasp of what those sheep or her farmland needed, but those weren't going to get her very far in the local society she wanted to be part of." He stopped, tangled in his own sentence.

"And was she an intuitive, Ernie? Did she... was the little house on her farm where she, I don't know, saw her clients? It's so like the one out back here that Mother uses..."

He shrugged. "Loretta said so. I'm not one to judge one way or the other."

At least that explained some of the rumors about her.

"Why are we here, Ernie? I know Mother and Loretta are friends but..."

"Loretta was like a big sister to your Mom while she was growing up. They've been close a long time."

"You guys never come to any of the parties, I never see you in town, I didn't know Mother and Loretta were this close."

"Oh, the party scene doesn't matter, and your mom knows it. She always invites us, and we always say we'll see her some other time. Who needs to stand around drinking gin with a bunch of people who want to spout nonsense in fancy clothes?"

He had a point.

The coffee gurgled and spit its readiness. "Mugs live in that cabinet above the stove and sugar's in the pantry on the first shelf." He opened the refrigerator and took out milk and a loaf of sweet bread. Together, we loaded the tray. Just before he pushed through the front room door, Ernie said, "You and me have some talking to do."

"I've got to resolve this first."

He swung into the living room without answering.

———

Loretta and Mother sat holding hands, two frail china figurines perched carefully side by side. Loretta had stopped crying. Ernie set the tray on the low, carved table in front of them. When everyone had a cup, he slouched into a chair. "They found her by the side of Levittown Road in her car. She'd been shot once, in the head." His voice was quiet, almost monotone.

The image punched a hole in my gut, and the vision I'd had in the bar flashed through my mind again. If I'd only responded when she asked what I'd seen. She'd known there was something; I could see it in her eyes. I could have warned her. She might still be alive.

Ernie went on. "That new police chief said it looked like an assassination; he thought the assailant had been hiding in the back seat. She was parked on a road she never drove, one that wasn't a direct route from town to her farm." He looked at Loretta. "Clara tells me she saw Hetty at The Peak. She left at about eleven-thirty or so." He turned to me. "You'll tell Detective DuPont?"

I nodded. It was the least I could do.

"They are impounding the car and checking the site for evidence. They have to do an autopsy, but we'll get her back when the investigation is over."

"That could take weeks."

"DuPont says it won't."

"How does he know?" It burst from Loretta, her terror and rage gunpowder fueling the verbal explosion. "They might never find who did this, and then what? We'll never get her back! It's two days to Christmas!"

Ernie reached across the table and laid a hand on his wife's knee. She grabbed it and squeezed. "Oh, Ernie." She pulled away from my mother and slid to her knees on the floor by her husband. "I'm so sorry." She put her head on his lap.

"For what, my love? You've done nothing."

"I'm falling apart. My daughter, if I'd only…" She could barely get the words out between her sobs.

"That's okay, sweetheart. I'm here, Constance is here."

She laid her head in his lap and he stroked her hair. Her fingers, wrapped around a wad of tissues, pressed against her lips, as if she could stop herself from weeping. I looked at my mother. She was cradling her coffee cup in her hands as if for warmth. We stayed like that for a long time.

CHAPTER 20

hat I really needed was some time to think. My vision of Hetty meant something; maybe I could make the link for Chief DuPont between my attacker and Hetty's, but I had to figure out how to persuade him a connection existed. He would want empirical evidence. I didn't have that, and sitting in Ernie and Loretta's living room wouldn't help me get it. I needed to find a way to get out and get quiet.

We were talked out by seven. We'd tossed around theories all night, but none of us had anything more than supposition. Hetty had been scared of Andrew Junior, and scared we knew each other. Junior had seen her fear; could he have killed her? Had he telegraphed some kind of message in our conversation that caused her to bolt? Had he texted or called her later? But we'd stayed a good hour after Hetty had left—oh!—long enough that Bailey and I functioned as Junior's alibi. If he needed an alibi. Plots of movies and TV shows swirled in my head, where murderers had just enough time, if... I reined in my thoughts.

No, Hetty must have connected with someone after she left the restaurant, someone she thought would allay her fears. Hetty was a loner; who could she possibly have called at that hour? Who did Hetty threaten and was her death related to Hugh's? We knew so little; even our speculations didn't make any sense. Loretta, worn out with crying, had fallen asleep on the couch. Ernie was working on stable business, and Mother was reading a book she'd plucked off their shelves. I volunteered to make a breakfast run.

"Maybe some cold cuts or soup for lunches and a few ready-mades so they don't have to think about dinner," Mother said.

I headed out, glad to be free for a few minutes, and drove to Whole Foods, stepping into the smell of warm bread and coffee. Before I bought pastry, I filled a cart with cheese, sandwich bread, sliced ham, salad makings, bottles of fancy fizzy water, and several cans of soup. The fresh ready-made casseroles weren't out yet, but frozen lasagna beckoned. I added two packages to my purchases. As I got into the line for pastry, a familiar voice called my name. I turned. Wendy Hankin, her hands on her hips, swayed slightly by a table in the café.

"Why are *you* here?" she demanded.

Startled, I said, "Why shouldn't I be here?"

"You're everywhere!" she exclaimed. "I see you at restaurants, on the street, at my country club bar, now here. Isn't anywhere safe from you? Stop stalking me!" she shouted.

Embarrassed. I pushed my cart out of line and walked over to her. I lowered my voice. "Wendy, I'm not stalking you. The last time I saw you was at the country club."

"That's not the last time *I* saw *you*. You were at The Peak last night. You rode with Mary Ellen yesterday. I was at the stables, too, and I know you know it. You need to stay away from me." With lightning speed, she moved in close and grabbed my coat sleeve. People stared at us as though we were an exhibit in the Natural History Museum: Neolithic Women Fighting. "I know you're trying to pin Hugh's murder on me."

I tried disengaging my coat from her fingers, but she was locked on like time-release vault doors. "Why would I do that?"

"You *know* why." She stabbed a finger at me. "So yeah, I had a little drug problem. So yeah, my husband shouldn't have helped me out from time to time, but just because Hugh threatened to report us if Gary didn't clean up his act, and Gary had to move his practice into the city and be supervised and go to anger management classes because of that time he hit Hugh, and I had to dry out at Betty Ford, which nearly bankrupted us even though *some people* think we're made of money, well, that doesn't mean I'd kill him." She shook my sleeve a little and my arm bones rattled.

Sounded like a pretty good motive to me.

"Besides it was years ago, and you're not going to prove anything following us around. Oh, and," she snapped her fingers in my face, "that sorry story about your mother and her medical records and what not, she's out of jail now, so you can cancel that appointment with my husband. Your mother has to ask him. He's not going to give it to *you*." She spat this last at me. "Besides," she muttered, almost to herself, "I know she kept a copy. Don't think you're going to blackmail us, too. There's nothing left."

She suddenly became aware that her behavior was attracting attention and picked up her coffee, but her hand shook so badly that she couldn't get her lips and the edge of the cup to meet. I wondered if she had raided her husband's stash this morning.

"Someone is blackmailing you? Who? And there's a copy of Mother's medical report?"

"Don't play innocent with me. I know Hugh told you about the DNA tests at your mother's Christmas party. It's all over town. Why do you think all this is happening?" She gave up trying to drink and put the cup down. The front of her blouse was decorated with little brown splatters. Her other hand was still locked onto my coat. Again, I gently attempted to disengage it.

"Wendy, I don't know anything about DNA tests." My mind was racing. I needed to get back to my mother. "Hetty Gardner was murdered this morning, and I have to take food to the family. You need to let me go."

She backed into a table, then sat down so fast I thought she would miss the chair and land on the floor. "Not another murder." At least she'd freed my sleeve. "You came here to ask me if I did it, right? That's why you're here. I know that's why you're here."

"Why would you kill Hetty?"

"I wouldn't kill Hetty and I don't know anyone who would. Gary certainly wouldn't. He doesn't have a motive either, and anyway, he was with me."

"He was with you when?"

"When Hetty was killed."

"Do you know when Hetty was killed?"

"No, but it doesn't matter because Gary is always with me."

I looked around. No Gary anywhere. "Where is he right now?"

"At work." She seemed to realize what I was saying. "Except when he's at work and then his tarty little nurse is his alibi."

That likely explained her affair with the podiatrist. "Gary's having an affair with his nurse?"

"Who told you that?" She nearly shrieked it.

"Calm down." I stepped back to my cart, grabbed a bottle of expensive water, and tried to get her to drink a little. "I inferred it from what you said."

"Oh." She sipped like a compliant child. "You're not a cop!" She crowed it loudly.

This was a revelation? "No, I'm not."

"I don't have to answer any of your questions."

"You never did."

"Leave me alone."

"Are you going to be okay? You seem a little agitated."

"Agitated, smagitated. I'm fine. Skedaddle." She waggled her fingers at me like anemone on a coral reef.

Maybe she still had that drug problem.

It would be a motive to kill Hugh, especially if he'd discovered Hankin was still dealing drugs to his wife. Maybe he was passing out "free samples" to other women, too.

—————

I dropped off the food and headed out again. I had one advantage no one else had and it was about time I used it, before anyone else got hurt. Maybe actively engaging the intuition would make the dreams stop—an added plus. Having physical contact usually sparked an image, but I hoped the intuition might activate from being at the murder scene.

Levittown Road was several miles northeast of Mother's place, almost at the border with the next town. The acreage there used to be cheaper, which is why Hetty's not-enormous inheritance from her father had been sufficient to buy her farm. Levittown Road ran a couple miles west of the farm road and didn't connect directly with it: she could have chosen two or three more direct ways to get home from downtown. That fit with the idea of someone in the car making her drive an unusual and slightly more secluded route.

Unsure where she'd been killed, I drove until I saw police tape, a couple of cruisers, and a tow truck, onto which a group of men were maneuvering Hetty's car. I pulled off to the side of the road, well away from the action.

As I pushed the car door open, the chief, in another nicely-cut suit, turned to look. Pete Samuels was helping the tow truck driver, and Joe Munson sipped a coffee, feet planted wide apart in that macho stance cops seem to learn in cop school.

As I walked closer, the chief said, "Nice of you to show up. I wanted to have a chat about your dinner last night." He watched as the driver hopped in his cab and turned on the winch. The car jerked slowly up the ramp.

"You're welcome, but I don't know anything."

Like much of Connecticut, the murder site was wooded and quiet. A heavy cover of trees bordered both sides of the long gentle slope, and the next house sat a good half mile away. I was surprised she'd been found here in the middle of the night. It was a pretty deserted stretch of road.

"Did you find other car tracks?" I asked.

"You doin' my job for me now?" The chief was still watching the car.

Pete yelled and the operator shut the winch down. He hopped out of the cab and began to secure the car to the truck and draw up the ramp.

"Just curious."

"Remember the relationship between curiosity and the cat?"

With the car secured, the driver jumped back in the cab, gesturing to Pete, who opened the opposite door and got in.

"Well, that's that. It's up to the forensics guys now," Munson commented to the air. He walked to one of the cruisers, got in, and pulled out to follow the truck. The chief gestured to the second cruiser. "Care to take a ride to the station?"

"I don't have anything to tell you. Bailey and I had dinner at The Peak last night, and Hetty arrived partway through our meal."

"Do you know when she left the restaurant?"

"About eleven-thirty. I wasn't paying much attention to time."

"How'd she seem?"

"Her emotional state?"

He nodded, his eyes hooded and watching.

"She was wary of us... there was, um, an incident when we were younger."

"Tell me," he said.

I did.

"You apologized?"

"I did."

Something softened, almost as if he approved of me, and I suddenly felt happy.

"Why do you think Bailey chose this particular night to apologize?"

"We'd been talking about it, then Hetty appeared. We'd waited far too long to say something: *carpe diem*."

"How did Hetty react?"

"She got angry, told us we couldn't make the hurt magically disappear. She was right and we started to talk about it, but Andrew Winters Junior interrupted us."

"What did he want?"

"To be social, I think."

"Have you been seeing a lot of Mr. Winters?" He folded his arms across his chest.

"We went to dinner once," I said. "He wanted to complain about his father."

He grunted. "How did Hetty and Mr. Winters get along?"

"I'm not sure," I said. "Junior was talking about his father's campaign and how loyal some of the campaign workers had been, and that's when Hetty freaked out, grabbed her stuff and ran out."

"Where were you between midnight and three a.m.?"

"I'm a suspect?"

"I have to ask." His brown face gleamed in the sunlight.

"Bailey and I hung out with Junior for another hour or so. Then I drove home and crashed on the couch, where my mother woke me at two to chat."

"No wonder you look like hell."

"Gee, thanks."

"Any time. So there's an hour-and-a-half window when your time is unaccounted for. Did your mother see you come home?"

"Not to my knowledge."

"Not that she's the most reliable witness," he muttered under his breath.

I stifled a laugh. "Trust me. I wasn't doing anything that took thought or planning during that ninety minutes."

He acted as if he hadn't heard me. "If we need anything further, we'll be in touch." He slid into his car, all business.

I wondered what he would think if he knew what I planned to do the moment he left. I might have to tell him, if we ever got further than growling at each other. I turned from his disappearing taillights and walked back to my car, feeling some trepidation. I hadn't tried this before, no matter what I'd told Bailey about scoping out Winters that night at his party. Asking for visions implied I had control, and I wasn't convinced controlling them was possible or desirable. How did I know my unconscious mind wasn't merely serving me up the answer I wanted?

I leaned against the door and shut my eyes, inhaling the cold dampness of snow vaporizing, the mud, the exhaust fumes. I tried to empty my mind, as Paul taught me, to let in other images. As I got quiet, I felt the cold metal seep through my jacket, the door handle press into my back. I let my breath slow, and tried to forget that I felt a little dumb standing with my eyes closed by my car on a deserted country road.

Then, it worked. I didn't get an image, as in the past. Instead, I got color: dark green, like the inside of a forest. It swirled around Hetty like a cloud in a fairytale, like ink in water. A thin strand of lighter yellowy green slithered through the cloud and disappeared. I opened my eyes. Colors. What the hell did they mean?

My cell phone rang. It was Mother.

CHAPTER 21

 half-hour later, I was seated in Ernie and Loretta's living room, chafing at the bit to get to my own agenda: the vision, the DNA report, Winken's strange accusations. But before I could, I had to deal with Mother's agenda.

Loretta looked completely washed out. Her hair hung in black and silver strands along her face, framing the pale freckles from her Irish heritage. The lines on her forehead and around her eyes were accentuated by the long shadows that stretched across the room from the front windows, where the sun was disappearing through the trees in early winter twilight. Mother sat by her side, holding her hand. Ernie had gone to make more coffee. We waited until he got back with the tray, mugs and a pot, and more of the sliced sweet bread.

"Zucchini," he said when he saw me looking at it. "Loretta grows about eighty pounds of it in the summer."

"Oh, Ernie." Loretta looked at him with a tired half-smile. "Don't exaggerate."

He shrugged and gave me an insider grin.

Loretta said, "I'm sorry to drag you back here, Clara. You must have other things you'd rather be doing, but Constance thought you should hear this directly from me." She'd been staring into her mug as she talked, but now she looked straight at me. "I know things have been difficult between the two of you for some time."

Oh, no. Not the make-up-with-your-mother talk. Not now.

Loretta used one hand to push her hair behind her ear. "Hetty and I had that kind of falling out, too, and we never got a chance to make it up before she..." She stopped.

"I know," I said. "It's okay."

"It's not okay—you and Constance need to fix what's wrong between you."

I looked at Mother. She looked at me and said, "I didn't tell her to say that."

"I'm saying it all on my own. I've watched this between the two of you for a lot of years, and you, Constance, are not without fault here." She shook her head. "But that's not why you're here." This time, she looked at Ernie and he smiled her some encouragement. "Constance mentioned that she's worried about your working on the Andrew Winters campaign. Those Winters... I want to tell you about Hetty, so you can see why you need to be careful.

"Hetty had been seeing someone," she said and I snapped to attention. "We probably never would have found out if old Uncle Roland hadn't died suddenly of a stroke in the middle of the night. He was her favorite uncle. She didn't answer at the house or on her cell and I was worried sick. She found all the messages the following morning, said she'd been out with a friend and had turned off her phone. Very unlike her: Hetty always wanted to be disturbed. It gave her a sense of belonging." She sipped from her coffee mug, made a moue of distaste and set it down.

"It was also surprising that she didn't want to tell us who he was. Hetty hasn't had—didn't have—many boyfriends in her life. She could have been pretty, but she didn't know how to present herself. No social graces. I showed her, but nothing stuck." She twisted her wedding ring around on her finger. "After her father died, she needed attention so badly. Ernie tried, but she never recovered. I guess one doesn't, but some people manage to go on better than others." She smoothed her skirt across her lap, plucking at a thread near the hem.

"At about that time, she began working for the Winters campaign—just some canvassing in her neighborhood, a couple of donations here and there, which she couldn't really afford since the farm was just starting to break even. Then, she attended two or three fundraisers to scope out likely 'targets.' That's what she called them, and that's when I started to get uneasy." She looked up at Ernie, and he took her hand and nodded. A little click fired in my brain.

"I pressed her a bit on this man's identity, and when she remained adamant about not telling me, I presumed he was married. Ernie and I also believe he was connected to the campaign, her reason for putting in so much time. She told me she would bring him home to meet us, but the time wasn't right. I tried to tell her being involved with someone married was a painful and disastrous choice, even if—or maybe especially if—the man did leave his wife. Hetty wouldn't listen. She said I didn't know what I was talking about." Her voice broke, and she paused to regain her composure. "I must have pressed too hard because she finally told me to mind my own business. We hadn't talked since."

She stopped. The wall clock snapped through several seconds. "When was that?" I asked.

"About when you returned home."

I thought about the campaign office. Would Winters Senior—just about the only guy who fit the description—risk an affair during the campaign? It seemed unlikely. He wanted this seat more than anything, and the voters didn't look too kindly on sexual peccadilloes. So who could it be?

Mother walked me out to the car, and I insisted we had to talk. "Two people have died, Mother. How much longer before we put our heads together?"

She agreed to meet me at home at the end of the day. Despite her urging, I wanted to put my time in at the campaign. I didn't know what she was going to tell me, but I was still collecting donor notes, and until I had answers, I didn't want to close down any options. Besides, something nagged at me in what Loretta had just said, something that went along with something Winken said, but I couldn't put my finger on it. That something, I was sure, was somewhere in those notes.

When I got home that afternoon, I left Mother to open the Chinese take-out containers, while I printed out the notes from my laptop. When I returned, she handed me a set of chopsticks and got herself a fork. She spooned precise, but very small portions of each dish onto her plate and ate them separately, savoring each bite and refusing to talk until she'd made her way through one full glass of wine. I drank a glass of seltzer. Last night's excesses were still with me, and I wanted a clear head.

Mother put down her fork. "Loretta's right, you know. You and I need to deal with our own conflict first."

No, no, no. First we needed to talk about how we were going to keep someone from murdering us in our beds. "Mother—"

She waved me off with her fork and poured more wine for herself. "Fine. Show me those papers."

I shuffled the pages into alphabetical order. I would get to the vision and the DNA in a moment. "These are names and accompanying data that I've, uh, borrowed from the Winters campaign files."

Mother looked horrified. "You've stolen their data? They could prosecute you."

I ignored her. "Something's not right. I'm not sure what it is, but you know these people. And something Loretta said... " I shook my head. It was right there. I just couldn't catch it.

Mother peered at me over the rim of her glass. The wine distorted her, as if half her face had aged faster, the jaw softening and warping. The lines had deepened around her eyes and mouth, enhancing that same sad expression of loss. As Loretta said, things happened to people and they never fully recovered. What had happened to Mother?

Sharply, a slash of light rent my vision and I felt as if I were burning. Where had that come from? Just as quickly, it passed, leaving only a sheen of sweat.

She saw, but she didn't ask, as usual. I pushed the papers across to her. She settled her glasses on her nose and started to read. About halfway down the first page, she frowned. "Get me a pencil?"

I rummaged in my purse and found a pen. She made a check mark and flipped to the next page, reading, frowning again, checking again. I cleared the table. By the time I'd packed everything away in the refrigerator and dishwasher, her glasses had slid to the tip of her nose and she was staring into space, ticking the pen absentmindedly against the wooden chair arm.

"Well?" I prodded. "You see them, right? Those notations? BRK? BSA? and so on?"

She nodded. "I think I know what they are. Can you call Bailey tomorrow? I'd like to run it by both of you, but I want to think about it a little more first."

"You know she's his campaign lawyer."

"That's why she should know."

"She'll be at Richard and Paul's tomorrow for Christmas Eve. We could talk there."

"I'm invited?" She looked genuinely surprised.

"It's Christmas, Mother."

"I know, but... I didn't assume you would want to spend it with me. I made plans with Ernie and Loretta."

"I'll call Richard to see if there's room for two more."

She looked grateful, so grateful I almost couldn't bear it. How could this be the mother I thought I knew? She was totally self-sufficient. She didn't need anyone or anything. She could have gone to Richard and Paul's whether I wanted her to or not. I turned away before she could see my tears.

Then, foiling me yet again, she swept the pages up and climbed the stairs to her bedroom, firmly closing the door. There would be no more discussion of anything tonight.

CHAPTER 22

hristmas Eve dawned brilliantly white and cold—unusual for Connecticut, which for the past few years had preferred its Christmases almost green and in the forties. Bailey was working; we would have to wait for Paul and Richard's party to confer. I was worried we might not have a chance to get away—Paul and Richard's parties could get very festive—but Mother reassured me that we would find time.

As for the other topics, she said, "It can wait until after Christmas." She raised an eyebrow. "It will be all right, Clara."

Screaming my frustration wouldn't help anything, so I shoved it down and hoped the dreams would cooperate with Mother's plan. The slug was still lurking, sloshing lazily at the back of my brain.

At seven, we arrived at the party: Richard and Paul were opening the first bottle of champagne, and playing Earth, Wind & Fire on the stereo. They'd just gotten glasses in our hands when the doorbell rang again. A blast of cold air blew in Bailey, Sondra, Joellen, Alcott, and Morrie. Sondra and Joellen were Richard's last remaining friends from the office, a pair of bottle blondes with expertise in computer languages I'd never heard of.

Alcott and Morrie, looking like a pair of mimes with their dark, slicked down hair and fair skin, had known Paul—and me—since grade school. They had barely gotten their scarves unwound when Loretta and Ernie arrived, bringing a large covered dish.

Everyone carried brightly colored packages and bags and bottles. Richard poured glasses of bubbly, everyone got kissed, and Paul took care of the food and directed the packages to the tree.

"We're so sorry about Hetty," Morrie said to Loretta, taking off his coat. The group hummed their agreement.

Loretta glanced at Ernie, her eyes tearing up. "We're still trying to figure out how to talk about it." She put her hand on his arm. "We don't even know what to say to each other yet."

Morrie responded by doing the perfect thing: he folded Loretta into a bear hug for several moments, then kissed the top of her head as he released her.

"Nothing I can say will make it better," he said. "Do you want us to talk about it tonight or not?"

She shook her head. "If you have nice memories of Hetty, yes, but I don't want to talk about her death. I want a little joy for us, for all the time we had with her."

They nodded, almost as one, and each of them hugged her on the way into the living room. We'd settled around the fire when the doorbell rang again. Richard and Paul glanced at each other, then at me.

"What?"

Richard shrugged coyly. Paul said, "Bailey mentioned that you'd probably forgotten to invite him yourself." He opened the door to Chief DuPont. "Shining Star" started playing. I looked daggers at Bailey.

The chief handed a large bottle of Bombay gin to Paul. "I thought, since you were entertaining Clara, you might need this."

Oh yeah, very funny.

Paul barely suppressed a smile. "Good thinking." Richard was already pouring another glass of champagne and making introductions. "Sandra and Joellen, Alcott and Morrie, this is Police Chief Kyle DuPont."

"Kyle is fine." He settled on a chair at the opposite end of the room from me, nodding in greeting when Richard's introductions swung around to my part of the circle. He was dressed casually in a dark grey V-neck sweater and black pants. A red t-shirt showed at the V and made his brown face glow. His shoes gleamed and he had on that thin Movado watch.

The group glanced from Mother to Bailey to Kyle, no doubt wondering about the state of the murder investigation. But they were too polite to ask outright.

A tray of rich goodies sat on the coffee table: dates stuffed with goat cheese and wrapped with prosciutto, fresh strawberries dipped in sugar, liver pâté crostini, baked brie, salmon mousse. People nibbled and gestured with their glasses, laughing and poking gentle fun at each other. Paul told a funny story about Hetty dressed as a chicken in a grade school play, something about tickling feathers and a sneezing fit she gamely turned into cock-a-doodle-doos. I even saw Mother and Loretta smile.

The political race provoked lots of speculation. The room leaned away from Winters and toward the Democratic candidate, Sherilyn Ambroise. She had cornered the black and Hispanic vote, and was now gaining among middle-class whites and class-conscious wealthy liberals. Winters had to be a little worried.

"You know Clara is working for Andrew Winters, don't you?" Kyle interjected. Ten interested faces turned my way.

"Not because I support him," I protested. Six of them looked puzzled.

Kyle looked satisfied, as if he'd driven out a piece of information in a successful interrogation.

Richard and Paul had invited him because they thought I was attracted to him, but was he attracted to me? We had so many complications standing in the way of any relationship, Hugh's murder and my pending divorce for a start. Yeah, I was a prize, all right. Why would he take a risk on me?

"Then whyever be part of the campaign?" Morrie asked.

I pulled myself back to the conversation. "It's long and complicated," I said.

Mother rescued me. "Clara's trying to help me." The interested expressions turned in her direction.

Sondra lowered her voice to a whisper, as if that would make what she said more palatable. "You mean because of the murder?"

My mother raised her eyebrows at me.

Sondra said, "Do you think Winters did it? Oh, wouldn't that just be dish? I would love to see that man go down in flames. He's so awful."

"Dish?" Richard shook his head.

"What makes him awful?" Kyle shone his charm in her direction, but his eyes were watchful.

Joellen answered for her. "He's just slimy. Can't you feel it coming off him in waves? Sliding off him, I guess, if it's slime!" She laughed.

"Ha!" I exclaimed, looking at Kyle triumphantly. "'Slimebag Winters.' You see? My pet name was totally appropriate!"

He looked bemused, though he hadn't lost his watchfulness.

"I can't even listen to him talk!" Sondra nodded her agreement. "Have you met his sister? She can be nice, but she always has an agenda. When I worked with her on a committee to help build a new children's playground, it was clear she was only on it to further her brother's career. Does she have any life of her own? I never see her without him."

"That's a little creepy, isn't it?" Patrick brushed long fingers through his slicked-back hair, releasing a torrent of it from its moussed perfection.

"What are you suggesting?" Morrie tried to look offended, but broke into giggles.

Bailey said, "I think we can safely rule out incest. For the record, I'm subbing for the lawyer who's supposed to be working for the campaign."

"What does a campaign lawyer do?" asked Joellen.

"Help the candidate avoid corruption, scandal and financial misconduct."

"How ya'll doin' on that?" the chief drawled, a little pointedly.

She shrugged. "It's Christmas. Can't we talk about something besides work?"

He laughed good-naturedly and let her off the hook, but it looked like a lawyer-cop standoff to me.

———

At dinner, I was place-carded next to Kyle. Paul sat to Kyle's right at the head of the table. Mother sat to my left, and after a speculative look at Kyle, engaged Loretta in a long chat about horses. Paul, when he wasn't helping Richard pour wine or serve courses, stayed fully focused on Sondra, seated to his right. Kyle dipped his spoon into the creamy scallop stew and ignored me, while I tried to ignore the occasional brushes with his lovely, strong shoulder.

About halfway through the soup, it occurred to me that this matchmaking had been done out of love. I hadn't succeeded finding someone on my own; perhaps I should allow my friends to do it for me. Plus, the little voice in my gut that sent out low growls when Andrew Junior or Pete Samuels inserted himself in the picture remained completely silent for Kyle—or crinkled up with silvery excitement.

He said, "You're not going to stop, are you?"

How could he know I'd been thinking about him? I licked a drop of soup off my spoon and set it on the charger. Richard was using his Christmas china and the deep green stripe on the rims reminded me of the color I'd seen at Hetty's murder site. "Stop what?"

"Trying to find out who killed Hugh and Hetty."

Not psychic after all. That was a relief. Two of us in one relationship would make for more stress than I could handle.

"Someone came after my mother and used Hugh's death to do it. Then they threatened me, and that night in the restaurant, I saw how frightened Hetty was."

"It's my job to solve those crimes, not yours."

"I'm not out to bug you, you know. I liked it better when you liked me."

"I still like you." His voice was gruff. From the corner of my eye, I saw Paul suck in a little breath. "I don't want you getting hurt, and you're doing everything you can to invite harm." He wiped a bit of soup from the corner of his mouth with the barest flick of the napkin.

"I'm sorry." He turned slightly in his chair. I don't think Paul was breathing at all, even though Sondra probably hadn't noticed he was hardly paying attention to her story about the South Norwalk Maritime Aquarium. "How about you tell me what you know?"

I breathed in and out three times as I considered this. Yes, I counted my breaths. I also counted to twenty while I was breathing. "How about you sit with Mother, Bailey and me later and talk through some ideas? I've, uh, 'liberated' some information from the campaign office, and Mother's found some anomalies. We wanted to see what Bailey thought."

"What do the Winters have to do with anything?"

"Probably nothing, but we've found some funny numbers, enough to take a look at. Plus, the photographs of Mary Ellen on Hetty's wall connect the players to each other."

I didn't know yet what the DNA or Hetty's affair meant.

"You bring me in, it's official."

"Listen as a friend rather than a police officer."

"They aren't separable like that, Clara."

"Nothing we have is hard evidence. It's all speculation."

He took in the sideboard covered with silver serving dishes, the red and green candles flanking the holly, evergreen, and red apple centerpiece, the flushed faces of my friends. I wondered what it would be like with him as part of this little family, if he would be comfortable, or if he spent his life watching other people for transgressions.

He said, "I'll think about it, but I can't promise you anything."

Richard whisked away Kyle's soup bowl. Paul leaned over with the wine bottle. "More?"

Kyle shook his head. "I've got to drive."

"Surely not for a while."

Kyle looked at me.

I said, "We're only on the first course."

Kyle nodded, and Paul filled his glass and then mine. When Kyle wasn't looking, Paul winked.

The scallop stew was followed by roast beef with crispy brown pan potatoes, gravy, braised leeks, Loretta's corn pudding, and Brussels sprouts with bacon. A basket of homemade cranberry bread made its way around the table. Dessert was chocolate and white mousses twirled around each other in a clear wine glass and topped with fresh raspberries. Paul had made extra thin sugar cookies and rolled them in tubes. By the time the Godiva chocolates and port arrived, I was too stuffed to touch them.

Luckily, Kyle and I got off the subject of my bad behavior and discussed movies (we both liked comedies and political thrillers and disliked horror films), music (almost anything but Wagner and gangsta rap, he said), and free time activities (running, travel, reading, gardening and cooking found common ground). I'd even coaxed out a couple of smiles.

After dinner, Richard and Paul insisted on a game of Charades, which was nearly impossible to play in their tiny living room. Kyle and I lost and were tasked with the dishes. While he washed and I dried and put away, I decided to pursue the intuitive image I'd had of him patrolling in the muddy aftermath of Katrina.

Besides, I'd drunk all that lovely wine and it was Christmas, and my friends had given me the wonderful present of having Kyle here.

"What happened in New Orleans?"

"What do you mean?" He was washing a knife, and his tone sliced with the same sharp edge.

"You left after Hurricane Katrina, right?"

He rinsed it, then ran his finger along the edge of the blade, as if to test it. "Yes."

"But your family's still there?"

"My mother and sister."

"Married? kids? Tell me about her."

"No."

"Okay," I said, drawing out the O and the K.

He handed me another knife to dry. I slid the towel down the blade and inserted it into the knife block.

He grumbled to himself, then lifted his hands from the water and rested them on my shoulders, suds and all. "Clara, you're not ready."

I leaned forward and kissed him. I blame it on the wine.

He didn't pull away immediately. Maybe things would turn around in my life and this nice man would like me and we could settle down and—the lips were gone.

"Look at your behavior over the past few days." He pulled his hands away, leaving foamy damp spots.

"I am a rule-breaker."

He shook his head, as if I didn't get it and handed me another knife.

"You're worried that my knowing a little about you and your sister will impact the town's perception of your objectivity?"

"As far as my judgment goes, this town needs to perceive me as unimpeachable. I'm a black man in a white town in a position of leadership. I'm a target. It's not that you're a rule-breaker, Clara. You're a loose cannon."

The criticism stung. "Loose cannon" implied I didn't know what I was doing. I set down the dishtowel. "I would think you'd want to hear our suppositions, just in case. Meanwhile, it's fine if you don't want to talk about your family. All you have to do is say so."

Kyle started on the pots. I could hear the sponge scratching at the metal, the laughter from the other room, the Christmas carols that had replaced disco, even the snap of the fire. The kitchen was warm and cozy, the pile of dirty dishes and pans shrinking, the lingering smells of the dinner in the air. Kyle's reflection in the window over the sink was fuzzed by the rising steam.

"I love red beans and rice. I miss the warmth and the sudden rain showers that come from nowhere and disappear just as fast. I miss the smell of the river and the lush landscape, the way smells are heavy in the heat and humidity. New Orleans was my home, until the hurricane took that away. I can't go back, and it's an ache, Clara. I did something that's got me blacklisted, and while I can visit my family, I can never live there again, at least not... for now."

A peace offering.

I leaned a hip against the counter. "Okay, then. How about a pact? When this is over—because it will be over—I'll take you to dinner, and we'll talk about the stuff that matters. In the meantime, I'll try to keep you in the loop for everything else. Deal?" I held out the hand covered in towel.

He grinned, the first, full out grin I'd seen on him that night. "Deal." He put his hand into the towel and shook. Then, he leaned over and, very gently, gave me a kiss on the cheek.

Woo hoo.

CHAPTER 23

ichard wobbled into the room, his champagne glass held aloft, queen-style. "Hey you two! You're taking an awfully long time to do the dishes!" He giggled a little and collapsed into a chair at the kitchen table. Morrie followed, putting his arms around Richard's shoulders and hugging him hard. He laid his cheek on Richard's head. "Hey, old man. What do the doctors say about you these days?"

Richard rolled his eyes. "Not much. Turns out I've got Lyme, so that's antibiotics up the wazoo." He snorted. "Whoopee. More drugs."

The stereo snapped off in the other room, and a round of "For He's a Jolly Good Fellow" started up.

Kyle finished the last pot and handed it to me before turning from the sink and drying his hands. "Does that affect your HIV?"

"Who knows?" Richard threw up his hands, unintentionally heaving Morrie off. Morrie smiled quietly and leaned on the wall behind Richard. "Everything pretty much does, it's *alllll* immune system. Maybe I should just cross my fingers. That should work, right? Yup. Just cross my fingers. More champagne?" He stood up and wobbled vaguely in the direction of the refrigerator. Kyle gently steered him back to the table and got the bottle. He sent a questioning glance toward me, but I didn't know what to do. I'd never seen Richard this plastered.

It didn't matter, because he forgot almost immediately.

"Morrie, my friend, this sucks. When we're young, we think everything is reversible. But some stuff, you never see coming and then you don't know what the hell you're supposed to do next." He squitched sideways in his chair and looked at Kyle. "Bet that's what Katrina did to you, huh?" He slumped forward again, tapping the table with his forefinger. "These days, they say HIV isn't a death sentence, but they don't tell you how to live with it. They don't tell you that people will still be scared of you, that you have to change how you think and eat and organize your life. Lucky days are when you forget about it for a while."

Richard plopped his elbows onto the table and dropped his chin into his palms. "Paul, now Paul. What would I do without him? That man loves me so much, and I don't deserve any of it. He keeps fighting for us, but sometimes, I just wanna give up, you know? Just put me in one of those flaming boats and float me out to sea like a Viking. That'd be the way to be sent off, right?"

I put my hand on his shoulder, and he rested his head in the curve of my hip. "Clara, sweetie, you've gotta find someone who loves you like Paul loves me. Dying is a bitch, and if you haven't shared whatever you get in this world with someone then who cares what you get? All those experiences go with you to the grave unless someone else carries the memory."

Morrie looked absolutely stricken. Kyle was still. I had huge knot in my throat like a scarf tied too tight. The song finished in the living room, and the chatter started up again.

"What did I come in here for?" Richard muttered, looking around vaguely.

"This, I believe." Kyle held up the champagne. "How about we bring it into the other room?"

Paul caught my eye as we entered. He rose quickly to help Richard to a seat, relieving Kyle of the champagne, and placing it safely out of reach on the sideboard. "Sorry," he whispered. "He's been like that recently. The pressure at work is getting to him."

I chastised myself for not being here to notice or to help, then felt overwhelmed by all the competing priorities. I turned away and saw Ernie helping Mother on with her coat. "Are you leaving?" I said. "I thought Bailey... I thought we were going to talk."

"I'm going to stay again with Ernie and Loretta tonight," she said. "We'll talk tomorrow." She tipped her head at Kyle, as if in warning.

I was too hurt by her leaving to pay attention. "It's Christmas. I'm your family."

She had the grace to look startled. "Yes, you are, although I've not heard you say that before. Tonight, though, Loretta and Ernie have lost their family, and they need someone with them. Loretta is my oldest friend." She started to reach for me, then paused, as if unsure of my reaction. "Loretta was here when you weren't, Clara. I owe her."

"Join us, Clara," Ernie suggested. "We have room." But Loretta's exhausted face and my own petulance stopped me.

"We'll have other Christmases," Mother said. Then, in the sort of strange turnabout that was her trademark, she gestured like the mother of my childhood, and like a good daughter, I stepped toward her. She kissed my cheek. "Merry Christmas, Clara."

Paul saw my face. "Why don't you stay here? You can run home for clothes tomorrow. We've got the space, it's late, and anyway, we could use the company." My first instinct was to demure, but then I reconsidered. I imagined that, when the person you loved was dying, being with him was the only place you wanted to be. It would also be a hard and lonely place. Maybe my presence would act as a buffer against the fear that this would be their last Christmas together, a fear—I suddenly realized—they must carry through every holiday, no matter how well Richard was doing.

After that, the party broke up. It was nearly one o'clock before they all drifted out the door, with kisses and promises to be back by early afternoon of the following day, even Kyle. At least I had that to look forward to, sort of. Paul banked the fire, and I helped him shepherd Richard off to bed after a large glass of water and three aspirin.

He came to find me after Richard was tucked in. I had crawled happily between the guest room bed's clean sheets and was leafing through a book of Mark Doty's poetry I'd found on the bedside table. Without saying a word, he sat down, put his arms around me, and began to cry.

———

Christmas dawned snowy. Everyone appeared earlier than expected to beat the storm. Paul, Richard and I were still in pajamas when the guests started arriving around eleven, so Paul made another batch of biscuits and more coffee and we opened gifts by the fire, listening to Aaron Copland's *Appalachian Spring* and Handel's *Messiah*. Richard, unchastised by his night of drinking, and Paul's remonstrance about alcohol's effects on his immune system, started on the champagne again when he started cooking, but promised to take it slower. It was unclear if he remembered the conversation in the kitchen the night before.

Mother arrived with Loretta and Ernie, on time of course. I still felt stung over her leaving me last night, even though I knew it was completely irrational, so I left the room and went into the kitchen to help Richard stir, chop, or sauté. He set me up at the kitchen table with a wooden board and let me hack at a stack of onions. Kyle wandered in a few moments later. Richard set up another board.

"Avoiding your mother?" Kyle asked.

"I'm a three-year-old."

"She's good at it," said Richard. "One of her specialties."

The onions started doing their good work and I swiped at my eyes. "Shut up, you. Your mother loves you."

"And your mother loves you," said my mother from the doorway.

Richard intervened. "Constance, you look lovely this afternoon." Mother's dark green suit and cream silk blouse were perfect. "They've already got me locked up in the kitchen, can you believe it? Do you need a glass of champagne? Some orange juice? No? Well, go grab yourself a chair and warm your toes by the fire. Hors d'oeuvres will be out in fifteen minutes." He gave her a big kiss and gently led her out the door.

I wasn't off the hook, only reprieved.

Paul came into the kitchen to pick up Richard's cooking duties while Richard schmoozed guests. My vision near Hetty's murder site still nagged at me, and if Mother wouldn't discuss it, at least I could talk to Paul. Kyle would get an earful, but better to shock him now.

"Um, Paul." Something in my tone of voice caused him to turn sharply. I nodded. He shrugged, in that way people do when they mean *it's your funeral.*

"I've started getting daylight dreams," our code for visions.

"Like what?"

"Like colors. Like a preview of a murder. Like lots of burning images. The sound of white noise."

"A preview of a murder?" Kyle stopped chopping, the knife suspended.

"I saw Hetty's attacker."

"Why haven't you told me?" He dropped the knife, and it clattered onto the board.

"It's a vision, Kyle, not an eyewitness account."

"Vision. Like voodoo and séances?"

"I'm not practicing it for money, but, yes, sort of."

He narrowed his eyes, sat back in his chair. "How long have you had these, uh, visions?"

"How often are you having them, Clara?" Paul asked.

"Maybe one every couple of days. Not often." For the moment, at least, fewer than I had before I ended up in Switzerland. "I'm not sleeping well, and I'm still having that, uh, same recurring dream." Kyle probably wasn't ready for visions of a bloody wave coming for me. "So... things aren't improving."

"No."

Paul put down his wooden spoon and turned off the flame under the pot he'd been stirring. "What else?"

"I brought the last vision on deliberately."

Paul's eyebrows rose. "You did?"

"I wanted to see if I could come up with something about Hetty's murder, something that might give me a sense of her. I got the color green."

Kyle's skepticism glowered at me across a haze of onion fumes.

Paul said, "Olive green? Neon green? Blue green?"

"Forest green. With a thin line of yellow green going through it."

"Did you see Hetty herself?"

"The color swirled around her, like ink in water or smoke in air. But the color strands were intense, not diluted."

He leaned a hip against the counter and frowned. I knew what the colors meant; I'd looked them up, but I wanted him to confirm it. Finally, he said, "Both dark green and yellow-green indicate jealousy, but you already knew she was jealous of you. Dark green is often related to ambition and greed; yellow-green, to sickness, cowardice and discord. What kind of sense does that make to you?"

"She was ambitious about her farm—and maybe a little social climbing. Loretta said Hetty was having an affair, someone from the campaign. Did you know that?" I asked Kyle.

"An affair?" Kyle picked up the knife. He sliced an onion in half and placed the halves flat-side down on the cutting board. "Or a relationship?"

"Loretta said 'affair.' You should ask her."

"I intend to. Thank you. Later." He severed the halves into fine little slices, swept the pieces into a bowl.

Paul slid his eyes in Kyle's direction. He said to me, "Maybe the ambition and greed had to do with harming you."

"You mean Hetty saw me as an impediment to her social climbing? And she killed Hugh to... do what? How did that help her cause?"

"She was jealous when you were children, right? Maybe her 'affair' from the campaign used her jealousy and social ambitions to manipulate her. That could cause the intensity in the colors you saw."

"But what did Hugh have to do with the campaign? I think Hetty killed Hugh because he rejected her." I told Paul about the photographs I'd seen in Hetty's cottage, and how her walls and furniture colors matched Mother's cottage. "Whatever's going on at the campaign is unrelated."

Kyle rubbed his hand across his eyes. He said, "Aren't you going in circles? Didn't you say to me last night that you thought they *were* connected?"

I brushed him off, confused, still wrapped in my remembered images from the vision.

"Clara, I think you need to let this go," said Paul. "I'm impressed at the images you've gotten, but it's easy to lose perspective, think you're acting logically when you're not. Hetty is dead because someone has a secret to hide, and whoever they are, they've targeted you and Constance, too. You're an intuitive, not an investigator. Use your gifts where they apply." He turned back to the stove.

"My point, exactly," Kyle chimed in.

I turned on him, furious, pent up with weeks of sleeplessness, blood-filled dreams, my mother's silence. "What have you learned? Do you know who killed Hetty? Who killed Hugh? Do you know who's targeting my mother and why?"

He remained unperturbed. "I can't share anything from the investigation with you, Clara. There's too much at stake if anything slips. I know you wouldn't mean to tell anyone, but it still happens."

"Right. You won't help me, and now even my friends are against me."

Furious, I walked out of the kitchen, put on my coat and boots, and grabbed my car keys. "I'm going home for clean clothes," I said to whoever was listening. "I'll be back in a half hour, in time for dinner. If I'm delayed, just go ahead without me." I felt childish, but if I stayed in this house, I would say something I regretted.

The snow wasn't too heavy yet, the road crews had plowed recently, and the ride home was easy. I pulled the Land Rover up by the front door, figuring I'd only be a few minutes. The door swung open silently, and I closed it just as silently behind me. Something about the house's emptiness was a balm to my anger. It bothered me that I'd told the chief last night that Hetty's and Hugh's murders connected to the campaign, but had forgotten it today. Just sleep deprivation, right? And how could a person think clearly when there were so many different threads to weave into an explicable pattern? Nothing fit. Not one thing. Hetty was so harmless. Why would anyone kill her? And how could I have known her all these years and not known she had a gift like mine?

Maybe her death had nothing to do with Hugh. Maybe some crazy client who didn't like her intuitive readings lured her to that country road. But I didn't believe that. This was a small town and two murders in two weeks had to be related. And what did the Winters know, and why would Mary Ellen threaten me to get Mother to do her bidding?

Paul and Kyle were right. I was thinking in circles, maybe making connections where there were none and ignoring the connections that were really there—but I couldn't stop.

I wandered through the living and dining rooms where we'd celebrated holidays when Father was alive. I missed him. I didn't think about him as much as I used to, which saddened me, but his voice echoed in my thoughts and his presence was strong in this house. For a moment, I even thought I smelled a bit of his aftershave. I shook my head. Olfactory hallucinations I could do without, but the scent lingered.

He'd loved the grounds, gardened them with pleasure. I still came across his books stuck in odd corners, and last week, in a little used drawer in the garage, his pipe, still redolent of the sweet tobacco he smoked. Mother even managed to keep some of his indoor plants blooming.

I turned, feeling a draft, as if he'd just opened the door and followed me in. I didn't believe in ghosts, but perhaps my thoughts made him somehow present.

That was ridiculous.

In the kitchen, I looked out at the snow-covered kitchen garden. The gardener handled it now, though Mother didn't bother with food crops any longer, only herbs. Maybe if I stayed, I would revive it.

Stayed?

I walked back down the hall, wondering if Father had known all Mother's secrets, and if so, what he thought. What story did Nat think Mother should tell me before it created a monster? I shivered and pushed open the door to what used to be Father's office, so caught up in my imagination that I half thought it would still contain his leather chair behind the big maple desk piled with gardening and landscape design books, all smelling vaguely of earth and crushed greenery. Even his scent seemed stronger in here.

Of course I knew Mother used this room now. She'd replaced the maple desk with a glass and chrome one, moved in some wooden filing cabinets, and installed a glass door leading out to the garden with stained glass panels on either side. The bookcases, though, were still crammed with his tomes, their little paper notes sticking out the tops and sides. His choices in paintings still adorned the wall space uncovered by books, and heavy leather reading chairs still flanked the fireplace.

What I should have noticed first was the person dressed all in black riffling through the top drawer of one of the cabinets.

"What are you doing?" I said it before thinking about whether or not attracting his attention was wise.

The figure spun around, startled. He had a fist full of papers, and his face was covered with a balaclava. Without saying a word, he threw the papers at me and lunged for the garden door. I ran to intercept him, but he got there first and yanked it open. Two steps behind him, I stretched out to grab his arm and dug my fingers in. He backhanded me and things went suddenly red and black. Falling across the doorsill was the last thing I remembered.

"Clara! Clara. Wake up."

Soft fingers probed my skull. I tried to pull away, but that felt even worse.

"C'mon. We have to get you inside. Help me."

Was the person talking to me? I cracked open an eye, but things stayed blurry.

"You'd better call Kyle and an ambulance. There's a lot of blood."

My blood? Maybe I'd dug my fingers into the intruder's arm deeper than I thought, but somehow, hazily, I remembered a lot of fabric between me and his skin. I tried to ask what was going on, but it didn't come out so well.

"She's mumbling. Is that a good sign?"

I finally heard the second voice.

"How should I know?"

Morrie and Alcott. I felt myself lifted up and deposited somewhat hastily onto the couch. "Jeez. She's heavier than she looks."

"Most bodies are."

"God, Morrie. She's not a 'body' yet."

"That's a lot of blood, though."

I lost consciousness again. What I remember next was a piercing light shining in my eyes.

"She'll be okay." New voice. "But we'd better take her in for observation. She might have a concussion, and it didn't do her any good to lie on that cold ground."

Things went black again.

CHAPTER 24

 woke in the hospital. Machines beeped next to the bed; footsteps hustled along the corridor, accompanied by quiet voices. Mother sat in a chair by the window reading a book. A vase of red and white carnations decorated the institutional gray table.

"I see you've decided to rejoin us," she said, closing the book and using her finger to mark her place.

I shook my head, too quickly. *Ow.* "This is worse than a hangover."

"Luckily, you'll recover," she said. "The rest of us may not," she muttered to herself.

"What happened?"

"Do you remember anything?"

"Not really. I remember going home to change. Then I started missing Dad, thinking about how we used to celebrate Christmas, the Christmas tree we'd drive to Newtown to chop down ourselves. Trying to figure out the murders. After that, not much."

"Morrie and Alcott found you in my office."

"Why did they come?"

"When you hadn't come back for an hour and a half, and you didn't answer your phone, we thought it a good idea to go find you."

"Thanks. What happened?"

"You were lying on the doorsill with your head cracked open. You'd fallen on the lip, so you hit not only the stone but also the hard metal track of the door. You've got a dent the size of the Marianas Trench in your skull."

"No wonder my head hurts." I rolled gingerly onto my side, so I could see her more clearly. "Oh." I sucked up a breath at the pain. At least a memory came with it. "I didn't fall. Someone was going through your files."

"I figured as much. My papers were all over the carpet. You might pry, but you are a more careful snoop. I've had to look hard over the past couple of weeks to determine what was out of place."

So I hadn't gotten away with anything.

"He threw those papers at me. What was he looking for?"

She scratched her finger inside the book, as if working at a blemish on the paper.

I said, "You know, but you won't tell me, yet I'm in a hospital bed and someone out there wants to shut us up. How much more risk are you willing to take to protect yourself?" That was definitely too much energy expended. My brain felt as if it would pound free of my skull. I groaned and rolled onto my back again.

She looked up, willing herself, perhaps, to the task. "It's a long story, but—"

The door swung open.

"Hello, Constance, Clara." The chief loomed in the doorway, his entrance unbelievably ill-timed. "I need to hear about your intruder."

"Could you, maybe, come back in a little bit? My head is killing me." Besides, Mother was just about to tell me what I'd waited fifteen years to hear. I pulled the blanket up to my shoulders.

He ignored my request, pulling out his phone to type notes. "Male or female?"

"Male, I think. His face was covered. Not much of a figure, if it was female."

"Height? Weight? Distinguishing features? Attire?" I did my best, but even his hands had been covered.

"He was searching the file cabinets?"

I nodded. Immediately regretted it.

"What was he was looking for?"

"Don't know." I glanced at Mother. Regretted that.

"Constance? Do you?"

Mother pursed her lips.

Kyle settled himself at the bottom of the bed. My head twanged with the movement. "It would be really useful if we knew what the intruder was looking for. That way, if, say, we caught him, we'd have leverage." He looked back and forth between us, waited out our silence.

Mother liberated her bookmark from a stack of magazines next to her chair. I could now see the book title: *Living with Grief.* Why would she still need a book like that, all these years after my father's death? She slid her sweater off the chair's shoulders. "Chief DuPont, I am going to take my daughter home and tell her a story. When I am done, I will tell you everything you want to know. It shouldn't take more than a couple of hours."

Kyle didn't look happy. "I have your word on that, ma'am?"

"You have the word of a Montague, Chief DuPont."

She didn't mean to, but she lied.

———

The doctor said I should stay another night in the hospital for observation, but Mother insisted we were going home. He cautioned me to rest for a few days and to let him know immediately if anything changed. I could come back in a couple weeks to have the stitches removed. They wheeled me to the hospital entrance, and I clambered into the car.

When we arrived home, she settled me in my father's old office on the couch, with blankets tucked around me, looking out at the fading winter light.

"I'll get us a cup of tea."

"I'm not an invalid, Mother. Just sit down and tell me."

"I know what you are. I'll be back in a couple of minutes." She left, delaying the inevitable. I wanted to hear, but after all this time and all this secrecy, maybe I didn't want to hear. Maybe that's why Paul kept the file from me, why both he and Kyle told me I wasn't ready.

Through the French doors, the doors through which the intruder had fled, I could see my father's formal garden, the snow-covered outlines of tiny boxwood in knotted formations around the slender stalks of rose canes. In the summer, their reds, mauves and pinks gleamed against the graveled path.

I missed my father so much. Just his steady presence had kept me on track through all those difficult years when it seemed Mother's goal was to make me feel small. He never interfered, and I had come to understand that whatever relationship I forged with her had to be because of my own backbone, not because someone else protected me. I wished he hadn't had to die for me to get it.

She carried in a tray with tea pot and mugs, sandwiches and cookies. She smiled ruefully. "I've not baked for a long time, so forgive the effort if it's not quite right. I needed something to occupy me while I waited for you to recover." She waved her hand at the papers and boxes. "Something besides this clean-up." Apparently she'd been reorganizing them.

I didn't ever remember her baking. I didn't even know she knew how.

She poured me a mug and handed it across. I sipped and picked up a sandwich. It was turkey salad. "Is this Richard's Christmas turkey?"

She nodded. "They said we could finish celebrating when you were better. I told them I would host New Year's. I'm not sure Richard is doing well." She seated herself across from me in a wingback chair. "You're up for talking? You'll tell me if you get tired?"

"Yes," I said, thinking I needed to call Richard.

"It's a long story, but it's about you and me, and our gift. I'm sorry I didn't tell you earlier, but when I'm finished, perhaps you'll understand why."

I wished she would get on with it. How bad could it be?

"When I was fifteen—" She stopped, pressed her lips together. The skin around them bleached out under the pressure. She suddenly thrust back her shoulders and started again. "When I was fifteen, I was raped. You're the result."

I couldn't breathe. I couldn't swallow. I couldn't feel any part of my body. *Rape? I was a child of rape?* How had she lived with that?

How would I?

A moment ago, I thought I was coming into a stronger, more centered self. Now I felt shame at having been born, at being the result of my mother's pain, as if I was at fault for what happened.

"Why did you keep me?" I whispered.

"Clara, I love you so much, and I am so sorry your life began that way, but I wouldn't trade you for anything. I only wish I hadn't had to experience what I did for you to come into the world."

Everything about my mother fell into sharp relief: the ambivalence, the coldness, the distance, the books about trauma and grief, the meditation, the therapy. Finally, she made sense. But now *I* didn't make any sense at all.

"You are the reason for Hugh's murder, Hetty's murder, the break-ins here. I know who's behind it, and I'm pretty sure I know why, but I can't prove it. I'm telling you so you'll protect yourself."

"From whom?"

"My rapist."

"You know who did it? Why isn't he in jail, rotting away in solitary confinement?" Rage welled up, momentarily relieving the shame that threatened to overwhelm me.

"I couldn't prove it, Clara. He paid off the doctor who examined me after the rape, and the ob-gyn I saw while pregnant. He's a powerful man."

"Who is it, Mother? You have to tell me who my real father is."

"He's *not* your real father. The man who raised you is your real father. This man conceived you in hate—and you must never—ever!—forget that."

"Who is he?"

She bit her lip again. Lights from a passing car flashed across the doors, probably the patrol car the chief had promised would regularly check the house.

"Andrew Winters," she said.

Something inside me, like a soft burrowing animal, hunkered down at her answer, as if it were satisfied that what it had known all along were suddenly proven true. The rage sharpened, but I focused it. I needed to know more.

My hands gripped handfuls of blanket. "What happened?"

"I made the mistake of telling Mary Ellen about my intuition. She told Andrew. I was so lonely, Clara. No one understood. And then my mother grounded me when she found out." She rubbed at a spot on the tray with her fingertip.

"Andrew cozied up to me. He sat next to me in class, offered to carry my books, ate lunch with me and your father. I started to get disturbing images, all about burning and fire." She laughed a little, like metal on slate. "Maybe he'll end up in hell...

"He finally got around to what he wanted, which was for me to use my gift to see if he should run for class president, if he should apply to Princeton or Yale, if he should run for local office after college. If he would ever be President. I was to become his personal fortune teller, and God help me if I got the answers wrong."

I held still, fearful any movement would throw her off her story and ignite my own brushfire of feelings.

"The previous year, the boy who ran against him in the school election got into a terrible car crash. He almost didn't walk again; he didn't make it back to school for the rest of the semester. Some people said Andrew tampered with the brakes on his car. He hadn't done it himself, he never does anything himself. He set up a favor system—he'd help you get a good test grade or get a bully off your back and you'd owe him—a sort of whispery economy floating just below the radar. No one would talk about it, because Andrew always knew if you'd stepped out of line and he made you pay."

"He raped you himself." Invisible question mark at the end.

She re-crossed her legs the other way. "It was a personal rejection. I'd wager it was the first and last misstep he ever made."

"What did you do when he asked you to predict the future?"

"You know it doesn't work that way. I only got the burning images, and I figured those didn't fit his plan. I very sweetly told him that I couldn't help him. He didn't ask again; instead, he found me after the honors convocation, the one event my mother had allowed me to attend. I was receiving an award for an essay I'd written about the mystic Julian of Norwich. Your grandfather was late picking me up, and Andrew offered me a ride home. I felt the fury billowing off him and told him my father would be worried if I wasn't there when he arrived. I wasn't anyway because Andrew manhandled me around the side of the school behind the dumpsters, forced me down on the filthy ground and ripped away my skirt and panties."

"Mother!" Shocked, I started to get up, but her hand locked me in place.

"You need to know he's vicious, Clara. I'll spare you the worst of it, but he slapped me repeatedly, until it felt like my cheek would crack open. My left eye swelled shut, my lower lip split. Broken glass on the asphalt sliced into my back; I needed stitches there and in my vagina. He bruised my face, wrists, upper arms, and thighs, and the ground scraped my back and thighs. The doctor spent a long time that night digging out glass fragments."

"How could the doctor see that and not turn Winters in?" Wasn't that medical malpractice? I was twitching from side to side, as if the movement would dispel my rage.

"Dr. Hankin had just been caught on the drug charges, and—"

"Hankin?!"

"Andrew's father persuaded the medical board that Joe deserved a second chance and the new practice in the city. It's probably why Wendy pulled that hysterical stunt on you in Whole Foods the other day. I would imagine Andrew's been pressuring Joe to keep his mouth shut.

"Joe did something for me, though, and that's what Andrew is after. Joe took tissue and semen samples. This was before rape kits were in common use, but he knew what to do: he wrote up and dated his report, and his nurse signed as a witness to my examination. Just before you arrived home, I finally managed to get some of Andrew's DNA by swiping a glass he set down at a party. I had a DNA test done, proving you're Andrew's daughter."

I nodded, remembering Dr. Hankin swabbing my cheek fifteen years before. I hadn't thought a thing about it. I'd gone in to make sure my vaccinations were up-to-date before leaving for France. Apparently, Mother had had it tested then, compared Andrew's to those results.

I thought, picked out the core piece of information. "Winters wants to be President."

"Yes."

"That's what the intruder was looking for. That report. The DNA test."

"Yes. And I don't know where it is."

"I took it from your cottage. It's in my night table upstairs."

CHAPTER 25

e stopped, encased in the kind of silence horror brings. All politicians weren't evil, but this one was, and he needed to be stopped.

"I'm sorry." I rubbed my hands down my thighs. I couldn't stop trembling.

"Sorry for what?"

"Because of me, you can't move on, you can't forget. I'm amazed you can bear to look at me."

"There were days I couldn't." She looked at me hard. "I was afraid you would turn out like him. You've carried your anger around for such a long time, and anger skews people. But you didn't. You try to do the right thing." At last, she reached her hand toward me and I took it. "I am honored to have you as a daughter, Clara."

I held my breath to prevent my tears. I couldn't even imagine what it cost her to say that, but I needed to absorb it before I could tell her the same. Even though I knew it was crazy, saying anything positive seemed like absolving Andrew Winters of responsibility.

"You think he killed Hugh?" I asked.

"Yes."

"Himself?"

"No. Not that."

"But why?"

"Those notations on the lists you gave me the other day? They correlate to constituents who are giving big private donations to his Political Action Committees, as regularly as once a month. Some of the donors began giving on significant dates. Joe Hankin started contributing shortly after he moved his practice into the city. That's thirty-five years of campaign donations, long before Winters declared for a national seat. Hankin supported him through council seats, local government, and the state senate. That's a pretty loyal donor."

My toe started tapping the floor in agitation.

"Then there's sweet old Melton Honey. He had a few business problems ten years ago or so, something to do with environmental regulations. The state was going to make him perform a very expensive clean-up, when suddenly the problems disappeared. Melton's regular donations started coming in shortly after that, but they came through his company, his wife, other company employees."

"So the 'B' in those notations is for blackmail? Winters is blackmailing his way into the Senate? Oh, for god's sake!" The trembling congealed into tension in my shoulders and jaw; if I held the blanket tight enough around me, maybe I wouldn't crack apart.

"Andrew would call it trading favors, just as he did in school."

"Right. I make your problem go away and, because you are so grateful, you fund my campaigns *for thirty-five years*? I understand a few donations, maybe even a one-time payoff, but these people are scared. These are incidents that could lose them their wealth and position and put them behind bars." I loosened my hands from the chair arms. "So what do the other letters stand for? BRE? BSA?"

Mother rubbed at the finish on her nail polish. "I'm pretty sure the RE is for the rape evidence that Hankin withheld. I'm not sure about the SA."

"The abbreviations indicate the infraction? SA was on Wendy's file. Substance abuse?"

Mother nodded. "That makes sense."

"What did Hugh have to do with all this?" My head had been spinning before being knocked out; now, it felt even worse. Stuff fizzled in the air like a blender full of poisonous fruit and ice.

"That's the link I haven't figured out. I told Hugh what I knew, but he was bound by doctor-patient confidentiality. He would never have shared any of this, and he would never have said anything to Winters. I keep circling it and wondering, Clara." She leaned forward to rest her elbows on her knees.

I got up to pace the room, moving gingerly from the French doors to the hall door and back again, weaving around Mother's boxes like a sheep dog trying to herd them. It was a path lit only by the light reflecting off the snow outside. Daylight had gone and an early moonrise cast eerie shadows in the room. The movement eased some of my jailed emotion. "Would anything cause him to break confidentiality?"

"Hugh was unimpeachable. He had to be or he'd lose all his clients."

"Paul told me he talked everything over with Maria."

She stood abruptly and flipped on a light. The brightness hurt my eyes. She was staring at me.

"Maybe someone *thought* he was going to break confidentiality," I said.

"What did you do with Hugh upstairs on the night of my Christmas party?"

I sucked in a breath. "What does that have to do with anything?"

"Don't be coy with me, Clara."

"You're blaming this on me? How original." The simmering rage billowed out. "It's not my fault your beloved Hugh died. Don't target me."

Suddenly dizzy, I grabbed the back of her chair for balance. I was lashing out not at her, but at the injustice of Andrew Winters getting away with *this* for thirty-five years.

Target.

That was the word that Loretta used that had been bugging me. That's how Winters referred to them the night I'd worked over Melton Honey. Did people really refer to their donors that way?

They might if they perceived them not as donors and colleagues but as blackmail opportunities...

"Clara, what did you do upstairs with Hugh?"

"*Nothing.* I did nothing but ask Hugh about you."

"About me?"

"I came home because I was worried, Mother. Because I've been having dreams for weeks about your running from something. Why do you think I've been so persistent? I'm trying to save you—because I didn't save Father."

She sat as abruptly as she'd stood, looking as if even the soft chair might break her in half. "Oh, Clara."

"Why does it matter what I did with Hugh?"

"If they thought he told you about the DNA link or... about the blackmail... they had to stop him before he did either of those things."

"Then why kill him *after* he went upstairs with me?"

"Maybe they figured his death would warn me to keep my silence and make sure you kept yours. And if he hadn't said anything, they'd eliminated the threat that he would tell anyone else."

"Who else would he tell? The press? You just said he wouldn't."

"He talked everything over with Maria."

I nodded. "What influence would she have over Andrew Winters?"

"None. But she knows someone who would, and I know him, too."

"Who?"

She shook her head. "That's enough for tonight, Clara. I need.... We'll pick this up later, when our minds are clearer."

I protested but Mother got up, the tray in her hands. I followed her into the kitchen and leaned against the counter, watching her place the cookies in a tin and rinse out the mugs.

"Go upstairs," she said. "I'll be along in a minute."

I trudged up to my bedroom, disheartened. We'd started to be honest with each other, but it hadn't lasted. Mother had spent a long time keeping secrets from me. But keeping secrets was human. Some things just belonged to us and no one else, except when others could get hurt.

Then again, the thought of Mother coming to kiss me good night felt strangely comforting. I put on cozy pajamas, a pair I'd found lurking in a bottom drawer. The pink flannel, pants and top were soft and almost sheer from wear. I wrapped myself in a red fleece robe and climbed under the bedcovers, suddenly chilled all the way through.

With a sudden rush of tears, I turned my face into the pillow, smelled the comforting lavender, burrowed into the sheets, hoping that, if I got far enough in, I wouldn't be the child of a rape victim. I wouldn't have terrifying dreams, or feel I had to save a woman I barely knew from a menace I didn't understand.

Mother's hand on my shoulder startled me. I crabbed back in the bed, nearly kicking her in my haste to scoot away. Half the bedcovers came with me, and before I was aware of it, I was at the edge, scrabbling for something to hold onto.

She grabbed my arm. "Clara! It's me!"

Breathing hard, we stared at each other. I shook my head, trying to clear the fog, and felt a deep, painful twinge from the gash. "I'm sorry. I don't know what I was thinking."

"I've spooked you, haven't I? With all this talk." She began to smooth out the bedclothes. I hunched back into the middle of the bed and propped myself up with pillows. She sat at the edge.

"Yeah." I felt tears threaten again, stopped talking until I regained control. "My skull *and* my brain feel cracked." I attempted a grin, thinking of the slug. Maybe that had been a warning.

"I wish Hugh were around," she said.

"He anchored you, didn't he?"

"Your father did, too." She ran her hand across the spread, a handmade flowered quilt she'd bought from an artist exhibiting at the Museum of Arts and Design. Bands of aquamarine and silver divided the flower blocks. "I'm glad you're home, Clara. It's good to have someone around I can trust."

I pulled my knees up to my chest and wrapped my arms around them. Being someone my mother trusted seemed like a lot of responsibility. Look at what had happened to the others: dead. I bit my lip.

She motioned to a glass of warm milk on the side table. "I put a little something in that to help you sleep." She kissed my forehead and got up. "Good night, darling."

Bathed in the first maternal love I'd felt in a long time, I drank the milk down until it was only a thin film coating the glass. Tucked under the covers, I should have slept dream-free. Instead, the moment Mother shut out the light, images started tramping furrows in my brain, like a circus horse on a tether, round and round and round. Only Mother's "little something" eventually knocked them down enough that I could rest in a sort of nether world, halfway between dreams and waking, halfway between truth and desire.

CHAPTER 26

other woke me at nine the next morning; we had to be at the church by ten-thirty for the funeral service. If we got there a little early, she said, she'd call Chief DuPont about the interview she'd promised him. I hoped the man Hetty had been having an affair with would be there as well. Somehow, I had to identify this guy; he might know what got her killed.

Between my general exhaustion and the bump on my head, I felt as if I were negotiating the world from inside a bad Halloween mask—the kind where you can't really breathe and it gets all steamed up and you have to press the mask to your face so you can see what's to the sides as well as straight ahead.

As I shut off the shower, the front door bell rang, a pealing set of tones meant to evoke Notre Dame. My father had installed the whimsy after an anniversary trip to Paris. A loud and imperious knocking followed the chimes, then the chimes rang out again.

I flung a towel around my head, threw on my robe, and ran down the stairs while tying the belt. Mother had gotten there first. Mary Ellen stood on the front step.

"Ringing once would have done the trick, Mary Ellen. No need to bring the house down." Mother's icy tones were never better employed.

"Let me in." She pushed past us, shutting the door quickly. She looked perfectly turned out as always, her white shirt tucked into black riding pants, her boots spit-shined. "I have to talk to you, Constance."

"Why should I talk to you?" She ran her hand through her hair. Not a strand dared fall out of place.

The cold floor tiles were frosting my bare feet, but I wasn't missing a second of this. I wiggled my toes to keep the blood flowing. Mother noticed. Mother noticed everything.

"Because no matter how much you hate me, you're curious."

"Whatever it is," Mother said, "I'm not going to stand here while Clara gets pneumonia. "Honey—"

Was she addressing me?

"—put some warm clothes on. Mary Ellen and I will be in the kitchen."

She faced Mary Ellen again. "I'm not talking to you without a witness, and you have twenty minutes, minus however long Clara takes to dress."

I hurried up to the bedroom, squeezing water from my hair on the way. I grabbed flannel-lined jeans and a heavy sweater and took them into the bathroom where I shimmied into them with one hand while using the hairdryer with the other. Five minutes later I was no glamour-girl, but I was presentable.

I rushed back down the stairs and into the kitchen. Mary Ellen and Mother had arranged themselves on opposite sides of the kitchen table, like opponents in a union negotiation. Sun streamed in over my mother's shoulders, probably blinding Mary Ellen. I imagined that Mother had directed her to that side of the table deliberately. Between them, a tray with the coffee carafe, mugs, sugar, and milk rested like the Berlin Wall. Neither woman was speaking. Mother flipped through the *Wall Street Journal*. Mary Ellen watched her.

"Want me to pour?" I asked. Mother nodded without looking up. She'd found the editorial page.

"Mary Ellen?" I asked. She nodded. I filled a mug and pushed it toward her, then poured one for mother. I poured one for myself and sat down. Mary Ellen doctored the drink with milk and three teaspoons of sugar, stirring vigorously.

Mother took hers black and reluctantly put the paper to the side. "Well?" She folded her arms.

Mary Ellen sipped her coffee. "You should stop meddling in our affairs."

"Meddling?"

"You're poking around where you don't belong, Constance, and Clara's doing it, too."

My mother let out a raucous laugh, like a drunken snort. "Please. You gave up all rights to ask me for anything thirty-six years ago when your sociopathic brother raped me in a parking lot. Thirty-six years that he's been running around free on this planet doing god-knows-what to who-knows-whom else. Thirty-six years that you've been backing his story and telling everyone in this town what a liar I am."

I'd never heard her so furious or raw or honest. It was painful.

Mary Ellen remained impervious, the ice queen in her ice castle. "If you don't, we'll make sure Clara's dear friend Paul is brought up on sexual harassment charges, and Clara's other dear friend Bailey loses her law license for conspiring with the Democratic candidate while working for Republicans. And then there's dear HIV-infected Richard. So many delicious possibilities for him." She said it all without a trace of emotion.

If I'd been a different person, I would have reached across the table and banged her head against the wall until her eyes glazed over and she died. The hatred shocked me. It felt a little too close to my Winters biology and too far from the person I wanted to be.

"And to prevent this, you want us to do what, exactly?" Mother's demeanor was as icy as Mary Ellen's. It was as if the threats hadn't registered.

"Clara will resign from the campaign. Can't have the scandal of a firing. You will burn the DNA report. Clara will stop running around town, talking to everyone she can find about Hugh's death and your past."

"Hugh's murder remains unsolved?"

"And Hetty's. So tragic." She pouted. "You know Andrew is obsessed. If you don't acquiesce, he will find a way to eliminate all the... obstacles."

"You mean he'd murder us, too?"

She shrugged.

I looked at Mother and Mother looked at me. Having watched a lot of TV, as far as I could figure in my TV-educated mind, we'd just witnessed a confession to plan murder and conspiracy. Maybe it didn't count if your brother was a lawyer.

"There are two witnesses here to your threats, Mary Ellen."

"Should I call Kyle?" I asked her.

Mary Ellen sneered. "Oh yes, let's get your little boyfriend involved. Your little *black* boyfriend. Let's just see who the judges believe in this town, me and my brother or that newcomer with his sketchy history."

Sketchy history? What sketchy history? Was that why he wouldn't talk about New Orleans?

Mother said, "All these years, Mary Ellen, and you're still his lackey. Don't you want a life of your own?"

"I've been a part of it from the start."

Mother's eyes turned ice cold and she leaned forward. "Yes, Mary Ellen. I have known all these years you sold me to your brother for a prom date."

I looked back and forth between them. "I don't get it."

Mother sighed. "Mary Ellen delayed your grandfather, telling him some story about her college prospects and how excited she was to be going to his alma mater. As I recall, you never did go to Princeton, did you?"

Mary Ellen didn't look ashamed or contrite. She looked the same as always: calculating. I wondered if she practiced that look in the mirror. *Aunt Mary*

Ellen. I shuddered, suddenly feeling her blood in my veins, and flashing on the blood dreams. Maybe that's what they'd meant—it was the blood that was coming for Mother—the blood connection she had with the Winters through me. My vision was suddenly filled with blood, and I shook my head to clear it, but I still felt it in the back of my throat.

I said, "You've done your duty. Is there something else you want?"

Mary Ellen's voice took on a wheedling tone. "Andrew wants to win. If there's some way you could tell me what the outcome of this election would be... if it were negative, maybe what we could do to change that..." She tipped her head to the side, shrugged her eyebrows, as if to say we knew what she was talking about.

Mother's chin went up.

Uh oh.

I thought about making more coffee. I thought about getting out of the kitchen. I thought about moving to Antarctica. I thought about all the lovely long, lazy days I'd had when I could do pretty much do whatever I wanted to do without worrying about the consequences. I thought about life before I knew how I'd been conceived, before I knew for sure that Mother had the same gift I did, before I remembered hurting Hetty and tried to apologize, before I met Andrew Winters. I thought about working in the garden with my father, about finding Mother's meditation house. And I thought about how everything in my life, and everything in my mother's life stemmed from this question, the one that Mary Ellen was again asking my mother, the one that had nearly destroyed her life thirty-five years ago.

Why is it that we have to keep answering the same questions? It's as if, in each new incarnation of the soul, a new torment must be overcome. It would be so much easier if we could deal with all the suffering in one lifetime and then proceed directly to "go."

And when I become God, I'm going to make it work that way.

I pulled myself out of my wandering thoughts. I wanted to put my head down on the table and take a nap, but Mother and I had to deal with the suffering embodied by Mary Ellen and Andrew Winters and their incessant greed for power. Mary Ellen was still talking. Mary Ellen was always talking. "If you'd just helped us all those years ago, Constance, your life would have been so different. You and I, we might still be friends." Was that cajolery I heard? "If you're unwilling, perhaps Clara...?"

In a split second, the temptation offered to my mother all those years ago became mine. I guess that's why they call it temptation. It's so silky and it seems that giving in will solve all your problems. Just this one time. Just this one thing. Just this, and everything else will be easy. No consequences. The snake in the Garden of Eden was female for sure—or at least spoke the male will with a female voice.

Then I realized that it offered absolution. I hadn't done the right thing by my father and I'd lost him. Mother couldn't give the Winters what they wanted; it would destroy her. But I could. I could get the Winters off Mother's back and my dreams off mine, and go back to Paris, far enough away that Winters wouldn't bother to come after me. He just needed the one answer, and I could supply it. I could save my mother. Finally, something made sense, something I could do to make it all come out all right.

Before I could think about whether using my intuition for the Winters was a good idea, I had to get everyone out of this room alive. The kitchen was filled with knives, hot coffee, heavy cutting boards, too many possibilities to count. If she did something, it would only make her appear more capable of having murdered Hugh, even though she couldn't have murdered Hugh, right? Because she'd said she hadn't murdered Hugh, and why would she, and anyway, it had to be one of the Winters because they were evil.

Stop.

I shook my head again. I must have looked like a wet dog.

I glanced at Mother. Her lips were parted, teeth bared, as if she was going to bite some part of Mary Ellen's anatomy off.

Okay, I would go with Mother's version for the moment. I said, "We're not fortune tellers, Mary Ellen. We don't see what *you* want us to see. Whatever intuition we get may have nothing to do with the question you ask, or we may get nothing at all. Asking us the same question over and over will not change the truth. Either way, threatening our lives is a prosecutable offense. A lawyer's sister should know that." I stood up. "Now, if you'll excuse us, we have to get ready for a funeral."

Mary Ellen seethed as I spoke, looking at Mother as if I were only the mouthpiece for her ideas. "It's not Hetty's funeral you should be worried about," she spat.

I followed her to the door and watched her stalk to her car, slam the door and spin angrily around the drive on her way out.

In the kitchen, Mother was still seated at the table, her hands clenched into fists, her teeth still bared. "Is she gone?" One of the fists held a small paring knife. Where had she gotten that?

I nodded and shoved my hands in the pockets of my jeans to keep them from shaking. Then I had to sit down because I couldn't breathe and my thighs felt funny, as if they were made of Spritz cookie dough. My head still pounded.

"Are you okay?" I asked.

"I haven't been okay for thirty-five years," she said.

"Mother, you need to put the knife down." She looked at me as if I had suddenly registered in her field of vision. "I saw her get in her car and drive out."

"Her energy is still here."

"It will dissipate."

"Only when she is gone."

"She is gone, I told you—"

"I mean forever. We have to get rid of them forever."

"Mother. Put the knife down."

She hadn't stopped staring at me. I was starting to feel like a bug under a glass cloche in the middle of a summer picnic. "For the last time," she said, "I didn't kill Hugh."

"I didn't—"

She wouldn't let me get my protest out. "Andrew won't stop until he has all the power he can possibly get, and that includes power over individuals and public power in office and the power that wealth confers." She put the knife on the table gently, as if it were a tender living thing. "That list you have? I can show connections; Kyle will have to investigate. Even if I can't prove them all, the scandal may be enough to stop that bastard's campaign."

"And if not?"

"I can't think about that."

"Should we tell the chief about Mary Ellen's death threats?"

"He'll be at the funeral. We'll tell him then." She looked up, her eyes fierce and dark. "I will smear Andrew and the Winters name like blood across the tabloids." She stood. "I'm going up to get ready." She left the kitchen and I heard her steps tapping across the hall's wood floor.

I put the knife carefully away in the drawer.

CHAPTER 27

other and I hurried from the car toward the service. The church, a grey stone Episcopal crowning Main Street, rose stark and forbidding from the snow at its base. Low clouds scudded just above its steeple and threatened more snow. Barely a minute before Hetty's service began, we slipped into the back row. From there, I could unobtrusively study the attendees. Most important, where was the chief, and who was Hetty's boyfriend? I started methodically scanning, row by row, wondering how I would know the boyfriend when I saw him.

The service began with a liturgical procession, the priest and choir filing down the aisle, while burning incense drifted up and carried, supposedly, the congregation's prayers to God. I wondered how many in the room believed that, and how many were here for show. American politicians had to say they believed to get elected; Winters would say whatever it took, but now I knew who he truly was.

After a hymn and some Biblical readings, the priest, solemn in his vestments and black stole, reminded us how central Hetty had been to town life over the past twenty years and asked if anyone wanted to speak of her contributions. A kind looking, middle-aged man with salt-and pepper-hair talked about Hetty's farm and meticulous care of her animals. The librarian praised her volunteer work with the kids on a community garden project. A brilliant red-head told us Hetty had been a good counselor, helping him after his wife passed away. The stories reinforced how little attention I'd paid her.

Hetty and I should have been friends. We'd had fathers die, we had stepfathers, our mothers were close friends, we both had an intuitive gift. Yet we'd never clicked. Why? What attracts us to one person and makes another unattractive? Look at Winters and his little bevy of women. How could they be drawn to a man who—to me—was so decidedly evil?

My attention was pulled back to the service, as Winters, unable to pass up a public gathering, lauded Hetty's work on his campaign in a brief and self-serving statement of mourning, keeping us all apprised that he was still running for office and still needed our support. He sat down, third row, right side, Mary Ellen and Andrew's wife Jennifer sandwiching him: Wonder Bread with bologna in the middle. I felt soiled by association. If he was my father, who did that make me?

Even though half the town had come, and many spoke warmly of her, Hetty didn't seem to have any friends. No one spoke of closeness, of a confidant who would be missed. She'd been an odd duck, hard to get to know, prickly enough to keep people at a distance. How had she managed to have an affair—and with whom? I surreptitiously observed the faces around me again, looking for men I recognized from the campaign, as well as obsessively checking every few minutes that the Winters remained together and seated. Mary Ellen made me want to sit with my back to a wall.

By the time we left, both the sky and Mother had cracked into sullen gloom. I hadn't seen the chief anywhere, although surely he'd attended. Mother, in charge of arranging the reception, refused to let me spend time after the service searching for him, snapping that she would call him later. I was a little relieved to be able to put off our revelations.

Mother had gotten a caterer and wait staff for the funeral luncheon, and rented everything else—tables and chairs, plates, glasses, linens. I thought Ernie and Loretta's house might pop like a dried seed pod, but Mother kept all the pieces under control, including persuading Loretta to sit and eat. I greeted and gave condolences and kept trying to figure out which man was involved with Hetty. I came up empty. I looked at the people eating and thought the shock and guilt we felt were only as real as the rented plates in our hands.

Most of the guests drifted away by two o'clock. Once, I saw the chief and tried to get his attention, but he merely waved. Later, I noticed Mother corner him and Bailey. Before I could find out her arrangements, Ernie cornered me. He looked exhausted.

"You and me, we need to talk."

"Now?" I said.

"Fifteen years is long enough to put a conversation off."

He led me to a small office created from one of the bedrooms. "This one's mine," he said. "Loretta's got the one next door. When we're ready for lunch, we bang on the wall." He tried to smile, but it didn't make it to his face. "Have a seat."

A desk faced the room's one window, and bookshelves lined two walls. More books lay stacked on the floor, and a well-used red leather wing chair hugged an arched floor lamp with a butterscotch linen shade. I slid onto the leather, braced myself. Ernie sat in his desk chair, a practical looking black job on wheels, and rolled toward me. "You're grown up, Clara. You've had fifteen years to sow your wild oats, figure yourself out. It's time you came home and faced your responsibilities."

"Ernie, I—"

He held up his hand. "You knew from the moment your father's will was read that this moment would come."

I thought about my father and how much he had loved his work, about all those trips he'd taken me on to show me his work in action. I remembered the smell of worms and dirt, the sharp citrus of green leaves, the silk and glitter of flower petals. I sank into memories, the crumble of dark earth across my palms, the sun's warm hand on my neck. And then, an image interrupted of my turning away from Mother, turning away from trying to persuade her that he needed help.

I'd abandoned him. The thought snapped me from the reverie, like an electric shock in my gut. "What do you want?" I asked.

Ernie gave me a funny look. "What you father wanted was for you to learn the business from the ground up. Sorry, bad pun." He shook his head. "Half of it is yours anyway; I've run it for you, sent your profits to your investment company, and not complained about it, Clara, but I'm not a young man anymore and the responsibilities are getting to be too much for me. The business is growing, and with Hetty gone, Loretta needs me. I need a partner I can trust—someone I can turn the business over to in another five years when I retire. That person should be you. If you don't want the responsibility, then we need to sell soon, while the market's good and buyers are interested."

I thought about what my nomadic life had netted me. Not much, as Bailey pointed out, besides experience and a soon-to-be ex-husband. I had, however, fallen in love with many parts of the world, and I'd organized my life abroad around visiting major gardens and making friends of their directors. Not being able to pick up and travel at a moment's notice daunted me, but if I had no meaningful purpose, where was the thrill?

"What would you think about making us a more international company? Specialty landscaping projects, big installations worldwide."

"I think, Clara, that if that's the kind of business you want to build, you've spent fifteen years setting up the contacts for it." He shook his finger at me. "You've got the education and the eye, but you have a long way to go before you understand what it takes to run a business like ours—especially if you want to work internationally. You need a year of supervised time on the job before the state will license you, and you need to start studying to take the LARE exams. CLARB offers the multiple choice part twice a year, and the next sitting is in March."

I stared at him, felt my world closing in. Could I really manage a business? Could I deal with this town permanently? Could I handle living close to Mother? What about Andrew Winters? What if I had to see my rapist father at Starbucks? Or as my senator in Washington? Getting far away from him was supposed to be my reward for using my gift to save my mother.

Ernie thought I hadn't understood him, "The L-A-R-E, Landscape Architect Registration Examination?'

I shook my head to clear it. "Right, CLARB, the Council of Landscape Architectural Registration Boards."

Ernie nodded and went on, as if I had agreed with him. "In the meantime, I'd like you to come to the office. We're shorthanded anyway; our technology guy just left for another job. It's a big blow, and it would be great if you could find his replacement." He shrugged. "That's just administrative stuff, but it's as good a place as any for you to start."

Wind and sun had creased Ernie's face, and those long delicate hands showed age spots and loose skin. I knew he was near sixty, so his willingness to give it five more years, well, maybe that was generosity on his part. He loved my father a great deal as did I, but a lot was at stake. "I need a few days to think."

I had to deal with Mother's situation first.

He nodded, rubbing his hand tiredly across his forehead, and in that moment, I really saw his age. It wasn't in the physical things; it was in a sort of sagging of spirit, of being worn down by too much responsibility for too long. Hetty's death would weight him now, too, as would the grief Loretta carried. That grief would always be a heavy piece of their souls. My feelings of guilt and loss around my father were still a heavy piece of mine.

Ernie said, "How about we give it a couple of weeks? Things will muddle along for a while with minimal guidance before I'll need to put out some fires. That gives you time to sort out things with Constance."

I guess he meant that I needed to make peace with her. I leaned across and squeezed his hand. "You're right, and I know you're right. It's time. I just need to let it all settle."

He looked at me for a long moment. "And," he said, "your mother needs you."

He was right about that, too.

———

By the time Mother and I sat down to review the blackmail scheme with Bailey, it was nearly five o'clock. A domestic dispute out on Alston Road required the chief's attention, so we started with Bailey; as campaign lawyer, she had the right to know what we'd found. I dreaded telling her, but I couldn't let her be blindsided either.

Mother said Maria was coming, too, but didn't say why.

We sat at the kitchen table, another pot of coffee in front of us. Bailey had changed out of her funeral suit into a pair of jeans with holes in the knees, a long V-necked sweater with a lace camisole under it, and a pair of spiky-heeled boots. I wanted to be her when I grew up.

My mother shoved the list toward Bailey. "There are irregularities in these campaign donations."

Bailey turned toward me, a hard look on her face. "You removed data from the office."

"You wanted to know if anything was off. You even asked me to use my intuition, said you were worried about Winters. Well, we've found something."

She started flipping pages.

Mother began getting containers out of the refrigerator. Hummus, carrot sticks, cheese and crackers, cold cuts and grapes appeared on the table. She put a plate in front of me and began filling it with food. "You've eaten almost nothing all day," she said.

"I'm not hungry."

"I don't care. You'll eat something because your body has been traumatized and I want you to heal quickly. We need to solve this and fast, so Andrew doesn't get elected, and we can all get on with our lives." Her sharp tone made me wonder if she regretted telling me about the rape.

Bailey looked up. "Andrew doesn't get elected? That's your goal?"

I ate a couple bits of cheese, realized I was ravenous. Maybe the increase in my blood sugar would deal with some of my wooziness.

As I ate, Mother told Bailey the story of the rape. Bailey's face snapped through emotions like one of those flip pads we played with as kids: pain, shock, horror, pity.

"Oh my god, Constance, all these years and you never pursued it? Why?"

"I didn't want Clara to have to live publicly with what had happened to me. We could deal with it privately, and we have. Until now. He thinks he's gotten away with it. He thinks he's invincible. Mary Ellen protects him. And I suspect he's getting bad advice somewhere." She paused, looked thoughtful. "Clara, don't you think it's interesting that Mary Ellen showed up on the morning of Hetty's funeral to ask us, well, what she did?"

Mother glanced at Bailey. I said, "Bailey knows about the intuition, Mother. Bailey has known for years."

Mother looked only mildly surprised and waved her hand like a wand. "I didn't want to, well... if she didn't know..."

"We get it."

Bailey tapped a long finger on the table. "You mean, Hetty supplied Winters with psychic predictions and when she died, he panicked?"

"He can't go twenty-four hours without a psychic's help?" I said. "I can't believe that. And anyway, why would he kill her if she was telling him what he wanted to hear?"

"Maybe she wasn't. Maybe she wasn't a fraud, like Hugh thought, and she'd started telling him the same truths I told him thirty-five years ago." Mother picked at a cube of cheese with her fingernail, crumbing it onto the plate.

Bailey frowned. "Hetty wasn't born when you turned him down."

"When he realized what I could do, he became obsessed with his future, but who knows what he did in those intervening years? He needed his narcissistic vision of himself confirmed—over and over. A whole industry of sham phone psychics and card readers and alternative therapists will give clients whatever answers they want."

I said, "That's why Hugh was trying to shut Hetty down? To stop her from reading for Andrew Winters? Was that revenge for you?"

"Oh, god, no. Hugh did think Hetty was a fraud. He worried that her attention-seeking behavior would get her in over her head." She folded her hands neatly on the table. "People who want that kind of information, some of them will believe anything, and they're willing to pay anything for it. If you give them the wrong answer, or you don't know how to read them or phrase what you tell them in a way that's easy for them to handle, well, it's a tricky business."

I looked at her questioningly.

"I have done a fair amount of research on the subject over the years." She shrugged. "Hugh encouraged it. I wanted to know how I could use the gift." She straightened in her chair, a proper lady. "However, nothing presented itself that was, well, appropriate."

"What did Winters want to know?" Bailey asked.

"He wanted to know how to achieve the Presidency. That's all he's ever wanted. Lord knows what would happen once those four or eight years were over. God forbid we would ever have to suffer through them."

Bailey threw her head back and let out a monster sigh. "Thanks, Clara. You've created the perfect storm. On the one hand, the partners and the election law guy are going to blame all this on me. On the other, if there's a trial, I'm the criminal attorney. Billable hours are always good news."

"That's cold," I said.

She laughed.

The doorbell rang. Mother went to get it and we heard low voices. A moment later, she and Maria walked into the kitchen. "Maria has news." She looked at me. "This is what I've been waiting on, Clara."

Maria sat down next to Bailey, looking tired, like part of her foundation had washed out from under her. Her long silver braid gleamed in the overhead light. Mother offered her coffee or wine, but she shook her head. "I'd rather just get this over with," she said. Then she told us that, just before Mother's fête, Hugh had closeted himself with an old friend, Vance Hardison, the Republican party boss for the entire Western district. Vance had tremendous influence, enough to investigate a candidate's ethics, even one as well established as Winters.

"Vance sat next to me at dinner," Mother said.

The silver-haired man.

I said, "So Hugh knew about the blackmail?"

"He pieced it together from client complaints," Maria said.

Bailey said, "But there's no evidence unless they testify, right?"

"Then we find someone to talk," Mother said.

Maria slid her hand down her braid. "We might find someone, but that only solves the blackmail. Two people have been murdered, one of whom I loved very much."

"Can you tie Andrew to the murders?" Bailey asked.

Mother said. "He never did his own dirty work."

"Someone got close to both Hugh and Hetty," Bailey said.

I scrubbed my face. "What about Hetty's mystery boyfriend? He was associated with the campaign." Something slid through my consciousness, a color, a dim flutter of green spiked with a thin drool of yellow.

"We don't know who he is," Mother said. Maria stared across the room at the clock, tapping her finger on the table.

Bailey picked off a couple grapes. "This stinks."

"In the meantime," Maria said, "we don't know who else threatens him, who else he thinks he might need to kill."

"Oh, yes we do." Mother stood and left the room. We looked at each other, then followed her into the library, where, as if we were in some nineteenth century novel, she pressed a button on her desk to slide open a panel in the wall. Behind: a fully stocked gun rack.

Where had *that* come from? I thought all the guns were stored in her closet safe. Apparently, Annie Oakley owned a whole other stash.

She pulled a shotgun down, cracked it to check the load, then pumped it. The bark resonated loudly in the small room. She hefted a Glock in her other hand.

"You got licenses for those things?" Bailey asked, casually offhand.

"Of course."

I kept my mouth shut.

"Do you remember how to shoot, Clara?" She handed me the Glock.

I extended my hand to take it—of course I would take it because Mother was handing it to me, even though I hadn't had a license in years. I didn't look at Bailey.

CHAPTER 28

other marched off to New York the next morning to deal with Dr. Gary Hankin, whom she deemed the most likely to cave under pressure. "He'll testify," she insisted. In her emerald green suit and four-inch heels, she had "dressed to kill" she said, and smiled evilly. I wondered if she'd tucked a pistol in her purse.

Maybe my bad feeling about her visit came from another almost sleepless night, afraid I would inadvertently set off the handgun she'd parked by my bedside. When I had finally drifted off, I dreamed of voodoo dolls, large and animate, bleeding from their pin wounds. It should have been zombie-funny, but I instead I ran and ran, feeling their breath, like a feather touch, between my shoulder blades. Now, in an empty, slightly frightening house with a head that still ached and a mind that felt as if it were floating free of my body, I wanted to blot the images out.

I needed somewhere quiet to *think*. I'd made the intuition work for me once; maybe I could do it again. I had to figure out who Hetty's boyfriend was. The meditation cottage was quiet, isolated, perfect—and Mother wouldn't use it today. I levered myself out of the chair, collected the gun, and drove there.

The stable yard was still. I parked and followed the path through the hedge, and, once inside, checked all the rooms. It looked as though no one had visited since I had last been there. The house had only two doors, both locked, and I would hear anyone trying to break in. I took the gun from my bag and dropped it in a kitchen drawer where it would still be easy to access, but I wouldn't shoot myself by mistake. I turned up the heat, brewed tea, then settled cross-legged on the floor, bean bag chair jammed between me and the wall for support, and began the breathing meditation Paul had taught me.

It was hard to concentrate. All these secrets. Whatever I had thought about my life before coming home had eroded over the past weeks. Michelangelo famously said he didn't sculpt, but merely revealed the image already in the marble. I, on the other hand, felt as if one more hit of the chisel would crumble the entire stone into dust. I drifted into half-awareness, returning to Mother's Christmas fête, arranging everyone at the dinner table, watching the eyes that watched me. Hugh to my right. Mother at the head. The polished, silver-haired man—Vance—to Mother's right. Hetty across from me. Hetty watching Hugh. Hetty with that long dissertation on sheep diseases by the Christmas tree, as if she were keeping me from something.

Hugh? I couldn't imagine Hugh as the boyfriend, especially if he thought she was a fraud. So maybe her photographs of Hugh weren't about her being in love with him, as I'd first thought, but some kind of monitoring, looking for something to get Hugh to lay off his attacks on her business. Maybe she needed that extra income from the readings to keep the farm going.

I let her photographs float through my imagination: Hugh, Mother, me, Pete Samuels, Mary Ellen. What did we have in common? Hugh, Mother, me: Hugh's murder. Pete, Mary Ellen, me: working the Winters campaign? I'd seen him that one night as security, if that's what he'd been doing there.

Was Pete Hetty's lover? I had a hard time seeing it, but maybe that's why I'd been in such pain on our date. It still didn't make sense. Why would my going upstairs with Hugh have provoked her to call Pete?

Why would Pete kill Hugh?

Then, with the kind of certainty that always came with intuition, I knew who could tell me. Hetty had been a loner, but even loners told someone when they fell in love, even if it was the person at the pharmacy counter. *Homeopathic remedies for sheep diseases.*

I scrambled up and headed across the yard.

Ernie looked surprised to see me. "What's up, Clara? You come with an answer about your Dad's firm?" He smiled, not believing his own words, and gestured for me to sit. Too antsy, I shook my head.

"Who was Hetty's vet? Someone who used homeopathic stuff."

He settled on the couch, grey lines etching his face. "David Warren. You know him, don't you? He was married to Mary Ellen Winters before he got smart."

I sat down suddenly.

"Warren's practice is in Stamford. He and Morty Hein are pretty much the only big animal vets around. David does dogs and cats too, to pay the bills, but I think he likes working with the horses and cows best."

"At the Christmas party, Hetty mentioned a natural remedy for her sheep. Could he have recommended that?"

"Sure. Warren uses natural remedies a lot. Hein doesn't think much of that 'new-fangled' stuff." He managed a grin.

"Did Warren attend the funeral?" I was trying to put a face to the name.

"Nice looking guy, grey-haired, tall. He spoke briefly about her and the farm." He stuttered over his words. I gave him a minute to recover, trying to recall the man.

"Were they close?"

"I wish I knew, Clara." He rubbed his finger around the diamond stud in his ear. "Hetty became a stranger. I don't think she let anyone know her."

Could Warren be Hetty's affair? If not, would he know if Hetty was having an affair with Pete Samuels?

Ernie let me look up the address in their phone book, and I hugged him goodbye on my way out.

———————

In Connecticut, one goes from lush, large properties surrounded by white fences or charming stone walls to public housing circled with wire fencing like a prison yard with disquieting speed, sometimes in the space of five or six city blocks. In this case, it took ten minutes from my secluded and seemingly safe enclave into the more urban area where Warren practiced. His office was well-located to serve farms like Hetty's, and the small pet owners that, as Ernie said, paid the bills.

Warren's clinic resided in a small, golden brick office building. A large apartment complex rose on the right, laundry hanging off its balconies, and on the left was an empty lot and a big hole where someone had started to build several years earlier. Piles of rock and rotting plywood lay stacked behind the eight-foot wire fencing, and flapping signs read, at intervals, "Keep Out." Given the amount of graffiti on propped-up plywood, the signs didn't seem to be working all that well.

I arrived just before noon, hoping to find Warren ready for lunch. He had already gone, but his friendly receptionist sent me the next street over to a deli where she said I'd find him sitting at a corner table reading the *American Journal of Veterinary Research* and eating a ham sandwich.

The deli was crowded, with a long line out the front door, and most of the tables filled with cops and road crews working their way through big sandwiches or plates of rice and beans. I edged through the din, trying not to bump too many elbows. When I pulled out a chair and sat down at Warren's table, he gave me a sad and bemused look and shut his magazine.

"Clara Montague."

Startled, I said, "You remember me?"

"Hard not to remember the daughter of the woman my ex-wife hates more than anyone else in the world." He quirked a corner of his mouth at me. From the silver hair, I guessed he was a little older than Mary Ellen, but his easy manner, dirty jeans and work boots made me wonder how she had ever said yes to his proposal. "It's a good thing she finally had a daughter of her own, took the edge off her jealousy."

My face must have shown my shock.

He said, "You didn't know Mary Ellen was jealous of your mother?"

I closed my mouth enough to form a word. "No."

"Didn't matter what your mother did, Mary Ellen had to one-up her, even if your mother never knew she'd been one-upped. Exhausting stuff."

My emotional fatigue at the revelations was so great at this point that the lump on my head felt like a minor wound. "That's not it," I managed to get out. "I didn't know she had a daughter. She—you have a daughter? How old is she?"

The girl would be my cousin. My trip from only child, isolated from her family, to having half-siblings and a cousin was giving me rope burn. Wait. That meant Andrew Junior was my half-brother. No wonder Mother and Mary Ellen had flipped out at my marriage proposal joke.

"Fourteen. Beautiful like Mary Ellen. Nice, like me." He smiled, the sad one again.

She'd been born after I left, but how could I not have known? "Do you have custody of—?"

"Emma."

"Mary Ellen never mentioned her."

"That was a condition of our divorce. Emma lived with me, and Mary Ellen couldn't interfere. I don't think she really wanted a child; Emma came late in the marriage. It's not true, but it felt like Mary Ellen filed for divorce the day she gave birth."

"I... I'm sorry."

"What can I do for you, Clara? I imagine it's not an animal problem you're here about." He picked up his sandwich and took a bite.

"You knew Hetty Gardner pretty well."

"No one knew Hetty well." He put the sandwich down and wiped his fingers on a napkin. "I knew her better than most, I guess."

"Did you meet when she started the farm?"

He nodded. I noticed his skin wasn't as sun-toughened as I expected for someone who worked regularly out-of-doors, and his eyes were a nice shade of pale blue, like Paul Newman's. I wondered if he wore a hat to protect his skin, or maybe he was always in the barn with the animals and so—*Get a grip, Clara.* I forced my brain back to the task at hand. "Ernie and Loretta told me Hetty was having an affair with someone close to the Winters' campaign. I'm hoping you can tell me who that person was." *Confirm who that person was.*

Warren leaned back in his chair. "Why should I do that?"

I breathed out in satisfaction. "So you *do* know."

"I'm about the only person on this planet the Winters can't touch. I know too much, and they know I know it, but I worked out my deal with the devil, and they leave me alone and I leave them alone. That was the price for keeping my daughter safe."

"You won't help me?"

"I didn't say that."

I looked around at the environment he'd chosen, so different from the one Mary Ellen inhabited. These were working people who figured out how to divide up the paycheck to cover their needs, who felt lucky to have jobs, even if they complained about them, and who didn't have time for the kind of games played by the Winters family. It seemed that Warren wanted to connect his daughter to this world—real people with real concerns. Andrew Winters pretended to understand it, made pretty campaign speeches reminiscent of trickle-down economics, but he didn't have a clue.

I reminded Warren about Hugh's murder and its connection to my mother. I told him I thought Hetty had alerted someone to my talk with Hugh, most likely the person she was having an affair with, and as a result, Hugh had been killed. I told him how Loretta had figured out that Hetty was having an affair with someone involved in the Andrew Winters campaign. I sputtered to a stop. I didn't want to tell him what I actually thought; I wanted to see if I was right first. If the intuition was working as well as I thought it was.

Warren's eyes glittered as I spoke, as if I'd awakened some sleeping dragon in him. When I finished, he leaned in so close I had to force myself not to skitter back. "You have the answer, Clara. It's just your basic assumption is wrong."

He smiled evilly, the most disturbing version of any smile he'd given me so far. Something I'd said gave him a triumphant, vengeful pleasure. He said, "Who is the person closest to the campaign, aside from Winters himself?"

"Mary Ellen."

He kept watching me.

It sank in. *Not Pete.* "Hetty was having an affair with Mary Ellen?" Shock nearly strangled my vocal chords.

"You'll notice I didn't tell you that." He wrapped up the remains of his sandwich, picked up his magazine, and strode laughing from the deli.

———

I sat in the Land Rover stunned by what I'd learned. Even though I had no evidence that Hetty called Mary Ellen the night of the party, the logical conclusion was that she did. I tried to assemble a reasonable scenario. Hetty saw me leave with Hugh and called Mary Ellen. Mary Ellen freaked out, believing Hugh would spill the beans about Mother's rape and the DNA report to me. She would assume—and she was right—that he wouldn't tell me all he knew the first time he saw me; I'd been gone for years. Why would he trust me right away? I should have figured that out, too, but I'd been caught up in the dreams.

Mary Ellen would also assume that I wouldn't hesitate to use information from Hugh to bring down the campaign. Was it Hugh's timing that got him killed? Did Mary Ellen realize that, if she got rid of him quickly, she could keep her precious brother's dream safe? And was she so impulsive or arrogant that she'd murdered Hugh herself? She'd already tried to get me to fall off a horse.

That's when I got scared. Until now, I'd been scared for Mother: scared because of the dreams, scared of losing her. Okay, I'd been scared for myself, too, but only because the dreams could overwhelm me, and staying here could drown me in the old stuff I'd run from. But Mary Ellen's willingness to engage in an affair with Hetty, someone she must have despised, merely to control her, told me she would do anything.

I pulled out the chief's card and called his cell number.

After I'd explained, he said, "Hetty could have an affair with anyone she wanted. I don't see how it's pertinent."

So I told him my theory about Hetty telling Mary Ellen about me and Hugh.

He didn't sound convinced. "Confidentiality rules would keep him from sharing any of your mother's personal history. Mary Ellen knows that."

"Unless Mother gave him permission."

"Did she?"

"I don't know. Can't you do something? Take Mary Ellen in for questioning?"

"Based on what? An affair? She's allowed to sleep with whomever she wants. There's no evidence she committed or conspired to commit murder."

I had to tell him everything. "Yesterday, Mary Ellen threatened to kill us. Mother was there when she said it, so there's a witness, and—"

"Mary Ellen threatened to kill you?" It exploded from the phone. "Why didn't you tell me this before?"

"I haven't seen you!"

"You have no phone? You and that damn mother of yours, every time I turn around you hand me some piece of information I should have had *weeks* ago!" The phone went silent again.

I said softly, "I'm sorry, Kyle. It's been a difficult decision. It hasn't been easy to learn I was a child of rape, and that Andrew Winters is my biological father."

"He *what*?"

"Mother didn't tell you?"

"It gives her motive, Clara."

"I just found out myself."

"She never told you?"

I said nothing. I don't think I could have said anything. The sympathy and tenderness in his voice called up such sorrow and hurt in me, I couldn't speak.

"Is there evidence?"

I told him about the DNA report, reassured him it was locked in Mother's safe where we'd put it after the Christmas break-in.

"Where's Constance?"

"She's gone to see Gary Hankin. She thinks he might testify against Winters about his blackmailing scheme."

The silence on the other end of the phone stretched across several galaxies, looped around and came back to swat me. *Right.* Mother hadn't told him about the blackmail, either. Obviously, she hadn't gotten around to that interview she'd promised. So I told him.

"You have proof?"

"That's what she's trying to get."

"Does Mary Ellen know about the blackmail?"

"We think so."

"I need you to listen to me carefully. Are you?" He waited.

"Yes, I'm listening."

"Good. Mary Ellen and I need to have a chat, but I can't detain her. Go home and lock the doors. When your mother comes home, keep her there. Don't go anywhere. Officer Munson will come stay with you. Don't let anyone else in—even if he's a cop. Call me on this number only. Don't call the station. I think I can finally prove which of my officers is dirty." He didn't even let me reply, just, mercifully, clicked off.

CHAPTER 29

turned the phone off and laid it face down on the passenger seat, then started to shake. *One of my officers...* Suddenly, Hetty's wall of photographs made sense: Hetty, Pete Samuels, Mary Ellen—what a weird trifecta. Mary Ellen to direct, Hetty for psychic predictions, Pete to do the dirty work. Win, place, show. But what was in it for Pete? He must be the man in the black balaclava. He had access to Hetty's dolls, and I figured all cops knew how to break into houses. Would he come after me and Mother? I could see Mary Ellen shooting off a deadly text as the cops arrested her.

I called Mother's cell, but it shuttled into voicemail. I left a frantic message. I got Hankin's office number from information and asked his receptionist if she'd seen Constance Montague that afternoon. She snipped about patient confidentiality and when I told her Mother wasn't a patient but a friend of Dr. Hankin's, she put me on hold and left me there. I disconnected and started toward home. Maybe Mother had already arrived.

The house was empty. I double checked all the rooms, locking doors behind me. Then, as I put the tea kettle on, Mother walked through the back door.

"Oh, Mother! I'm so glad you're okay. The chief—"

"You're making tea?" She nodded at the kettle, shrugging out of her coat. "Would you make me a cup while I go change?" She had faded since her tart exit this morning. Even her suit had wrinkles in it.

I relocked the back door, flopped teabags into two mugs and leaned against the counter with my arms folded, waiting, trying not to feel cranky and worried. Whatever discussion she'd had with Hankin would have been difficult at best.

I sighed. The truth was, despite whatever reconciliation we reached, she would still be the same woman with the same flaws. They might soften and ease, but they wouldn't disappear. And that went for me too. I had never been easy to live with.

The kitchen was bright with harsh winter light. The heavy table gleamed, except where I'd left crumbs this morning. The broom closet door stood slightly ajar, in its shadows a chaos of mops and brooms. I crossed the room and shut the door.

Mother came in again, wrapped in a fleece robe with thick slippers on her feet. She'd washed her face. I filled the mugs. "Are you hungry?"

She shook her head. "I just need to sit with you. Is that all right?"

"Sure." I pulled out a chair, puzzled. She didn't say anything for a long time, just sipped. I left her in peace, delaying my tale and Kyle's. We were safe for the moment.

After a while, she reached for my hand and held it. I practiced breathing, calming my anxiety, and watched the sun play with the shadows. My thoughts slowly stilled. Into that emptiness, an image slowly built of the woman sitting before me: I saw her lying on a raft, floating. A long thin cord tethered her to something outside my vision. She wept and her tears flowed off the raft and melded with the sea, raising her higher and higher, until the tether cut at her wrist and the cord began to pull her toward the deep water. She shifted in her chair and the image disappeared. "He said he would testify."

"That's good, Mother. The chief can build a case." The first nail—why didn't she seem pleased?

"It was awful." Tears pooled in her eyes. "It brought back so much... of that night. He wouldn't stop apologizing for the deal he'd made with Winters. He kept saying he was just trying to protect his family, and surely I understood that." She pressed her finger over one of my breakfast crumbs and absently lifted it from the table. The tears spilled over, and she hunched a shoulder into her cheek to wipe them away.

"I've never been angry at him. I always told myself I understood why he didn't turn Winters in, but today, he seemed groveling and weak. I felt dirty demanding that he stand up and do the right thing, even though he should have done it years ago." She frowned, sniffed. "I know that doesn't make any sense." She rubbed the crumb between her fingers until it was powder. "I did it anyway, and I made him sign a statement. I know it won't stand up in court, but—oh God, Clara. I'm as bad as Andrew." The tears came on again. I reached for a napkin.

"You're nothing like him," I said, "and with Hankin's testimony, the police can make Winters pay." I paused, hoping she'd respond with a smile, but she just stared at the table top. Instead, I told her what I'd discovered about Hetty and Mary Ellen.

"How could I not know Mary Ellen had a daughter?"

"You've been gone a long time, Clara. You probably forgot. Mary Ellen is so relentlessly single, and Emma was born only a few months before they split.

David hasn't brought that child around, ever. Mary Ellen's not allowed to see her, not after almost killing her."

"She almost killed her own daughter?"

She looked up. "Hugh diagnosed postpartum depression, but who knows. David filed for divorce right after it happened, and Mary Ellen was so furious in court that the judge ordered therapy and gave David full rights and custody." Mother allowed the glimmer of a smile.

"David told me *she* filed for divorce."

"I'm sure that story was part of their agreement. Mary Ellen would want to leave, not be left. Anyway, Hetty and Mary Ellen were free to engage in..." she waved her hand vaguely, "...whatever they wanted. They were consenting adults."

I spoke slowly, tying the strands of the story together. "So we know Mary Ellen would do anything for Andrew, even create an opportunity for him rape you, to teach you a lesson. She also knew Andrew was blackmailing his friends for campaign funds. Maybe she even came up with the idea; it sort of sounds like her. Then, she takes Hetty as a lover to persuade her to do readings for Andrew, and because, after I come home, she realizes she can use Hetty to get close to me and find out what I know. Well, at least before I got her to put me on Andrew's campaign. Anyway, that didn't work, but when Hetty saw Hugh and me getting cozy, she called Mary Ellen—who then called Pete to kill Hugh." I sat back, a bit stunned.

"Pete? I've known him since he was a boy."

"People change, Mother." Although she did have a point. Why would a cop kill someone? What could be in it for Pete?

She mulled it over. "Okay, so I can see the connections to Mary Ellen, but there's no evidence Andrew was behind any of this. He could plead ignorance."

"That's the hole we've got to fill. If the chief can get Mary Ellen or Pete to talk..."

"Mary Ellen will never talk." She scrubbed at her nose. "I suppose I should call Kyle, too, let him know Hankin will be a witness."

I handed her the house phone just as the doorbell rang and she disappeared into the other room with the phone.

By the time I reached the front door—after checking the steps and yard from behind the curtains in the front rooms—Bailey was stamping her high heels free of snow and squirming out of her cashmere coat. I shut, locked and bolted the door behind her and set the perimeter alarm. She followed me into the kitchen, tossed the coat over a chair and flopped sideways into another. "You can *not* believe what is going on. The cops took Mary Ellen in for questioning. Right from the campaign office! They said—and I quote, 'In connection with the murder of Hetty Gardner.' Winters flipped out. When Jennifer tried to calm him, he slapped her hand so hard he almost ripped it off. She cowered, literally, and it didn't seem like a new pose."

"You didn't go to the station with her?"

"She didn't ask for me. I bet they use John. He's got more experience." She rubbed her finger across the remaining breakfast crumbs.

I brought her up to date on what I'd discovered. Each time I told it, it made more sense, except Pete's motivation.

"Maybe Mary Ellen was paying Pete off," she said, "or maybe she was sleeping with him, or maybe she was paying him off *and* sleeping with him." She grinned.

"It's not funny. Hetty and Hugh are dead."

"You're right." She wiped her hand across the table, and my mother came back to hang up the phone. She greeted Bailey, walked to the back door, and put on her boots.

"Where are you going? We have to stay inside. I've even set the alarm."

She turned it off. "I'll only be a minute. I'll stay on the property." She stepped out into the cold. In her bathrobe. I cocked my head at Bailey, and she shrugged.

"Who was she talking to?"

"The chief." I filled her in on Mother's meeting with Gary Hankin.

"Why would Hankin talk now? Winters must have the same hold over him as always."

"Guilt, apparently."

"Doesn't make sense. You sure Hankin's not playing her?"

"She says he signed a statement."

"Mmm." Bailey wasn't convinced.

I twisted to look out the back door for Mother, but she wasn't in view. What could she be doing out there?

Bailey coiled herself forward. "Listen. Mary Ellen isn't doing this alone. Somehow, Andrew is behind it, and making that connection is key. If she doesn't confess, you got nothin'."

"Mother says she won't confess. Why would she drag Andrew into it? He's her reason for living. Do you think she'll confess?"

Bailey went sideways in her chair again, crossed her legs. "No way. She'll take the bullet for him."

"Of course, she *is* crazy, so maybe she did do it all by herself, thinking Andrew would reward her, or she'd be the power behind the throne, or whatever." I shook my head. I told her about the boy who'd defied Andrew and ended up in the hospital when his car crashed. "He's the sort of man who would pimp his sister to the highest bidder to get into office."

"You're babbling."

"I know. I think I need a glass of wine." I stood and crossed to the wine rack.

"Oh yeah, that's going to help—but while you're up..." She gestured that I should bring her a glass, too. "Who's your weak spot?"

I took the bottle to the counter where I could see out the window. Mother was nowhere in sight. I put down the corkscrew and went to the door. I could feel Pete out there, like a prickle at the ends of my fingertips. Kyle had said there was a dirty cop.

Bailey persisted, oblivious to my concern. "Who's the person most likely to give if you press on them? The one who has the information you need?"

"Is this how lawyers think?"

"All the time. C'mon, Clara. Who knows what's going on inside the Winters clan?"

I turned and breathed it out in a sigh. "Jennifer."

"Right." She smacked the table, startling me. "How do we separate her from the herd?"

"I'm a sheep dog now?" I began putting my boots on, distracted.

She rolled her eyes. "Stay with the program. What's the next campaign party sort of thingy?" She drummed her fingers against the wood, red nails clicking. "New Year's Eve. Right. I'll get a couple of invites."

"If they hold it with Mary Ellen in jail."

She waved her long fingers in the air. "She'll be out in a couple of hours. No way John lets her stay there. Can't have the sister of a Senate candidate locked up. And this time, there's no convenient photo of her at a crime scene, as there was with your mother."

"Right. And since the police have likely told Mary Ellen that I reported her death threat, she'll throw me out of her party on my butt." I shoved my arms into a sweater I'd grabbed off the hook by the door.

"What are you doing?"

"Mother's been outside in her bathrobe for, I don't know, ten minutes? It's really cold out there, and the chief said to stay in the house. Pete Samuels could be on our property for all I know. I'm going out to make sure she's okay."

I yanked open the broom closet, looking for a weapon. Buried behind the mops was an old shovel, something the gardener probably disdained in favor of a new, less rusty version. It would do.

Bailey looked alarmed. "I'll come with you."

"Stay here, please. If I'm not back in fifteen minutes, call the chief." I dropped my cell phone into my pocket. "I'll call if I find her. Arm the house after I'm out. He got in twice before because I forgot." I gave her the code.

I opened the door and followed Mother's footprints in the snow across the kitchen garden to the gate in the wall. It was propped open with a sturdy stick, which I appropriated as an easier weapon to wield than the shovel. To the left a hill sloped toward the pond and, to the right, the back meadow abutted the road. The grounds spread across three acres, and my father's garden, its graceful shrubs, sculptures, and carefully designed private nooks, created enough quirky hiding spots that she could be anywhere, as could anyone who wanted to harm her.

Her footprints led toward the right. I stepped through the open gate and walked quickly, hugging the wall to its end, where a hedge screened the driveway. I paused, listening, but heard nothing except the whisper of car tires on the road. I closed my eyes, letting the silence soak in, hoping the intuition would tell me if I were out here alone or not. Nothing concrete, but something didn't feel right.

I took a deep breath and ran across the open expanse, following Mother's footsteps. I was the perfect target against all that white. A red shadow flitted at the edge of my vision and I snapped my head to look. A hawk, above me, cruised for small prey. As I looked ahead again, I heard a high-pitched whine by my ear. I dove for the gazebo, landing by Mother's feet and dropping my stick. It was useless against a gun. She fell to her knees next to me, and I yanked her to the floor. "Get down!"

"Clara, what is the matter?"

"Someone just shot at me." Staying below the benches, I scrabbled out of sight of the meadow, dragging her with me. Surrounded by trees on three sides, the gazebo made a cool spot on a warm summer day. Now, those three sides of trees protected us from the shooter. He could only come from one direction if he wanted to aim with any accuracy. I dialed the chief.

"Sit tight," he said. "We'll be there in five."

Five minutes was a long time. Another bullet pinged off the metal roof of the gazebo. I said, "Probably Pete and Mary Ellen think killing us will eliminate the evidence against them. Maybe they think the police will conclude you killed Hugh, and then killed yourself."

I listened, hard. Was that a footstep, crunching in the snow?

I looked at Mother. She huddled, shivering, tears running down her face. "So many lives I've destroyed, Clara—all for a stupid principle. If I'd just told Andrew what he wanted, anything, I could have made it up—how would he have known?—none of this would have happened."

I didn't believe that, but I had come to understand regret. I shrugged out of the sweater and draped it around her shoulders. "He wouldn't have let you stop—and if you lied, or your predictions weren't true, he would have harmed you—as he did." Besides, if anyone should sacrifice, it should be me. If the only way to save my remaining parent was to give Andrew Winters what he wanted, then I would do that. The gazebo seemed to tip, as if in a storm.

A crackle startled me. A foot stepping on leaves under the snow? I peered around the corner of the bench, but I couldn't see anything, except another sudden rush of red.

"Oh, Clara, we've wasted so many years. I didn't know how to love you when your life had started in such a... terrible way. Your father was so gentle and kind. I wanted to be like him but I couldn't let go of the rage and fear I felt every time I looked at you. If I let go, if I loved you, Andrew would have a wedge to use against me, so I drove you away." Her shivering intensified.

We had to have this conversation *now?* My tension rippled out into my fingers, and my grip tightened on her arm. She winced.

This reconciliation business was hard. She was vulnerable, something she'd so rarely been with me, and I could respond from my anger or from the intent behind her words to reconnect, to make what was wrong between us right again. If she got shot or froze to death, that would be a bad start.

"I think Pete is getting closer. We've got to go through the woods. Maybe we can circle around to the drive." If hypothermia didn't get us first.

A small gate led out the back of the gazebo. It probably hadn't been opened since father installed the folly thirty years ago. I pushed on it slowly, hoping it wouldn't squeal, and then, squeezed through behind Mother. Snow started to fall, tiny flakes like little prickles of ice on the skin.

"Use the trees for cover," I whispered, scanning the woods. I didn't see anything, but my training was in plants, not tracking killers.

Thud. Something lodged itself in the tree next to my head. I ducked and ran, dragging Mother by the hand. "This way," I hissed. If we could get to the road, maybe we could flag down a passing motorist. Surely, Pete—it had to be Pete—wouldn't kill us in front of witnesses?

That's when I heard sirens. Bullets started flying randomly, Pete's last ditch effort to get us. I tugged Mother to the ground and started crawling. We were still a hundred yards from the road. I scrabbled in my pocket for my phone and dialed Bailey.

"Where are you? What's going on?"

"Tell the cops we're in the woods behind the gazebo and Pete's shooting at us."

Mother screamed. I looked up. Pete stood over her, his gun pointed straight at her head.

"No!" I yelled, moving to block his shot.

He racked the slide, and smiled at me, triumphant, his teeth gleaming in the dim light. "You want to go first?"

"The chief knows you're working with Mary Ellen."

"The chief knows squat. The chief is a stupid, Southern hick from Louisiana who thinks he knows this town. I know who's who and what's what. And I've always known how to work the pretty ladies, haven't I, Mrs. Montague? I had you fooled, didn't I? Nice little Petey, that sweet boy. Too bad that's the only way you saw me." His snide energy rippled out. "I should have been Chief of Police. I'd worked for it, knew all the right people, even gave a good interview, but no, you had to go all affirmative action. Stupid. Mary Ellen will make me chief. Mary Ellen is smart."

Even the birds were silenced.

"Put the gun down, Pete," the Kyle DuPont said. "There's nowhere to go."

Pete's face went blank. Then a welter of conflicting options played across his face.

"It's not worth it," the chief said.

Slowly, slowly, Pete put the gun on the ground.

Inside, Bailey had blankets, wine, a hot pot of tea. Kyle held a chair for Mother, wrapped a blanket around her shoulders and pushed a tea cup at her. "Mrs. Montague, are you okay?"

She nodded. "I'm fine."

He crouched by her chair with his hand on her arm. "Are you sure?"

"Mother," I said, suddenly angry now that we were all safe, "Why did you go outside? We were nearly killed."

"Chief DuPont suggested that my telling him about the rape and Gary Hankin earlier might have saved Hetty's and Hugh's lives."

"You said *what*? She could have died out there!"

The chief looked at me, with real pain in his eyes. "I didn't say—"

"It's what you meant." Mother shot me a look like the old days—tough as steel girders. "It's okay, Clara. He was doing his job."

Bailey filled a mug and pressed it into my hands. Its heat made me realize how cold I was.

"It's not okay," I said, but subsided into a chair.

The chief nodded. "Officer Munson will stay with you tonight."

"You've got both Mary Ellen and Pete Samuels. Why are you still worried?"

He leaned back in the chair and tugged on his suit jacket. "Mrs. Montague, for thirty-five years, you've kept your mouth shut. Whether or not you want to see it that way, you've done your rapist's bidding. Now, you're challenging that." He glanced briefly at me. "You should be prepared for another attack, and that attack will most likely be on Clara, because he perceives her as what you love most."

"But Clara is his *daughter*."

"I believe he feels his children with Jennifer are his only true family."

I almost launched myself out of my chair to dial Air France. The Seine. The wine. The Louvre. Escape, blessed escape. But another stronger piece of me, a newer piece, knew I couldn't abandon Mother. She needed me. I'd abandoned my father, but I wouldn't abandon her. If the chief couldn't find a reason to arrest Winters in the next twenty-four hours, I would act. I couldn't live like this, waiting until something broke in the case.

"Fine," Mother said. "I'm not risking Clara's life and I'm not risking my own. Not for that man."

I kept my mouth shut.

CHAPTER 30

ary Ellen refused to talk. So did Pete. I made a phone call, made a promise. Then I made preparations, including persuading Paul to hand over Mother's file.

New Year's Eve opened with clear black skies salted with a thousand stars. Curled in my favorite chair, I could see them through the bedroom window.

I didn't understand what created people like Andrew or Mary Ellen. It wasn't parental neglect, since people built dynasties and media corporations even when their parents ignored them. It wasn't excess privilege, since privileged people also endowed museums and fed third world children. Some people were just born wicked, and if life handed them a butterfly, they pulled off its wings.

I stood. Ten o'clock. Too early, but I slid into my long black wool coat, picked up my keys, and drove to Mother's meditation cottage, reviewing each scenario I'd considered as I drove. None of my ideas was surefire, and none of them safe. Finally, I breathed deeply, letting the clarity and depth of the beautiful winter sky fill me. Intuition would have to bridge whatever holes logic and planning had missed.

When I pulled in, Ernie and Loretta's lights were out. I parked the car out of sight behind one of the barns and made my way to the cottage with a flashlight. The protective circle of hedges felt menacing tonight, but the snow that had fallen over the past couple of days revealed no other footsteps.

Inside, I flipped on the lights and walked the rooms to ensure everything remained in its place, then sat on the floor with plenty of pillows behind my back. Paul had taught me some new relaxation exercises. They helped, but I still jumped out of my skin when someone knocked. I crossed the room, intuition on high alert, feeling every fiber in the carpet through the soles of my shoes.

I opened the door. "Andrew." I could see an aura around him, the violet aura of visionary thinkers. I was obviously seeing things.

He was dressed in a tuxedo, but he'd pulled the tie loose and worn hiking boots rather than the fancy dress shoes he must have sported at his New Years' Eve party. He had arrived nearly an hour and a half before the time Mary

Ellen and I agreed on, but the boots showed he wasn't all impulse. I needed to remember how smart he was. His face wore a self-satisfied smirk. "I figured you'd come around eventually. Smarter than your mother." He stamped the snow off his boots and looked around the room with greedy interest. "Mary Ellen regaled me over the years with tales about this spot." He took in the limited furniture, the turquoise and white color scheme, the pillows on the floor. "Charming."

The word dripped with disdain. I breathed in and out slowly, trying to hear past the white noise enveloping me. I had to quell it to do the reading, or I wouldn't get accurate images. "Come into the kitchen," I said. "We can discuss the terms before we get down to business at midnight."

"That midnight crap sounded like bullshit. Did you make that up?" Niceties over, he slithered from his civilized skin.

"Midnight 'crap'?"

He yanked out a spindly kitchen chair, hitting the leg on the wall and leaving a mark. "That New Year's midnight was the ideal time for intuitive practice because you could see more clearly."

Beneath the impatience, I heard the first crack—a crack I intended to wedge open like the entrance to a secret cave. He had waited for this moment for thirty-five years. Hetty served her purpose, but the Montagues doing his bidding was sweetened whipped cream on his dessert. If gave him that triumph, I wouldn't have any more dreams. I wouldn't have to deal with him again. He might win his Senate race, if he kept his momentum going, but his opponent had raised support and several surprisingly large infusions of cash. She'd spent a lot of time in working class neighborhoods, earning her media buzz. He needed to know if his blackmail would be exposed, and what magic he could work to keep that from happening. My visions could tell him. I was his daughter—I would be genetically tuned to him. A wave of white noise washed over me.

"Of course I didn't make it up," I snapped. "It's too serious for you to take this lightly. Here are my terms. I'll give you intuitive guidance for your Senate campaign, but once you're elected, we're done."

He waved his hand in agreement, an agreement I could see in his eyes he had no intention of keeping.

"I have a few questions first." I opened one of the files on the table.

"You going to make me write it all down and sign it, like your Mama did with Hankin?" He held a spoon by the neck and spun it on the table top.

"Those are the terms," I repeated.

He leaned over the table, his eyes locked on mine. "Go on, girl."

"How did you persuade Dr. Hankin to ignore his medical ethics?"

He snorted with laughter, a thousand stones pounding the rocky shore. "Why the hell do you care about Hankin's ethics?"

"I didn't say I would explain."

He waved at the walls. "And you happen to have little recording devices scattered all over the place."

The installer had assured me no one could find them. "You're welcome to check." I shrugged, thinking I only knew what kind fathers were like—and my kind father was dead. The desire to have him standing next to me overwhelmed me. Father would know how to handle this man.

Winters studied me, hate and mirth mixed in his eyes, and I remembered the snaky arm at that first fundraiser. He'd known then who I was, and he'd made a pass at me, to see how I'd respond.

I wasn't this man's daughter. I wouldn't ever be, despite our shared genes. He would always let his darker passions dominate.

"Gary Hankin was an idiot, like most people around here. Too stupid to do right by themselves and always coming to my family to rescue them. Early on, Gary tangled himself up in some legal snafus. He was taking drugs home to his lovely wife, and selling samples off the books to his friends. Had himself a nice little side business going, which financed his wife's drug habit. He was dumb enough to sell to an undercover officer. I negotiated a settlement, and Gary moved his practice out-of-state." The spoon still spun round and round, Winters's fingers tight against its neck.

"He's given you a lot of campaign contributions."

"Payment for services rendered. His contributions to my campaign have indicated his gratitude." He sneered, a snake curving around its prey.

"How did Wendy's drug habit start?" All I had to do was be a good listener. A captive listener.

"A little issue during my father's time. Gary 'lost' some records as a favor to us"—his eyes flicked from the spoon to me—"and Wendy was so afraid someone would find out, she needed pills to stay calm. Stupid. No one found out in thirty-five years."

I shrugged. "I have." I opened Hugh's file on my mother.

He looked unsurprised. "Your mama finally break down?"

"Yes. But it's corroborated by Hugh's notes. Did you know that therapists make a second set of notes following therapy appointments? They're called 'shadow notes,' and they record the parts of the session the doctor or patient doesn't want in the public record." The chief was combing those files in search of evidence that Hugh had figured out Winters' blackmail scheme.

He waited.

"Hugh's notes document my mother's claim of rape."

"Hearsay," he tossed off.

I shut that file, slid another out from under it. "DNA doesn't lie. Wendy needed those pills because her husband hid evidence that could convict you of raping my mother and fathering me."

He was proud of himself. "My father cut the deal to lose those records; I cut the deal to save Hankin's business, rescue Wendy, and fund my campaigns. Whatever Hankin says he still has, he's lying."

Perhaps only Mary Ellen knew about Mother's recent DNA tests. "What about Hugh?"

He went back to spinning the spoon by its neck. "That was Mary Ellen's thing. Hugh threatened to use some party boss out west to screw my campaign. I didn't believe Hugh had the balls to go to this guy, but Mary Ellen freaked—something about the women on Hugh's client roster. She thought they'd all whined to him during therapy and he'd concocted some conspiracy idea. Hugh didn't have the brains for that, but she decided he had to be dealt with anyway."

As if Winters himself was off the hook.

"Dealt with how?"

"Hugh always checked his messages last thing at night in case of emergencies. She got Pete Samuels to leave a message saying the cops wanted to consult him ASAP on a night she knew he'd be out late at your mama's Christmas party. When Hugh called back, Pete knew he was home. He went and took care of things. It's so easy to fool people."

"Yes, it is," I agreed. "And Hetty?" A third file was filled with her photographs. "Were these taken at your suggestion?"

"Hard evidence is so useful when you're persuading people to contribute money, isn't it? Hetty got a little carried away with the assignment, then got uncomfortable." He waved a dismissive hand. "Too late, sweetheart."

He glanced at the clock. "That's all you get. Do the reading now. I can't miss my entire New Year's party, and I don't give a crap about the midnight thing."

I pulled open the kitchen drawer nearest me and removed a pack of Tarot cards. I shuffled and laid them out between us. I tried to calm myself, but the white noise kept amplifying.

Images flickered in amongst the snow: the burning, the blood, the voodoo dolls, my mother on her knees in the gazebo, Pete standing over her with a gun. They swirled into colors: the green and sickly yellow of Hetty's aura, the purple around Andrew, the swarming red and buzzing white I kept seeing. I turned over the cards: Death, the Devil, the Tower, Strength—reversed—the Hanged Man—reversed—the ten of swords. He stared at the layout. "What does that mean?"

I almost laughed at the righteousness of it and felt myself lift free for the first time in weeks. The white noise faded, and with it the longings, images, conflict. The dreams would stop now.

I said, "It means you can leave."

For the first time, surprise crossed his face. "What?"

I raised an eyebrow, sure of myself, centered. I knew the right path, no matter the outcome. "Really, Andrew. Did you honestly believe after all the damage you've done to my family that I would give you what you wanted? Even the cards refused to do that. This reading tells me you'll fail. That's what Hetty's readings told you, too, and all those years ago, that's what Mother's readings told you. You didn't want to hear it, but you've destroyed yourself." I stood. "You can leave now."

For a moment, he sat stunned. Then he launched himself across the table at me.

CHAPTER 31

 had a momentary flash of burning as if hell's floor had opened and the fires were rushing up to consume us. Then it was gone, and I'd lost my advantage. I'd been prepared for violence, but before I could raise my arms to defend myself, Winters toppled me off the chair and onto the floor. "You little slut! I'll teach you—"

He gripped my wrists with one hand and tore at the neck of my t-shirt with the other. It ripped at the shoulder and side seams, exposing my bra and skin. "Where's the wire?" he yelled. "Where is it?"

"There is no wire. Get off me!" He started pulling at the bra.

No, no no! Not that!

He levered himself onto me, his knees pinning my wrists to the floor. I squirmed, but he slapped my face and pulled the pants down my hips.

"I should have eliminated you when Mary Ellen heard you were talking to Hugh!" His fingernails ripped at my skin. He scrabbled around my back, pulling the pants low over my butt while I struggled to loosen my arms from his grip. "You aren't containable, like your mother. You'll tell the world." As he fumbled at his belt, getting the fitting loose and whipping it from the belt loops, the pressure on one of my hands lessened and I wrenched it free, slamming it into his nose—a move I remembered from some self-defense class. He howled. I pushed him off, yanked up my pants and jumped to my feet.

"You bitch! I won't be able to speak in front of a camera for weeks." He grabbed my leg, and I fell to my knees, just missing the counter with my head.

The gun. He'd listen to that.

I reached for the drawer, kicking at him. I wasn't paying attention to where I kicked, but when I heard him scream, knew I'd hit something tender. I yanked the drawer open, felt for the gun, then snatched at it. He seized the waistband of my pants and tugged. The fabric ripped. I swung my arm hard and slammed him on the side of the head with the gun. His grip relaxed and he slumped to the floor.

I hoped I'd killed the bastard.

God, I hoped I hadn't.

Hanging onto the counter, I clambered to my feet. I could still walk, despite the pain in my knees and back. I had to get help. I zipped up my sweatshirt over the torn t-shirt, and wrapped myself in my coat, stuffing the gun in the pocket. Then I stumbled out the door and across the drive to the main house. Gentle snow had started to fall, and a thin new coating lay over the old.

Ernie answered the door, bleary eyed. "Clara! What's the matter? Is Constance all right?"

"Mother's fine. You've got to come. I hit Andrew Winters and I think he needs medical attention." I punched buttons on my phone to call Kyle.

"Are you okay?" Ernie asked.

"I'll be fine."

Ernie nodded without asking any further questions, a measure in that moment of how much he loved my father.

Kyle picked up. I said, "Please come. Andrew Winters just attacked me." I told him where I was.

"Are you safe?"

"Yes."

"Ernie?" Loretta called from the top of the stairs.

"It's okay, honey, go back to bed."

"Ernie, the cottage is burning!" She rushed past us and into the kitchen for the phone.

We ran across the grass as police sirens wailed up the drive. I hoped fire sirens wouldn't be far behind. Had Andrew gotten out? How had the fire started? The flames leapt and cackled like a priest at an Inquisition burning, smoke twisting black and pungent into the blacker sky. But as we burst through the hedge, Andrew wasn't the Winters we found. Instead, a triumphant Mary Ellen stood, holding a red plastic gas can.

"Mary Ellen! What are you doing?"

She turned sharply, her face etched with hard black and gold lines from the fire. "You're supposed to be dead. I blocked the doors!"

"Andrew—did he get out? Is he with you?" I panicked. The ribs of the cottage stood out like a whale carcass on the beach.

"Andrew's in there?" Her face melted in the heat, and she sagged to the ground. "Oh god. I thought—he wasn't supposed to be here. It's only eleven."

"He came early."

"Nooooooo!" She lunged at me swinging the gas can wide, as if to strike me. A strong hand came out of the darkness and seized her arm mid-swing.

"I'll take it from here."

Before she could twist to see who it was, the chief had locked her hands into cuffs. "You can tell the rest of your story at the station, Ms. Winters." Joe materialized from the edge of the fire and took her arm.

That left me to face the chief. "I'm sorry. I didn't know it would get so out of hand."

"That's the nice thing about you, Clara. You're always willing to apologize after you've done something horrendous—like burn down someone's house."

"Actually, it was my mother's house. Well, she rented it from Ernie and Loretta. She probably won't need it any more. I mean, we have a big house—"

And then I couldn't really breathe properly because I'd been folded into a hug, strong arms around me, and stupid me, like a baby, started to cry, huge gulping sobs that I couldn't get to quit, and I was getting his really nice coat all damp and snotty. I pulled away to wipe my nose. The chief pulled a handkerchief from his back pocket.

"Sit down," he said. "The firemen have the blaze under control and they'll call when they need me."

We sat on Ernie and Loretta's porch. Light from the flames backlit the hedge and we could hear the firemen as they yelled to each other. Flakes of snow spun and melted above the fire in the midnight air. "Tell me what happened," he said.

I told him how I'd offered Winters an intuitive reading if he would tell me about Hankin, how I'd had surveillance equipment installed, and how I planned to give the police the recording so they could investigate and toss Winters in jail forever and ever. And ever. But when the tarot offered up only death and failure and I just laughed, he had freaked out and I'd been afraid he was going to rape me like he'd raped my mother—

"Rape his own daughter?"

I tried to shrug, but it came out like a convulsion. "He kept ripping at my clothes." The chief pulled me under his arm and I told him Winters kept asking about a wire, so maybe it wasn't rape after all and I'd fought him off with the nose thing, and then I'd smacked him on the side of the head with the gun in the drawer.

"Gun? You brought a gun tonight?" The chief, suddenly tense, cut through my babble.

"It was in the drawer."

"Do you have a license?"

"Mary Ellen threatened me, so Mother armed me. I didn't know what to do with it, so I threw it in a drawer and forgot about it."

He shook his head at the image of my mother arming me. "Did you discharge the weapon?"

"If you mean, did I shoot it, then no. I grabbed it by the barrel. Do you want it? Here." I pulled it out of my pocket and started to hand it to him.

"Put it away, Clara. We'll deal with it later. What about the license?"

"I haven't had a license in years. Mother does, though."

I felt him relax. "I can work with that. Her place, her license, her gun. No one needs to know otherwise, Clara, okay? Carrying without a license is a one-year mandatory minimum."

"In jail?" I squeaked.

"In jail."

"Is it over? Will this get Mary Ellen put away?"

"Catching someone in the act is a pretty good guarantee."

"She didn't mean to kill him."

"She meant to kill you. I heard her say it."

"So did I." Ernie sat next to me on the porch steps. "I'll testify, too."

I said, "I didn't mean for him to die. He was my biological father...even if he was... do you think I could be insane like that?"

"You have your moments." The chief's dry chuckle comforted me.

When Loretta came out and shooed us all into the house, I realized I was shivering. She put a blanket around my shoulders, and I sat on the couch with my teeth chattering at the rim of a teacup until my gut unlocked. Somewhere in there Mother showed up and the chief left, the firemen and the ambulance corps finished their work, and then sometime around seven-thirty, the sun came up officially on the first day of the New Year.

CHAPTER 32

'd made it home for a couple of hours of blissful, dreamless sleep before Mother woke me for a shower. I dressed in velvet leggings and a thick, creamy, hand-knit sweater. Two cups of French press coffee later, I was just about steady on my feet. Mother, looking happier than she had since I'd arrived home, installed me in the solarium with a blanket over my knees.

"The guests will be here in a few minutes and you can play hostess. The caterer already arrived, so there's nothing to do."

The chief appeared, shaved and showered, a half-hour early to update us, but Mother left him alone with me after promising coffee. The sun shone over last night's crust of snow and in the windows like stage lights, making the room cozy and warm.

Mary Ellen still refused to talk and had hired a big name New York lawyer to represent her. However, Jennifer had shown up at the police station about an hour after Mary Ellen's booking and offered to talk about twenty-five years' worth of dirty Andrew Winters deeds. Without Andrew there to cow her into submission, she wanted a clean start for herself and her children. The chief studied my face. "You were the target. You were the target ever since you and Hugh had your, uh, discussion."

I felt my face heat up like an electric burner. He laughed. "Hetty saw you go upstairs together and called Mary Ellen. The Winters were already planning to kill Hugh because he'd pieced together the blackmail scheme, but now they weren't sure what Hugh told you. Andrew knew he could keep your Mother quiet by threatening your life, but you," he shook his head slightly, "were a wild card. You left all those years ago because you hated your mother. You even told Mary Ellen that at lunch."

"You couldn't possibly know what I said to Mary Ellen."

He grinned. "The job of a small town cop is to be in everybody's business. I have spies everywhere, and that waiter is a terrible gossip. Very useful for keeping track of Ms. Winters. Did you know she set that barn fire as a test run?" He shook his head again. "I know more about people's lives around here than anyone should." He paused, unhooked his fingers and then hooked them up again. "The point, Clara, is that they hired you onto the campaign to find out if you knew about the blackmail. If you did, Mary Ellen had plans."

I pushed the sleeves on my bulky sweater up, as if letting in some cooler air would ease my sudden claustrophobia. "There's one thing I don't understand. Winters told me Pete killed Hugh. But Pete told me there was female DNA on Hugh's body, implying it was Mother's."

"Pete didn't know whose it was, until Hetty died. Her autopsy revealed healing scratches, and her DNA matched the sample found on Hugh. Maybe Hetty got physical, and Hugh pushed her away. We can only guess, since there's no one left to tell us what happened."

I remembered how Hetty had looked at Hugh at Mother's fete, her burning eyes—and the long distance shots on the cottage wall. She had stalked him, at least a little.

"Then the threat escalated. You turned Mary Ellen in for her sins, and we caught Pete. When you offered the reading, Mary Ellen took her chance."

"What about Hetty?"

"Poor Hetty." He rubbed his thumbs together and looked out at the snow. "Jennifer claims Hetty knew about the rape—overheard your mom and Loretta talking years ago. When she needed help getting clients and making a name for the farm, she went to Mary Ellen, who, at first, ignored her.

"Finally, Hetty pulled her trump card. To keep her silent, Mary Ellen seduced her and implicated her in their blackmail scheme with those photographs. When you and Bailey apologized, Hetty grew a conscience; Mary Ellen decided she was a liability and had Pete kill her. What a screwed up family, even Jennifer. I'll never understand how people stand by and watch injustice be done."

"But what was Pete's motivation? Did he really want to be chief of police?"

He rubbed a thumb along a crease in his slacks. "Soon after I arrived, he told me he deserved my job. I didn't pay it much mind; some guy always thinks he deserves more than he's getting." He shook his head, pulled his gaze from the purity of the winter scene and looked at me. I looked at him.

"There's an old nature/nurture debate," I said. "Until recently, I would have told you I was my father's daughter because of nature. Now, I know I'm my father's daughter because of nurture."

He seemed about to speak when Mother poked her head in. "Some of the other guests have arrived."

David Warren and Andrew Winters Junior walked into the solarium accompanied by a teenage girl. She was the spitting image of Mary Ellen.

I slid to my feet and put out my hand. "You must be Emma."

She ducked her head, her face reddening. She looked briefly at David, who nodded slightly. She stuck her hand awkwardly into mine, but gave it a surprisingly firm shake. "I'm sorry about Mum—what she did," she said.

I looked a question at David, but he shook his head slightly. Then I remembered fifteen, the weight of responsibility.

"It's not an issue," I said.

"She killed your father." She glanced at David again. It was the kind of glance I would have given my own father.

"My father was a landscape architect who died fifteen years ago. I didn't know Mr. Winters." And in that moment, fifteen years of guilt lifted free. I gestured at the couch. "Please sit down."

Shyly, she took a spot at the other end of the couch from me. David chose a chair not too close to his daughter but not too far either. I turned to Andrew Junior. "I'm so sorry," I said.

Tears filled his eyes. "Mom's been telling us stories. I didn't know how bad it was—for her. He—" He pressed his fingers to his eyelids to stop the trickle and spoke through his own darkness. "My sisters wanted me to tell you they were sorry. They couldn't face you."

"Another time. We have time. We're family." He opened his eyes and moved as if to hug me, then stopped himself. I folded him into my arms. "We'll figure it out." Over his shoulder, I saw Mother watching from the door.

Paul and Richard arrived next, followed by Bailey. I made them all sit down and take glasses of champagne. Richard's color was better, and Paul told me later that the antibiotics and the de-stressing had helped put him on an even keel. Loretta and Ernie came soon after, looking worn out, but more peaceful than I'd seen them in several days. Nat Mueller and his wife, and Maria Leiber landed last, coming into the solarium with Kyle, who had disappeared a few moments before. They were laughing over the packages he was carrying. The larger had a red and gold bow on it, and he deposited it in my lap. Then, he sat down next to me—right next to me.

Inside, under layers of gold tissue, was a beautiful red silk shawl embroidered with creamy white flowers. "They're magnolias, the state flower of Louisiana," he said. "Merry late Christmas." I let the heavy fabric slide through my fingers. The workmanship was exquisite.

"Where did you get this? It's beautiful."

"Mama makes them." I could hear his pride. "She put us all through school with her embroidery. Neiman Marcus picked her up as a vendor in the eighties and she's still selling strong."

"I'd buy one," Maria said. "They must sell out before they hit the stores. I've never seen anything quite like it."

"She can't work as fast as she used to, even with the people she's hired to help, and well, Katrina didn't help any."

I suddenly saw that image again of Kyle surrounded by Katrina's muddy detritus. Why couldn't he go back to New Orleans?

"I'd love to meet her," I said. Bailey gave a quiet, giggly whoop.

"Now's not a good time," he said shortly, then covered it with a smile that didn't quite reach his eyes.

Mother came into the room with an array of cheese and little quiches arranged on a silver tray etched with whirly designs. She set it on the coffee table and moved a poinsettia to a side table, where it shimmered in the sunshine.

Kyle handed her the other box. "There's one for you, too, ma'am." Mother carefully removed the paper to reveal a smaller scarf with a design of green ivy on a gold silk background.

"It's lovely, Kyle. Thank you."

Emma said with round eyes, "Is he your boyfriend?"

Kyle guffawed. "A date might be a good idea."

Her mouth formed an "oh," but she looked at me as only a teenager in awe of a woman with a handsome boyfriend can be. I would treat that awe gently. Maybe we could do some sister outings—shopping or a play in the city. Something else to think about in the new year. I handed her the box. "Feel the fabric. Isn't it luscious?"

I turned back to Kyle. "Thank you. I feel very honored. May I have your mother's address, so I can thank her?"

He nodded his assent.

I added, "You never know. She might like me so much she decides to relocate."

"If I keep my job, after all the damage you've done in this town."

Mother said, "I don't think that will be a problem."

He looked at her, the question on his face.

She grinned ruefully. "With the Winters out of the way, I've the influence, you know."

"Except for me," Nat chimed in. His wife patted his leg. "But I'm thinkin' of running for Senate, now that the Republicans need a candidate. Ya think I gotta shot?" He grinned and winked at me.

Kyle leaned back and crossed his legs. "Mama would like you all a whole lot. She likes integrity. I sure wish I could persuade my family to leave New Orleans."

The doorbell rang and Mother stood, hastily untying her apron.

Richard raised an eyebrow at me. Paul and Maria leaned in to sample the cheese, and began passing quiches and napkins. I would find out what had happened in New Orleans later.

I heard talking from the hall, then Mother beckoned to me from the doorway. I pushed off the blanket and padded across the room in my socks. Reaching the hall, I was suddenly self- conscious about my lack of footwear, as standing there was the handsome silver-haired man from Mother's Christmas fête. The one she hadn't introduced me to.

"Vance Hardison, meet my daughter Clara. Vance and I have been seeing each other for about a year now."

"Vance?" The name rang a bell, but I couldn't place it.

Mother said, "He's the President of the Association of State Democratic Chairs and Chair of the Montana Democratic Party."

"Hugh's friend! Hugh told you about Andrew Winters, and you started the ethics investigation."

He smiled and held out his hand. "It's a pleasure to meet you, Clara. I've heard a lot about you." It was a perfect hand, manicured and lightly tanned. A Philipe Dufour watch glimmered at the edge of his white shirt cuff, which extended the requisite half inch beyond the end of his suit sleeve. The suit itself was a gorgeous navy wool, pinstriped wispily with silver-grey. The fact that he wore a pair of Timberland work boots made the outfit eerily reminiscent of the last time I'd seen Andrew Winters, but Hardison's mischievous smile trumped any misgivings. He knew exactly what Mother said about me, he knew what I'd said about Mother, and with all her faults, he loved her. I surprised myself by hoping it worked out.

I turned to Mother. "Well, well. A boyfriend, hidden away all this time and no one knew. Weren't you the clever one!"

She gave me a cool look. "Do control yourself, Clara. Really."

Ah. That's the woman I knew and loved.

"It's lovely to meet you, Vance. Come have some champagne." I wrinkled my nose at Mother and led the way back into the room.

Maria leapt up. "Oh, Vance. You made it! I'm so glad." She hugged him hard and he patted her back, resting his cheek against her mass of silver hair.

"I'm sorry about Hugh," he said. "I'll miss him terribly."

She pulled away. "It's not the same without him, even though we spent so much time apart. I talked to him every day, you know?" Her eyes brimmed.

"I know." Hardison clasped her upper arm until she patted his hand and sat down again. Then he made the rounds, meeting everyone and getting a glass of wine. I could see why he had risen so high in politics. Each person he talked to got his complete attention. When Mother introduced him to Nat, she suggested they discuss Nat's candidacy for Senate.

Nat looked as if he'd gotten caught in his own joke. "I—"

"Oh, stop," Mother said. "You know you want it. You've been reading books on campaign finance for months." She went back to her hard chair across the room, the queen orchestrating her court. Hardison settled onto the ottoman, looking as at home as a polar bear on his favorite iceberg.

"So Clara," Bailey practically squeaked in her excitement. "Are you sticking around or what?"

"I'm going to Paris," I teased her, trying to keep a straight face. "I leave in early January." I paused, then decided I was being too mean when I saw her face close in. "Want to come? I've got tickets for Fashion Week."

She looked unsure, as if she couldn't decide whether this was a prelude to my leaving again or a way for us to spend some time together. I smiled. "When I get back, I'm going to work with Ernie at father's company. Well, my company. And Richard has agreed to work for us as our new IT chief."

Bailey leapt from her seat and fell on me in a giant hug. "Yes, I'll go to Fashion Week! Are you kidding? Oh, I'm so so happy. So-so-so happy." She curled in next to me.

"Where will you live?" Mother refused to meet my eyes.

I took a deep breath. I'd rehearsed this, but it was never the same when you had to say it, especially not when a lifetime of difficulty weights the words. I knew what I wanted, but I didn't know if Mother felt the way I did: that we had come to some kind of accord, a place from which we might be able to move forward as adults, flaws and all.

Everyone was waiting, watching me expectantly. I said, "That depends on you. I can find a place, if that's more convenient, but I would prefer to stay here, with you, for now—until the divorce is final and while I learn the business."

The room held its breath.

"You can stay here as long as you like." She shrugged in that offhanded way she had that indicated it didn't matter one way or the other what I chose. She wouldn't meet my eyes.

"I'd like that very much," I said.

When Mother looked up, her eyes were filled with tears.

CLARE MONTAGUE WILL RETURN IN:

THE FALLEN

Coming in 2021 from Woodhall Press

ACKNOWLEDGEMENTS

 would like to thank the following people, who have been instrumental in this book coming to life, and I thank them with all my heart:

Carol Randel, for multiple draft readings and friendship. Rebecca Hussey and Rick Magee, for encouragement and reading at an early stage, and Rick for keeping me straight with the bike stuff. Mat Johnson, for putting on a great workshop that helped me focus Clara's motivations.

Steve Waldinger, Shapiro, Gettinger and Waldinger, Mount Kisco, New York, for legal advice. All law errors are my deliberate and willful twisting of the legal system to fit my own devious ends. Ross Seyfried, for saying thirty years ago, "Figure out what the end is; then work your way back," and for answering all the gun questions. Rosemary Harris, Joanne Dobson, and Reed Farrel Coleman for giving feedback on parts or all of the manuscript. Donna Miele for the name of a charity when I needed one. The MFA program at Manhattanville College, for reconnecting me with a community of writers and reminding me to keep at it, no matter what.

And to my husband Van, without whom the world just wouldn't exist.

ALSO FROM LAUREL S. PETERSON

Talking to the Mirror

That's the Way the Music Sounds

(Re)Interpretations: The Shapes of Justice in Women's Experience (Co-Editor)

Oysterville: Poems (Editor and Contributor)

Do You Expect Your Art to Answer?

COMING SOON FROM LAUREL S. PETERSON AND WOODHALL PRESS

The Fallen: *A Clara Montague Mystery,*

Book 2

WWW.LAURELPETERSON.COM

ABOUT
LAUREL S. PETERSON

Laurel S. Peterson is a Professor of English and served as the first poet laureate of Norwalk, Connecticut. She is an editor of the literary journal, Inkwell. Among her works are two poetry chapbooks, *That's the Way the Music Sounds* and *Talking to the Mirror*, and a full-length poetry manuscript Do You Expect Your Art to Answer? She co-edited a collection of essays on women's justice titled *(Re)Interpretations: The Shapes of Justice in Women's Experience*. During her three year tenure as Norwalk's Poet Laureate, Peterson organized the audio and poetry chapbook project *Oysterville: Poems*, a collection of poems from local Norwalk poets. She and her poet husband live in Connecticut. Find out more about Laurel's work at her website www.LaurelPeterson.com

ABOUT WOODHALL PRESS

Our mission as a press is to represent diverse and imaginative literature from contemporary authors.

Woodhall Press was founded in 2016 with the publication of a single book that needed to be out in the world. *Mentoring Teenage Heroes* is an innovative and unusual book that defied categorization. We now have over thirty titles in print and continue to look for riveting essays, unforgettable stories, and powerful works that defy categorization.

Our publications include essay collections, flash nonfiction collections, children's books, novels, poetry collections, and novels that contain poetry. Recent publications include *Fast Funny Women,* a flash nonfiction collection edited by Gina Barreca; *Songs From a Voice*, a novel, by former Maine Poet Laureate Baron Wormser; *Seven Drafts,* a guide to self-editing by Alison K. Williams; and *A Perfect Facebook Life*, a collection of poems and micro-memoirs by Ann J. O'Connell.

Two of our 2020 novels, *Catchlight* by Brooke Adams Law and *Sorrow* by Tiffanie Debartolo, received Kirkus Starred reviews and were each named to Kirkus Reviews' Best Indie Books of 2020.

Woodhall Press also publishes the biannual Fairfield Book Prize in association with the Fairfield University MFA program.

Please visit woodhallpress.com for more on our books and submission information.